BABY SURPRISE
BY
KATE CARLISLE

AND

THE SECRETARY'S
BOSSMAN BARGAIN
BY
RED GARNIER

"We can talk about sleeping arrangements later," he said easily, moving closer. "It's great to see you, Julia."

Smiling tentatively, she said, "Really?"

He skimmed his lips along her hairline and breathed in her fresh scent. "Yeah."

She sighed and closed her eyes, clearly swayed. "But what about your rule?"

Watching her closely, he lowered his head toward hers. "What rule is that?"

Her eyes fluttered open as she whispered, "Once you've finished with a woman, you never go back."

Cameron frowned. "I told you that?"

Nodding solemnly, she said, "It was the last time I saw you. You said you had a great time but you wouldn't call. You said you didn't want me to get the wrong idea." Her voice quavered as his lips hovered within millimeters of hers.

"I'm an idiot," he said, cupping the nape of her neck in his hand.

With a smile, she gazed into his eyes. "You said it's a long-standing rule of yours."

"Rules are made to be broken," he murmured, and covered her mouth with his.

Dear Reader,

Years ago, wealthy young widow Sally Duke adopted three troubled boys, Adam, Cameron and Brandon. She gave them love and affection, strong values and a sense of family they'd never had before, and they grew up to be confident, handsome and powerful businessmen.

Now it's payback time. Sally Duke wants grandbabies and she's willing to play hardball to get them! You may have already read Adam Duke's story. Now, in *Sweet Surrender, Baby Surprise*, it's Cameron's turn to face his mother's matchmaking machinations. When he runs into lovely pastry chef Julia Parrish, he has no idea that their last romantic tryst resulted in the birth of a darling baby boy—but Sally knows!

The dramatic central California coast is the setting for my Duke brothers stories. As a California girl myself, I've grown up spellbound by the rugged beauty of the cliffs, the Zen-like dignity of the singular palm tree wavering in the wind, the power of the ocean waves pounding against the shore. But mixed in with all that power and ruggedness is the laid-back relaxation that California is famous for. My three handsome heroes have their own easygoing style and it works well for them— until they're confronted by love!

I hope you enjoy Cameron and Julia's story. Please stop by my website at www.katecarlisle.com and let me know.

Happy reading!

Kate

SWEET SURRENDER, BABY SURPRISE

BY
KATE CARLISLE

Published in Great Britain 2011
by Mills & Boon, an imprint of Harlequin (UK) Limited,
Eton House, 18-24 Paradise Road, Richmond, Surrey TW9 1SR

© Kathleen Beaver 2010

ISBN: 978 0 263 88318 3

51-0911

Harlequin (UK) policy is to use papers that are natural, renewable and
recyclable products and made from wood grown in sustainable forests. The
logging and manufacturing processes conform to the legal environmental
regulations of the country of origin.

Printed and bound in Spain
by Blackprint CPI, Barcelona

To the wonderful Susan Mallery, with love and thanks for being a true and generous friend. Drinks are on me!

One

All Cameron Duke wanted to do was rip off his tie, grab a beer and get laid, not necessarily in that order. He'd been working too hard for way too long on the current Duke Development project and he was damn tired of living in a hotel suite.

On the other hand, he reasoned as he slid his key card into the door slot, he couldn't really complain about it. After all, he owned the hotel. And the owner's suite of the Monarch Dunes resort hotel was two thousand square feet of luxury: all the comforts of home with a wide terrace, fantastic ocean views and room service. Nope, he couldn't complain about that.

As he stepped inside the foyer of his suite, Cameron vowed that as soon as the hotel's international catering conference was over, he would go fishing. The resort was up and running to capacity, so it was time for him to take off for a few weeks, get away and do nothing. Maybe he'd rent a houseboat up on Lake Shasta, or grab a raft and float down the King River. Or maybe he'd just make a few calls….

Not to put too fine a point on it, he definitely needed to get laid.

Pulling his tie loose, he dropped his keys on the foyer side table, placed his briefcase on the marble floor and stepped into the living room, where every light in the room was turned on.

"Now, what's wrong with this picture?" he muttered, knowing he'd switched the lights off when he left two days ago.

Not only was every light on in the suite, but the drapes were all closed. Housekeeping knew he preferred the drapes to stay open in order to take advantage of the incredible Pacific view. The room was on the top floor of the Craftsman-style hotel, and the double-paned windows were tempered glass and lightly tinted. It wasn't as if anyone could see inside.

He shrugged out of his suit jacket. Maybe there was someone new working in Housekeeping. They must've left the lights on and closed the drapes without knowing his preferences. It could happen. But it wouldn't happen again.

Taking a few steps into the room, he saw a strange paperback book, opened and facedown on the coffee table. Then his gaze focused in on another foreign object draped over the arm of the couch.

Moving closer, he carefully picked up the soft bit of fabric. Pink, trimmed with paler pink lace around the edges. Lingerie. Expensive. Absurdly feminine. He fingered the fancy silk and the lightest scent of orange blossoms and spice wafted up and enveloped him. The fragrance was vaguely familiar and his groin tightened as an inexplicable need arose in the pit of his stomach.

"What the hell?" He tossed the camisole back on the couch. Not that he didn't appreciate a nice bit of feminine adornment as much as the next guy, but right now he was more concerned with how in the world it got in here.

"Beer first," he decided, and cut through the spacious dining room to get to the kitchen. That's when he saw the high heels. Sexy ones. Red. Tucked under the dining room table.

He hated to repeat himself, but *what the hell?*

Red high heels? It had to be a joke. Something like this was right up his brother Brandon's alley. And if Cameron hadn't already been annoyed at having his quiet evening interrupted, he might've managed to laugh about it.

He moved cautiously past the bar into the kitchen. No, Brandon wasn't hiding there, waiting to jump out and yell that Cameron had been *Punk'd*. But that didn't mean his brother wasn't around somewhere. Cameron grabbed a beer from the refrigerator, twisted the cap off, took a long, slow drink, then stared at the row of empty baby bottles lined up next to the sink.

Baby bottles?

"Okay, that's enough," he said, then shouted, "Brandon? Where are you?" There was no answer.

"I know you're in here somewhere," he said as he walked through the double doors and down the wide hall toward the master bedroom.

That's when he heard the singing.

He froze. A woman's voice, slightly off key, singing some old song about piña coladas and getting caught in the rain. Some woman was singing in the shower. His shower. In his bathroom.

He glanced at his navy polo shirt neatly tossed over the back of the chair in the corner. Those were his running shoes tucked under the chair, too.

Good. He was in the right suite. Which meant that some woman was definitely in the wrong one. Cameron swore under his breath. This had to be Brandon's work. It would be just like his brother to hire a woman as a "surprise." It was the only explanation, because without the approval of a family member, there was no way the front desk would ever allow a strange woman into his room.

He stood listening to the soft singing and wondered what his next step ought to be. He should probably be a gentleman and wait for whomever it was to finish her shower, dry off and put some clothes on before he kicked her out. But then, he'd never claimed to be a gentleman.

Besides, he wasn't the one guilty of breaking and entering. And showering. So he stood at the entrance to the bathroom and waited as the water was turned off and the shower door opened.

One incredibly shapely, bare, wet leg emerged at the same time as a well-toned, lightly freckled arm reached to grab a towel. Cameron pulled one off the rack and handed it to her. "Allow me."

Her scream was shrill enough to peel the paint off the bathroom wall.

"Get out!" she cried, then dropped the towel in her anxious rush to cover herself up.

"Funny, that's just what I was about to say to you," he told her.

Cameron wasn't normally a voyeur. He should've moved away from the door immediately and given her some privacy, but he couldn't. All he could do was gawk like a school kid at her wet-dream-inducing breasts. High, round orbs with tight pink nipples that he imagined would fit perfectly in his hands. And his mouth. His imagination didn't stop there. He wanted to reach out and touch the smooth skin of her stomach, then let his fingers wander down to the delicious patch of dark blond hair at the apex of her curvaceous thighs.

A spark of light drew his gaze back to her navel, where a small diamond twinkled. She had a pierced belly button. For some reason, that made him smile.

"Will you stop staring and get out of here?" she shrieked as she grappled with the towel, finally covering up those spectacular breasts of hers.

Show's over, his rampant libido thought mournfully, and he brought his gaze back up to her face. Whoa. He would know those flashing dark blue eyes anywhere. They belonged to the one woman he'd never quite been able to get out of his mind.

"Hello, Julia," he said.

"What do you think you're doing here, Cameron?"

He leaned back against the doorjamb. "Well, since I live here, I was thinking I'd throw some shorts on, have another beer and watch the football game." He folded his arms across his chest. "A better question might be, what are *you* doing here?"

She huffed out a breath as she stepped fully out of the shower, the towel wrapped around her like a terry-cloth shield. "I was told this suite would be unoccupied for the next two weeks."

"I seriously doubt anyone on my staff told you that."

"Well, it's true," she grumbled, then walked into the bedroom and over to a small open suitcase on the luggage rack near the window.

He took a sip of beer as he watched her pull out some clothes. "Maybe when you're dressed, we should have a little talk about boundaries."

"Oh, stuff it," she said irately, but her hands shook as she pushed her wet, wavy hair back off her face. "Why are you here, anyway?"

"Me?" He probably shouldn't be smiling still, but after all, he was just a man, and she was gorgeous. "Last time I checked, this was my suite."

"But you're not supposed to be here!"

"Honey, I own the place."

Gripping her towel together with one hand, she pushed past him to the walk-in closet to dress quickly. She emerged less than a minute later, dressed in loose shorts and a T-shirt.

Cameron swore under his breath. If she thought putting on clothes would decrease his desire to stare at her, she was wrong. The small, thin shirt outlined her breasts vividly and Cameron was even more intrigued now than before.

"So, you ready to explain what you're doing here?" he asked, wondering if it was getting hotter in here.

Fluffing her hair with her fingers to dry it, she began in a calm voice, "Look, Cameron, Sally said that—"

"What?" Every nerve ending in Cameron's body

began to twitch and not in a good way. "Wait a minute."

Hearing her invoke his mother's name was not a good thing. Sally Duke, the incredible woman who had adopted him when he was eight years old, was a force of nature. Cameron was well aware of her mission to get her three sons married off and knew she wouldn't be satisfied until the deed was done. Damn it, if Sally had something to do with Julia being here, Cameron was in for nothing but trouble.

"Exactly what does my mother have to do with you being wet and naked in my bathroom?"

Julia gazed at him warily, seeming to gauge his temper. "Um, absolutely nothing. I misspoke."

"You *misspoke?*" he drawled. "About my mother? You're kidding, right?"

"No, I'm not kidding," she said, and straightened her spine in righteous anger. Which caused her breasts to thrust forward. Her wet hair had dampened the T-shirt enough that it molded even more firmly to her skin. But she didn't seem to notice as she persisted. "You're not supposed to be here. And since I was given a key by your hotel management, I think it's only right that you should leave."

"Trust me, that's not going to happen." He prowled toward her, studying her every move. "Now exactly what did my mother tell you?"

Her eyes widened and she took a step back. "Never mind. On second thought, I think I'll just pack my things and get out."

"Not yet," he said, grabbing her arm. "I want to know what my mother has to do with you being here."

"All right," she said as she tried futilely to pull away.

"Sally said you'd be gone during the conference and that I would be more comfortable in a suite than a regular room. She told your manager to give me the key."

Her words sent icy tendrils of pure dread down Cameron's spine. Yes, he'd originally planned to stay up north another two weeks, but he'd called Sally yesterday to tell her his plans had changed and he was coming back tonight.

His mother had set this whole thing up.

Did Sally really think that Cameron would take one look at this woman, fall on his knees and beg her to marry him? If so, then Mom was doomed for disappointment.

But as Julia squirmed to pull away from him, Cameron's lower body came to life in a big way. Did it really matter, in that moment, what his mother had done? No. He'd deal with Mom later. Much later.

Right now he had his hands on a lovely, skimpily dressed woman. A sexy woman he'd once known in the most intimate way a man could know a woman.

Holding her close, he again caught that intriguing fragrance of orange blossoms along with something deeper, something exotic. He'd never forgotten her, never forgotten her scent, despite his every effort to do so.

He could still remember meeting her that first time. Talk about lust at first sight.

It all happened after his mother had discovered Cupcake, Julia's bakery in Old Town Dunsmuir. Mom had tried her pastries and cupcakes and had insisted that her sons try them for themselves. They all agreed that her products were incredible and soon thereafter, the Duke resorts began carrying Julia's line of pastries, cookies and breads.

Julia had been invited to attend a one-day vendor orientation at one of the Duke resorts up the coast. She'd planned to stay through the long weekend as a guest of the Dukes. That was where Cameron first saw her, walking across the lobby on her way to the hotel lounge. He'd approached, she'd shown equal interest, and they'd ended up spending that long weekend together.

And that had been the end of it.

She'd haunted his dreams on more than one occasion, but Cameron had refused to contact her again. He had a steadfast rule when it came to women. Once the affair was over, he always made a clean break. He never went back, never looked back. It was safer that way, and simpler. For both parties. Otherwise, women tended to get the wrong idea and hold out hope of a relationship growing. Cameron didn't want to hurt anyone so he stuck to short-term affairs with women who knew the score.

He remembered receiving a few emails from Julia, asking him to call her. He'd thought about it, wanted to, but personal experience had taught him that renewing the affair would only lead to disaster. For her sake as well as his own, Cameron had ignored her requests and eventually, she stopped contacting him.

But here she was, he thought, a year and a half later. In his hotel suite. Wearing those sexy shorts and a practically see-through top. And a belly ring. She gazed up at him with her startling blue eyes and in that moment, he wanted nothing more than to watch those eyes go dark with passion, to taste her lush lips again as well as every other part of her stunning body. Was he honestly going to kick her out of his suite?

Was he nuts?

"Look, I'm sorry," he said in a soothing tone as he ran his hands up and down her arms. "My people must've forgotten I was coming home today. It's late. We can both stay here tonight and I'll find you a room in the morning."

Her eyes clouded with worry. "I suppose I could sleep on the couch."

"We can talk about sleeping arrangements later," he said easily, moving closer. "It's great to see you, Julia."

Smiling tentatively, she said, "Really?"

He skimmed his lips along her hairline and breathed in her fresh scent. "Yeah."

She sighed and closed her eyes, clearly swayed. "But what about your rule?"

Watching her closely, he lowered his head toward hers. "What rule is that?"

Her eyes fluttered open as she whispered, "Once you've finished with a woman, you never go back."

Cameron frowned. "I told you that?"

Nodding solemnly, she said, "It was the last time I saw you. You said you had a great time but you wouldn't call. You said you didn't want me to get the wrong idea." Her voice quavered as his lips hovered within millimeters of hers.

"I'm an idiot," he said, cupping the nape of her neck in his hand.

With a smile, she gazed into his eyes. "You said it's a long-standing rule of yours."

"Rules are made to be broken," he murmured, and covered her mouth with his.

A soft moan escaped her throat as she melted against him. He used his tongue to urge her to open for him and she relented. He thrust into her warmth and felt as though he'd come home. The problems of his world faded and all that mattered was her taste and his need for more.

Wrapping her arms around his neck, she pressed herself even closer. Sweet, was all he could think. Sweet and warm and passionate. He'd missed her, he realized. He shoved that thought away as her tongue teased and tangled with his.

He heard whimpering and wanted to hear more. Wanted to hear her shout his name. Wanted to hear her begging, demanding, crying out for...

Crying?

Cameron stiffened. Yes, that was definitely the sound of someone crying somewhere. Outside? Next door? That was odd, since it was almost impossible to hear anything going on outside the suite. The walls of all the rooms were reinforced and soundproofed.

But there it was again, muffled but discernible. He eased back a few inches to make eye contact with her. "Did you hear that?"

"Yes, I did," Julia said, pushing him away and glancing around. Her eyes were sharp as she seemed to be waiting for it to happen again. But there was nothing, and after a moment, Cameron pulled her back into his arms.

"Must've been next door," he whispered, then proceeded to plant soft kisses on her lips, across her cheek, grazing her ear before moving to taste her sexy neck.

She groaned as Cameron maneuvered his hands down her back until he gripped her supple bottom. He pressed his rigid length against her as his mouth devoured hers, then began to guide her toward the bed. He was hot, hard and ready for her.

"Oh, Cameron," she whispered.

"Yeah, baby, I know." He sat on the edge of the bed and eased her closer until she was standing between his legs. He reached for the hem of her T-shirt and began to pull it up, just as a sudden, wailing scream filled the hotel suite.

Julia moaned loudly as she eased out of Cameron's arms. A million and one thoughts raced through her mind all at once. First, the baby needed attention. She'd foolishly left the baby monitor in the master bathroom when she was so rudely interrupted by Cameron, but she knew that if little Jake was fussy, she'd hear him from anywhere in the suite. After that initial scream for attention, he was quiet, but experience had taught her that he wouldn't remain so for long.

Her other million thoughts were all centered around the realization that Cameron would finally meet Jake. She knew it would've happened eventually, but since he hadn't brought up the subject tonight, she was fairly certain that Cameron, stubborn to the end, had never looked at her emails and therefore, had no idea about the baby. Well, she really hoped he liked surprises.

She headed down the hall toward the bedroom door to face the inevitable. "I'd better take care of this."

"Take care of what?" Cameron asked, coming up behind her and wrapping his arms around her waist.

"The noise you heard before? The crying?"

"The noise from next door? I don't hear it now," he said, and continued his sensual onslaught by kissing her neck, then nibbling that most sensitive spot behind her ear.

She couldn't help but sigh deeply. Her skin tingled everywhere Cameron's amazing lips touched her. As his hands worked their magic over her body, Julia recalled that everything about Cameron Duke excited and delighted her.

But why in the world had she trusted Cameron's staff when they'd promised he would be away this whole time? But even his mother had insisted it was safe to stay in the suite. Julia should've known by the twinkle in the older woman's eye when she insisted that Julia stay in Cameron's suite, that she was being set up.

Her first instinct had been to leave Jake at home with the nanny while she traveled to the conference. But their nanny had a chance to go on a cruise with her daughter, and many of Julia's old friends attending the conference were bringing their families with them. They'd all wanted to see little Jake. For that reason, plus the fact that she missed her baby when he wasn't with her, Julia had decided to bring Jake along, too.

It figured that Cameron would cause all her plans to go awry. It wasn't as if she *never* wanted him to see the baby, but there was no getting around the fact that this was going to get very awkward, very quickly.

"Mmm, that feels so good," Julia murmured as she turned in Cameron's arms and kissed him with all the ardor she could muster. It wasn't a hardship. The man was incredibly sexy and handsome as sin. He seemed taller than she remembered, and definitely stronger. More confident, too, if that were possible. His dark green eyes watched her with a predator's gleam. She shouldn't have found it so absolutely thrilling, but she did.

But damn him for showing up like this! It was just her bad luck, which was the only kind of luck she'd ever had when it came to Cameron Duke.

She'd met him eighteen months ago and willingly succumbed to his charms. They'd had an incredible, torrid four-day affair. Weeks later, she realized she was pregnant.

She'd tried to do the right thing and contact him, but Cameron had all these damn rules about women. Sure enough, true to his word, he never looked back, never contacted her again.

She'd tried emailing him a few times, but it was sadly obvious now, he'd never read any of her messages. And maybe it was just as well. With his so-called rules regarding relationships—or rather, the obsessive need to avoid them—she'd come to the realization that Cameron Duke wouldn't want to have anything to do with raising a child.

She could just imagine what he would think of her for bringing the baby here, especially when he found out Jake was his. Cameron was a decent man so it wasn't as if he would toss her and Jake out of his suite. But he might accuse her of setting this whole thing up and there was little doubt that he would deny the baby was his.

"Oh," she whispered as he pressed himself closer to her. It was getting impossible to think straight with the delicious onslaught of his mouth and hands, but Julia was starting to wonder if she might possibly distract him long enough to get Jake settled. Then she could deal with everything tomorrow morning. Perhaps it was cowardly, but she could live with that.

Whatever she did would have to happen fast, before

her baby decided to take matters into his own chubby baby hands.

"Look, Cameron," she said, finally catching her breath. She needed to get him out of the hallway, now. "Why don't you go get a fresh beer and I'll just slip into something more—"

"I don't need a beer, Julia," Cameron said, running his hands down her sensitive thighs. "I just need this."

"Mmm, me, too," she said as she moved her fingers along his tight, muscled shoulders. "But first, I need a minute to freshen up."

"You took a shower ten minutes ago," he reminded her as he nuzzled her neck. "You're fresh as a daisy."

She moaned, then reluctantly wriggled out of his grasp. "But I really need to dry my hair."

"Yeah?" He brushed a few curling strands away from her face. "It looks fine to me."

"Thanks, but I don't want to catch a cold."

He looked at her skeptically. "Right."

She smiled brightly. "So how's that fresh beer sounding?"

"What?"

"Beer," she repeated. "In the kitchen. And didn't you say you wanted to watch the football game?"

"Yeah, sure. But—"

"Go ahead, then. I'll be right there." She tried to push him toward the living room but the guy was like a brick wall. Unmovable.

"What's going on here, Julia?"

Just then, Jake cried out, "Mama, Mama!"

Cameron's eyes widened.

So much for distractions. She could tell from the tone of Jake's cry that he wasn't hurt or hungry, but that didn't make this moment any easier. "Fine. Look, I didn't want to have to—"

"Okay, I definitely heard that," Cameron said, ignoring her words as he stepped around her handily. "I think it came from the other bedroom."

"No, no, no." Julia jogged just as quickly around to stop him. "It's probably just a cat. I'll take care of it."

"A cat?" Cameron frowned as he glanced down the hall again. "I don't think so."

The baby cried out again and Julia sagged against the hallway wall.

"Aha!" Cameron said and walked toward the second bedroom.

She dashed in front of him and blocked the door. "This is none of your concern, Cameron. Why don't you go turn on the game?"

Cameron was staring at her as if she'd gone insane. Maybe she had. Seeing him again was causing her to behave completely contrary to her usual sensible self. She could blame him for that, too.

"Move it, Julia."

She held up her hand to stop him. "No way. This may be your suite, but you're not going in there without me."

"Then open the door." His look said he wasn't going anywhere until he'd investigated what he'd heard.

"Fine," Julia said. He'd been bound to find out sometime. The most important thing now was to make sure Cameron didn't upset Jake. She huffed out a breath as she pushed the door open slowly. "But it's not what you think. I mean, it is, but—"

"Oh, really?" he said, stepping into the room and spying the portable crib. Julia followed and saw Jake wearing a great big grin on his face, gripping the railing with both hands as he bounced on the mattress.

"Because I think it's a baby." Cameron turned and glared at her. "What do you think?"

She walked over to the crib, smiled down at her son and whispered, "Looks like a baby to me, too."

Jake's little cheeks were red with exertion and Julia felt a sharp ache in her heart. He held out his arms and his knees began to wobble. "Mama, Mama."

"Hello, my darling." She bent to pick him up and perched him against her shoulder, rubbing his back. "That's better. Don't worry, sweetie, I'm here. That's my good boy."

"What in the—?" Cameron's tone held a dangerous edge. "Julia, is this your kid?"

She smiled and kissed Jake's soft cheek, inhaled his warm, powdery baby smell, then turned to face Cameron. "Yes, he's mine. And yours. Cameron Duke, I'd like you to meet Jacob Cameron Parrish, your son."

Two

Cameron immediately stepped back two feet and smacked his elbow into the doorjamb.

"What the hell kind of a joke is this?" he demanded, rubbing his elbow. *Damn, that hurt.* "Trust me, it's not funny."

Apparently, someone disagreed as the baby let out a gut-deep laugh and clapped his hands together. "Ba-da-ba!"

Cameron frowned at the little guy, then glared at Julia, who seemed to be holding back a smile. That set him off even more. He wasn't about to be played for a fool.

He knew the game. This wasn't the first time a woman had tried to pin a paternity suit on him. That was the downside of having a lot of money. The upside was, he wasn't an idiot, despite what he'd told her earlier in jest. He had plenty of lawyers and he knew how to deal with this nonsense. "Not that I believe one word of your story, but the kid's not exactly a newborn. So why'd you wait so long? If he's really mine, why didn't you tell me before now?"

"You're kidding, right?" Julia laughed sardonically. "Cameron, I emailed you a number of times asking you to call me. In the last message I sent, I told you everything. So what part of 'I'm having your baby' didn't you understand?"

His eyes narrowed and he moved in closer. "And what part of 'I don't believe you' do *you* not understand? This is the oldest trick in the book. If you think you're going to get money from me, you're crazy."

"I don't need your money," she said crossly, then lowered her voice as the baby began to fuss. "I was just trying to let you know you were going to be a father. But you couldn't return one lousy email. You couldn't make one stupid phone call. No. You've got *rules*."

She patted the baby to calm him down as she paced the floor in front of the crib. She rounded and came right up to Cameron, clearly riled as she poked him in the chest to emphasize her words. "But you know what? Maybe it's just as well that you ignored Jake and me. With your lifestyle, you probably wouldn't make a very good father anyway."

He grabbed hold of her slender hand before she could take one more poke at him. "Don't you ever insinuate that I would turn my back on my own child."

He dropped her hand and watched her swallow apprehensively. "I didn't. I just meant—"

"I would never hurt my own child," he said through clenched teeth. "I know what it's like to live with a—"

Cameron stopped abruptly and raked his hand through his hair. "Hell, never mind."

What was wrong with him? Except for his two brothers, he'd never told anyone about his childhood. He'd buried it all in the past, right where it belonged. And that ugly childhood was the very reason why he took every precaution to avoid bringing a child into this world. That's why he knew this one couldn't be his.

"I'm sorry," Julia whispered.

Cameron pulled himself together, then turned and said calmly, "Never mind. The fact remains, I don't believe you. We took precautions. I always take precautions."

"Yes, I do, too. But nothing is 100 percent effective." She looked down at the baby in her arms. "Obviously."

"I don't know what game you're playing," Cameron persisted, "but this is not my kid."

"Baba, dada," Jake said, enthusiastically wiggling in his mother's arms. "Dada, ba-boo, dada." He grinned and a tiny dimple appeared in his right cheek.

Dada? Cameron frowned and self-consciously scratched his own right cheek, suddenly ill at ease on a whole different level. "Tell him to stop saying that."

Julia laughed. "He's just babbling. It's the first sound babies make. It doesn't mean anything."

Jake kept bobbing and grinning and the little dimple grew deeper. Cameron gritted his teeth. So he happened to have a dimple in his right cheek, too. Didn't mean a thing.

"Come on, sweetie," Julia whispered to the baby, and turned back toward the crib. "Let's see if you'll go back to sleep after all this excitement."

"No! Baba! Dada!" Jake cried, waving his arms and turning to Cameron for help.

"Looks like he wants you to put him to bed," Julia said wryly, and before Cameron could stop her, she thrust the baby into his arms.

"Hey, I'm not—"

"Baba," Jake said, grinning as he bounced in Cameron's arms. "Dada."

Abruptly, the little boy stopped moving and stared meaningfully into Cameron's eyes. Cameron couldn't help but stare back as emotion washed over him. Confusion, affection, anger, frustration, joy, pain. Wonder. Cameron and Jake both blinked, then continued to stare, and Cameron felt as though he were gazing into his own soul. And where had that thought come from? This was just too weird. It couldn't be happening to him. How could he be a father? It was the last thing on earth he ever intended to be.

Jake yawned and closed his eyes. He rested his head on Cameron's chest, his tiny fist gripping Cameron's shirt as though he were claiming ownership. Cameron touched Jake's soft baby hand with his own larger, stronger hand, and felt something shift inside. He tightened his hold around the baby's back, only because the kid might suddenly decide to try for a swan dive if he wasn't careful. That was his story, anyway.

"He's sleepy," Julia said quietly. "Just lay him down on his back and rub his tummy a few times. He'll be fine."

"Sorry, pal, but your mom has spoken," Cameron said in a low tone. He leaned over the crib and laid the baby down on the soft mattress. Cameron ran his hand over Jake's head. The kid's blond hair was impossibly soft.

Jake didn't whimper or balk, but stayed right where he was. He stuck two fingers in his mouth and continued to stare up at Cameron in pure fascination.

Cameron had to admit Jake was a darn good-looking kid, but that didn't make him his son.

Aw, hell. Who was he kidding? One look at the little guy with his shock of golden blond hair and the shape of his dark green eyes, not to mention the dimple in his cheek—though Cameron hated the word dimple, for God's sake—and anyone would see it, plain as daylight. The kid was Cameron Duke's.

Still, he couldn't shake loose the idea that Julia Parrish was playing him for a fool. Who was to say she hadn't gotten herself pregnant on purpose? Everyone knew the Dukes had money, so maybe she was looking for a handout. Cameron would never shirk his duty to his son, but that didn't mean he was going to make it easy for Julia.

As the baby's eyes closed and he began to sleep, Cameron led the way out into the hall. As Julia closed the door to the bedroom, Cameron turned and said sharply, "I'll want a paternity test."

She froze. He could see he'd shaken her. What? Did she expect him to just believe her with no proof? But watching her now, he remembered how her face had always been an open book. He'd known exactly what she wanted by her facial reaction to everything he did to her, everywhere he touched her. She'd been so forthright about how much she enjoyed his touch. Did she have a dishonest bone in her body? he wondered.

Of course she did. Most of the women he'd dated did.

"Fine," she said grudgingly. "We'll do a paternity test."

Cameron's mind jolted back to the present. "Okay. Good. I can get it done tomorrow."

"I start my conference tomorrow," she said, leading the way into the living room. Cameron watched her backside move with a graceful, long-legged sexiness. He remembered that, too.

She picked up the book she'd left on the coffee table and turned. "I won't be able to take the baby to the doctor until I get back to town."

"Wait a minute," Cameron said, her words sinking in. "You're here for the conference?"

She looked at him like he'd grown another head. "Of course I'm here for the conference. Why else would I be staying here in your hotel room?"

To seduce me into paying child support, Cameron thought, but didn't say it aloud. He wasn't a fool. Sometimes he needed to remind himself of that fact. He coughed to cover his hesitation. "We have a nurse on call at all times. I'll have her come by the room tomorrow to draw blood."

"Okay." Julia shivered visibly and rubbed her arms.

"What's wrong?"

She sighed. "I know it's necessary, but I hate the idea of Jake having his blood drawn."

"It's important," he said, then tried not to cringe himself at the thought of that needle going into Jake's arm. Cameron was already having second thoughts. He'd only insisted on the paternity test to punish Julia, but she wouldn't be the one getting stuck in the arm with a needle. No, that would be Jake, who seemed way too small to have to deal with stuff like that.

Who was Cameron kidding? Jake was his child. The blood test wouldn't be necessary.

He wasn't happy about the way Julia had sprung the news on him, but he believed her. He wouldn't tell her tonight, though. Better to let her squirm for a few hours. He'd tell her in the morning after he'd had a few strong shots of caffeine.

"Fine." Julia swiped the sexy camisole off the chair cushion and grabbed her high heels from under the dining room table. Then she headed into the kitchen and began gathering the baby bottles on the sink.

"What are you doing?" he asked.

"I've got to pack our things."

"Wait." Cameron grabbed hold of her arm before she could go any farther. "No packing. You're staying here."

She looked up at him. "We can't stay here, Cameron. *You're* here."

"Exactly," he said decisively. "That's why you're staying here, too."

She gave him that big-eyed incredulous look of hers again. Why he found it so sexy, he couldn't say. Maybe he enjoyed the challenge she provided.

Shaking her head, she said, "If you think something's going to happen between us, you're wrong."

"Honey," he drawled. "I think we proved awhile ago that it definitely could happen."

"Now, look—"

"You're right, though," he continued. "It's not going to happen tonight." With a casualness he didn't feel, he let go of her arm and walked into the living room. "But you're still staying here."

"Okay," she said, following him. "I'd rather not

disrupt the baby tonight anyway. We'll move to another room in the morning."

An irrational shot of annoyance ran through him and he covered it by grabbing another beer from the refrigerator and popping the top off. "You don't get it, babe. You're staying here until the paternity test is completed. In fact, you might as well stay through the conference. There won't be any rooms available anyway."

She gritted her teeth. "I gave my room away when your mother insisted I stay here. I don't suppose it'd still be available."

"It's not, trust me," he said. "Besides your conference, we've got a golf tournament here this weekend."

She flashed him a frown of frustration. "But you own this place. You should be able to find another room for me and Jake."

"I could, but I'm not going to," he said flatly, then pointed toward the back bedroom. "If that *is* my son in there, I don't want him staying anywhere but here. With me. And we'll know the truth soon enough, won't we?"

"I think that went well," Julia muttered to herself as she slipped between the sheets of the twin bed in the guest room. Jake was sleeping soundly, completely unaware of the drama going on around him. She was gratified to hear his innocent baby snores and wished more than anything that he would never have to be touched by unhappiness of any kind. She knew she couldn't shield him forever, but for now, he didn't need to know that his mommy and daddy were in such an emotional twist over him.

She tried to concentrate on her son, tried to picture his soft little hands waving in the air and hear his funny belly laugh, but visions of Cameron kept interfering. She winced as she remembered how easily she'd melted in his arms. How could he still wield that kind of power over her? She'd known that one day she would have to confront him with the reality of Jake, and she'd steeled herself for that moment. But he'd caught her unprepared. Now he knew how susceptible she was to his charms. He knew he could wiggle his finger and she would come running.

It was humiliating to know that he was right.

In a matter of hours, she would have to tangle with him once more. Would she come running to him again? Or would she be able to withstand his immense allure? It was almost as if he'd put a spell on her.

Yawning, she fluffed her pillow and tried to settle her active mind by breathing deeply for a count of ten. She knew she would need all the sleep she could get if she expected to put up a good fight tomorrow.

Cameron stretched, then tried to turn over onto his back—and landed on the floor.

"What the—?" he grumbled. Where the hell was he?

His brain slowly engaged and he groaned as he remembered exactly where he'd slept last night. Moving slowly, he pulled himself up off the living room floor, then sat on the couch with his elbows resting on his knees.

After Julia had gone off to bed, he'd finished his beer and tried to watch the football game, but it had lost its appeal. So he went to bed where he tossed and turned, unable to sleep with the knowledge that Julia was sleeping in the room just across the hall. He wanted her in bed with him. Wanted her lush body pressed against his. Wanted to bury himself in her silken warmth.

But you can't always get what you want, he thought. Not right away, anyway. He was a patient man and he would have her in his bed soon enough.

Last evening, though, that thought had not been conducive to a good night's sleep. So Cameron had come out to the living room couch, thinking he'd zone out on late-night television. He finally fell asleep and now he regretted it as he stood and tried to stretch out his spine. Damn, his couch looked spacious and luxurious, but spending the night on it had been a tactical error. His back was whimpering like a whiny schoolgirl. He stood and stretched and tried to remember when, exactly, had he turned into such an old man? He was barely into his thirties.

Determined to work out and get rid of the aches and pains, he slipped on a pair of gym shorts and sneakers, then left the suite for a brisk twenty-minute run around the resort grounds.

Forty-five minutes later, after a hot shower and two cups of coffee, he felt a whole lot better. A good thing, because he would need to be in peak condition to deal with the new occupants of his suite.

"Dada!"

Speaking of.

"Good morning," Julia said as she carried Jake into the room. She had him in some kind of space-age kid carrier and without thinking, Cameron took it from her and placed carrier and baby up on the breakfast bar.

She was dressed in a sleek, navy pinstriped suit with

a crisp white blouse and black heels. Her wavy blond hair was tamed back into a simple ponytail. And why he found that look so damn sexy, Cameron couldn't figure out, but he knew he was on a slippery slope, watching her walk around the kitchen as she grabbed an apple for herself and warmed a bottle for the baby.

"Dada," Jake whispered, gazing up at Cameron's face.

"He says that a lot," Cameron said, staring at the kid. He realized as he spoke that Jake's repetition of the word *dada* didn't bother him half as much as it had last night.

"It feels good on his tongue," Julia explained, then blinked and quickly turned toward the coffeemaker.

Cameron laughed as she crisscrossed the kitchen, her cheeks blushed pink after realizing what she'd just said. Obviously, she hadn't thought about the words before uttering them, and now he could think of a few things, too, that would feel good on *his* tongue.

"I've got a conference panel in forty minutes," she said briskly, back to business after a few hurried sips of coffee. "I've arranged for a babysitter to watch Jake for the day, and she should be here any minute. But if you'd rather not have anyone in the suite while you're here, I'll understand. I can check with the concierge for another place to—"

"It's fine if the babysitter stays here."

"Okay." She nodded. "Good. Thanks."

"Did you sleep well?" he asked.

"Wonderful, thank you," she said, and rinsed her coffee mug. "You?"

"Like a rock," he lied.

"That's great."

Well, this was awkward. He leaned against the bar, watching as Julia put the mug in the dishwasher. Then he glanced over at Jake, whose eyes were closed. He was already sleeping peacefully, Cameron realized. Must be nice.

The doorbell rang and Jake's eyes flew open. His mouth quivered in a pout, and Cameron realized he was about to cry.

"Hey, kiddo, it's okay," he said softly, and stroked his tummy. "Shh. Don't worry. Doorbells scare me, too."

Jake stared up at Cameron as though his words were written on stone tablets. A wave of something powerful swept through him and he felt as if he just might be the most important person in the world in that moment.

"That must be the sitter," Julia said, her voice a little hoarse. "I'll go let her in."

Ten minutes later, the babysitter and Jake were ensconced in the back bedroom, and Julia was ready to leave. She had her purse strapped over her shoulder and she carried a soft leather briefcase. She looked like a lawyer instead of the best pastry chef on the Central Coast. Cameron walked her to the front door and opened it.

"I showed her where everything is and gave her my card in case she needs to call me," Julia said nervously. "I won't turn off my phone."

"Everything will be okay," he said, and leaned against the door jamb, blocking her way out. "Look, we haven't talked about the paternity test yet."

"Oh," she said. With a frown, she dropped her briefcase and folded her arms across her chest. "I was hoping you'd changed your mind about that."

He narrowed his eyes. "You don't think I'm handing

you a child support check until I've verified that Jake is my son, do you?"

"I don't need child support, Cameron," she said testily. "You can keep your money."

"Yeah, that's what they all say."

Her lips thinned in anger. "First of all, it's Jake's comfort I'm concerned about. Do you have any idea how many immunizations he's been through in his short nine months? I've lost track of the number of needles he's had to suffer through. But don't worry, you'll have your damned paternity test. Second of all—"

"Look, Julia, I—"

She held up her hand. "Just let me finish before you say anything else you'll regret later about the money thing. Do yourself a favor, go online on Google and look up the Parrish Trust. When I get back, we'll talk about money."

"Fine." He realized he'd pushed her a little too far, but where did she get off thinking he'd just accept her word on everything?

She picked up her briefcase and started to walk out, but stopped again and glared at him. "And as long as you've got your computer fired up, you might want to take a look at those emails I sent you a while back. They just might paint a different picture than what you think is going on here."

"Julia, I'm not—"

"And while you're at it," she said, pulling a flowery scrapbook from her briefcase, "I brought this to show some friends, but you might want to take a look at it first."

He stared at the thick journal, then began to thumb through it casually. There were photographs of the baby affixed to the pages, along with handwritten passages describing the pictures. Frowning, he gazed at her.

"And one more thing," she continued before he could say anything. "You caught me in a weak moment last night, but it won't happen again. We're willing to stay here with you for the next ten days, but there's no way I'm having sex with you. That's a deal-breaker."

With that, she left the suite in a huff.

Three

That's a deal-breaker.

Sex? A deal-breaker? Not in this universe, Cameron thought. He could recall Julia melting in his arms last night and knew it was only a matter of time until he had her in his bed.

After she left for the conference, Cameron pulled his computer out of the second bedroom and set everything up in the dining room. That way, he wouldn't disturb Jake when it was nap time later.

Cameron couldn't get Julia's irate words out of his head so, with great reluctance, he finally did as she suggested and went online to research her family business.

Now, he sat back in his desk chair and stared at the computer screen. A thousand different thoughts ran through his mind, but the first thing he did was pick up the phone and call his company's tech department.

After putting in a request that they immediately recover the emails from Julia he'd deleted more than eighteen months ago, Cameron hung up the phone and went back to gazing at the online information he'd pulled up on Julia Parrish and her family.

It was disturbing to read that Julia's parents had died in a small plane crash when she was ten years old. There were pages and pages devoted to her parents' philanthropy, but almost nothing on young Julia Parrish until she opened her popular bakery shop in Old Town Dunsmuir Bay four years ago.

Did she have other family in the area? Who had been responsible for raising her? Cameron found more questions than answers and knew they would have to talk about these and other issues tonight.

Aside from the news of her parents' death, the most shocking fact about Julia Parrish was that the woman was almost as wealthy as Cameron was. So why was she slaving away making cupcakes for other people?

It turned out that the Parrish Trust was one of the biggest and most influential charitable organizations in the state. The trust funded or underwrote everything from children's television to scientific research to humanitarian efforts on behalf of children everywhere. Cameron had heard of the Parrish Trust, of course. Who hadn't? But he'd never connected the dots from the trust to Julia, never had any reason to. Now, though, he had a reason.

No wonder Julia didn't care about Cameron's money. No wonder she'd given up on trying to contact him. She didn't need Cameron Duke's support. The mother of his son was worth millions.

He didn't know how he felt about that. He supposed it wasn't a bad thing that little Jake would never want for anything in his life. In fact, that was definitely a good thing. But Cameron wanted to be the one to provide those things for his son. And he would. As soon as Julia got back to the suite, they would talk. He would tell her she didn't have to worry anymore about being the sole provider. Cameron was ready and willing to step in and take care of things from now on.

"Oh, that'll fly like a lead balloon," he uttered, then shrugged. Didn't matter what she thought. Cameron was Jake's father and he would be responsible for him. Besides, why shouldn't Julia take a break and let Cameron shoulder some of the burden for a while? It's not like he was forcing her into a marriage. God forbid. Neither of them wanted that.

Although, now that he thought about it, a marriage between Cameron and Julia would be the best thing for Jake.

"But that's never going to happen." He shoved his chair back from the table. If Cameron didn't do relationships, he sure as hell wouldn't ever do marriage. And that was okay. Jake would thrive with two parents who cared about him. They didn't need to be living together in order for the kid to have a good life.

Cameron hadn't exactly grown up with great role models. Quite the contrary, his dad had been a lousy excuse for a parent and a miserable marriage partner to his mom. Cameron had always said that if his parents were what marriage was all about, he wasn't interested.

And if his unhappy parents weren't enough of a reminder that marriage was out of the question for him, there was also the sacred pact he'd made with his brothers. He would never break that pact, ever.

Cameron could still picture the day, shortly after his eighth birthday, when he arrived at Sally Duke's big house on the cliffs of Dunsmuir Bay. At first, it was unsettling to learn that Sally had rescued two other boys from foster care along with Cameron, and that she expected all of them to become a family.

Those early weeks he spent getting to know Adam and Brandon were bumpy, to say the least. A pecking order needed to be established, so the three boys fought for supremacy over everything: toys, food, television shows, Sally's attention. They bickered and clashed just like eight-year-old boys were supposed to. At the same time, they worried that Sally might dump them back on the state coffers. It wouldn't be the first time for any of them. But they didn't know Sally Duke.

One day when she'd heard enough arguing, Sally banished the boys to the custom-designed tree house she'd had built for them. She told them they could come down when they'd learned to behave like friends and brothers.

Cameron, Adam and Brandon spent hours in that tree house, and eventually their worst secrets were unraveled and shared. Brandon's drug-addict mom ran off and his dad used to beat him until the man was killed in a bar fight. Adam's parents abandoned him when he was barely two years old. He was raised in an orphanage before being thrown into the foster care system.

Cameron finally confessed that his own father was a violent man and his mother bore the brunt of it. Not that she was all that loving, given her appetite for alcohol and drugs. Cameron knew she had lied and stolen and worse to support her habit, but he blamed his father for turning her into an addict. He still had nightmares of his mother screaming from the beatings his father inflicted. Even worse, Cameron could never forget hearing his old man hit his mom while yelling that he was doing it because he loved her. And he would never forget waking up and finding them both dead. He was seven years old.

When Adam and Brandon heard that Cameron's dad thought he was showing love by beating the crap out of his mother, they both were disgusted. That led to the pact.

First, the three eight-year-olds swore loyalty to each other. Next, they made a sacred vow that they would never get married and have kids, because it was clear that marriage turned people mean and stupid. Married people hurt each other and their kids.

Finally, they vowed to make Sally Duke proud that she'd chosen them.

From that day forward, Sally let them know in a hundred different ways that they'd fulfilled their third vow—and then some. They'd all grown up to be honorable, successful men and she couldn't be more proud. Of course, now Sally had come up with some cockamamie plan to marry the brothers off so they could give her a bunch of grandkids. And despite all of his diatribes, Cameron had just given her exactly what she wanted.

"Oh, man," he said aloud. The realization had him rubbing his knuckles against his chin. "Wait'll Mom gets a look at little Jake." He chuckled in anticipation of the scene that awaited him when Sally heard the news.

Of course, she might be a little disappointed that he had no intention of marrying Julia, but she would just have to live with it. Cameron would never marry, that was all there was to it. He would never want to destroy someone else the way his parents had destroyed each other.

It's not like he'd been a martyr to his fate. Cameron had tested the waters more than once, in spite of the boyhood pact. But things had never worked out, to put it mildly. There had been plenty of women in his life and a few attempts at serious relationships, but they'd been disastrous. He'd used those as strong reminders that he'd come from bad stock and things would never change. He wasn't willing to put someone else through that kind of pain, let alone experience it again himself. No, he was meant to go it alone, and that suited him just fine, thanks.

He stood and checked his wristwatch. The babysitter had taken Jake for a long walk around the hotel grounds so Cameron could have a short meeting with his brothers here in the suite. They were due any minute.

They would soon find out they were uncles, Cameron thought. So much for sacred pacts. But at least Cameron hadn't been the first brother to break it. That honor went to Adam when he married Trish James last month.

The doorbell rang and Cameron greeted his brothers, then led the way to the kitchen. "You guys want beers?"

"You have to ask?" Brandon said, swinging the refrigerator door open and grabbing three bottles from the shelf.

"How's Trish?" Cameron asked Adam, knowing his brother had brought his wife along for a quiet, romantic weekend at Monarch Dunes.

"She's great," Adam said with a smile. "She ran into Mom and her friends downstairs so they're probably relaxing at the pool by now."

"Relaxing?" Brandon laughed. "We'd better get this over with so you can rescue her."

"Good idea." Adam sat at the dining room table and opened a thin binder of notes and spreadsheets.

Cameron and Brandon joined him at the table where they discussed some last-minute scheduling items that had arisen over the hand-off of priority projects from the Monarch Dunes resort to the Napa Valley property.

"You've done a great job with Monarch Dunes, bro," Brandon said, tipping his beer bottle in Cameron's direction.

"Thanks," Cameron said. "Napa's looking good, too."

The three men had found out years ago that the best way to run their development company was to put each brother in charge of a particular property from start to finish. The Monarch Dunes property had been Cameron's baby from day one and he'd run the project much as he ran his life: with military precision.

The multifaceted, multileveled Craftsman-style resort, located forty miles south of their home town of Dunsmuir Bay, was already completely booked for the next three seasons and on its way to becoming the premier destination spot along California's Central Coast.

Cameron had had a hand in every decision along the way, from the expansiveness of the lobby that opened to a spacious terrace overlooking the ocean and cliffs, to the placement of the greens on the state-of-the-art championship golf course that wound around the wide perimeter of the hotel.

"My staff is more than ready to have me move out of here," Cameron admitted. "They've started saluting me when I ask them to do something."

"When you *ask* them to do something?" Adam said sardonically. "More like barking out orders, I'd say."

Brandon shook his head. "Once a marine, always a marine."

With a shrug, Cameron said, "Hey, I just prefer to have things done the right way, so let's get back to business." He read his notes off a legal pad. "I'll let my assistant know that the Napa grand opening will be pushed back one week to coincide with the grape harvest and crush. She can coordinate schedules with the Napa staff."

The Dukes' Napa property was being built adjacent to the acres of vineyards and the winery they'd purchased years ago. The white wines were already being marketed all over the country and the reds were on the verge of reaching world-class status.

"Good," Brandon said and walked toward the kitchen. "Hey, what's this?"

Too late, Cameron realized Brandon had picked up the scrapbook Julia had given him earlier. "It's nothing. I'll take it."

But Brandon was already thumbing through the pages. "Dude, these are baby pictures. It's a baby album."

"Who's the baby?" Adam asked, moving around the table to see what Brandon was looking at.

Hell. Cameron reached for the book. "I'll take that."

"I don't think so," Brandon said and whipped the book away.

Adam pierced Cameron with a look. "Was there something you wanted to share with us?"

"I'm not playing this game." Cameron held out his hand and waited calmly until Brandon gave him the thick scrapbook. "Okay, I'll see you guys later."

"You're kidding, right?" Brandon said, both hands fisted on his hips. He turned to Adam. "I saw a shot of a pregnant woman. And an ultrasound photo."

"So what?" Cameron said. He wasn't about to let his brothers see anything else in the book before he'd had a chance to thoroughly view every page.

"What's going on, Cam?" Adam asked quietly.

Feeling cornered but knowing there was no way out, Cameron sat back down at the table. "Fine. I was going to tell you anyway."

"Well, let's hear it." Brandon pulled out his chair and sat.

"I have a son."

Stunned silence greeted his announcement. Brandon blinked a few times, opened his mouth to speak, but ended up saying nothing.

Adam's eyes narrowed. "Mind repeating that?"

Brandon folded his arms across his chest. "I knew that was an ultrasound."

Cameron glared at Brandon. "No, you didn't."

"Yeah, I did." Brandon lifted his shoulders philosophically. "I'm smarter than I look."

Adam and Cameron both laughed, easing some of the tension in the room.

"I think you owe us some explanation after dropping that bomb," Adam said.

They'd only torment him until he spilled everything, so he gave them the abbreviated story of Julia and baby Jake.

"You never read the rest of her email messages?" Brandon said incredulously. "Weren't you curious? I would be."

"Yeah, well, I've got more control than you," Cameron said, his tone slightly defensive.

"Control *issues,* you mean," Brandon replied.

Adam chuckled. "I think we should check out some of those messages."

"I told you I erased them all," Cameron said, not willing to add that he'd also taken steps to recover them. By now, they were probably waiting in his email in-box.

Adam grabbed Cameron's shoulder and said, "Maybe so, but you've got the baby book. Let's check it out."

"I don't think so."

"Dude, we're your brothers," Brandon said. "We can add some objectivity to the situation."

He had a point. They both did, as much as Cameron hated to admit it. In fact, it seemed fitting that they were there with him, considering that bits of their sacred brotherhood pact were crumbling to dust by the minute.

Against his better judgment, he opened the book. His brothers pulled their chairs up close to look at the photo on the first page. It was of Jake, taken in the hospital within an hour after he was born.

"He looks like a grizzled old man," Brandon said.

"No, he doesn't," Cameron argued.

Adam sat back. "Babies always look like that. You've got to consider where they just came from."

"Oh, man," Brandon said, flinching. "That's just rude."

Cameron chuckled as he turned the page and gazed at a number of early photos of Jake, some with Julia holding him. He wondered who had been operating the camera. He was dismayed to realize that it should've been him. But he'd completely ignored Julia. It grated on him more and more as he turned the pages and saw his good-looking little boy growing bigger and bigger.

"Oh, man, he's in heaven," Brandon said, as they stared at the shot of Jake enjoying his first barbecued chicken. Julia wrote next to the picture that the chicken had been pureed for Jake and he'd eaten it quickly, but then he'd taken his time enjoying the sauce. Cameron had to laugh. Jake's little face and hair were smeared with red sauce and he flashed the camera a big, toothless grin.

"Looks just like Cameron when he eats barbecue," Adam said, and even Cameron had to laugh at that one.

He turned to another set of pictures. Julia had titled them Jake's First Immunizations and described how the nurse's assistant had taken the pictures while Julia held and comforted the baby.

"Uh-oh, this is gonna hurt," Brandon said, wincing. Cameron did the same. The first photo showed the nice doctor holding a small syringe. Several more shots documented Jake's expressive face as it scrunched up in preparation for something bad to happen. The last picture showed the dam bursting. Jake's face was purple with rage, his eyes were shut tight and his mouth was wide open. He was obviously screaming in terror and pain.

Cameron could almost hear the screams.

"Man, that's just cruel," Adam said, averting his eyes from the book.

"I completely feel his pain," Brandon agreed, rubbing his arm where the needle would've gone in.

The next page showed the look of happy shock on the baby's face as his mother took him into the ocean for the first time. He stared at Julia frolicking in a brief bikini, looking so lush and sexy he had to stifle the urge to stroke the page.

With a start, he realized his brothers could see her as well, and immediately turned the page.

"Hey, wait, not so fast," Adam complained.

"Yeah, slow down," Brandon said. "That photographer is really talented. I want to see more of the ocean."

"Yeah, right," Cameron said, shaking his head. He knew what his brothers wanted to see more of and he wasn't about to give them what they wanted. Nobody was going to look at Julia in a bikini but him. His brothers would have to learn to live with disappointment.

"Come on, Cam, go back to that last shot," Adam said, then added in a reasonable tone, "We really should get to know Jake's mom better."

"You've both seen enough," Cameron said, and closed the book.

"Fine," Brandon said, and sat back in his chair. "But I still wonder why you didn't get in contact with her when you got her messages."

Cameron turned and glared at him. "All I saw in that first message was a woman demanding that I call her. Who needs that? So I deleted the ones she sent after that."

"Seems a little harsh," Brandon replied.

"Oh, come on. You've dealt with obsessed women. What would you have done?"

Brandon frowned but said nothing.

"He has a point," Adam said reluctantly.

Cameron expelled a long, slow breath. "I did what I had to do at the time."

"Yeah, been there," Brandon said with a sigh. He'd spent ten years in the NFL and knew what it was like to be stalked by an obsessed woman or two. Or three. "I guess I can't blame you. But she looks so normal."

"Don't get me wrong," Cameron said. "I liked her a lot. But then the messages started. That first day, she sent four emails. Four. Seriously, she showed all the signs of a desperate woman who'd talked herself into something that wasn't there. Like, we had sex and suddenly she was in love or something, demanding that I call her. She even sent me a letter, but I threw it away unopened. I wasn't willing to buy into any of it."

"I guess I see your point," Adam admitted.

"Thought you might," Cameron said. "Then all of a sudden, the emails stopped coming and I figured she got the message."

"Guess she gave up on you," Brandon said with a shrug.

That didn't sit well with Cameron, but he said nothing.

Adam gazed at him. "So where do you go from here?"

"I'm working it out."

"Yeah?" Brandon chuckled. "Good luck with that."

Cameron's jaw tightened and he shot his brother a scornful look. "I'm in complete control of the situation."

"Ah, the famous Cameron control," Adam said, nodding sagely. "So now she's living here with you for the next ten days or so. I have a feeling your legendary control is going to be tested to the max."

The way Adam chuckled, Cameron imagined he'd had his own share of control issues. And knowing Trish now, he was pretty sure his brother had already lost that battle. Strangely enough, Adam didn't look like he minded one bit.

Cameron was glad his brother had found happiness, but marriage and a family weren't on Cameron's agenda.

Adam stood and slipped his binder into his briefcase. "Trish is going to want to see the baby."

"Hey, me, too," Brandon said. "I want to meet my nephew."

"How about if we swing by tonight?"

"Tonight's not good," Cameron said quickly. He needed to prepare Julia for the family onslaught. "I'll set something up for tomorrow night."

Ten minutes after his brothers took off, the babysitter returned with Jake. Cameron watched her carefully as she changed the baby's diaper and fed him his bottle. He asked a few pertinent questions and had her show him some of her techniques, then he gritted his teeth and told her she could go for the day. He was ready to take over.

"It's just you and me now, kid," he murmured to Jake after the woman left. Cameron lifted the baby into his arms and spent a few minutes walking Jake around the suite. They stood at the window and stared out at the cliffs and the ocean beyond. Cameron pointed out a few landmarks up and down the coast.

"Can you see that bit of land jutting out into the ocean?" Cameron said, pointing northward. "That's where we live."

A seagull flew high over the ocean and Cameron said, "Can you wave at the bird? Sure, you can. I'll help you." He grabbed Jake's wrist and moved it up and down in a waving gesture.

"Smart boy," he murmured, and breathed in the powdery scent of clean baby.

No, marriage and family hadn't been on Cameron's radar, but now that he had Jake to take care of, he was already mentally planning to do everything he could to contribute to the boy's welfare. Jake would never want for anything as long as Cameron had a breath left in his body.

He was amazed to realize that he'd already developed strong feelings for the little boy. He wouldn't call it love. He wasn't sure he would ever be ready to take that step and say those words. Maybe it would be better for Jake if he never did.

"Dadadada," Jake gibbered.

"Hey, kiddo," Cameron said, and gave him an affectionate squeeze. "Let's see about getting you something to munch on."

They walked into the kitchen where Cameron found some Cheerios for Jake and crackers for himself. He put Jake in his high chair and watched the baby amuse himself with the little O's.

Despite the violence of his early years, Cameron had lucked out when Sally Duke adopted him. Through her strong and loving influence, Cameron learned to trust again. Even though his father had warned him that nobody would ever find him worth a damn, Cameron knew he was capable of giving and accepting love. He'd been with plenty of women all through high school and, even though he couldn't say he'd loved any of them, he'd certainly felt affection for them and knew the feelings were reciprocated.

Then, in his senior year, he met Wendy, a beautiful girl who fell for him, hard. One night, she told him she loved him and demanded that Cameron say it, too. In one of the dumbest moves of his life, he told her he loved her. But he didn't, and soon after that, he tried to break it off as gently as he could. Wendy went wild. She tried everything to force him to take her back, even tried to turn his friends against him. Then she tried blackmail, threatening to tell his teachers that he cheated on his exams. Cameron ignored her, so she finally went to the police and pressed charges, accusing him of abusing her. That was the final straw.

Given his early upbringing, Cameron was the last person who would ever physically abuse anyone. Wendy didn't know that, but Sally Duke did. She circled the wagons and hired a lawyer. In the courtroom, Wendy broke down and admitted she was lying. She recanted the charges, but the damage had been done.

Cameron could still feel the anger and adrenaline that shot through his system as the judge cleared his name. If things had gone the other way, would he have reacted violently, like his father?

In a desperate attempt to channel the fury he knew was inside him, he joined the marines. And he vowed that he would never again give anyone the power to destroy him in the name of love.

But now there was Jake. And there was Julia. What was he supposed to do about them?

* * *

Julia finished her food allergies workshop and stayed over to answer all the questions from the audience. Even after she left the meeting room, several of her attendees followed, peppering her with more. This was the part of the conference she loved—glad to pass on the things she'd learned from her own mentors and teachers over the years. She considered it a tribute to her mentors and teachers that she was now able to share the knowledge they'd generously given.

She bid her students goodbye and entered the lobby, then stopped abruptly. Sally Duke stood with two other women by the concierge desk, fifty feet away. They were all dressed casually in Bermuda shorts, colorful T-shirts and walking shoes.

Julia didn't know whether to avoid Cameron's mom or confront her. After all, Sally had to have known Cameron was due back last night, yet when they'd run into each other yesterday, the older woman had blithely assured Julia that Cameron would be out of town for the duration. After all her careful planning, Julia couldn't believe she'd walked right into a trap.

If Julia had known otherwise, she might've thought twice about attending the conference at all. And she definitely would've left Jake with their nanny back in Dunsmuir Bay.

Feeling like the worst kind of coward, Julia skulked away to avoid another run-in with Cameron's lovely mother. As she scurried down a long hallway toward the bank of elevators at the far end of the hotel, Julia thought back to that moment the day before when she and Jake had first arrived at the resort.

She'd been pushing Jake in his stroller while a bellman followed with a luggage trolley stacked to the top with Julia's suitcases and conference supplies and piles of baby paraphernalia. From across the wide-open lobby, someone had cried out her name.

"Julia, what a delightful surprise!"

She'd been shocked to see Sally Duke standing there when she turned to look. Normally, she would've been happy to see her Dunsmuir Bay friend. After all, Sally Duke had put Julia's bakery on the map when she'd insisted that her sons carry Julia's products in all the Duke resorts.

But before Julia had even been able to say hello, Sally had bent over to take her first look at baby Jake. Julia would never forget her own sense of apprehension as she watched the older woman's reaction to the baby. Would she recognize the strong resemblance to her own son?

Julia had hesitated, then said, "Sally, this is my son, Jake."

"Oh, how wonderful." Sally knelt down in front of the stroller, grabbed hold of Jake's foot and said, "Hello, you little darling. I'm so happy to meet you."

Jake giggled and his dimple popped out on his right cheek. Sally gasped and her mouth dropped open. She stared at the baby for another moment, then looked up at Julia with tears in her eyes.

"It's impossible," she whispered.

There was nowhere to run, nowhere to hide. Maybe Julia was overdramatizing things, but she could barely breathe.

"Is it true?" Sally asked.

"What are you talking about?" Julia tried for casual, but she stumbled on the words.

"Oh, honey," she said softly. "He's Cameron's, isn't he?"

Julia felt her own eyes water as she slowly nodded.

"I thought so," Sally said, gazing back at Jake and touching his nose playfully. "That little dimple is better than a DNA test."

Julia had smiled, but her worry had increased. She could only hope Cameron took it this well when he finally learned the truth.

When Sally looked up again, she sniffled and said, "I'm in love with him already. Thank you so much." She wrapped Julia in a tight hug.

Completely distressed, Julia swore Sally to secrecy until she could break the news to Cameron herself.

"He doesn't know?" Sally had asked in shock. "Why on earth haven't you told him?"

Julia hastily explained that she'd tried, but Cameron had never called or returned her messages.

Sally rolled her eyes in exasperation. "Why am I not surprised? I'm sorry Julia, but my son can be stubborn."

Then Sally promised Julia that she wouldn't say a word to Cameron. Her lips were pursed in determination as she called over the hotel manager and told him to put Julia and the baby in Cameron's suite. Julia had protested, but Sally managed to convince her that Cameron would be gone for the next two weeks.

"He'll never know what happened," Sally had said with an innocent smile. "Trust me."

Julia let herself into the suite and was surprised by the silence. There were no lights on, no sounds of activity anywhere. Back home, her house was never this quiet. Had Cameron taken the baby somewhere? Maybe Sally Duke had followed through on her promise to babysit and rushed up here to take the baby off to play.

Julia left her briefcase and purse on a dining room chair and considered pouring herself a glass of wine. The thought was irresistible but she would check on Jake first, then see about the wine.

It had been a long, intense day. She would have to talk with Cameron's mother eventually.

The fact that Sally had set them both up still baffled Julia. And she had to wonder what Sally would think when Julia told her that Cameron had discovered her in his shower.

"Maybe I won't go into quite so much detail," Julia muttered to herself. Removing her high heels, she walked down the hall to the baby's bedroom and still didn't hear anything. When she pushed the door open, the first thing she saw was the empty crib. She suffered a moment of consternation as she wondered where her baby could be. The room was dim with the lights off but the drapes were open, letting in the dusky twilight. Looking beyond the crib to the twin beds, she finally spotted Cameron laid out, with little Jake sprawled on his chest, sound asleep. Cameron's big hands were splayed protectively across the baby's back, holding him in place.

Julia's heart stuttered in her chest as she tried to swallow the emotional lump in her throat. Had she ever seen anything more beautiful than the sight before her?

Oh, she was in such big trouble.

She sighed, wondering if she could possibly be a bigger sap than she'd already been over Cameron Duke.

There was no way she would fall for him again. Hadn't she learned her lesson about commitment-phobic men? Besides, she and Jake were doing just great on their own, thanks very much.

But now Cameron was back in the picture and he'd made a few things quite clear. First, despite his apparent affection for Jake, he didn't yet believe that the child was his son. Second, he'd like a repeat performance of the wild affair they'd had the last time they were together. But Julia had her child to consider now, and she was no longer interested in sex without love. Cameron wasn't about to open his heart to her, let alone fall in love and marry her.

And she was fine with that. She'd grown a lot stronger in the year and a half since Cameron had refused to answer her messages. She was happy. Her life was full. She neither wanted nor needed Cameron Duke in her life anymore. No, the only thing she needed right now was someone who could convince her that everything she'd just told herself wasn't a big, fat lie.

Four

Cameron heard a sigh and his eyes flew open. Julia stood a few feet away, staring down at him and Jake. She was still dressed in her serious business suit but she looked softer, almost more fragile now than she had that morning. He didn't budge from his position as he whispered, "He's asleep."

"I see that," she said quietly. "So were you."

"Nope," he countered. "Not asleep. Just resting my eyes."

"Ah." She smiled. "We should probably wake him up now or he won't sleep through the night."

Cameron frowned. "I never thought of that."

"That's okay, you didn't know," she said, walking to the edge of the bed.

Cameron patted and stroked Jake's back. "Hey, buddy, mom's home. Time for some grub."

The baby stretched and grunted. Cameron watched as he blinked, then stared into Cameron's eyes and began to whimper.

"Shh," Cameron said, as Jake's lips quivered. Concerned, Cameron shifted his gaze to Julia. "Why is he going to cry?"

"He's always a little crabby when he first wakes up from a nap," Julia said, reaching for the baby. "He's a bit disoriented and probably needs his diaper changed."

"Again?" Cameron frowned, feeling strangely bereft without the weight of the baby on his chest. "But the babysitter took care of that before she left."

"I'm sure she did," Julia said, smiling as she snuggled Jake against her shoulder. She slipped her feet into a pair of flat shoes she'd left by the bed. "But knowing Jake, I'd better check anyway."

"Okay," Cameron said, standing and stretching. "I'll watch what you do. Just so, you know, in case you're not around, I'll know what to do."

"Oh." She seemed taken aback, as though the thought had never occurred to her that he was capable or interested in taking care of the baby. "Okay. Good idea."

Sure enough, Jake needed a clean diaper in a big way. As Julia handled the task with an efficiency Cameron could only marvel at, she asked, "Did you speak with the nurse?"

It took him a moment to figure out what she was talking about. Then, for some reason, Cameron decided he wasn't quite ready to concede that Julia was right about Jake being his son. He'd let her squirm for a bit longer. "Oh, for the blood test? Not yet."

She sighed. "I don't know why you can't see it. Your

mother knew Jake was your son within seconds. And before you jump to any conclusions, let me assure you that I didn't say one word to her. She just knew."

"My mother?" Cameron frowned. "She saw Jake?"

As she maneuvered Jake into some kind of stretchy blue pajama thing, Julia related what Sally had told her the day before.

"Okay, I'll admit my mother might have a scheme in mind," Cameron said, watching her. "That still doesn't mean Jake's my son. I mean, I can't imagine I'm the only guy you've ever…" Cameron couldn't continue with that thought. He didn't want to picture Julia with other men, not that it was any of his business what she did or who she did it with. He just didn't want to think about it. He coughed to cover his uneasiness. "Anyway, as I said before, we used protection. So you want to tell me how this could have happened?"

Julia raised her gaze to meet his. "Of course we used protection, but for goodness' sake, Cameron. Don't you remember how many times we did it that weekend? Something was bound to happen."

Yeah, he remembered. And even after all this time, Cameron's groin still stiffened at the memory of that red hot meeting of lips and tongues, hands, skin, bodies.

"Anyway," she said, after taking a deep breath, "you can blame your mother all you want, but we both know how *this* happened." Still blushing, Julia hoisted the baby up into her arms and rushed out of the bedroom. "I'll go warm a bottle and start his dinner."

Cameron followed, unwilling to end the conversation just yet. "Come to think of it, we wouldn't have met in the first place if my mother hadn't demanded that we carry your bakery stuff in our hotels."

She turned. "True. But that was almost two years ago now. Do you really think your mother was thinking at the time that we would...oh, never mind." Her chagrin was obvious as she hurried away from him and went to the kitchen. She placed the baby in his carrier on the bar and made sure he was secure, then walked over and opened the refrigerator door.

"That we would what?" Cameron asked provocatively. "That we would fall into bed the first night we met?" He came up close behind her and wrapped his arm around her waist to stop her in her tracks. "Or that we would spend seventy-two hours making love over and over again, until we passed out?"

He moved even closer. Her curvaceous bottom pushed against his erection and she moaned.

"Do you remember?" he asked.

"Yes," she whispered. "Thank God for room service or we might've starved."

He laughed, then groaned as she pressed into him. He kissed the skin beneath her ear. She stretched her neck to give him more access and he ran his tongue along her jaw line. "Do you remember drinking champagne in that big tub?"

"I remember," she whispered.

"God, you smell so good." He turned her around and kissed her cheek, her chin, then covered her trembling lips with his. Her mouth parted and he delved inside, exploring her moist heat with the sweep of his tongue. She sighed and he plunged again.

The doorbell rang and they both jumped, then stared at each other in disbelief.

"This is crazy," Julia muttered, and grabbed a bottle from the refrigerator shelf.

"Who the hell can that be?" Cameron groused and stalked to the door. He took a moment to compose himself before he opened the door.

"Hello, darling," his mother said.

"Yoo-hoo! Hi, Cameron," Beatrice said, waving behind her.

"We want to see the baby," Marjorie said. "We're not interrupting anything, are we?"

Cameron shook his head as the three women sashayed into the suite. They had been friends longer than Cameron had been alive. They still played cards together every Tuesday. Beatrice and Sally both volunteered at the hospital and Marjorie still worked as Duke Development's Human Resources manager.

"Hello, ladies," he said, and closed the door behind them.

"Are we too late?" Marjorie asked, glancing around the room.

Sally followed her gaze, then turned to Cameron. "We were hoping you'd let us babysit while you two kids ran out and grabbed some dinner."

Julia poked her head out from behind the kitchen bar. "Oh, no, that's not—"

"Sounds great," Cameron said immediately. "Give us five minutes and we'll be ready to go."

"They railroaded us," Julia grumbled as she sipped her chardonnay and nibbled on a carrot stick from the relish tray.

Cameron glanced around at the other tables in the elegant dining room of the Monarch Dunes. He was happy to see that there was a full house tonight, but the space still felt intimate. Stylized sconces along the sage-green walls cast dramatic shadows on the cathedral ceiling. Around the large room, screens and plants created a sense of privacy and exclusivity for the diners. The service was attentive yet discreet. And the food was excellent, naturally. The Duke brothers insisted on it.

"Do you really mind being out tonight?" he asked.

"Oh, no." She glanced around, admiring the room and the view. "Of course not. Everything is lovely."

"Good," he said, resting back in his chair. "Take a sip of your wine and relax."

She complied. "It's wonderful."

They were seated at a table along the glass wall overlooking the golf course and the cliffs and ocean beyond. It was a beautiful night, with a crescent moon and a million stars in the sky. The crystal glassware and silver flatware caught the candlelight and cast rainbow shards on the pristine white tablecloth.

He gazed at her through the glow. "I'm glad you like it."

Sighing, she said, "I just don't want Sally to think I expect her to babysit."

"Get used to it," Cameron said with a sardonic grin. "Now that she knows about Jake, you'll have a hard time keeping her away."

"I know," Julia said, smiling. "She's already threatened to pitch a tent on my front lawn so she can see him every day."

Cameron raised one eyebrow. "I'll talk to her if she gets pushy."

"Oh, goodness no," Julia said, and reached out to touch his hand in reassurance. "I think it's wonderful. I don't have any family so the thought of Jake having a grandmother to dote on him is like a dream come true."

Cameron held on to her hand when she tried to slip it away from his. "Speaking of family, I did what you suggested and looked up the Parrish Trust."

"So you know I'm not looking for a handout."

"No, I guess you're not," he said. "But when I was looking at the trust information, I saw that your parents died when you were young. I'm so sorry."

"Yes, they died in a plane crash. It was devastating. I was ten years old and had no other family to live with."

"What happened to you?"

She smiled wistfully. "I had a nanny who'd been with me since I was born, so the judge allowed her to stay with me. My court-appointed guardians were two of my parents' lawyers and they moved into our house."

"You're kidding. You had lawyers for guardians?"

Julia grimaced. "Yes. And it was just as businesslike an arrangement as you can imagine. You know, I finally read my parents' will a few years ago and it made me feel like one of their properties. I know they loved me, so I blame it on the lawyers. It's just how they used to write these things. The bottom line was, neither of my parents had siblings so there were no relatives who could take me in."

"Be thankful you weren't put into the foster care system."

"Oh, I am," she said in a rush. "My nanny, Rosemary, was great. She was like a mother to me."

"You were lucky to have her."

"Yes, I was." Julia fortified herself with another sip

of wine. "But two years later, she died suddenly. Cancer. It was overwhelming. I cried for weeks."

"I'm sorry." He squeezed her hand lightly.

She nodded. "The trustees hired another nanny but she didn't do much. I was too old by then."

"You were only twelve."

"I always felt like a grown-up," she said, smiling as she broke a breadstick in half and munched on it. "My parents traveled quite a lot for their foundation so I was used to spending time alone. It was okay. I was a self-sufficient kid."

Cameron sipped his wine. "You were lonely."

"Oh, please," she said, waving the comment away. "Don't make me sound like some poor little rich girl."

"Why not?" Cameron's tone was so compassionate that Julia felt her eyes sting. Good grief, would she burst into tears merely because someone showed kindness to her?

"Because no one cares," she said. "Boo-hoo, all the money in the world but no one to love her. It's such a cliché."

"Clichés are true for a reason." Cameron put down his wineglass. "Some things are more important than money, Julia."

Did he mean *love* was more important? Julia wondered, but wasn't about to ask him out loud. Instead she said, "I agree, but it's easy for people with money to say it's not important. So rather than annoy my friends, I keep it simple and don't talk about myself."

"Except to me," Cameron said, and his lips twisted in a grin.

She frowned as though she'd just realized the same thing. "So it would seem."

* * *

The baby was asleep in his bed when they returned to the suite. Sally and her friends assured them they'd had the time of their lives and wanted to do it again. Then they said good-night.

"Would you like a nightcap?" Cameron asked, as he headed for the dining room liquor cabinet.

"I have a long day tomorrow," she said, tossing her sweater over the dining room chair. "But I wouldn't turn down a cup of hot chocolate."

"That's not quite what I had in mind, but okay." He shut the cabinet and followed her into the kitchen. "I'm not sure we have all the ingredients."

"We do." She pulled a slab of chocolate down from the cupboard and began to break it into chunks.

"Where did that come from?"

"I brought it with me," she said.

"You always travel with your own supply of chocolate?"

She looked at him as though he were a dimwit. "Of course."

"Oh, right, guess you never know when you'll be called on to make dessert."

"That's right." She placed the chunks in a small saucepan, added a touch of water and put it on the stove.

"That's it?" he said, his tone dubious.

She pointed to the pan, then the fire. "Chocolate. Hot. Equals hot chocolate."

"It seems like cheating."

She rested her fist on her hip. "You think I should carry cocoa beans and grind them to dust first?"

"Something like that."

She laughed. "This skips a step or two."

He gave her another skeptical look, then stared at the pan. "I'm not sure about this."

She stirred the mixture slowly. "Because you've always made it with cold milk and chocolate syrup."

"Well, yeah," he said, biting back a grin as he leaned against the bar. "Anything else is just un-American."

"Don't judge until you've tried it," she said mildly, adding some more drops of water as she continued to stir.

"It's starting to smell good."

"Here, you stir," she said, handing him the spoon as she turned down the fire slightly. "I need to make whipped cream."

"I suppose you brought that with you, too."

"Always." She pulled a container from the fridge.

He couldn't hold back his smile. "I like the way you travel."

She reached into a drawer and pulled out her own hand mixer, poured cream into a bowl, threw in a heaping spoonful of sugar, and began to mix it up. Less than four minutes later, she had a bowl of thick, pillowy whipped cream. She poured the creamy chocolate into two small coffee cups, added a dollop of whipped cream on top, and handed one to Cameron.

"Sip the chocolate through the cream," she instructed. "That way, you get the hot with the cold, but you don't dilute either."

She stood inches away, watching him as he tried the concoction. He watched her, too, as he sipped the hot, creamy chocolate through the cool, soft whipped cream. It was possibly the most sweetly decadent thing he'd ever eaten.

"Well?" she said.

He stared at her and wondered what the chocolate and whipped cream might taste like when licked off her breasts.

"It's almost immoral, it's so good," he said, his voice husky.

Her cheeks began to turn pink again and he found he enjoyed making her blush. He also savored watching her realize the direction his thoughts were traveling.

She coughed to clear her throat. "So, you like it?"

"Like it?" He took another long sip and emptied the cup. "Yeah. I'd suggest you package it, but I'm afraid it might be banned in thirty or forty states."

"I'll take that as a compliment," she said demurely, and placed her cup on the counter. "Thank you."

"No, thank you. It was delicious." He put down his cup and reached for her. "I want to taste it on your tongue."

Before she could utter a word of protest, his mouth consumed hers.

The heat was instant and overwhelming. The sweetness of her mouth was incendiary. Pressing her against the kitchen wall, he kissed her again and his tongue swept inside, tangling with hers. Now he tasted the need in her. Now he sensed the surrender he'd craved from the first moment he'd seen her in his shower, her long legs wet and warm, her breasts firm and round. He wanted her with a fervent passion he hadn't felt in months, maybe years. Maybe since the last time he'd been with her.

He ravaged her mouth again and again, sweeping and plunging and reveling in her heated depths. She wrapped her arms around his neck and raised herself so that the apex of her thighs pressed against his burgeoning erection. He held her there with one hand while he shifted his other hand up to cover her breast. She moaned and he knew she wanted him as much as he wanted her.

His body shouted at him to take her here, now, against this wall. Tear off her clothes and plunge into her over and over again until they both slid to the floor from sheer exhaustion. He couldn't remember feeling like this, couldn't remember ever needing a woman this much, as much as he needed another breath. Maybe more. She was his. Now.

Julia broke away to take a deep breath. "Oh, Cameron, I can't…"

"I know." He ran his mouth along her exposed jawline and down her neck, sucking and nibbling his way to her shoulders. He began to unbutton her blouse, pulling the fabric back to feast on her soft skin.

"Cameron, please," she murmured. "I…I'm sorry." She pushed away. "I can't do this. I can't…"

He groaned. "You can. You did. Watch. I'll show you."

She pressed her hand against his chest. "I know how it's done. I just…"

His brain clicked into gear and with great reluctance, he shifted back a step. "You mean you're not ready to do this."

"Oh, I'm ready," she said with a contrite smile. "But I'm not stupid. I know how you feel, Cameron."

"I think it's pretty obvious how I feel," he said, carefully pressing himself closer.

It was her turn to groan. This felt too good, but she had to stay strong. "I mean, how you feel about *me*. You think I'm lying to you. You think I set you up and I'm trying to trap you into fatherhood."

"No, I don't."

"*Yes,* you do," she said calmly. "You have rules. I have Jake. We need to get through the blood test before we can even think about…well, I should go to bed."

Crap, he thought. The damn blood test. He really was a dolt.

"Julia, listen to me," he said with all the sincerity he felt in his heart. "I do believe you. I know Jake is my son. I haven't ordered the blood test because I know you're telling the truth."

Her shoulders sagged a little. "You're just saying that because we're this close to jumping into bed together."

"I'm not just saying it," he insisted, then gave her a sideways glance. "But is it working?"

She smiled softly. "I would love to be with you more than anything tonight. But it won't help matters at all. In fact, it'll just complicate everything."

He studied her for a moment and saw in her wide, expressive eyes a mix of storm clouds and uncertainty. And more than a remnant of passion. "I say we go with the complications."

Now Cameron could see a touch of sadness there in her eyes. It felt like a punch to the gut.

"I don't want to be with you simply because I happen to be the woman staying in your hotel suite."

"But you *are* the woman staying in my hotel suite."

"Exactly," she said. "Which makes me convenient, that's all."

"That's not what I meant." He swept his hands through his hair in frustration. "I'm saying all the wrong damn things. Let's start over. I believe you, Julia. Jake is mine. I know you weren't lying. And I want you. I desire you. *You.* Not some woman sleeping in my suite."

She stared up at him, searching his face for answers.

"I want you, too," she said finally. "And I'm glad you believe me. But I know you have your rules. I know that once we leave here, you won't want me anymore. And I can't go through that. I won't. Not again."

Staring back at her, he saw the resolve. He also saw that if he continued his tender assault, he could melt away her reserve. But at what price? It wouldn't be what she wanted, what she needed right now. With great reluctance, he stepped back. "You're wrong, sweetheart. But I'm not going to convince you of that tonight, am I?"

She slowly shook her head. "I'm sorry."

"You and me, both." He couldn't help but lean over and kiss her full, ripe mouth once more. "Sweet dreams, Julia."

Five

His freaking rules.

Talk about being hoisted by his own…whatever. Cameron punched his pillow, knowing once again that he wouldn't get much sleep tonight. It was just as well, because he needed to spend some quality time mentally kicking himself. And he really needed to rethink a few things. Like those rules of his. It's not that he would change them because, frankly, they worked. But he certainly wasn't going to talk about them anymore. Especially not to a woman who might've been lying in his bed this very minute, were it not for him and his big mouth.

Screw the rules, he wanted Julia.

How could he convince her that he believed her? He should've told her immediately that he knew Jake was his son. He'd known it almost from the first minute he'd seen the handsome little kid. But hell, that wasn't even Julia's point, was it? He smacked the mattress in disgust.

Whatever her point was, he still wanted her. Rules be damned. But if he tried to tell her that, she would think he was just saying it to get into her pants. And while that may be true…no, damn it, it wasn't.

He *liked* her. He liked her mind, and her sense of humor, and her integrity. Okay, he liked her pants, too, and everything inside them. Nothing wrong with that.

And besides, she was the mother of his child, so they'd be seeing each other at least once or twice a week for the foreseeable future. And since he'd be coming by to see Jake all the time anyway, why shouldn't they have a…a what? A relationship? An understanding? A regularly scheduled booty call?

Sounded good to him.

Oh, right, he thought. Even Cameron was smart enough to know she would kick his ass into next week if he suggested that scenario.

But she wouldn't keep him from seeing Jake. No way. Cameron would let her know in the morning they would need to work out a custody arrangement.

And now that he thought about it, he would have to make sure his house was baby-proofed. He made a mental note to call Housekeeping the next day and tell them to take care of it.

But just baby-proofing the house wouldn't make it a home for Jake. He would have to transform one of the bedrooms into a room for the little guy. A bed shaped like a race car. A computer. And toys. A football.

He would put up a fence around the pool immediately,

but he would also teach Jake to swim as soon as possible. His son would be a champion swimmer.

He would build a super-deluxe swing set on the side of the house, with a slide and monkey bars to play on. And Jake would need a dog. A big one.

Cameron was just beginning to doze off when it occurred to him that the thought of Jake visiting once every few weeks didn't appeal at all. Maybe Julia and Jake should simply move into his sprawling home on the cliffs overlooking the bay. The place had six bedrooms. There was plenty of room for all of them and the kitchen was big enough for Julia's baking stuff.

Whoa. In a flash, Cameron threw off the covers and sat on the edge of the bed. "Am I insane?"

What was he thinking? He wasn't fit to be a father. And he had no business inviting Julia to move in with him. Hadn't he been through this before? Had he forgotten about Martina?

Years ago, long after the fiasco with his high school girlfriend Wendy, he'd left the marines and gone to work with his brothers to start up their development company. Through business acquaintances he met the very attractive Martina Moran. He thought he'd learned his lesson where love and women were concerned, but once he met Martina, his good sense flew out the window. She came on strong, and almost as a test of his own will he began dating her.

Their relationship flourished and he thought he might be falling for her. Anxious to prove he'd grown as a man and was no longer subject to his father's cruel legacy, he proposed, and Martina said yes. Cameron thought he might be able to finally relax and looked forward to many happy years of married life.

He had been young, stupid and oh, so wrong.

It turned out that Martina had been using Cameron to make another man jealous. Her scheme worked and that man, trust-fund baby Andrew Gray, had begged Martina to marry him. She walked out on Cameron as fast as her Jimmy Choo shoes could carry her.

Cameron had taken Martina's betrayal as a message from the fates. His birthright could no longer be ignored and he had to force himself to accept that he was, indeed, a bad risk, a loser and irretrievably flawed. It was a hard lesson to learn, but it was for the best that he'd vowed never to give in to love again. It could end only in disaster.

He was older now, but was he any smarter? Could he actually make this work with Jake and Julia? Did he really have any choice in the matter? Jake was his son and Julia was Jake's mother. He was determined to make it work. Julia would have to understand that it was all for Jake. As long as they both had Jake's best interests in mind, everything would be fine.

He lay back down and as he drifted into sleep, a plan began to form in Cameron's mind.

It was an effort just to slide the key card into the door slot, Julia admitted the following evening. She was exhausted. She hadn't slept well the night before and she'd just spent one of the most grueling conference days ever. She was looking forward to a glass of wine and a long soak in the tub after she got Jake settled for the night.

But as she stepped into the foyer of the suite, she was instantly assailed by the sounds of controlled madness. Music was playing and people were laughing and talking. Was Cameron having a party? Where was Jake?

Julia had just spent ten long hours working the conference. She was not in the mood for a party. Could she possibly get away with sneaking straight through to the hall and disappearing into the back bedroom?

But that would be a spineless act of cowardice. Julia considered the alternatives and decided she was okay with that.

Before she could make her move, though, a woman about her age walked into the living room and spied Julia lurking in the foyer.

"You must be Julia," she said with a smile. "Cameron's told us all about you."

And what was that supposed to mean? Julia wondered.

"Hello," Julia said, trying not to eye the other woman with too much suspicion. Not only was she drop-dead gorgeous and tall, with thick brown hair and perfect skin, but she looked really nice and friendly.

Was Cameron dating her? Not that she would blame him; the woman was lovely. But did he have to rub Julia's nose in it? Had he invited his friends over for a party? Julia was more convinced than ever that slinking off to the back bedroom was the way to go. She had no place here among Cameron's friends.

At that moment Sally Duke marched into the living room. "Trish, where is—" She stopped when she saw Julia and cried, "Oh, she's here!"

"Hi, Sally," Julia said, now thoroughly confused.

"Come in, sweetie. We've completely invaded your territory and you must be beat after that long day."

"That's okay," she said weakly.

"Come meet my boys and have a glass of wine. You've already met Adam's wife, Trish."

"Not exactly." Julia turned and smiled much more warmly and extended her hand to shake the other woman's. "Hi, Trish."

Trish ignored the handshake, instead pulling her close and giving her a hug. "I'm so glad to meet you. Jake is precious. We're all so lucky Cameron found you both."

"Thank you. I'm happy to meet you, too."

"I'm relatively new to the family, too," she said, linking her arm through Julia's. "Adam and I just got married a month ago."

"Oh, how wonderful. Congratulations."

"Thanks. We're really happy."

"Well, of course you are," Sally said with a wink. "I wouldn't have planned it any other way."

They both laughed, then Trish glanced at Julia. She must've been wearing a look of sheer bewilderment because Trish quickly said, "It's complicated."

Sally laughed again. "But you'll hear the whole story eventually. Come meet my sons."

Sally grabbed Julia's other arm and she and Trish led Julia through the dining room and up to the kitchen bar.

The first thing Julia noticed was that the spacious kitchen area was literally dwarfed by three big, handsome men, obviously Cameron and his brothers, who chatted and laughed with Sally's girlfriends, Beatrice and Marjorie.

The next thing Julia noticed was that the largest of the brothers was holding her baby over his head as though Jake were a paper airplane about to be launched across the room. Jake screamed with laughter and excitement.

Julia, on the other hand, had to take some deep breaths in order to remain calm. This had to be Brandon who was holding Jake. Cameron had told her he used to be an NFL quarterback.

"I want to hold him," the third brother said. By process of elimination, this was Adam. Without waiting for an okay from Cameron, Adam reached over and grabbed Jake mid-flight.

Jake cooed with delight.

"Hi, Jake," Adam said, staring up at the baby. "Welcome to the family."

Brandon reached up and tickled Jake's stomach. "Hey there, kiddo. You're pretty happy to be here, aren't you?"

Jake giggled and his little legs bounced back and forth.

Brandon turned and thumped Cameron on the back. "He's awesome."

"Yeah, he is," Cameron said, taking the baby from Adam. Just for a moment, he held Jake close to his chest, and Julia could almost see his heart on his sleeve.

The moment passed and Cameron swung the baby up above his head so his brothers could get another good look at him. Jake continued to smile and coo at the men, thrilled to be flying in the air. Cameron brought the boy down to eye level and with a note of pride, said, "Notice how handsome he is? Looks just like his father."

"Aw, don't insult him like that," Brandon joked.

Adam laughed. "Yeah, this is a good-looking kid."

"Funny, very funny," Cameron said, and lifted his son up again.

"Dada!" Jake cried.

The room went silent. Julia watched the brothers exchange glances, then they all broke out in grins. Adam slapped Cameron's back. "Congratulations, Dad."

Cameron exhaled heavily. "Thanks, I guess."

"Yeah, congrats," Brandon said. "Can't wait to meet the little woman."

Trish coughed to get their attention. "The little woman?"

"Mama! Mama!" Jake cried. He waved his arms and kicked his legs as the three men slowly turned.

Julia had been marveling at the lovely camaraderie among the brothers and their willingness to bring Jake into the fold, but now she laughed at the abashed expressions on each of their faces. She reached out to pat Jake's cheek as he bounced in Cameron's arms. "Hi, punkin'. Are you having fun?"

The baby burbled and wriggled as Brandon shrugged. "Hey, I'm a big guy. Everyone looks little to me, not just women."

"Nice try, Ace," Adam drawled.

Ignoring him, Brandon thrust his hand toward Julia. "Hi, I'm Brandon, Cam's much smarter and more handsome brother."

Julia shook Brandon's large hand. He was as big as a bear and, like his brothers, one of the most handsome men she'd ever seen. He had shoulders as wide as the refrigerator and wavy, light brown hair an inch too long. He pushed his hair back, but several thick strands flopped onto his forehead, giving him an irresistible, bad boy look. Brandon looked powerful enough to snap a man in two with his bare hands, but he couldn't have been more gentle with Jake.

Adam stepped forward. "Hello, Julia. I'm Adam Duke."

She shook hands with the tallest and most serious of the three brothers. Adam was dark haired and sophisticated, with a strong jaw and piercing blue eyes that focused completely on her. Julia's first thought as she shook his hand was that Trish was a very lucky woman indeed.

"Adam's frightening the womenfolk again," Brandon said, and picked up his beer. "Listen, Julia, if you get scared and need a hug, I'm your man."

Julia laughed, and Trish rolled her eyes in amusement.

"Nobody's hugging her but me," Cameron muttered as he handed Julia a glass of crisp white wine. She smiled her thanks as his two brothers ribbed him.

Conversations overlapped as Cameron opened another bottle of wine. Everyone wanted to hold the baby, and Jake was perfectly happy to be passed around from one family member to the next. Not just the women, but Cameron's brothers also demanded quality time with their new nephew.

Julia took a sip of the wine and felt her muscles and nerves relax. A half hour had passed, she realized, and instead of feeling worn out, she felt energized. She'd never been around such a boisterous, fun group. If this was what family was all about, she would love to be a part of it always.

The doorbell rang and Sally ran out to see who it was.

"That'll be room service," Cameron said in a low voice behind her. "I hope you don't mind, but I invited everyone to stay for dinner."

"I don't mind a bit," she said, turning to smile at him. "Your family is wonderful. You're so lucky."

"I like to think so," he said, staring at her intently.

"I should help get things together," she said, feeling her cheeks burning. Cameron was the only man who could make her blush simply by looking at her.

As she gathered utensils, plates and napkins, she sized up the three Duke men. Cameron's brothers were both gorgeous, but Cameron eclipsed them both with his tall, leanly muscular body, clear green eyes and beautiful smile. And that adorable dimple in his cheek was like the cherry on top. No wonder she was always blushing when he was around.

As the room service crew worked swiftly to set up dinner, Julia settled Jake in his high chair, placing Cheerios and soft baby carrots on his tray for him to munch on while she warmed his dinner.

Then, to everyone's delight, she whipped up a modified chocolate mousse by combining the remaining chocolate bars, whipping cream and sugar from last night and adding egg yolks and vanilla. Within ten minutes, dessert was chilling in the refrigerator and everyone sat down to eat.

All through dinner, they laughed and talked over each other, sharing lots of old family stories with Julia. One story would lead to another, and Julia couldn't remember a time when she'd laughed so much.

After the dishes were removed, Cameron made coffee, and Julia served her chocolate mousse to rave reviews. She had to laugh because it was one of the simplest things she could've made.

Back at the table after clearing the dessert dishes, Julia felt a little twinge in her heart at how readily the

Duke family and friends had welcomed her and Jake into their lives. She watched as Cameron finished giving Jake his bottle and raised him to his shoulder. He rubbed the baby's back a few times and Jake favored him with a rousing belch. Everyone laughed and cheered.

Julia's breath caught as Cameron squeezed her thigh under the table. "You having a good time?"

She gazed at him. "The best ever."

These people, this moment, were exactly what Julia had dreamed about her entire life, she realized. It was the warm family circle she had always wanted to be a part of. Could it really be this easy for a dream to come true? Was she foolish to think she could honestly trust her heart to these people and this man?

Cameron had been watching her closely all evening. He didn't want to crow too loudly, but his plan was working to perfection, even better than he could've envisioned.

Leaning closer to Julia, he said, "Walk with me outside for a few minutes?"

"I should put the baby to bed first," she said.

"Oh, do you mind if we do it?" Trish asked, pushing away from the table. She stood and touched Adam's shoulder. "We should practice, you know."

Adam's eyes widened as he stared up at Trish.

"Excuse me," Brandon said, glancing back and forth at the two of them. "Do you two have an announcement to make?"

"I don't know," Adam said, his eyes narrowed on his wife. "Do we?"

She smiled innocently. "Of course not, but it never hurts to be prepared."

Adam's cheeks puffed out. Shaking his head, he stood and grabbed hold of Trish's hand. "Don't ever scare me like that again."

Everyone laughed, and Cameron handed the baby to Trish. "He's starting to fade into dreamland."

"He's so sweet," Trish whispered, then looked at Julia. "We'll be careful."

"He's pretty sturdy," she teased, tucking Jake's collar under his chin. "And he does love to get his diaper changed."

"Yeah," Cameron said with a laugh. "Good luck with that."

He led her out to the living room and opened the sliding glass door. Julia stepped out onto the terrace and he followed her. The evening breeze lifted her wavy blond hair and she pulled her lightweight jacket tighter around her waist. Cameron squelched the urge to wrap her in his arms and shield her from harm.

It's just a little wind, he thought, knowing she could take care of herself. But ever since he'd hatched his plan in the early hours of the morning, he'd been advancing, both mentally and physically, toward protective mode. He'd already called his housekeeping service to take care of the baby-proofing of his home. They'd also assured him they would have the swing set erected and ready to go within the week. Now he just needed to arrange for the baby's room to be fixed up. He was hoping Julia would be amenable to helping him with that job. They could go shopping together. Women loved to go shopping, right?

"What a beautiful view," she said, gripping the balcony rail as she stared north at the forest of towering redwood trees silhouetted against the night sky.

Cameron's gaze was focused on her. "Yes, it is."

Julia turned and saw that he was looking at her. It was too dark to see if she was blushing, but Cameron had no doubt her cheeks were pink. He wasn't sure why that made him smile. He just knew he hadn't met a woman capable of blushing in a long time.

"Are you having a good time tonight?" he asked, as he rested his hands next to hers on the railing.

"Yes," she said, and her eyes twinkled in the moonlight. "Your family is just wonderful. I'm so grateful that they've welcomed Jake."

"They've welcomed you, too, Julia."

"I know," she said, laughing softly. "They're so kind. I'm thrilled that Jake will grow up surrounded by a warm and loving family."

"Is it going to bother you to have us all clamoring to be with him?"

"Absolutely not," she said firmly. "That's the best thing in the world for him."

"I'm glad you said that, because it's something I've been thinking about all day."

"What do you mean?"

"I'm trying to figure out what's best for Jake."

She gazed up at him. "You are?"

"Yes," he said, smiling down at her. Damn, she was a beautiful woman. Sometimes that realization snuck up and knocked him upside the head. "I want Jake to be a part of my life, Julia. I want the very best for him."

She nodded warily. "I want that, too."

"Good," he said, pleased that his plan was working out so well. "Because I think you and I should get married."

Six

"What?"

He knew he'd caught her off guard, so her shriek shouldn't have been such a big surprise to Cameron. But it still managed to ring in his ears. He grabbed hold of her hands in a romantic gesture he hoped she'd appreciate. "I want us to get married, Julia. You and Jake will move into my home. We'll be giving Jake a great life."

Julia's eyes turned dark. "Jake has a great life."

"It'll be even better if we're together," he said with all the patience he could muster.

"No," she said, shaking her head. "Absolutely not."

Not appreciating her tone, he stepped a foot back and folded his arms across his chest. "Are you going to keep me from seeing my son?"

Taken aback, she stared wide-eyed at him. "No,

of course not. We can arrange some sort of visitation schedule. You can—"

"I don't want visitation," Cameron said. "I want him."

"That's not possible," she cried. "I'm his mother. He's been with me his entire life and I'm more than capable of raising him on my own. You can't take him from me."

"I don't want to take him from you," Cameron said quickly, annoyed that this conversation wasn't going the way he'd planned. Nothing seemed to go according to plan with Julia. "I'm asking you to marry me so we can raise him together."

She stared at him for a moment then asked, "What planet did you come from and what have you done with Cameron Duke?"

"That's not funny."

"You're right, it's not one bit funny. I don't know who you are. Where did you dream up this idea? There's no way I'm going to live with you."

"Why not?"

She spluttered in shock, but finally managed to speak in complete sentences. "Because you don't want me, Cameron. You never look back, remember? What happened to your rules? What changed overnight that you suddenly want me around?"

He swallowed hard and thought fast. "Look, people adjust, Julia. Rules are meant to change with the times." He was being perfectly reasonable, why couldn't she understand?

"Well, isn't that mature of you?" she said, a little too snidely for his taste. "But that still doesn't mean I'm going to move into your house to play nanny while you go about your business."

"Nanny?" He frowned. "Who said anything about you being a nanny?"

"Oh, come on, Cameron. I'm not a complete idiot. You want Jake, so you need me there to take care of him."

"No, that's not true. I want you, too."

"Jake and I are perfectly happy in our own home. With *our* nanny. You can visit anytime."

"I don't want to visit, I want to live with my son and his mother. I want you to marry me. Why is that so hard to comprehend?"

"Because you're using me to get to Jake," she said, her voice quivering with emotion. "And I won't be used."

That's when it sank in. Julia was afraid. Damn it. Once more, he was being a dolt. She seemed to bring that quality out in him. Leaning back against the concrete balcony wall, Cameron pulled her close and ran his hands slowly along her spine, trying to soothe her. "I swear I'm not using you, sweetheart. I wouldn't do that. I'm just asking for a chance to live as a family. You, me and Jake."

She sighed, then looked up at him. "Cameron, you don't love me."

His eyes widened before he could stop the reaction. She wanted love? From him? He blew out a breath, knowing he could never give her that. But there were plenty of other things he could give her.

"Julia, I admire you," he said gently. "I respect you. I like you a helluva lot. I want to be with you. It's pretty obvious we're both hot for each other. That's a major plus, right? I think we could have a great life together. But I...I just don't do love. I'm sorry."

She tilted her head and studied him keenly. "Do you love Jake?"

He frowned. Did he love his son? Could he? He thought about it, remembering those moments when he and the little guy had stared into each other's souls. He already had a bone-deep connection to the boy. Was that love? Did it matter? Cameron didn't think so and Julia would have to deal with that.

"Jake is my son," he said. "I'll protect him with my life."

Julia nodded without speaking. She'd seen the look of awareness that had passed across Cameron's face when he'd considered whether he loved Jake or not. Julia knew that look. She'd seen it in her own face when she looked in the mirror while holding Jake. It was the look of parental love. Cameron might not be able to say the words, but she knew he felt them.

She didn't dare admit that she was tempted by his loveless proposal. What would that make her, besides desperate? Did she really want a family so badly that she would abandon the possibility of love forever?

A while later, she wandered through the rooms of the suite, visiting with the people she'd already begun to wishfully think of as her family. At the same time, she considered Cameron's words. He liked Julia. Respected her. They were hot for each other. But was all that enough to make them a family? On the other hand, there were probably plenty of other families that had started out with less.

A family was something she'd dreamed of for most of her life. She'd always imagined what fun it would be to have brothers and sisters to play with and talk to. Cameron's brothers and Trish would fulfill that desire. And with Sally, she would have a mom to share her deepest dreams and secrets with. They could go shopping and have lunch together.

"And we could braid each other's hair," she muttered, disgusted with herself. Good grief, was she so needy that she would marry Cameron just to have lunch with his mother?

With a sigh, she walked into the second bedroom just as Trish snapped the last snap on Jake's jammies.

"We did it," Trish said, gazing at Adam with just-ifiable pride.

"You were brilliant," he said. With one hand, he held Jake securely on the changing table while he reached for Trish with the other and planted a kiss on her mouth.

Julia sighed again. It was such a romantic move.

Trish noticed her then. "Oh, Julia, he was a perfect angel."

"And he looks relatively undamaged by the whole experience," Julia quipped. "For that, I thank you."

"Thank you so much for trusting us with him," Trish said.

Adam kissed her temple and she beamed at him. They were so clearly in love, it almost hurt to watch them.

Could Cameron ever love her that much? she won-dered, then rapidly banished the foolish thought from her mind. Wishing for things that would never come true wasn't her style. Long ago, she'd trained herself not to wish for too much and to be happy with whatever she had, because things could always change for the worse in a heartbeat.

After Adam and Trish left the room, Julia laid Jake in his crib and rubbed his tummy until he settled.

"Sweet dreams, my darling," she whispered, and watched him drift off to sleep. He'd always been such a happy baby, and relatively easy to care for. Now Julia wondered if she was robbing her son of a closer relationship with his father by saying no to Cameron's proposition. Cameron had said he would protect Jake with his life. But was that enough on which to build a marriage? Could she be content, knowing that Jake would have a doting father who protected and cared for him?

As she switched off the light, Julia remembered the other point Cameron had made to sweeten the deal. They were hot for each other.

"So true," she murmured, and felt a jolt of desire in her lower stomach at the thought of the two of them in bed together. The image was so vivid, she had to stop for a moment, take a deep breath and let it out slowly, before she was able to walk into the living room. Her eyes instantly sought and found Cameron, who watched her with an intensity she'd never experienced from a man before.

Julia's laid-back facade turned to dust as Cameron's blazing awareness scorched her from across the room. Oh, yeah, they had heat. The question was how long could they make it last?

Cameron scrunched his pillow and wondered if he would ever sleep again. In keeping with his plan, after their guests had left, he'd led Julia to her bedroom door where he'd kissed her good-night and walked away.

"For the third damn night in a row," he said. Once

again, he lay in bed wide awake, wondering what the hell was wrong with him. He was a marine, he'd led warriors into battle and faced the enemy, but walking away from Julia a few hours ago had been the hardest thing he'd ever done.

But it was for a good cause, he reasoned. His plan was working. Leave her wanting more. He'd give Julia another few days, but in the end, she would come to see that marriage was the best thing they could do for little Jake.

None of that seemed to matter to his libido, though. He stared at the moonlight streaming in through the window and resigned himself to another sleepless night. All for the good of the plan.

It was impossible for Julia to avoid Cameron in the morning, not when he was sitting at the dining room table, eating toast as he fed Jake his breakfast of rice cereal and mashed bananas. She wondered how he'd picked up the baby's routine so well in less than three days. Was the babysitter giving him private lessons?

She also wondered if she would ever get a decent night's sleep again. It was bad enough that Cameron had dropped a bomb when he asked her to marry him. But then after that, when she'd gotten all hot and bothered and tempted by the way he watched her so intently, what did he do? He kissed her chastely and dumped her off at her bedroom door.

She hadn't slept a wink and it was all his fault.

"Jeez, kiddo," Cameron muttered, grabbing Jake's hand before he could smear bananas in his hair. "They go in your mouth, not in your hair."

Despite her somewhat surly mood, Julia bit back a smile. "Nice save."

He looked up and grinned and Julia's heart took a sharp dip. "Thanks. You off to the conference?"

"Yes," she said. "The babysitter should be here in five minutes."

"Okay, good," he said, as he took a cloth and wiped cereal off Jake's neck. Jake giggled and Cameron gave his nose a light tweak. Jake pounded his tray in delight and Cameron stroked his head affectionately. "Yeah, you're pretty tough, aren't you, pal?"

Julia's first baking demonstration was to begin in less than twenty minutes, but how could she leave when Cameron and Jake were having so much fun bonding, eating, playing? It was all so domestic. So normal and comfortable. So...desirable. She'd wanted this so badly, for so long, and now it was happening. How could she leave? Not just today, but ever? How could she give this up?

The man and the baby laughed in unison and Julia stared, mesmerized. Dear God, was there anything more sexy than the sight of this strong man taking care of her baby?

The tears came from nowhere and Julia tried to sniffle them away. She had to go. Leave. Quickly, before her brain exploded from confusion, from distraction, from yearning. From love. Not to mention lust.

She took another deep breath and let it out, then leaned over and kissed Jake's cheek. "Bye-bye, sweetie. I love you."

Without thinking, she kissed Cameron as well, right on the mouth. Realization hit her and she tried to break off the kiss, but he grabbed her arm and kept her close, lengthening the contact until she gasped for air.

Breathless, she managed, "Um, bye."

"Bye-bye, sweetie," Cameron said, grinning brashly as she backed out of the room and rushed out of the suite.

The meeting with the new investors had gone smoothly, Cameron thought, as he slipped their business cards inside the pocket of his suit jacket. Now he had an hour to kill before he met with his managers for their weekly lunch. Strolling down the wide hall to the conference center, he found the demonstration room he'd been looking for and walked inside.

"Can you taste the difference?" Julia was saying as she wandered up the aisle, holding a large bowl and handing out samples to the attendees on small plastic spoons.

"It's so bright, it practically glows," she said cheerfully. "I love that. And see how sticky it is? That's from the egg whites. This type of frosting takes longer to make, but look at the stiff peaks. It's gorgeous, isn't it? Worth the extra effort, don't you agree?" Julia popped a sample into her mouth. "Mmm, and so sweet, it melts on your tongue."

Cameron was hard in an instant. It didn't seem to matter that the room was filled with people, or that she was dressed conservatively in sensible heels, slim navy pants and a pale blue shirt with a cook's apron tied securely around her waist. He wanted her now. He could imagine her in just the apron and heels and his hardness intensified.

Gritting his teeth, he wondered how an innocuous,

twenty-second description of cake frosting could make him want to pick her up and toss her onto the nearest flat surface where he could plunge into her hot, moist core?

Maybe it was her vocabulary. Sticky, stiff peaks? Melts on your tongue? Damn, just what was she teaching these people?

At that moment, Julia saw him and stopped in her tracks. His gaze narrowed in on her and he wondered if she could see what she was doing to him.

Her eyes flashed with awareness and she had to cough to clear her throat. "We'll take a ten-minute break now, and when you come back, I'll reveal the secret ingredient for making the ultimate buttercream frosting."

Cameron ignored the stream of attendees drifting past him and stared directly at Julia until the room had cleared and she approached.

"What a nice surprise," she said with a smile. She still held the bowl of frosting and scooped out a small spoonful. "Want a taste?"

"Yeah," he growled. He grabbed the bowl and spoon and put them on the nearest desk. Then he clutched her upper arms, pulled her close and kissed her. He could taste the sweetness on her lips, her tongue, and wanted more. Wanted all of her. Here and now.

She reached up and wrapped her arms around his neck and he knew she could feel his length pressing against her.

"Where can we go?" he demanded. "Right now. Where can we be alone?" He didn't know why he was asking her. Hell, he owned the place, he ought to be able to come up with something. But with her clinging to him, his mind was a sieve. He couldn't think, couldn't focus, couldn't do anything but take as much of her sweet heat as she could offer.

"Cameron," she whispered, panting for air. "My students will be back in a minute."

"I want you now," he said, as if she couldn't tell from the rock-hard pressure against her. His mouth covered hers in a move of possession so demanding that she could only comply, opening to allow him entry so deep that he wondered vaguely where he left off and she began.

"Cameron, I...I want you, too," she said on a gasp of air. "But we'll have to wait."

"I can't wait much longer," he muttered, then took her mouth again, sweeping inside to savor more of her moist warmth.

"Tonight," she promised when they broke off the kiss.

"Tonight," he echoed, just as the doors swung open and her students filtered back into the room.

"And we'll talk," she added.

"Yeah, we'll talk."

Seven

Julia stepped inside the suite and glanced around the quiet, empty living room. Were Cameron and Jake taking a nap again?

A sudden, distant whoop of laughter made her smile, and she followed the shrieks and giggles all the way back to the bathroom attached to the second bedroom. Taking one cautious look inside the room, she burst into laughter herself.

Jake sat, surrounded by floating toys and securely tucked into his sturdy bath ring seat. The seat was suctioned to the bathtub's surface so he couldn't go anywhere, but he could splash up a storm. And that always made him happy.

Cameron, on the other hand, was drenched. "Partner," he said, as he soaped up a washcloth and swiped it across

Jake's shoulders and back. "We're going to have a long talk about water conservation one of these days."

Julia smiled. She'd spent the morning going over all the pros and cons of a marriage to Cameron Duke, but when he'd walked in on her frosting workshop earlier, she forgot everything she'd been thinking. The look in his eyes as he'd stared at her told her everything she needed to know. Maybe he didn't love her yet, maybe he would never use the *L*-word with her, but in that moment, in his eyes, she had seen something so intense, so real, so elemental. Part of her wanted to take that leap of faith, to be part of his life, to be a family with him and wanted to experience his passion every day for as long as it lasted. But another part of her was holding back, worrying and wondering if a loveless marriage to Cameron was perhaps the worst thing she could commit to, for both of them.

Cameron looked up at her then, his face dripping water. "Do you want to take over here?"

"No, you're doing great," she said, and made her escape.

An hour and a half later, the dinner dishes were in the dishwasher and a sleepy Jake was tucked into bed.

Cameron tugged Julia's hand and they tiptoed out of the baby's room. He led her into the living room where he'd left their half-full wineglasses and a small plate of her homemade cookies. "Let's sit here and talk."

"Okay," she said, visibly nervous. He wasn't sure why. She held all the cards in this transaction, didn't she know that?

When the idea had first occurred to him to have Julia and Jake move in, the thought of asking her to marry him was the furthest thing from his mind. After all, from the time he was eight years old, he had vowed never to get married, ever. Of course, he'd also vowed never to have children. So much for the vows of an eight-year-old boy. Now, not only did he have a kid, but he fully intended to move that kid into his home and marry his mother—if that's what it took to get them there.

He hoped he'd made the case last night, that their marriage would be built on respect and a mutual desire to raise Jake in a two-parent home. And lots of hot sex, of course. That was a key point of the negotiations.

And that was a hell of a lot more than most people started with.

"Cameron, I've—"

"Sweetheart, just—"

She laughed self-consciously, and Cameron said, "Go ahead. Tell me what you were going to say."

"Okay," she said with a nod as she brushed her hair away from her face.

"Here, let me do that," Cameron murmured, and ran his fingers through her thick, luxurious strands, lifting and pushing them back. He used the movement to come closer and breathe in her feminine scent.

"That feels good," she whispered.

"God, you're beautiful," he said, clutching her hair lightly in his hands as he stared into her vivid blue eyes. A few errant wisps of hair got loose and he smoothed them back behind her ears. "Your hair is every color of the rainbow."

"I know," she said shyly. "It's so odd."

"It's lovely." He bent to kiss her neck. "And it always smells great."

"Thank you," she said. Her eyelids fluttered closed

and she moaned as he kissed her once more. "You're distracting me, you know."

"I know," he said, as he nuzzled her neck. "Give me a minute."

She touched his cheek. "Cameron, I'll never say what I need to say if I don't do it right now."

"All right," he said in resignation, and sat back against the cushions. "Go ahead."

She took a deep breath, looked him directly in the eyes and said, "Okay. It's just that I…I've decided that, yes, I'll marry you."

He'd always known—hoped—he'd be able to talk her into it, but he hadn't realized until that moment how immensely important it was that she agree. He felt himself loosen up as his muscles relaxed and his chest lightened, making him realize he'd been tense enough to crack in half.

"Did you just say you'll marry me?" he said, checking to make sure he'd heard her correctly.

"Yes," she said, smiling tentatively. "Yes, Cameron. I'll marry you."

"Good. That's settled." He swooped her off the couch and onto his lap, then cut off her next sentence by kissing her deeply. His hands traced the length of her spine as his mouth claimed her as his own. His body absorbed the waves of shivers radiating off her as she met his fervor wholeheartedly, opening for him in a charged meeting of lips and tongues and anticipation.

He savored the taste of her and wanted to feel her skin against his. Now.

Julia must've had the same thought because she wriggled off his lap and turned to straddle him. "Touch me," she demanded.

"Great minds think alike," he murmured, as he slid his hands under her sweater. Lifting it up and off her in one movement, he inhaled sharply at the sight before him. She was braless. Her breasts were exposed and they were perfect. Fuller than he remembered, ripe and round, her dusky pink nipples erect as if waiting for his touch.

With both hands, he cupped her breasts, using his thumbs to tease her nipples until she moaned and pressed her hands over his. He gave in to temptation and moved to take first one breast, then the other into his mouth, licking, sucking and nibbling as she whispered words of urgent need.

Delicious, was all he could think. His senses were spinning out of control. Her skin was silken. She smelled like a field of delicate flowers and tasted like the sweetest sin.

Julia's hands moved to his head and clutched him to her breasts, urging him to indulge more.

Any thoughts of taking things slowly disappeared as he drank her in, moving back to her succulent mouth where she met him hungrily, opening for him to sweep in and take.

Scorching a path down her neck, he kissed his way across her shoulders and back to her breasts, which demanded more attention from him. She moaned as her hips moved back and forth, pressing against him insistently. His erection strained for release. He was dangerously close to losing it and she and her sexy body weren't helping matters.

"You're killing me," he growled. "Wrap your arms around my neck." Gripping her bottom with both hands, he levered himself off the couch and stormed down the hall to the master bedroom where he laid her on the bed.

She leaned up on her elbows and watched as he rapidly stripped off his clothing. Her eyebrows rose as his erection was unfurled. He could see the hunger in her eyes and it empowered him. He prowled closer, naked and rigid, until he stood between her legs. Bending over her, he unzipped her pants and pulled them off, leaving her in nothing but an incredibly hot, black lace thong.

"Is it my birthday?" he wondered aloud.

"Did you make a wish?" she asked, her eyes twinkling with promise.

"Yeah. It just came true."

She licked her lips in an unconscious move that almost undid him. Then she blinked in surprise as he knelt at the end of the bed and shifted her legs onto his shoulders.

"I have to taste you," he muttered, and kissed her most delectable spot. When he thrust his tongue into her, she arched off the bed with a feral cry.

"You're mine now," he murmured, and proceeded to brand her, licking and plunging over and over until she was writhing on the bed. He used one finger to enter her moist core and she groaned with pleasure.

"Now, Cameron," she cried. "I need you inside me now."

He lowered her legs carefully, then stood and walked across the room, leaving her moaning in protest until she noticed him putting on a condom. Then he was back. He knelt on the bed and stroked her again with his fingers to assure himself she was truly hot, moist and ready for him.

"Please, now," she whispered, pulling him closer.

"Yes, now," he said and entered her swiftly and completely. She gasped and he planted his mouth on hers and kissed her fully, swallowing her cries, sweeping within, his tongue matching his own surging thrusts as he buried himself within her.

She drove him to the edge, but his innate self-control pushed back from the brink. Pumping harder, faster, he moved deeply into her, so deep that he might've lost himself in her. It didn't matter. Pulling his head back, he watched the storm gather in her eyes as he stroked again, craving more, demanding all. When at last he saw her head whipping back and forth in surrender and heard her cry out his name, he buried his face in her neck and kissed her skin. Gathering the last of his strength, he thrust again, then again, and finally gave himself up to the abyss and tumbled, free-falling, into her arms.

They were married three days later on the cliffs of the Monarch Dunes resort, overlooking the ocean. The day was sunny and bright, the ocean was a calm, deep blue, and the grass was sparkling green after an overnight light spring rain.

All in all, it was impossibly romantic, or it would've been, if not for the fact that the groom didn't love the bride. And the lawyers on both sides who'd insisted on drawing up a prenuptial agreement. Cameron and she had signed the final documents that morning.

But Julia refused to dwell on the gnawing details as she listened to her new husband declare, "I do." A minute later, he wrapped her in his arms and kissed her senseless in front of the small crowd of well wishers, and all seemed right with the world.

She'd found a beautiful white dress to be married

in. It wasn't exactly the bridal gown of her dreams and maybe the white was a bit of a stretch but it was a lovely off-the-shoulder summer frock that she could wear again. Cameron looked handsome and strong and sexy in his tuxedo. Sally and Trish had found an adorable matching tuxedo for little Jake to wear.

"I'd like to make a toast," Adam said, and everyone raised their glasses as he proceeded to give a stirring speech.

"Cheers," the guests cried, and Cameron and Julia took sips of the expensive champagne. The diamond on her finger twinkled and she smiled. The day after she'd told Cameron she would marry him, he had presented her with the most beautiful ring she'd ever seen. Then he'd made love with her so tenderly, so sweetly, she'd been brought to tears. Yes, she knew Cameron didn't love her, but she couldn't fault him for putting on a really good act.

Julia had been consumed by both the catering conference and the sudden wedding plans, so Sally had taken on the task of inviting friends to the wedding. Many of Julia's friends were there today, and for that alone, she fell in love with her new mother-in-law all over again.

Cameron's two brothers were sharing the best man honors. Sally had held Jake quietly through the ceremony and the toast, but now the boy cried for Cameron to hold him.

"Come here, cowboy," Cameron said, and hoisted Jake into his arms, putting an immediate stop to the whimpering. Holding Jake securely in one arm, Cameron put his other arm around Julia, then leaned in to kiss her. "Thank you. We'll be happy, you'll see."

"I know," she said, smiling. Then she was whisked away for a hug and a kiss on the lips from Brandon.

"Welcome to the family, gorgeous," he said.

She smiled up at her handsome new brother-in-law. "Thank you, Brandon."

"I'd like to welcome you, as well," Adam said, then hauled her into his arms and kissed her soundly.

Dizzy, she almost stumbled but caught herself. "Whew. Okay. Anyone for cake?"

Cameron scowled at his brothers, but Sally laughed as she linked arms with Julia. "They're a formidable trio, aren't they?"

"I'll say," Julia said, still breathless.

"This is a delightful party," Sally said, giving her a quick hug before she left to join her girlfriends at the champagne bar.

Julia watched as other guests wandered over to the nearby tables where all sorts of hearty hors d'oeuvres shared space with numerous bite-sized desserts. Many of them were made following her own recipes so she knew they were delicious. She wished she'd had more time to prepare for the wedding, but things had turned out pretty well, under the circumstances.

Most importantly, she and Jake were now part of a family, and that made all the last-minute preparations worth it.

Her old friend Karolyn Swenson walked over and gathered her close for a hug.

"I'm so glad you could make it," Julia said. They'd known each other since grade school and Karolyn was her manager at the bakery.

"How could I miss it?" Karolyn said, gripping Julia's

hands in hers. "I still can't believe you're married. You actually went and did it."

"I did it," Julia said, and met her friend's gaze. "Be happy for me?"

"Of course, I'm happy for you," she said, then whispered, "He's gorgeous. I assume he's your baby's daddy. Jake looks just like him."

Julia gave a start of surprise. "Yes, he's the one. And he'll be a great dad. We're going to be a happy family."

"Then that's all that matters, isn't it?" Karolyn hugged her again, and Julia had the feeling her friend was trying to reassure her that she'd done the right thing.

As Karolyn walked away to find a glass of champagne, Julia's resolve slipped. Was having a family all that mattered? Julia had thought so when she told Cameron she'd marry him, and again when she said "I do" a while ago. But honestly, how would she know? She hadn't had a real family in almost twenty years. But it's what she'd always wanted, so she would have to take it on faith that she was doing the right thing. Faith, and Cameron's vow that the three of them would have a wonderful life together. As vows went, that was a good one.

"I brought you a fresh glass of champagne," Sally said.

Julia turned and smiled her thanks and the older woman entwined her arm in Julia's.

Sally sighed. "When I see the way Cameron looks at you, it warms my heart."

Julia counted to five to ease the sudden tension she felt. "I know we'll be really happy together."

"Of course you will be." Sally patted her arm. "Now

look, you and I were friends long before we became family, right?"

"That's right," Julia said with a tentative smile.

"So I want you to tell me the truth. You do love Cameron, don't you?"

Julia blinked. "Love him? Why, of course I…"

Sally studied her for a moment. "Was that a yes?"

"Oh, God," she said lamely. It was impossible to lie. The fact was, she and Cameron had talked about his inability to love her, but as for whether Julia loved him or not…

What she knew for sure was that she wanted to be part of his family more than anything. She respected and cared for him a lot. She wouldn't have agreed to marry him if she didn't.

Her shoulders sagged. "I don't know."

"You don't know?" Sally asked. "Interesting. It didn't come up in conversation before you took the plunge?"

Julia bit her lip. "Well, yes, it did. But not in the way you think."

"I suppose I appreciate your honesty," Sally said. "But I'm going to go out on a limb and say that I won't be surprised if someday soon, you and Cameron both realize that what you're feeling for each other is love."

Julia grabbed Sally's hand and squeezed. "I hope you're right. But for now, please know that I'm happy. Really, really happy."

"I'm happy, too, sweetheart." Sally blinked back tears, then smiled and surveyed the crowd. "I'll be honest. Once my sons were grown, I worried that they would have a hard time finding women who would love them for themselves and not for their money or position."

"I imagine you've suffered through some scary moments over that issue."

"You'd better believe it." She winked at Julia. "But I don't have to worry about that with you, do I?"

Julia laughed. "No, I don't think anyone can accuse me of marrying your son for his money."

"What's so funny?" Cameron said, coming up behind her. He wrapped his arm around her waist and pulled her close to his side.

"Sally was just saying that nobody can accuse me of marrying you for your money."

He chuckled, then thought about it for a moment. "I guess nobody can accuse me of that, either."

"So it's a win-win," she said and smiled at him.

"Absolutely," he murmured, and smiled back. Then he tightened his hold on her, pulling her even closer and resting his forehead against hers.

Sally looked on with interest, then said something about getting more champagne and walked away, leaving the newlyweds alone for a moment.

He stared into her eyes. "Have I told you lately how beautiful you are?"

She sighed. He was so handsome, and he'd been so good to her and Jake. It wouldn't take much more for her to fall in love with him.

She stopped, stunned. What was wrong with her? Hadn't she just confessed to Sally that she hadn't married for love? She needed to get a grip. He was handsome and a nice guy, so all she was feeling was lust, not love. She glanced around as she cleared her throat. "It looks like everyone's having a good time."

"Thanks to you," he said. As his brothers came over

to talk to him, Cameron absently took hold of Julia's hand and kissed her knuckles.

She sighed again. It had just been a momentary lapse, she assured herself. It wouldn't happen again. She could blame it on the wedding itself. Weddings were romantic, that was a given. Everyone here, including his mother, had automatically assumed they were in love. And why wouldn't they? She and Cameron had just repeated vows to love and honor each other. They were married now. Both of them wore shiny new wedding rings. They'd put on quite a show.

But that's all this was. A show. A sham, really. Cameron was not in love with her, never would be. And if she thought about it, she couldn't really be in love with a man who didn't love her, could she? No. And if she found herself wishing, just once in a while, that he really did love her, then she was a bigger fool than anyone.

It was time for her to face the fact that all she had with Cameron Duke was a marriage of convenience. With benefits, of course. Rather nice benefits, to be sure, but those were a far cry from love everlasting. And the sooner she accepted that reality, the better off she would be.

Eight

That evening, Sally took the baby and all his baby necessities to her room for Jake's first sleepover. For Sally, it was an adventure. For Julia, it was an excuse to worry.

Cameron ordered champagne to go with some of the hors d'oeuvres they'd brought back from the wedding ceremony. Julia changed out of her white dress and into something cozier while Cameron poured the champagne.

As she walked into the living room, she stopped abruptly. "Did your mother take the wet wipes with her?"

"I don't—"

"I'd better check." She turned and ran back to the bedroom, then returned after a few seconds. "I guess she got them."

"Julia, relax," Cameron urged, and handed her a fresh glass of champagne.

"You're right, I'm being silly." She took a sip and started to sit down on the couch, then jumped up. "Oh, no. I forgot to give her the brush for washing out the bottles."

"Sweetheart, my mother is not going to wash baby bottles."

"Oh, God, of course not. What was I thinking?" She took another sip of the champagne, then sighed. "I guess I just miss him."

Feeling relaxed, Cameron leaned his elbow on the mantel. "Hey, at least you've had him around for the past nine months. How do you think I feel? I just…"

He cut himself off as he saw Julia's eyes narrow in on him like a heat-seeking missile. He wondered if it was possible to snatch the words back, but it was too late. She turned on him like a rabid dog. "So you still blame me for keeping him from you?"

"No, I don't," he insisted with a firm shake of his head.

She walked right over and smacked his arm. "All it would've taken was one lousy phone call, but you were too damn proud to give an inch."

"You're right, sweetheart. But at the time, it seemed like you were a little obsessed."

She stopped in her tracks and turned on him. "Obsessed? I was not obsessed. I was—" she flailed her arms, trying to find the right word "—I was driven."

He realized they'd never truly discussed all her emails or his blatant disregard of them. Tonight didn't seem like the most opportune time to delve into it, but the subject wasn't going to go away. "Look, you sent me four emails in one day, Julia. I'd call that a little obsessive."

She folded her arms tightly across her chest. "So you actually saw my emails."

"Yes, I saw them," he said reasonably. "I opened the first one where you demanded that I call you. And I almost picked up the phone, but then I noticed you'd sent three more in rapid succession and I figured you were a little, you know."

"Obsessed," she said pointedly, and continued her pacing.

He shrugged. "I guess. But that's all in the past. Let's forget about it and enjoy the evening."

But she wasn't ready to let it go. He was troubled that she was no longer fuming but instead looked a bit forlorn. "I was pregnant and alone, Cameron. Nobody would've blamed me for being a little obsessed."

"I don't blame you," he said. "I'm just explaining how I felt at the time. In hindsight, I wish I'd called you, but back then, I was being cautious."

"Oh, because so many women are obsessed over you?"

He wasn't about to explain to his lovely new wife that there actually had been a few dangerously obsessed women over the years. Right now, Julia was venturing into perilous territory and Cameron didn't see a safe way out.

"Look Julia, you're upset and—"

"You're darned right I'm upset."

"Then let's sit down and talk about—"

"Never mind, Cameron," she said, pacing away from him, then whirling around. "I'm sorry, but I can't do this right now. I need some time to think. I— I'm sorry." She turned and ran down the hall to the second bedroom where she went inside and closed the door.

"That did not go as planned," he muttered, staring down the hall, almost not believing what had just happened. He'd screwed things up royally. He wasn't sure how, he just knew this was his fault.

The fact was, they were married now. They shouldn't be fighting, they should be having sex. Rubbing his forehead in frustration, he walked to the wet bar and poured himself a healthy shot of Scotch. Holding the glass up, he toasted himself. "You're a knucklehead." The whiskey burned all the way down his throat. And so did the realization that he'd hurt her.

But she'd caught him off guard. He was so used to Julia being reasonable and smart and funny, he hadn't recognized the signs. She'd worked night and day to put together the wedding. And she'd been worried about the baby. He didn't realize how worried, so he hadn't helped matters one bit.

Fortified by several more generous slugs of Scotch, he flopped down on the living room couch, thinking he'd watch the football game. But he dozed off before he ever had a chance to switch on the television.

Something was pounding against his head. Had he really had that much to drink last night?

"Dada!"

Cameron opened one groggy eye and saw a blurry-looking Jake, up close, smacking his little hand against Cameron's forehead.

"Hey, buddy," Cameron whispered, grabbing his hand. "Let's use our indoor voice, okay?"

"Dada," Jake cried in excitement, then bobbled and plopped back on his well-padded butt.

Cameron's vision began to clear and he could now see Julia standing a few feet away, her arms folded across her chest, shaking her head at him.

"Don't yell," Cameron said in surrender. "I know I'm a slug and deserve your wrath, but I want you to be happy and I want us to be together. I apologize for everything. Can we start this whole thing over?"

She smiled, enjoying the moment. "I'd like that."

That night, Cameron was determined to seduce his wife. This time, he did everything right. The baby was off to spend the night with Sally again, he'd stocked up on more champagne and ordered a small platter of appetizers. And there was Julia.

Sitting on the couch, he framed her face with his hands and gazed into her eyes. "Forgive me, Julia."

"Of course," she said simply.

"I don't really want to get too far into it," he said, "but I've lived with anger in my life. Let's make a pact never to go to bed angry again."

She searched his face and must've found whatever it was she was looking for, because she nodded. "It's a deal."

"Good." He kissed her. Then he reached inside his pocket. "I have something for you. A token of my feelings for you, as well as my gratitude, and…well. Here."

He pulled out a slim blue box and handed her the gift.

"No." She stared at the box, then looked at him,

her forehead creased with concern. "I didn't get you anything."

He chuckled. "Honey, I already got the best end of the deal. I got you and Jake."

She carefully unwrapped the baby-blue jeweler's box and opened the lid. Inside was an exquisite diamond necklace. In shock, she whispered, "Oh, Cameron, it's gorgeous. But…why?"

"Because I wanted to give you a little something to remember this evening. Now let me put it on you."

"It's hardly 'a little something,'" she murmured, but held her hair up as he slipped the necklace around her neck and fastened it.

He kissed the back of her neck, then she turned to show him how it looked. "It's perfect. Just like you."

She smiled as she ran her fingers hesitantly over the necklace. "You shouldn't have done it, but thank you."

He poured champagne, then they made slow, easy love on the couch. Afterward, they moved to the bedroom and started all over again.

Much later, they were both too wide awake to sleep, so they talked for another hour. Cameron asked her questions about her pregnancy and Jake's birth. She told him about the baby's milestones. He wondered about their nanny and she told him all about the older woman who took such good care of Jake. They talked about her bakery and her schedule these days.

He asked her why she specialized in cupcakes at her bakery. She shrugged, told him that people liked cupcakes, then changed the subject, asking him how it was to grow up with two brothers. He regaled her with Sally Duke stories. Cameron found himself laughing more than he ever thought he could.

The laughter turned to kisses and they ended up making love again.

The next morning, they shared a quiet breakfast on the terrace, wearing matching robes. He was pleased that she still wore the diamond necklace.

"Do you want more coffee?" he asked, lifting the carafe.

"Yes, please." She glanced around, a puzzled frown on her face. "Is that water running?"

He listened, then grinned. "It's the waterfall."

"You have a waterfall?" Standing, she walked to the balcony railing and looked out at the resort grounds. "Is it by the beach?"

"Not exactly." He joined her at the railing and pointed out a large, thick copse of trees and shrubbery next to a rocky mound halfway across the expanse. "It's a pool. Very private. We rent it out for parties occasionally, but we don't advertise it. It's part of an underground spring, so the water is naturally warm. I had a grotto built around the pool, with a waterfall. It's pretty nice."

She sighed. "It sounds wonderful."

"It's secluded and romantic." He wrapped his arms around her. "Maybe we'll check it out before we leave."

"I have only two days left of my conference, so we'll have to…oh, my God."

"What is it?"

Her eyes showed a spark of fear. "What day is this?"

"Tuesday."

"Cupcakes," she cried. "I have to bake cupcakes." She slid the terrace door open, then stopped and shook her finger at him. "You distracted me."

"I hope to God I distracted you," he muttered, following her into the suite.

"Oh, you know what I mean." She circled the kitchen, opening cupboards and slamming drawers. "The demonstration is today at two o'clock. I have to start baking now."

"Why don't I just send my assistant to the store to buy a few dozen cupcakes?"

She stared at him, her mouth agape in horror. She waved him off as she raced down the hall. "You don't get it."

"Babe, relax," he said, strolling after her. "I can help."

She stopped abruptly. "Very funny, Cameron."

"Hey, I'm a good cook," he insisted, scowling as he trailed her into the master bathroom. "Ask anyone. I'll pit my chili recipe against anyone's, any day of the week."

"Your *chili* recipe?" she said. "Cute."

"Okay, those are fighting words." His eyes narrowed as she ignored him, whipped off her bathrobe and stepped into the steaming rush of water.

"So maybe we'll fight later," he muttered, then threw off his robe and followed her into the warm shower.

The kitchen bar became an assembly line with all three of Julia's professional-strength mixers arranged side by side.

On another counter, she'd lined up all the ingredients she would need, as well as the bowls, spoons, measuring cups and spatulas she would use to blend everything together.

Cameron had called Sally to ask if she could keep

the baby for a few more hours while he and Julia baked cupcakes. Sally and her girlfriends were thrilled. Jake could sit in his bouncer while the women played canasta by the pool.

"Okay, let's get this show on the road," Cameron said, all business as he tied a cook's apron around his waist. "How much flour do you need?"

"Baking is slightly different than cooking," Julia said warily. "I won't be offended if you just want to sit at the bar and offer moral support."

"You're kidding, right?

She sighed. "Okay. We'll need three cups of flour in each of those three large glass bowls."

"Fine." He reached for one of the glass measuring cups and the bag of flour.

"Oh, use this plastic cup, not the glass one."

"What's the difference?"

She held up the two different measuring cups. "One's for liquids and one's for solids. You can fill this one to the top and level it off." She demonstrated how to level it off using the thin, straight handle of the spatula.

Cameron considered that, then nodded.

Twenty minutes later, Cameron had flour in his hair and egg on his shirt. He'd spilled sugar on the floor and had to sweep it up. His apron was smeared with chocolate splotches and butter stains.

Julia's apron was spotless and she hummed a perky tune as she briskly washed the bowls and utensils. What was wrong with this picture? Cameron shoved the broom into the utility closet as Julia turned the water off and dried her hands.

"As soon as the third batch is in the oven, I'll start the frosting." She dried one of the large bowls in preparation for the next step. "Maybe you can add the sprinkles at the end."

"Sprinkles?" He slammed the closet shut. "Now that's just demeaning."

Julia laughed. "You're so wrong. Sprinkles are a critical part of the operation."

"I'll show you a critical part," he said with a growl as he grabbed her from behind.

Her protest landed somewhere between a scream and a giggle. Then her eyes flared as Cameron managed to ease her blouse off, then handily relieved her of her blue jeans.

"What have you done?" she asked, glancing down at her pristine apron, which was all that remained of her clothing. It was still tied neatly at her waist. "How did you do that?"

He waved his hands. "Magic." Scanning her from head to toe, he said, "Very nice. Now turn around."

"I don't think so," she said, backing away from him.

He ripped his apron off and unbuttoned his shirt as he stalked her. Her back hit the kitchen wall as the oven timer buzzed.

"Perfect timing," she said, and made a sideways move toward the oven.

Cameron held her in place. "Stay right there." He pulled the second batch of cupcakes out of the oven and placed them on a rack, then slipped the third batch in and set the timer for fifteen minutes.

"I have to start the frosting now," she said.

"Not yet." He pulled her close and turned to switch places with her, so now his back was against the wall. He slipped his hands under her apron and clutched her exposed backside, shaping it with both of his hands. "This is what every guy watching your baking demonstrations has been fantasizing all week."

"Don't be silly—oh," she said, her protest fading as he cupped her bottom and lifted her. She wrapped her legs around his waist and moaned as she sank onto his rigid length. "Oh, Cameron."

"I told you I knew my way around the kitchen."

Julia's conference ended two days later. Cameron enlisted the help of most of the bellman staff to load up two cars with suitcases, Julia's kitchen equipment and the baby's gear. Then they caravanned back to Dunsmuir Bay.

Cameron pulled into the tree-lined driveway that led to his two-story, Craftsman-style home overlooking the cliffs and parked his Porsche next to the three-car garage. He jogged to Julia's minivan, slid opened the back door and stepped into the car to take Jake out of his car seat.

"We're home, buddy," he whispered as Julia gathered her purse and keys and climbed down from the driver's seat. "Hope you like it here."

Holding the baby, Cameron led Julia to the carved-oak door leading into his home. She stopped and gazed out at the wide lawn that rolled all the way to the cliffs overlooking Dunsmuir Bay.

"It's beautiful," she said, shielding the sun from her eyes.

"Yeah, it is," he said, staring at her as the baby bounced in his arms.

Julia felt her cheeks heat up from his intense gaze.

She swallowed self-consciously. "I think we'll be very happy here."

"Good," he said, and kissed her. "Let's go inside."

"Okay."

Cameron swung the front door open, then stopped, blocking the entryway.

"Is something wrong?" she asked.

"Everything's perfect," he assured her, "but I want to do this right. You hold Jake, okay?"

Julia grabbed hold of the baby, then Cameron bent and lifted both her and the baby into his arms and carried them into his home. Once inside, he kissed her again. "Welcome home."

"Thank you," she whispered. "You can put us down now."

"Oh, yeah." He grinned and kissed her one last time, then gave the baby's forehead a smooch before letting them go.

As Cameron placed the baby in his rolling bouncy chair, Julia gazed around, taking in the large living area. Peg-and-groove hardwood floors spanned the length of the room from the front door to the wide wall of glass on the opposite side. The ultra-modern kitchen was open to the room and the vaulted ceiling rose up two floors, making the space feel even bigger. Along one wall, the wide staircase led to the second floor.

Spacious rugs covered the living room area where several chairs and sofas were arranged to create a number of conversation areas. A river-stone hearth and fireplace was built into one wall, lending the room a warm, cozy feel despite its massive size.

"My housekeeper had everything baby-proofed,

but we'll go through and double-check to make sure everything's extra safe for Jake."

"It's beautiful, Cameron," she said, making a beeline for the opposite end of the space where the dining room connected to the kitchen. She was curious to see where she would spend much of her time every day.

In the dining room, she stared through the thick glass wall at the ocean. There were whitecaps on the water today and sailboats dotted the horizon. "Spectacular."

"And the view from the kitchen is just as nice."

"Nice?" she said, smiling as she checked out the fabulous views. The kitchen walls were painted a dark gold, maybe too dark for her taste, but that could be changed. "It's gorgeous. And huge. I can watch the waves crash while I bake. This place is a showcase."

He laughed. "Is that a genteel way of saying it's not exactly comfortable?"

"Are you kidding?" she asked, her eyes wide. "It's very comfortable. It's a real home."

"I like to think so." He glanced around the kitchen. "I spend most of my time in here or out by the pool. There's a den upstairs where I like to watch TV, although sometimes I'll use the set in the living room." He was rambling, she realized. Was he nervous? "Anyway, I hope you'll feel at home here."

"I already do." She wrapped her arms around his waist and laid her head against his shoulder. After a moment, she leaned back and added, "Although it's awfully clean."

He raised an eyebrow. "Again that doesn't sound like a compliment."

"Oh, it is," she said laughing. "I'm just so used to the clutter of my old place. It's up in the hills and it's big and old. I love your home much more." *Because you're here,* she thought. And because this was a real home, not a mausoleum. She looked around some more, then grimaced. "I just hope you know what you're getting yourself into. With Jake here, your lovely clean home will deteriorate into a jumbled mass of toys and clutter."

"I can't wait," he insisted, and followed her back into the living room as she explored the space. "It'll be fun."

"No, I mean it," she said, strolling over to run her hand along the back of the dark gray sectional. "He's like a tornado."

"This place can handle it," Cameron said. "And if you don't like anything, we'll get rid of it. I want you both to be happy and comfortable here. Believe me, I'm not tied to anything in this room."

She sighed. "I hope not, because Jake's stuff seems to multiply and take over rooms. It's scary."

Cameron laughed. "It's okay, Julia. It'll be an improvement from the way it is now."

She glanced around as the baby began to bounce and wiggle. "You mean, neat and clean?"

"*Too* neat and clean," he clarified. "I'm glad Jake's here to liven things up."

She shrugged and watched as the baby rolled and bounced his way across the Persian carpet. "Don't say I didn't warn you."

"That was a waste of three days," Brandon muttered as he slid into the back seat of the limousine and slammed the door shut.

Adam took off his sunglasses and slipped them in

his pocket. "The first two days were worthwhile. It was just today that sucked."

"True," Cameron said with a nod. "But now we know who we're dealing with."

"Yeah," Brandon said. "Idiots."

The head of one of their subsidiaries, Jeremy Gray, had set up the meeting in Delaware earlier that morning, thinking the two companies might find enough common ground for a merger. It hadn't worked out, to say the least.

"I'm scheduling a meeting with Jeremy first thing tomorrow morning," Adam said, pulling out his cell phone. "I want to know what the hell he was thinking, setting this up. That group won't be ready to take their operation nationwide for another two years."

"If ever," Brandon added.

The rest of the drive from the airport was made in relative silence. Cameron was dropped off first and after grabbing his suitcase from the trunk, he thanked their driver and told his brothers he would see them in the morning.

He was tired but happy to be home. He'd always enjoyed traveling for business, but this time he had to admit he was beat. More than that, he'd actually missed his new family. It had been disconcerting to find himself in the middle of a business meeting, checking the time and wondering what Julia and Jake were doing right at that moment. He refused to read too much into his feelings, though, chalking it up to the fact that the newness of being part of a family hadn't worn off yet.

Stepping inside the house, he paused for a moment and listened for their voices. Then he took the stairs two at a time and found Julia in Jake's room, putting the baby to bed for the night. She whispered sweet nothings and rubbed Jake's stomach for a minute before winding up the colorful wizard mobile over his bed and wishing him sweet dreams.

Cameron leaned against the doorjamb, taking in the warm, homey scene. When Julia spied him, she let out a muted cry, then raced over and pulled him out into the hall where she wrapped herself around him. "I'm so glad you're home."

"Me, too." He breathed in the sultry scent of her.

"Do you want dinner?" she asked.

"No, I had something earlier at the airport. But I could go for a beer. Then bed."

They walked downstairs arm in arm. "What have you been up to while I was gone?"

"You'll see in a minute," she said, her tone light-hearted.

In the kitchen, he headed for the refrigerator, then stopped. He glanced around the room. It took him a few seconds before he realized what was different. "You painted my kitchen. And where's my refrigerator?"

She smiled brightly. "It's just a few shades lighter than it was, but it makes a nice change, don't you think? And your refrigerator is in the garage. We can still use it for storing drinks and frozen foods, but mine was practically brand-new and it's so much bigger and laid out better. I didn't think you'd mind."

He opened the new refrigerator to look for a bottle of beer. It took a minute before he found them stacked neatly along the door. He twisted the cap off and took a long drink. "You could've asked me."

Her smile dimmed. "It was a spur-of-the-moment

decision. I guess I should've warned you, I make them sometimes. And you weren't here."

"You could've called."

"I didn't want to bother you while you were in meetings." She sniffed. "Besides, you made it clear you'd be too busy to talk much."

"We talked last night," he pointed out. "You could've told me then."

Her lips compressed in a tight frown. "We were discussing other things. I forgot."

Oh yeah, he thought, recalling the conversation. They'd had phone sex. He took another sip of beer, then muttered, "Well, next time let me know."

"Fine."

She sounded annoyed. *Join the club,* he thought, and tossed the bottle cap in the trash can, which she'd moved to the opposite side of the room, closer to the service porch. Irritated now, he said, "Look, just ask me before you make changes to my house."

"And here I thought it was *our* house now," she said as she wiped off Jake's high chair. "My mistake."

"I didn't mean it like that."

"No? Well, it sounded *like that.*"

"Sorry, but I've had a long, frustrating day."

"And I haven't?"

"That's not my point."

"Oh, did you have a point?"

Yeah, she was definitely annoyed. But so was he. "I'm just saying that this is the kind of decision we should both have a hand in making."

"Fine." She threw the sponge down. "I'll call the painters and have them change it back to the way it was. Then we'll discuss it."

"Don't be ridiculous."

"Oh, now I'm being ridiculous?"

"Well, you're not making much sense," he said. "I'm just saying it's important for us to—"

"I'll tell you what's important," she said, wagging her finger in his face. "Me. That's what. I'm important. And my work space is important. Call me a temperamental artist, but I need to enjoy the space I work in. And that means the kitchen. Your refrigerator wasn't efficient and the color of this room was too dark for me. I didn't feel creative, I didn't feel like it was mine. It sounds stupid, but it's true. So I changed the color and made it mine. Now I can work here. That's the bottom line. So live with it."

"I'm trying to live with it, Julia," he said, wrapping his hand around her finger to stop her from jabbing at him. "But don't expect me to roll over and let you change everything that's mine, just because you…" He hesitated.

"Oh, don't stop now," she said, inches from his face.

But he had to stop. *Everything that's mine,* he'd just said. Damn. She was right. His house was *their* house now. And she needed to feel comfortable here. He'd get used to the new refrigerator. And why did he care what color the kitchen walls were? He didn't, but Julia did. And looking around, he could see that it actually did look better, lighter, brighter in here now.

Besides, her scent was driving him nuts. Why were they fighting? He couldn't remember, but one thing was for certain. He was a fool to start a fight when he'd been traveling for seventy-two hours straight.

"Why don't you put stickers on anything that's yours,"

she continued angrily. "Never mind, we'll just assume *every*thing's yours."

He moved a half inch closer and took a deep breath. "You smell like flowers. And lemons."

"Don't change the subject," she chided, then added defensively, "I made lemonade."

His eyes narrowed in on her. "I like lemonade."

He had her cornered against the chrome door of the ultra-modern refrigerator. She tried to edge sideways. "I'm going to bed."

"Not yet." He held her shoulders to keep her close. "You forgot something."

"What?"

"This," he said, and kissed her, his mouth taking hers in a rush of heat and an explosion of taste and need.

When she groaned, he lifted her up onto the counter. Sliding his hands up the insides of her thighs, he spread her legs. Then he pulled her closer to the edge and knelt before her.

"Cameron," she whispered.

"Shh," he said, then kissed the inside of her knee and moved higher, to her thighs, first one side, then the other. Hearing her moan in pleasure, he used his tongue to part her sensitive folds and plunged deeply. Her wild cry satisfied his masculine pride as he delved deeper, pressing his lips to her, sliding his mouth and tongue against her slick center, licking and suckling.

She was intoxicating. He couldn't get enough of her. When she screamed his name, he didn't wait a second longer. He stood and, watching her closely, unfastened his jeans, shoving them down his legs. Her eyes flashed at the sight of his impressive erection.

"Come to me," he said, lifting her up and onto his

stiff length and slowly lowering her until he filled her completely.

Her lusty sigh pushed him to the limit, but he forced himself to go slowly. At first. But she was so hot, so tight, so ready, that he began pumping into her with an urgency that brought him close to the edge of his control. Moments later, she cried out and he fused his lips to hers as he drove himself to join her in a climax so intense, he had to wonder if they might both go up in flames.

They leaned against the kitchen counter, holding on to each other like drunken sailors. Cameron wasn't ready to let her go just yet. He vaguely remembered fighting about something, but now it seemed nothing more than a prelude to some of the best sex he'd ever had.

"I might regret asking," she said, resting her head on his shoulder as she lazily stroked his back. "But I need to know what you're thinking right now."

He looked around, then met her gaze. "I was thinking I really like the new paint job."

After the kitchen confrontation and its pleasurable aftermath, Cameron and Julia settled into a routine. He was amazed at how easily the three of them were adjusting to life together in his home.

Even though there were staff bakers at her store doing the yeoman's work of making the products she sold every day, Julia liked to bake her signature delicacies at home. She was up early every morning, kneading and mixing and baking and frosting, so Cameron got into the habit of joining her.

"Almost like a real marriage," he muttered, and caught

himself wincing at the words. This wasn't what he'd had in mind when they entered into this arrangement.

He hadn't counted on caring about her so much.

And it was getting more and more difficult to keep from letting his feelings show.

"I can't believe my kid likes carrots for breakfast," Cameron said, looking baffled as he fed Jake another spoonful of pureed carrots.

"He likes everything." Julia poured herself another cup of coffee.

"Yeah, but carrots? Go figure." He loaded another bit of carrot mixture onto Jake's spoon, then turned as a thought occurred. "Maybe we should start a vegetable garden."

"Good idea," she murmured. Her eyes widened. "A vegetable garden? With carrots. Oh, my God, carrots and carrots." She grabbed the pad and pen by the telephone and scribbled a note.

"Well, we could have other stuff, too." Cameron shrugged as he lifted the spoon up in the air and made like an airplane toward Jake's mouth. "Cucumbers, tomatoes, lettuce, maybe some different kinds of peppers."

She put down the pen and sat forward. "No, carats, like diamonds and rubies. And carrots. And tomatoes and cucumbers. A garden. For kids. And a museum for the diamonds and the art and, oh, everything. That's it."

"That's what?"

She jumped up and planted a kiss on Cameron's lips. "You're brilliant."

wouldn't do it, but a huge vegetable garden would. Kids could grow and harvest their own vegetables and have fun while they learned some healthy lessons. Julia had whipped up a business plan in no time flat and scheduled a trustees' meeting to go over her ideas.

On Cameron's first tour of the place a few weeks earlier, Julia had mentioned casually that the main residence was more than thirty thousand square feet. The lawns, gardens, pools, rare trees, bowered rose garden and other botanical delights comprised ninety acres of prime real estate overlooking Dunsmuir Bay.

With Sally Duke as his adoptive mother, Cameron had grown up with money and luxury, but this was something else. To be honest, Cameron couldn't help thinking that this amazing house, with its massive grounds and stunning views, would make one hell of a Duke resort.

But this was Julia's show, and it was now showtime.

"Thank you for being here with me," she whispered to Cameron as they watched a stretch limousine wind its way up the long driveway.

"Wouldn't miss it for the world," he said. As he dipped down to kiss her cheek, he added, "I've got your back."

The limo driver parked and four older men in dark suits climbed out. As they approached, Julia grabbed Cameron's hand. He could feel the nervous energy coursing through her.

Why his strong, independent wife felt she needed backup was a mystery to him. After all, this was her home, her decision. Not only that, but it was her money, her heritage. So who cared what these fat cats thought? Apparently, Julia did.

As the four men came closer, Julia smiled and patted Jake's butt for luck, then strolled over to greet the trustees. Cameron handed the baby over to the nanny, who took Jake inside. Then he followed Julia and greeted two of the lawyers he recognized from past business deals around town.

"So, Duke," said Dave Saunders, an overfed blowhard Cameron had never liked, "why aren't you turning this place into one of your fancy hotels?"

"Who says I'm not?" he said pleasantly.

The four men exchanged glances and Cameron earned a skeptical look from Julia. He winked at her as if to urge her not to take any of this too seriously.

So these were the four almighty trustees Julia believed were in charge of her destiny. No wonder she thought she needed backup.

After the introductions were made, Julia led the entire group across the wide lawn to the first of many spots on the property for which she had plans.

As a light breeze stirred the leaves, the men stopped to gaze up at what looked like a smaller version of the ancient Greek Acropolis built into the hillside.

One of the men chuckled. "Ah, the famous Glen Haven Folly."

"Seems a waste of good real estate," Saunders mused.

"And money," a third man added with a significant nod to the others.

"My father had it built for me when I studied ancient Greece in third grade," Julia explained briefly.

One of the men sniffed. Another muttered, "Must be nice."

Cameron stifled the urge to smack the guy upside his head.

Julia ignored the sarcasm and pointed forward. "Now we continue along this path to the western end of the meadow."

As they passed an old wrought-iron gate built into an ivy-covered stone wall, Cameron stopped to look through the gateway. He hadn't noticed it on his first visit. Inside the thick wall, row after row of tall hedges were aligned in a circular pattern that covered a wide stretch of green lawn. Intrigued, he took another, closer look.

"Whoa, is that a maze?"

Julia stopped and turned. "Yes."

"That's incredible," he exclaimed. "You grew up with a maze in your backyard?"

She glanced over her shoulder and saw that the four men had stopped to wait for them.

"Now what?" said Harold Greer, the oldest trustee.

Cameron smiled. "We'll just be a minute, gentlemen."

Glaring at Cameron, Julia said, "Yes, it's a maze."

He pulled her closer to the gate and peered through. "This is amazing. Is there anything in the middle?"

She sighed. "A life-size chess set."

Cameron turned. "You've got a life-size chess set in the middle of the maze?"

"That's right," she said defensively.

"With life-size chess pieces? Like French royalty or something?"

"Or something," she said through clenched teeth.

"French royalty, they wish," one of the other trustees muttered.

"It's shrubbery, Duke," Dave Saunders said with a sneer. "Get over it."

Greer sighed. "Miss Parrish, is this going to take all day?"

Julia cringed. "I'm so sorry, Mr. Greer."

Cameron's eyes narrowed. From her tone and the surreptitious looks she'd been sending the tight-assed trustees for the past half hour, this wasn't the first time she'd felt the need to either defend or recoil from her late parents' supposed profligate style. And right then he wished she'd never set up this meeting. He wanted to sweep her up and carry her away from their hypercritical opinions and high-handedness.

In his years of dealing with these kinds of guys, Cameron had learned not to take them too seriously, especially when he was the one holding the purse strings. But Julia had grown up under the control of people like these men. They'd been in charge, running her life, making decisions. As strong as he knew her to be, she'd clearly never stood up to these men before. No wonder she was nervous.

"Excuse us for just a moment, gentlemen," he said, then took hold of her hand and pulled her away, back around the bend of the thick wall.

"What do you think you're doing?" she asked in a furious whisper.

After checking to make sure they were far enough away not to be overheard by the trustees, Cameron said, "Why are you trying so hard to impress these guys?"

"Their opinions are important."

"They work for you," he said, pointing at her. "They should be trying to impress you so they keep their jobs, but they're not. What's going on here?"

Her chest rose and fell slowly. "It's not that simple, Cameron."

"It *is* that simple," he said. "These guys have no say over your decisions."

She shifted uncomfortably. "Yes, but they've worked for my family trust for years. If they think I'm spending money unwisely…"

"You're not," he insisted.

"And you're not helping," she added irately, folding her arms across her chest. "Going on and on about the maze and the stupid chess set. What was that all about? I need you to focus."

"Trust me, I'm completely focused on the thought of chasing you naked through that maze."

"Cameron." Flustered, she peered around to see if he'd been overheard. "I'm trying to be professional here. These guys have never thought of me as anything but a frivolous trust-fund baby. Maybe I don't need their support exactly, but I would like to have their respect."

"Respect?" He frowned. It hadn't ever occurred to him that his wife wouldn't be respected anywhere she went. And that thought just pissed him off. "Okay, I'm going to share some insider information that I think will put everything into perspective for you."

She scowled. "Oh, this should be good."

"I don't offer this sort of strategy to everyone, you know."

"Just get on with it." She tapped her foot. "They're waiting for us."

"Let them wait," he said, then lowered his voice. "I've known Dave Saunders for years. I went to college with him and I've done business deals with his firm. If he has two drinks, he starts taking his clothes off and dancing. The guy's got a gut on him that won't quit, and he's a bad dancer. Overbite, little fist pumps, the whole deal."

She smothered a laugh. "Stop it."

"I'm serious here. Just do me a favor—the next time he dismisses your opinion or makes you feel less than amazing, I want you to picture him in his baggy underwear, doing the hully gully. It's not pretty. Will you promise me you'll do that?"

"I hope it never comes to that," she said solemnly as she tried to suppress another giggle.

"I hope not, too. But this is a tried-and-true business strategy. You'll thank me for it later."

She gazed at him, then gave him a quick hug. "Thank you."

"No problem." He jerked his head toward the trustees. "Go give 'em hell."

Taking a deep breath, she said, "I suppose you're going to want to check out the maze after this."

His eyebrows shot up. "You know I am."

She cocked her head to look up at him. "And I bet you'd never get lost in a maze, would you?"

"Not a chance."

"I didn't think so." She paused, then her eyes glittered with determination. "So he's got the overbite going and everything?"

"Oh, yeah."

With a quick nod, she said, "Thanks. I appreciate it."

"Like I said, I've got your back."

Cameron watched as she composed herself, then turned and rejoined the trustees. She had once told him that she refused to play the poor little rich girl, but Cameron hadn't known the half of it. She'd come from one of the richest families in the state, but she'd grown up lonely and starved for affection, living on a massive estate with no one to talk to but the hired help.

And she'd had to deal with snot-nosed lawyers like these guys her whole life. Men who thought they knew more than she did about everything. But they couldn't be more wrong.

As Julia showed the trustees where she planned to plant the half-acre vegetable garden and the spot she thought would be perfect for a barn and petting zoo, Cameron realized he was going to have a good time watching her prove just how wrong they could be.

It had been several weeks since the meeting with the trustees. Julia had turned the museum plans over to a project management company, and while she still kept an eye on things at Glen Haven Farm, she was finally able to return to her early-morning baking schedule. The nanny showed up every morning in time for Julia and Cameron to go off to work. Some days, Cameron worked in his office at home, and on those days, Julia came home early and gave the nanny the afternoon off.

One afternoon, Julia arrived to find the house empty. It was sunny and warm, so she followed her instincts and walked through the kitchen to the sliding door that led out to the patio. Sure enough, her two men were in the pool.

Cameron was holding on to Jake who was wrapped securely in a bright yellow life jacket decorated with cartoon characters.

"Ready?" Cameron asked.

"Da-da-da-da!" Jake blubbered excitedly.

"One, two, three," Cameron shouted, then bounced Jake on the water, causing a wave to form and splash against his daddy. Jake shrieked with laughter.

Julia laughed, too. The wave was tiny, but Cameron pretended to be drenched in water to make Jake laugh. Her two men looked so adorable together, her heart was in danger of melting.

Was it possible to be more in love than she already was?

"Oh, no," she whispered. Her knees were suddenly weak, so she backed up and slid into the nearest patio chair. Her eyes began to tear up. It was just the bright sunlight, she thought. There was no way she could possibly be in love with Cameron Duke.

Oh, of course, she *loved* him. That was inevitable. But she couldn't be *in love* with him. That would ruin everything.

Dear God, how could she be so stupid? Staring at Cameron playing with Jake in the pool, she had to admit to herself that it wasn't all that hard.

"Don't be ridiculous," she retorted aloud. That was lust, pure and simple, and nothing more. The man was capable of turning her on with a wink of his eye. Didn't mean she was in love with him.

Hadn't she worked all this out at the wedding? All they had was a marriage of convenience. Falling in love was *not* convenient. It wasn't part of the plan.

So why was her heart beating so fast? Why were her knees so weak? Maybe she was coming down with the flu. Anything but the alternative.

Jake's little screams of delight kept her anchored as her mind spun out of control. She needed to reel it back in, now. Because it couldn't work. Cameron would never reciprocate her feelings, so why would she endanger their relationship by insisting that he do just that?

She wouldn't. Even if it meant lying through her teeth, she would never admit that she was in love with her husband. And didn't that sound absurd?

"I'm going to make lemonade," she said, waving to Cameron and Jake before going inside. As she cut lemons and began to squeeze out the juice, she watched through the window as Jake giggled at Cameron's antics. He really was the best father, she thought.

She recalled the diamond necklace Cameron had given her while they were still at the hotel, to thank her for agreeing to marry him. Then the night they'd moved into his house, he'd slipped a matching diamond bracelet on her wrist.

Was it dangerous to read anything into the fact that he gave her lovely gifts whenever wonderful things happened in his life? It had already occurred to her that this wasn't about the jewelry. It had to be something more than just a gesture. His gifts always seemed to come from a warm, loving place within him. Within his heart. Was it Cameron's way of telling her he loved her?

"Oh, there you go again," she said irately, pounding half a lemon onto the juicer and squeezing it to within an inch of its life. "Snap out of it."

Cameron Duke took care of what was his. She was his wife; Jake was his son. Cameron would do whatever it took to keep them healthy and happy. He would protect them with his life and make them feel as if they were the most important people in the world. Which made him all the more special to her. If that meant she was a sap, so be it.

Julia sighed as she added sugar and stirred it into the mixture of water and juice. Was it any wonder that she'd fallen in love with the man? Now she would just have to keep that realization hidden deep within her heart so that Cameron would never learn the truth. Because Cameron Duke would never allow love to be a part of his plan.

Nine

"It looks like they're going to catch on fire," Julia said in a worried tone.

Cameron and his brothers stood around the barbecue grill cooking sausages, burgers and steaks. They didn't seem to notice the billowing clouds of smoke that enveloped them as they laughed and talked and drank beer.

"But they never do, honey," Sally said dryly as she placed folded cloth napkins and plates on the patio table. "It's a male ritual. Don't try to make sense of it."

"Don't be too concerned, Julia," Trish said, stopping to give her new sister-in-law's shoulder a comforting pat before continuing to add utensils and glassware to each place setting. "You won't have to worry about Jake joining them in the manly smoke, at least for another year or two."

Julia shuddered and stroked Jake's head, then sprinkled a handful of Cheerios onto the tray of his bouncy chair. They had been living with Cameron for two months now, and Cameron had decided to celebrate the milestone with their first official family barbecue.

The late spring day was sunny and warm, so they'd all spent quality time in the pool before starting dinner. Everyone had dried off and changed into shorts, shirts and flip-flops. Sally, with her blond hair pulled back in a neat ponytail, sipped Julia's homemade sangria.

Julia had baked hot dog and hamburger buns that morning and now she placed the large, plastic-wrapped cookie sheet on the sunny side table near the grill.

Sally shook her head at the sheet full of buns. "Now I know you're a baker, but it still amazes me that you baked these yourself just for us."

"Of course I did," Julia said. "They're so easy." She glanced back at the buns on the table. "I'm hoping the sunshine will warm them instead of sticking them in the oven. What do you think?"

"I think that's a stroke of genius," Trish said. She finished with the utensils and picked up her glass of fizzy water. "I would beg you for the recipe, but why? My new sister-in-law owns a bakery."

They all laughed. "I'll bake them for you personally anytime you want."

"Don't tempt me," Trish said.

Julia headed for the sliding glass door leading to the kitchen. "Anyone for more sangria?"

"I'd love a glass," Sally said.

"None for me, thanks," Trish said easily. "It's not good for the baby."

Sally leaned over the table to straighten a fork,

but froze in mid-move. She turned and stared at her daughter-in-law. "No."

"Yes," Trish said, her laugh filled with joy.

"Oh." The older woman's eyes misted as she clasped her hand over her mouth in shock and wonder.

Julia felt her own eyes dampen, as well. "You're having a baby?"

Trish nodded, still grinning.

Sally grabbed Trish in a warm hug. "Oh, I'm so happy."

"That's wonderful," Julia said, and laughed as she joined in the hug fest. In that instant, her heart was so full of love for these two women and the baby yet to be born. She couldn't begin to describe how grateful she was to be a part of this family and this thrilling moment.

Sally covered her face and began to cry in earnest. "I'm just overwhelmed. And overjoyed. I never thought... and then Julia and Jake came into our lives, and now Trish, and a baby, and... Oh, will you look at me, carrying on?"

"It's wonderful," Julia said, sniffling.

Trish and Julia linked arms with their mother-in-law and they all put their heads together.

"This is the most fantastic day ever," Sally whispered, then her eyes lit up. "And little Jake will have a cousin to grow up with."

Julia sniffed as tears began to flow again. "Oh, great. Now you've got me going again."

Sally patted both of their cheeks. "You girls are both such a gift."

Seconds later, Cameron walked over and saw Julia sniffle and wipe her eyes. He peered at her, then noticed his mother was crying, too. Alarmed, he grabbed Julia's arm. "What's wrong? You're all crying. What happened? Is it Jake?"

"No, no," Julia said quickly, then laughed. "It's good news. It's Trish. She's going to have a baby."

He broke out into a grin, turned and pulled Trish close for a big hug. He kissed her right on the lips and said, "That's great news, honey."

"Thanks, Cameron," she said, smiling.

He jogged back to the grill and punched his brother in the arm. Then he gave him a brisk hug.

"What's up?" Brandon asked.

"They're having a baby," Cameron explained.

Brandon choked on his beer, and Cameron thumped his back. When he'd recovered fully, Brandon grabbed Adam in a bear hug. "Congratulations, man."

Adam laughed. "Thanks."

The three brothers clicked their beer bottles together in a toast just as Sally rushed over to give Adam a ferocious hug.

"Lots of hugs going on around here," Cameron said.

Sally turned and said, "I just can't help it." Then she hugged Adam again. "Oh, sweetie. I'm so happy for you."

"Thanks, Mom," Adam said, unable to conceal his grin of masculine satisfaction.

"Glad he's not shooting blanks?" Brandon said wryly.

"Oh, you," Sally said, and smacked his arm lightly. "Just wait till it's your turn."

"Whoa. Threats?" Brandon gave her an incredulous

look. "Sorry, Mom, but you'll be waiting a long time for that day."

"We'll see about that," Sally muttered, then gave him a pointed look before turning back to join the girls.

Brandon's shoulders shook violently and he glanced at his brothers. "Did anyone else feel that sudden chill?"

"Yeah, I saw that look she gave you," Cameron said, his lips twisted in a wry grin. "I'd say you're screwed."

Brandon glared from one brother to the other. "Whatever happened to our sacred vows? We made a pact. Blood brothers forever, remember?"

"We're still blood brothers," Adam said amiably, then took a long sip of beer. "Always will be."

"Yeah, but come on," Brandon groused. "First, there's your marriage. I could almost handle that. But then Cameron went and did it. That blew my mind, I've gotta tell you. And now, more kids?"

"Stuff happens," Cameron said by way of explanation. What else could he say? He couldn't figure it out, either.

Brandon shook his head. "And now I'll have Mom on my case, bellyaching for me to do the same. And that's never going to happen."

"You think not?" Adam said.

"Never," Brandon said decisively, and pointed his beer bottle at both of them. "I understand you two are feeble-minded amateurs when it comes to women, but I'm a professional. I've got standards to uphold."

Adam threw back his head and howled with laughter. "Standards. That's a good one, bro."

"Yeah." Cameron patted Brandon's back. He understood standards. They were a lot like rules. Sometimes both were meant to be broken. "Lots of luck with those standards."

"You guys are killing me," Brandon muttered, then slugged down the rest of his beer. "Getting so you can't trust anyone anymore."

"Why don't you just tell him how you feel?" Karolyn asked as she filled the refrigerated display case with more freshly wrapped sandwiches from the Cupcake kitchen.

"I don't know what you're talking about," Julia said. She grabbed a large tub from the busboy tray behind the checkout counter. "Lynnie took a break so I'm going to bus the tables out front."

"You're avoiding the conversation," Karolyn whispered.

"Yes," she admitted. "But I'm working, too."

Karolyn rolled her eyes and went back to tucking and folding the small, white boxes used by customers to carry home their bakery goods. The word Cupcake was embossed in navy blue on the top, under the outline of a fluffy cupcake.

The white box and the navy-blue ribbon tie had become an iconic symbol in Dunsmuir Bay. When mothers arrived home carrying a Cupcake box, children turned into angels. When the boss showed up at the office with a Cupcake box, it was better than getting a promotion.

Julia stacked empty latte cups, pastry plates and utensils in the tub, then wiped down the tables. She greeted three of her customers who always met here for lattes and a snack after their morning workout, then answered a question about the sandwich special of the day.

Glancing around the café area, she assured herself

that everything was clean and tidy. She was proud of what she'd created here. Even before her customers walked inside, they could smell the mouth-watering aroma of baked bread, puff pastry and sweet chocolate chip cookies all the way down the street.

Julia returned the filled tub to the busboy tray behind the counter just as Lynnie finished her break.

"Julia," Karolyn called from the kitchen. "Can you come back and check on the cheese bread?"

Julia made sure Lynnie was ready to work and checked that her young assistant's apron was tied securely to cover the tacky saying on her T-shirt before walking into the kitchen. Karolyn grabbed her arm and pulled her all the way to the back door leading to the tiny, fenced-in patio.

"Now, sit," Karolyn said.

Julia glanced around at the colorful flower boxes and miniature potted lemon trees that decorated the space. "No cheese-bread emergency?"

"No."

With a slow, heavy exhalation, Julia sat at the small table they'd set up for staff meetings and coffee breaks. "All right. What do you want?"

Karolyn pulled another chair around to get closer. She grabbed Julia's hand and squeezed it. "I'm worried about you."

"I'm perfectly fine," Julia countered breezily. "Business is booming. I'm married to a gorgeous man who is a terrific father. We have a wonderful life. Cameron loves Jake, and it's so sweet to see them together. He treats me like a princess. He's sexy and attentive and warm, and I'm…I'm happy."

"Honey," Karolyn said, shaking her hand to get her

attention. "Don't you think he deserves to know you're in love with him?"

"Oh, God." Julia dropped her chin to her chest in defeat. "I never should've told you why we really got married."

"I'm your best friend. Who else can you share your deepest, darkest, dumbest secrets with?"

"True," she mumbled. "But why do you think I'm in love with him?"

"It's only written all over your face. *All* the time," Karolyn said. "Even Lynnie made a comment the other day, and you know she doesn't notice anything unless it's dressed in black leather and pierced in twenty-seven places."

Julia laughed, then sobered immediately. "What, exactly, did Lynnie notice?"

"That you're humming all the time, that your eyes have taken on a dreamy glow, that you leave early now. You never used to leave early." Karolyn leaned close and whispered, "She thinks you're in deep."

"Of course I leave early," Julia said, pouting at the idea that she was so transparent, even her employees were starting to notice. "I have a baby at home."

"That never stopped you from working all hours before." Karolyn grinned. "And you still have a devoted nanny who will stay all night with Jake if you need her to."

"Oh, God, even Lynnie noticed." Julia laid her head on the table. "That's pitiful."

"Sad but true," Karolyn said.

"What am I going to do?"

"You're going to go home and tell him you love him,"

Karolyn instructed. "And if he's got any guts at all, he'll tell you the same."

Julia stared forlornly at her friend. "He doesn't love me, Karolyn."

Karolyn laughed. "Oh, Julia."

Julia blinked. "It's not funny."

"Honey, he's so in love with you, it's ridiculous."

"No, he's not."

"I saw him at the wedding. He was smitten then, and it's even worse now."

Julia pursed her lips in discontent. "He wants me, I know that. But *want* isn't love."

Karolyn sighed. "Every time he walks into the bakery, the air becomes charged with electricity between you two."

Julia shook her head. "That's just lust."

"You can ignore the signs, and he might deny it to kingdom come, but take my word for it, Cameron Duke is a man who's in love with his wife."

The following Friday, Sally babysat Jake so that Julia and Cameron could attend a hotel-owners conference at Monarch Dunes.

Unlike her last visit when she had Jake with her, plus her own conference to attend, plus a wedding to organize, Julia was able to relax. Cameron made sure of it by arranging for her to spend the time being pampered at the hotel spa while he attended meetings. Julia couldn't remember the last time she'd spent a day in such luxury, with a mani-pedi, a facial and a massage. By the time she dressed for the owners' annual charity ball that evening, she felt completely fluffed and refreshed.

She blew her hair out straight so she could wear it

up in a sleek, smooth style, instead of her usual loose waves. After stepping into the strapless burgundy gown Trish had helped her shop for, she fastened the gleaming diamond necklace around her neck and slipped on the matching bracelet. She'd brought her mother's diamond studs to wear in her ears.

Checking herself in the mirror one last time, Julia took a deep breath and walked out to the living room. There she saw Cameron, dressed in the elegant tuxedo he'd worn at their wedding, pop open the champagne and fill two glasses with bubbly gold liquid.

"That looks wonderful," she said. Whether she was referring to the frothy champagne or her husband, she couldn't say, but both were true.

He turned to hand her the glass, then stopped. And stared. The fiery intensity she saw in his eyes left shivers on her skin and heated up her insides.

"Wow," he said on an exhalation.

She smiled, delighted by his reaction. "Thank you."

"No, thank you," he murmured, and touched his glass to hers. "Let's pass on the party and stay here."

"Aren't you the host of this thing?"

He grimaced. "Okay, we'll stay half an hour."

"Just long enough to dance one slow dance," she said, and sipped her champagne.

"We can do that right here," he said, taking her in his arms and swaying in place. After a moment, he chuckled. "You'd never know it from this, but I was actually forced to attend cotillion at an early age."

She gasped. "So was I."

"And we both survived," he said, grinning at her.

She laid her head on his shoulder. After a moment she whispered, "Mmm, you're a very good dancer."

"It's easy, with you in my arms," he said, as he planted slow kisses along her neck. "I didn't think you could possibly be more beautiful, but tonight you are."

Julia looked up at him, at his eyes smoldering with need, and felt her heart tremble. If she told him she'd fallen in love with him, what would he do? Would he be shocked? Angry that she'd broken the rules? Could he admit the same back to her? Staring at him now, Julia wondered if it was only wishful thinking, or could she really see her feelings reflected in his eyes?

"We'd better go now or we'll never leave the room," Cameron said gruffly. "And don't get too friendly with anyone at the party. We'll be in and out of there in thirty minutes."

As they moved through the party, greeting friends and business competitors, Cameron kept Julia's hand gripped in his. She was so stunning, every man in the room had their eyes on her. No way would he let her loose in this crowd of sharks.

"There's the man of the hour," someone said.

Cameron turned and grinned at his old friend Byron Mirabelle, owner of the prestigious Pinnacle Hotels chain. The two men exchanged hearty handshakes and Cameron introduced him to Julia. "Byron specializes in small, luxury hotels in the mountain states of Colorado, Wyoming and Montana."

"Got one going up near Park City, Utah, next year," the older man said proudly.

"That's fantastic," Cameron said. To Julia, he added, "Byron was one of my first mentors in the business."

"It's so nice to meet you," Julia said.

"And you're just the lady I've been wanting to meet," Byron said, and pointed his finger at Julia in accusation.

"Me?"

"Yes, you," Byron said jovially. "You're the reason my wife won't stay anywhere else but the Duke resorts when we're in California."

"But I'm..." Julia shot Cameron a look of puzzlement, then stared at Byron. "Why?"

Byron slipped his arm through hers. "Because of those chocolate croissants you make for the Dukes. We can't get them anywhere else."

"Oh, that's so sweet." Julia laughed as she patted his arm.

Byron leaned closer. "Personally, I'm partial to your apple fritters. My goodness, I could eat them all day long." He frowned and slapped his gut a few times. "I think it shows."

"I like those best, too," she confided.

As Cameron watched his stunning wife interact with his friend, he felt a wave of tenderness so overwhelming he almost stumbled backward. Suddenly, his chest felt so full of emotion, he could hardly breathe.

What the hell was that?

Was he having a heart attack? He didn't think so. He wasn't in pain. Quite the opposite, in fact. He felt warm, fulfilled, happy. Bizarre.

Hell, he didn't know what was going on, but he knew he needed to move.

He left Julia and Byron chatting while he walked to the bar and ordered a shot of good Scotch. As he sipped the drink, he decided the best thing to do right now was to get Julia and slip out of here, take her back to the room and make love. And tomorrow, he couldn't wait to drive home and see Jake. He didn't know when it had happened, but he'd become a family man, and Julia and Jake had become the most important part of his life.

Cameron felt someone touch his shoulder and he turned.

"Hello, Cameron."

His back went rigid. "Martina."

"Don't you look handsome," she said, her voice as sultry as he remembered. She wore a black-lace dress that barely covered her impressive cleavage, which she used to great advantage by leaning close to him as she batted her eyes. "I was hoping I'd see you here tonight."

Cameron gazed at her with detachment. He had loved Martina once, or so he'd thought. Now, he looked at her and felt…nothing.

"So, where's Andrew?" he asked. And more important, where the hell was Julia? He peered over the heads of the crowd, trying to see where his wife and Byron had disappeared to.

Martina's lips curled in a pout. "Andrew's not coming. It's just as well. I've missed you, Cameron. How have you been?"

"Couldn't be better," he said tersely.

"Oh, I'm glad." She walked her fingers up the lapel of his tuxedo. "To be honest, I was hoping I'd find you here alone. Maybe you and I could go somewhere and… and talk, or perhaps…"

"Or perhaps what?" he said, and carefully removed her hand from his jacket. "Perhaps cheat on your husband? Make him jealous? I don't think so."

"Oh, Cameron, don't be bitter," she said, and gripped his arm. "I—I can't pretend anymore. Andrew and I are divorcing."

"Sorry to hear it." He didn't look at her, but instead continued to scan the room, searching for Julia.

"I think you should know," Martina said in a low voice. "The reason we broke up is I…I've never gotten over you, Cameron. I want you back."

He choked on a laugh. "That's rich."

"There you are," Julia said brightly, touching his shoulder. "Byron's such a doll. Oh, hello."

With some relief, Cameron turned and wrapped his arm around his lovely wife. "Martina, this is my wife, Julia."

"Your…what?" Martina opened her mouth, then shut it. A wise choice.

"Hello, Martina," Julia said graciously, though Cameron could feel the tension in her body. She had to have seen the other woman hanging on to him.

"How do you do?" Martina said coolly, but Cameron saw two red spots appear on her cheeks. He'd seen her get angry before and knew the signs.

He leaned closer to Julia and whispered, "I think our half hour is up."

"All right," she said, then smiled at Martina. "Nice to meet you."

"Yeah, same here." Martina did an about-face and faded into the crowd.

Julia gazed up at him. "A friend?"

"Hardly," he said. "Let's get out of here."

* * *

They took the long way back to their suite, walking along the beach. It was a typical, late-spring evening in California and a mild breeze tickled Julia's skin. The tide was out and the waves lapped softly on the shore. She carried her heels in her hand and waited for the right moment to ask Cameron about Martina, the woman he'd been talking to. Julia had heard the last of their conversation. She knew the woman wanted him back.

Her words had sent dreadful chills of fear down Julia's spine. But then Cameron had laughed at Martina, and Julia could only hope that tonight would be the last they would ever see of the woman and her imposing cleavage.

"Let's go this way," Cameron said, taking her hand and guiding her to the stairs that led up to the hotel. When they reached the top, he veered off the path toward a large grove of trees. As they got closer, she heard water rushing.

"Is that the waterfall?"

"Yes," he said, pointing. "It's over by those trees."

She squeezed his hand. "Let's find it."

Clouds moved in the night sky, revealing a full moon as they wandered through the forested area. After a few minutes, they came to a rock-covered hill. Carved into the base was a small, stone-lined pool. Water cascaded over the smooth boulders and splashed into the pool, which was lit from under the surface, giving the water a mystical blue glow.

"It's beautiful, like a tropical lagoon," she said, and gazed up at him. "Can we go in?"

Touching her cheek, he smiled at her. "I was hoping you'd want to."

She angled her head to catch a glimpse of something across the pool. "It looks like there's light coming from behind the waterfall."

"That's the grotto." He grinned and pulled her close. "It's every man's fantasy. Want to see it?"

Shooting him a dubious look, she said, "Do I want to see every man's fantasy? I'm not sure."

With a laugh, he ran his hands up and down her arms. "It's really just a spa, but it's awesome. Secluded, warm and well-lit."

"How do we get there?"

His lips curved up. "We swim."

She laughed nervously. Glancing around the smooth rock terrace, she saw a wide chaise longue with towels and bathrobes laid out. "Are those for us?"

"Yes."

"Will anyone see us?"

"No," he said confidently. "I've made sure of it."

That brought a smile to her face and her shyness disappeared. "Then let's go swimming."

He kissed her bare shoulder as he reached for the zipper of her gown and slowly lowered it. "I want to make love with you."

She shivered from his touch. "I want that, too."

"Are you cold?"

"Not at all."

"Good." He let go of the burgundy silk and it slid down her body. She stepped out of the dress and Cameron picked it up and draped it over a chair. He turned and stared at her in her high heels, a red thong and matching red strapless bra.

"You take my breath away."

She closed her eyes on a sigh. "Touch me, please."

He complied, but took his time, first running his hands down her spine, up her arms, then down again, shaping her hips and thighs lightly with his fingers. He stood behind her, kissing her neck and back as he moved his hands over the soft skin of her stomach. He stopped to toy with her tiny, jewel-encrusted belly ring, then his hands glided up to skim the sides of her sensitive breasts.

She groaned. "Cameron, I need…"

"I know, baby. I need that, too." His hands molded her breasts and he used his thumbs to massage her responsive nipples to a hard peak. When she moaned, he unlatched her bra and let it fall. She writhed in his arms as he pressed his hard length against her lower back. Then, turning her, he knelt and slowly slipped off her thong before parting her thighs.

"Oh," she gasped, as he kissed her inner thigh. He brushed his lips against her most sensitive skin, then used his tongue to touch her deeply. She was trembling with desire, didn't think she could take any more, when he stood abruptly and lifted her in his arms.

"We'll swim later," he growled, and gently laid her down on the soft chaise. Watching Cameron rip off his jacket and shirt, Julia experienced a moment of potent clarity as she realized her feminine power. It was exhilarating to watch him peel off his trousers to reveal his enormous erection.

She held up her arms to welcome him. He knelt on the chaise and paused to slip on a condom. Then he pinned her arms over her head and aligned himself with her body. Under the night sky, she lifted her hips to allow him to glide into her depths and once again claim her for his own.

* * *

Later, in the quiet stillness inside the grotto, Cameron lay replete once again in Julia's arms. After making love outside on the chaise, they'd spent time playing under the stars in the warm pool. Then, with much laughing and splashing, they'd dipped under the rushing waterfall to enter the hidden grotto. After floating in the sparkling waters of the heated cave, they made love again on the very private bank of the inner lagoon.

Cameron grinned as he lifted his head and kissed her. "You realize you just fulfilled my greatest fantasy, right?"

She laughed. "I love you, Cameron." As soon as the words were out, she gasped and covered her mouth.

Cameron froze. What did she expect him to say? He wasn't about to tell her he loved her. He wouldn't do that to her, knowing it would ruin everything. And just in case he'd thought he might have a chance to live and love like a normal man, Martina's appearance earlier that night had reminded him that things would never change. He would always be a terrible risk.

"Well, I guess I said the wrong thing." Julia stirred away from the warmth of their combined body heat. She grabbed one of the towels stacked nearby and wrapped it around her. Then she stood and looked down at him.

"Wait," he said. "Don't go."

"Why would I stay, Cameron? Look, I didn't mean to say it, but now that I have, I'm not sorry. I'm in love with you. But you've completely closed down. How do you think that makes me feel?" She tightened the towel around her. "I'm going back to the room."

He grabbed her hand. "Julia, I care about you."

"I know you do. But I'm not sure that's enough. Not anymore."

"Julia, I can't…" Hell, what was he supposed to say? He'd told her before, he would never love her. Now she was trying to change the rules, but he couldn't let her. She didn't know the consequences. And what she didn't know could hurt her. He pushed himself up and stood at the side of the pool. "Look, I told you from the beginning that I won't…"

"I know, I know. You don't do love."

Her tone was flippant enough that he grabbed her arm. "That's right, and you should be glad of it. You—"

"Let me guess," she said softly, sadly. "I broke the rules, right?"

He ground his teeth together. "Yeah, you did. We had a deal, remember?"

"I don't remember any deal, Cameron." She removed the towel and tossed it on the rocks, then took the steps one at a time, her glorious, long legs sinking deeper into the water.

"I'll go with you," he said.

"I'd rather be alone for a while."

"Too bad." He slid into the water and grabbed her hand.

"Cameron, I think you've said all there is to say."

"No, I haven't."

Turning to glare at him, she said, "What else is there?"

"Just this." He stared into her eyes because if he looked at her gorgeous breasts, he'd probably begin to whimper and admit something he'd be sorry for later. "I'm glad you're in love with me, Julia."

"What?" Her forehead crinkled in confusion. "Why?"

"Because it'll help our marriage run more smoothly."

Her mouth gaped. "What is that supposed to mean?"

"Just that if you're in love with me, you won't be tempted to give up on our marriage. And that's a good thing for all of us."

"Listen, you arrogant bigheaded fool," she said, and jabbed his chest with her finger. "I was never tempted to leave you, but you're pushing it. And don't for one minute think that I don't know the truth."

"What truth?"

"That you're just as much in love with me as I am with you. You can fight it all you want, deny it all you want, but someday you'll admit I was right. I just hope it won't be too late."

Then she dove under the water and swam away.

Ten

She was in love with him.

Cameron would never admit it out loud—because he valued his body parts—but he was more than thrilled to hear Julia say she loved him. Yeah, he could see she was a bit annoyed with him, but she would get over it. After all, he reasoned, she was in love with him. Now they could go on from here with an even stronger marriage and a great family life. Maybe someday, they'd give Jake a little brother or sister. Who knew?

Did that make him arrogant, as Julia had accused him of being? Cameron chuckled as he switched the power level on the hose in order to wash down the cars. It had been two days since they'd returned from Monarch Dunes. Two days since Julia had confessed she was in love with him, then turned around and told him he was arrogant for insisting that this was a good thing.

No, he wasn't arrogant. He was smart. Smart, for recognizing that what Julia wanted most in life was a family. Smart, for deciding that Julia and Jake should live with him and be that family together. And smart, for avoiding the fall into love that had ruined his parents' lives and left Cameron wary of ever getting too close to anyone for fear that it might destroy them.

And if he'd ever had second thoughts about opening his heart and accepting that he might be in love, it had only taken the unexpected and unwanted presence of Martina at the party to remind him why that was a bad idea. Had he honestly thought, way back then, that he was in love with her? She was an empty shell compared to Julia.

But seeing Martina had stirred up other memories as well, ones he truly didn't want to revisit. Memories of the myriad mistakes he'd made in ever thinking he was worthy of love. Memories of Wendy, his high school girlfriend, who had upended the notion of love so badly that it had almost ruined his life.

Cameron turned off the water and reeled in the hose. Then he grabbed a chamois and began to dry off the cars.

No, he thought. Whether she knew it or not, Julia was much better off without his love. She could have his affection, his respect, his admiration. Hell, she could have his body, too. She could have just about anything she wanted, but she would never hear Cameron admit to loving her. Doing so would just lead to another disaster his heart couldn't afford.

It wasn't enough for her. Not anymore.

Julia folded the laundry, then opened the dryer to

toss in yet another load. She usually didn't mind these household chores. In fact, she generally enjoyed the quiet simplicity of such uncomplicated tasks. But today, nothing was making her happy.

It had been a week since that night in the grotto, and Cameron was still acting as if nothing had happened, nothing had changed. And maybe nothing had changed—for him. But for Julia, the whole world had shifted.

She had thought it would be enough to go through life married to a considerate husband and a wonderful father for her baby. She had agreed to the wedding, agreed to move into his home. Now she wanted more.

Maybe he was right, maybe it wasn't fair of her to change the rules in midstream. But she couldn't help it anymore. It wasn't just that the rules had changed. It was that Julia herself had changed. She had told him she was in love with him and now she needed him to admit the same.

But he wouldn't. He couldn't. They'd discussed it again last night and she had demanded to know why. What had happened in the past that made him refuse to love her now?

She'd even swallowed her pride and asked him if his feelings had anything to do with that woman she'd met at the formal party. Martina. Was he still in love with her?

Cameron had laughed and brushed off her question, saying only that she was barking up the wrong tree, and left it at that. He wouldn't tell her anything more, wouldn't give her any reason for it.

And now she could actually feel her heart breaking. For herself and for him. And for Jake. All this time, she'd tried to convince herself that it was enough to have a family, an attentive husband, a darling baby. But she'd finally come to the realization that it wasn't enough. She wanted it all. And she deserved it all.

The following Saturday, Adam and Trish threw a small party for a few friends to celebrate their pregnancy. Julia brought homemade breads and dessert and helped Trish with the dinner. Later in the kitchen, she stacked the dessert plates.

"Can I wash the dishes?" Julia asked.

"No, no," Trish said easily, hanging the potholders on their hooks. "Adam and I like to clean up the place by ourselves once our guests go home. It's fun to spend the time together, talking and laughing about the evening and planning our next get-together."

Just then, Adam walked into the kitchen and slipped his arms around Trish's waist. "I missed you. Are you done in here?"

"Yes." Trish beamed at him and he kissed her, then laid his cheek against her head.

Later, on the ride home, she turned to Cameron. "It must be wonderful for you to know your brother Adam is so happy."

Cameron glanced at her sideways as he drove down the highway. "Never really thought about it, but I suppose it's nice."

"Nice?" She laughed. "Cameron, the man is so head over heels in love with his wife, he can't see straight."

Cameron held up his hand. "Okay, I know where this is going and we've been there before. For the last time, I'm telling you that we have a great life together. Why can't you just let it go at that?"

He reached for her hand and squeezed it. It was an affectionate move, meant to reassure her that he cared. But oddly enough, she had to blink back unexpected tears that threatened to fall. She refused to cry, refused to act like more of an idiot than she already was. But was it so idiotic to want all of him? She wanted his heart, not just his name. If that made her a fool, then so be it. At least she would be a fool for love. The thought made her smile all the way home.

But the next day, as she put the breakfast dishes in the dishwasher, she felt her world closing in on her. She had to sit down for a minute as she wondered if she was actually sick or if it was just her heart breaking.

"Good grief," she murmured, standing up with determination. She shut the dishwasher door and turned it on. "When did you become such a drama queen?"

Why couldn't she just let it go? But she couldn't. She'd fallen in love with Cameron and all those strong feelings had wormed their way into her heart. She had to do something about them because she was pretty sure that if she continued to live without love, she would lose herself.

With a sigh, she remembered there was one person in the world she could talk to about her problems. She changed Jake's diaper and got him dressed, then packed him in the car and drove to Sally's house.

"What a nice surprise," Sally said when she opened her front door.

"I hope you don't mind that we stopped by without calling."

"Are you kidding?" she said. "I love it. Come in."

"Thanks."

Sally led the way through her comfortable, stylish living room to her big sunny kitchen. "Don't ever think you can't drop in on me. I love seeing you."

Jake blew bubbles and cooed as he bounced in his carrier.

"Yes, my little darling." Sally tickled his belly. "I love seeing you, too."

She pulled a pitcher of iced tea from the refrigerator, poured two glasses and placed them on napkins on the kitchen table. "Now sit and tell me what's going on. Are you feeling okay? You look a bit down."

Julia shook her hair back and held her shoulders up. "I don't really know where to begin. I suppose I'll start by saying, I'm in love with your son."

"I assume you mean Cameron," Sally said dryly.

Julia choked on her laugh. "Yes, of course."

"Okay, then yes," she said, chuckling. "Of course I know you love him, despite your inability to admit it at the wedding. It makes me so happy to hear you finally say it."

Julia began shredding her napkin. "But he doesn't love me, Sally."

"What?" Frowning, Sally sat back in her chair. "Honey, of course he does. He loves you very much. I can tell with every look he gives you. I've never seen him so happy."

"Why won't he tell me, then?"

"Tell you what?"

Julia gave Sally a look of frustration. "Why won't he tell me he loves me?"

Sally took a slow sip of her tea. "He's never told you?"

"No," Julia admitted, and buried her face in her

hands. "And I feel so stupid, so needy. It's making me sick inside. We actually agreed, when we got married, that love wouldn't come into it."

"You did what?" Sally sounded sincerely shocked.

"Oh, I know what you're thinking," Julia said. "But it seemed like the right thing to do at the time. We married in order to provide Jake with two parents who lived together and loved him. And I was just so happy to be a part of your family, I had to do it."

"Oh, sweetie." She sniffled.

"But now I've fallen in love with Cameron and I've told him, but he insists he's not in love with me. And the thing is, Sally, we're so happy otherwise. So maybe I should just stop whining and be content with what I've got."

Julia sat up straight and looked at her mother-in-law with resolve. "But I can't. I used to think I could be happy without love, but I want it all, Sally. I want him to love me."

"Oh, dear." Sally jumped up from the table and stooped down next to Julia, where she rubbed her arm and patted her cheek. "He does love you, sweetie. Believe me, I know my son. He's not an easy man, but he's worth the battle."

"He really is," Julia said through a light mist of tears.

"Now, you need to stop worrying so much."

"I'm trying."

"Good girl," Sally said. "Now try harder."

Julia laughed, then took hold of Sally's hand and squeezed it. "But I need to ask you something really serious, and I hope you'll keep it between us."

"Anything, sweetie."

Julia bit her lip, then took a deep breath and said what she'd come here to say. "Is there something about Cameron that makes him not want to love me? Oh, that sounds so stupid but I need to know. Is it something about me? Or is it him?"

"Oh, my," Sally said, pushing herself up. She began to pace around the kitchen as she talked. "Poor Cameron. Your question makes me wonder if this whole thing might be because of his father. He was a horrible man. I never got the complete story because the records were sealed, but I knew he was violent. I don't want to alarm you, but I did find out that the man killed Cameron's mother, then killed himself."

"Oh, that's awful. Cameron's never said anything."

"No, he wouldn't. But he was so unhappy when he first came to live with us."

"Oh, God," Julia whispered, as she considered the sad little boy he'd been back then.

"Then, when he was a senior in high school," Sally said, "he met a girl." She told Julia about Wendy. "He always blamed himself for her horrible behavior."

"But that's not fair," Julia cried.

"No, but that's Cameron. I'll never forget it when he told me it was his fault and that his father was right."

"Oh, dear."

"Maybe I shouldn't have told you all this," Sally said, frowning. "I don't want you to worry that he might hurt you. He wouldn't."

Julia's eyes widened in disbelief, then she started to laugh. "Hurt me? Cameron? He doesn't have a violent bone in his body."

Sally smiled. "It's true. He never was much of a fighter. Oh, sure, he went and joined the marines, but it wasn't because he was looking for a fight. My theory was that his early childhood was so chaotic, he was always seeking more control and order in his life. I think he appreciated that aspect of the military."

Julia made a face. "Well, he certainly likes to control things, doesn't he? But still, he wouldn't hurt a fly. He's the most gentle man I know."

"Yes he is," Sally said, then smiled slyly. "But I'm thinking you might need to ruffle his feathers a bit before he comes to that realization for himself."

Julia frowned at her for a moment, then slowly, understanding dawned. "Oh, Sally, you're a wise woman."

She splayed her hands out. "That's exactly what I keep telling my sons."

Cameron brought her a beautiful butterfly pin made of yellow diamonds and sapphires.

"Oh, Cameron, it's lovely," she said. "But why?"

"No reason."

She took a deep breath. "Are you sure it's not because you're in love with me?"

"Julia…"

"I know, I know." She held up her hand. "It's okay, I know you won't say it. But I do want to make sure of one thing. You love Jake, right?"

"What? Of course I do," he said and stared impatiently out the window.

"I'm glad to hear it, for your sake and Jake's."

"What are you getting at?" he asked.

She placed the lovely pin back in its cushioned jewelry box. She smiled at him and her tone turned blunt. "It'll just make the custody agreement easier to deal with once Jake and I move back to my house."

"Once you—what?" Stunned, he spun her around to face him. "What's that supposed to mean? You're not moving out. We're married. You're not going anywhere."

She clasped her hands together. "I thought it would be enough, Cameron. But it's not. You're a wonderful man, kind and attentive, and so good with Jake. You're an amazing lover and a great friend. But you don't love me, and I want a husband who will love me."

"I'm your husband," he bellowed, then remembered the baby and lowered his voice. "This is all wrong, Julia. You're trying to change the rules again."

"I don't think I am," she said quietly. "I just think that from now on, I'm following my own rules."

"And what are your rules, Julia?" he said, with just a hint of sarcasm.

"There's only one rule, so far," she said. "I deserve to be loved."

"I can give you almost anything," he bit out, "but I can't give you that."

"Even though I know you love me?"

"You're wrong, babe. I don't love you."

She struggled to catch her breath. He'd never denied it quite that harshly before. But she would get through this. "All right then. I guess that's it."

"I'm sorry," he said, rubbing his neck in frustration. "But you made me angry. Look, I don't want to hurt you. Ever. And that's why…" He stopped.

"That's why…what?" she asked finally.

"That's why I'll never tell you I love you."

She sighed and prayed for patience. "Cameron, you've given me more than fifty thousand dollars worth of jewelry."

"Exactly," he said, as if he were praising a bright six-year-old. "Doesn't that prove that I care about you? Haven't I treated you well and given you things to remind you of our good times together? Can't that be enough?"

"All those things are a sign that you love me," she said pleasantly. "So you might as well just say it."

"Look, I won't do this," he said, pacing the room. "You keep going over this same issue and it's never going to turn out to your satisfaction."

"You're right, and that's why I think we need to separate for a while."

"No." His fists bunched up and he gritted his teeth, seeming to struggle for the words that would stop her from making demands while also explaining why things had to be done his way. Finally, he composed himself enough to speak. "Look, I grew up in a bad place. My father was…"

"Your father?" she prompted after a moment.

"Was a jackass," he said with force. "Violent. Mean. My mother suffered for it."

She winced. "Did he hurt you?"

He laughed without humor. "Once in a while. Didn't mean anything. Mostly he took his rage out on my mother. And that's a fact I'm not exactly proud of."

"Why?"

"I didn't protect her, did I?"

"How old were you?"

He shrugged. "Six, seven. Doesn't matter. I couldn't stop him. But the worst part was that every time he hit her, he would yell that he was doing it because he loved her."

Julia cringed as she finally saw the reason behind Cameron's reluctance to admit love. "That's awful."

"He *loved* her," Cameron repeated, his face a mask of revulsion and pain. "And he showed his *love* by beating the crap out of her."

"Oh, Cameron," she said, and reached out to touch his shoulder in a move meant to comfort him.

He flinched. "No. Don't."

"But—"

"Don't you get it?" He stepped back from her. "I have that same violent streak buried somewhere inside me. I know it's there. So I'll never give in. I'll never love. Believe me, I've tried. It didn't work. In fact, it ruined people's lives. I'm a bad risk. Do you understand now?"

"But you're not anything like your father," she said gently.

"It's not that simple." He raked his fingers through his hair. "Look, I know you want to hear the words, but I'll never say them. And I'll never feel them, either. I care about you, Julia, but I refuse to hurt you like my father hurt my mother. I couldn't live with myself if that happened."

Julia would never say it aloud, but she was already hurting. Bleeding. For him. "Do you remember our wedding night?"

He seemed taken aback by her non sequitur. "Of course."

"I was so angry with you."

He grimaced. "Yeah, I know. For good reason."

"I stormed out and you spent the night on the couch, remember?" she persisted. "I think I hit you at one point."

"You were pissed off."

"But nothing happened."

"Well, sure it did," he said, looking at her as though she'd lost her mind. "The next night we had a great time. You don't remember?"

She rolled her eyes. "Yes, I remember that part. But I'm talking about when I was so angry. I was yelling at you, and I could tell you were angry, too. But you didn't hit me back. And the same thing happened when I painted the kitchen. You were furious with me."

"Yeah, so?"

"Why didn't you hit me?" she persisted.

He frowned. "Look, you're upset right now, but you've got to know that I would never hit you—"

"That's right!" Her eyes lit up. "You would never hit me because you're so *non*violent, it's ridiculous."

"No, that's not why," he muttered, walking away. "I'll never hit you because I don't love you."

Julia was startled. But then she began to laugh.

"It's true," he said, then turned and pointed at her in warning. "Don't push me, Julia."

Still laughing, she walked right up to him and pushed his chest, hard. He didn't budge. Julia shook her head and wrapped her arms around him, whispering, "I'm pushing you, Cameron, but you would still never hit me. I know you wouldn't. It's not in your makeup."

Resting her head on his chest, she held him tightly and took a moment to mourn the traumatized young boy he used to be. And she felt herself falling more in love with the strong, generous man he was today. The stubborn, ox-headed man who refused to recognize love when it shoved him in the chest.

After a long moment, she lifted her head and gazed

at him. "Do you remember when you asked me why I always baked cupcakes?"

"Yeah."

"I told you that after my parents died, whenever it was my birthday, Cook would give me a cupcake to celebrate the occasion. What I didn't say was that Cook told me it would be a waste of time and energy to bake an entire cake just for one little girl. So every year, I got that one cupcake."

Her shoulders trembled at the memories and he tightened his hold on her.

"One sad little cupcake with one candle in the middle," she said, and tried to laugh about it. "In my mind, cupcakes began to symbolize my life. And now I can see they symbolized my loneliness."

"Oh, baby," he murmured, and rubbed her back.

"Sometimes I would go into the kitchen and beg Cook to let me help with the baking, just to be near another human being in that big old drafty mansion. After a while, I discovered I was really good at baking."

"You're more than good at it."

"Thanks," she said. "I used to bring cupcakes to school sometimes and I saw how they made everyone feel better, especially myself. It was nurturing and fun to bake for other people and it kept some of the loneliness at bay."

She stepped away from Cameron's embrace and looked him in the eye. "It might've been a brilliant business decision to start a bakery that specialized in cupcakes, but now I'm thinking of changing my business plan."

"Yeah?" he said, sounding almost afraid to ask what she had in mind.

"Yeah," she said adamantly. "I'm not going to settle for cupcakes anymore. I want the whole damn cake."

She told him she needed space to think about things, then packed her bags and Jake's baby gear.

Cameron was beyond pissed off that she was leaving and taking Jake with her. "This is absurd, Julia. I don't want you to go."

"You can stop me with a word," she said lightly, though he could see her eyes were bright with tears. "No, make that three words."

He stared at her, his mouth a firm, thin line, saying nothing.

Awash with a sudden wave of grief, she nodded. "That's what I thought." She put Jake into his baby seat. "Say bye-bye to daddy."

Jake bounced in his seat and waved his hands. "Dada!"

Cameron stared after them as they drove down the driveway and disappeared, leaving him with nothing but his famous grip on control.

Eleven

Barely one hour later, Sally was knocking on his door.

"Come on in, Mom," Cameron said, holding the door open for her. "You want a beer?"

"Of course I don't want a beer," she said, dropping her purse on the living room chair as she followed him into the kitchen. "Cameron, what is going on? You two looked so happy. I was so proud of you for finally accepting love into your life."

"It wasn't what it looked like, Mom." He shrugged. "We had an arrangement."

"Oh, don't be ridiculous," she said, waving his words away. "Arrangements. Good heavens. You kids today."

"Mom, I don't—"

"Look me in the eye and tell me you are not head over heels in love with Julia."

He gritted his teeth and stared her in the eyes. "No."

She narrowed her gaze. "No, you won't tell me or no, you're not in love."

He folded his arms across his chest defiantly. "I'm telling you I'm not in love with her."

She blinked in surprise. "My goodness. Well, I guess I'll be going."

"No need to rush off," he said, a little desperately. "You want to go for a swim or something?"

"No, I got what I came here for."

"Mom," he said, shaking his head. "I'm sorry."

"I am, too, dear," Sally said, and collected her purse as she headed for the front door. "Cameron, you know I love you very much."

"I love you, too, Mom."

"I'm glad, because there's something I need to say to you." She turned and he could read the disappointment in her eyes. "It's been a long time since you lied to me, Cameron Duke, but you're lying now. To me, and to yourself. You are nothing like your father and you know it. Now, I didn't raise a fool, so stop acting like one. You get that wonderful girl and her darling baby back inside this house or heads will roll."

Damn, they didn't call her the Steel Camellia for nothing, Cameron thought ruefully. After his mother left, he took some time to brood for a while. Sally was wrong about the whole lying thing, of course. But he'd been the good son and had allowed her to say what she needed to say.

Now, alone in the house, it almost felt good, necessary even, to wallow in the pain. It had only been a few hours, but he already missed Julia like he would have missed a number of key body parts. More, in fact. Somehow, over the last few months, she had become an essential part of his life, like breathing out and breathing in. So now how was he supposed to live without breathing Julia?

But he would do it. And maybe it was better this way. He'd warned her from the start that he didn't do the whole love thing, and she'd tried to change the rules. She was asking too much, making demands. Cameron Duke didn't work that way. Nobody changed his rules but him.

Still, he missed Julia and Jake like crazy.

He was well into his second beer when the doorbell rang again. He wasn't surprised to see Adam and Brandon let themselves into the house, but he was shocked to see Brandon carrying a small white box with the word Cupcake stenciled in navy blue across the top.

"What are you doing with those?" Cameron asked irately.

"I stopped by Julia's store and bought them," Brandon said with a grin. "Hey, now that you and she are breaking up, I'm thinking she might want to go out sometime." He took a bite of a red-velvet cupcake and moaned, then slid into a dining room chair. "Holy smokes. You let her and these cupcakes get away? Dude, you're nuts. I'm calling her tonight."

Cameron started toward him with both hands fisted. "If you want to live, you'll think twice about that."

Adam grabbed Cameron's arm before he could get any farther. "Don't be a fool."

"Why not?" Cameron asked. "That seems to be the popular opinion of me right now."

"Well, a fool is what you are," Brandon said matter-of-factly, and took another bite of the cupcake.

"And you're a dead man," Cameron said, folding his arms across his chest.

Adam laughed. "Look at you."

Cameron glanced down at himself, then snarled at his brother. "What?"

"You're standing there making threats, but we all know you would never hurt Brandon."

"Don't count on it," Cameron muttered.

Adam shook his head. "Even when we were kids, you never threw the first punch. Ever."

"True enough," Brandon said with a shrug.

"Whereas, Brandon used to get into fights all the time," Adam grinned. "Remember?"

Brandon smiled at the memories, then glanced at Cameron. "You never fought about anything unless some kid hit you first. Even then, you'd do whatever you could to prevent another punch."

"Yeah, always the diplomat," Adam said. "I only remember one time when you were actually forced to defend yourself."

"Yeah," Brandon said, then laughed. "And that was only because Jerry Miles was going to beat the crap out of me."

"I should've let him."

"But you didn't," Adam said pointedly. "You entered that fight with grim resignation. There was never any blood lust with you. You never enjoyed it, never got into it. And you never will."

"Yeah," he muttered. "Maybe."

"No, not maybe," Adam shot back. "Don't you get it?

You're not a fighter. You're not violent. You're nothing like your old man and you never will be."

That Saturday, Sally brought Jake over to Cameron's house so he could spend the day with his daddy. Julia had an emergency at the bakery, Sally explained, so she had agreed to bring Jake by.

That's when it really hit him how much he missed Julia, more than he'd ever thought possible. So much that it hurt him physically.

He took Jake swimming in the pool. After some serious splashing and laughing, they got out and Cameron dried Jake off. He let him crawl in the thick grass of the yard while Cameron quickly dried himself off. Then he watched in amazement as Jake crawled to the fence and used it to lever himself up off the ground. He stood all by himself in the grass and took his first step.

"Dada!" Jake cried, then plopped back down on his butt. He laughed and Cameron swooped him up with delight.

"Jake, what did you do?" Cameron asked, astounded by his son's ability. "Can you do that again? Can you walk by yourself like a big boy? Here, I'll help you."

Cameron steadied Jake, who stood where he was for a few seconds, then took a tentative step. He began to wobble and finally fell on his knees. This time, he screamed bloody murder. Cameron picked him up to comfort him.

"That's okay, buddy," he crooned as he hugged the little guy. "We'll just kiss it and make it better. All better."

Jake shuddered and sniffled as Cameron soothed away his pain.

"Hey, you're getting to be a real big boy," he murmured, patting his back. "Come on. It's all better now. All better. And just wait till your mama hears what you did."

The emotion hit him so fast and hard, Cameron almost fell to his knees himself. Julia needed to know that Jake had walked. He raced into the house to call her immediately. Who better to share this special moment with?

As Cameron picked up the phone, he rubbed his chest, recognizing the heavy feeling. He'd felt it that night at the big party, while watching Julia as she talked to his friend Byron. Now the feelings seemed to come in waves and they filled his chest with so much warmth, he had a hard time catching his breath. It wasn't pain. It was an emotion he'd never felt with any other woman but her.

He stared at the phone for a few seconds, then put it back in its cradle. What would he do when Jake had another special moment? Would he rush to call Julia? And what would happen when Jake started walking for real? If Cameron wasn't there, would Julia call him to describe his every movement, bit by bit, over the phone? Was Cameron prepared to miss all those special moments of their lives?

And what would happen if Jake fell down again? What if Cameron wasn't there when Jake cried? Who would kiss and make it better?

And what if something happened to Julia? Who would kiss her and make her feel better when she was hurt? She'd spent much of her life having no one around to do that for her. He was ashamed to admit that he hadn't come forward to do it for her, either.

Would she find someone else? Someone with the guts to stand by her side and love her as she deserved to be loved? Would some other man move into Julia's life and take Cameron's place?

Would Cameron really sit on the sidelines and let that happen?

"Hell, no," he swore. If anyone was going to love Julia, it was going to be him.

"Damn it, Julia," he muttered, grabbing his keys and Jake's diaper bag. "I warned you."

He drove up into the hills above Dunsmuir Bay to Glen Haven Farm, Julia's home. She and Jake had their living quarters in the east wing. It was a nice set-up, with three bedrooms, a couple of bathrooms, a good-size sitting room, as Julia called it, and a great old kitchen. It was comfy and lived-in, unlike the rest of the big old house.

He still couldn't picture the little girl she'd been, trying to grow up in what was more like a fine arts museum than a home. But that was okay, because he was determined to make sure she wouldn't live here much longer.

Holding Jake securely in his arms, Cameron rang the doorbell and waited for the maid or housekeeper to open the heavy double doors.

Instead, Julia showed up, looking beautiful and sexy in jeans, sneakers and an apron spotted with chocolate smears. "Hi."

"Hi," Cameron said, and gazed into the dark blue eyes he'd fallen for the first time he ever saw her. He'd settled on a plan of action on the drive over here. He'd worked out all the right things to say, and just how to say them. But when faced with his fate, he simply blurted, "I love you, Julia. Please come home."

He watched her swallow, then she bit her lip as her forehead furrowed in a frown. "I'm sorry. I'm not sure I heard you quite right. Could you maybe repeat that three or four more times?"

"I'm in love with you, Julia," he said. "I love you more than anything in the world. I want you and Jake to live with me and I want more babies and I want a dog. A big one. But more than anything else, I want you back, Julia. I love you so much. Come back home and don't ever leave me again."

She tilted her head. "Once more?"

He laughed and grabbed her in a fierce embrace and she kissed him with all the love she could muster. "Of course I'll come home. I've just been waiting for you to ask."

"Mama!" Jake giggled and waved his hands.

Cameron's heart was bursting with joy. "I love you more than anything. Will you marry me all over again? We'll have a huge, fancy wedding. You can wear a designer dress and we'll invite a thousand people. There'll be a gigantic cake. I promise we'll do it the right way this time. Just please come home with me. I love you."

She kissed him again with her arms still wrapped around him and Jake. "Silly man. You still don't get it. I don't need another wedding, Cameron. I already have everything I've ever wanted right here in my arms."

* * * * *

"Your new wardrobe is in the plane. There's a room in the back. *Change.*"

Of all the high-handedness, of all the *arrogance!* Of all the bosses in the world—she had to be in debt to *Marcos.*

While the jet motors hummed in the background, Virginia slipped into the slinky patterned dress inside the windowless little room at the back of the plane. The clothes were divine. She couldn't in her right mind stay annoyed at a man with such exquisite taste. Her knight in shining armor.

Enthralled by how slight and satiny the dress felt against her body, she ran three fingers down the length of her hips, wishing there were a mirror to visually appreciate its exquisite plunging back. *And how is this necessary to his plan?* she wondered.

Gathering her courage with a steady inhale, she forced herself to step outside.

And there was nothing to pry his glimmering eyes away from her, no shield from the scorching possessiveness flickering in their depths...

Dear Reader,

This book, my first Desire™, was an adventure to write. Adventure in the sense of me, being immersed in this wonderful story, bravely struggling to adjust my vision to something that would do justice to the wonderfully provocative Desire line. Believe me when I say this was no easy feat when you start with a stubborn hero like mine!

Marcos is a ruthless man, and so stubborn he wouldn't bend to my ideas no matter what I did or said. He always won. Powerful in character and in will—he's determined to get what he wants and he always gets his way. But despite the constant headaches from the man, I realized there was always one constant in him. No matter what he did, or where he was, or what I demanded that he do, Marcos wanted Virginia with a passion. A passion that could make *any* woman, even this author, tremble.

As I wrote, I learned to see our heroine, his lovely assistant Virginia, through his eyes. And boy, how I grew to admire Virginia's quiet strength! Just to work for her powerful boss and remain sane seems like a Herculean task. And where I, author and supposed master of this story, failed to domesticate our billionaire hero, Virginia succeeded with her quiet loyalty and determination to get ahead in life.

Her boss wants her. He always has. He wants her bad enough to help her, bad enough to bend for her. He wants her bad enough that, this time, Marcos Allende will get more than he bargained for.

Enjoy,

Red Garnier

THE SECRETARY'S
BOSSMAN
BARGAIN

BY
RED GARNIER

Published in Great Britain 2011
by Mills & Boon, an imprint of Harlequin (UK) Limited,
Eton House, 18-24 Paradise Road, Richmond, Surrey TW9 1SR

© Red Garnier 2010

ISBN: 978 0 263 88318 3

51-0911

Harlequin (UK) policy is to use papers that are natural, renewable and
recyclable products and made from wood grown in sustainable forests. The
logging and manufacturing processes conform to the legal environmental
regulations of the country of origin.

Printed and bound in Spain
by Blackprint CPI, Barcelona

Red Garnier is a fan of books, chocolate and happily ever afters. What better way to spend the day than combining all three? Travelling frequently between the United States and Mexico, Red likes to call Texas home. She'd love to hear from her readers at redgarnier@gmail. com. For more on upcoming books and current contests, please visit her website, www.redgarnier.com.

This book is dedicated to the fabulous Desire editors,
who provide endless wisdom, advice and inspiration.
Krista, Charles, and Shana—
Thank you for the gift of writing for your line.

And to Diana Ventimiglia,
who believed in me since the beginning.
You're fondly remembered.

One

She was ready to beg him.

Virginia Hollis shuddered. She wrapped her arms around herself and stared out the back window of the sleek black Lincoln as it wound along the darkened streets of Chicago. People strolled down the block, hands in their pockets, chins neatly tucked to their chests to shield their faces from the biting wind. Men held cell phones to their ears; women struggled with their shopping bags. One glimpse made it seem like such a regular evening. An ordinary night.

But it wasn't ordinary. It couldn't be.

Because Virginia's world had stopped turning.

The men who'd knocked on her door this morning had had a message for her, and it had not been a kind one.

She inhaled deeply and glanced at her simple black dress and the delicate strappy heels on her pink-toed feet. It seemed important for her to look nice—not just respectable, but sophisticated, noble—because the favor she was to ask was anything but.

And she could think of no one else to ask but *him*. God. Just thinking of humiliating herself like this in front of *him* made her stomach churn.

Nervously, she tugged on the pearl strand draped around her neck and tried focusing on the city again. The pearls were smooth under her fingers, genuine and old, the only thing Virginia had been able to salvage from her mother's belongings.

Her father had lost it all.

Bet by bet, he'd lost the cars, the antiques, the house. Virginia had watched with a combination of helplessness and rage. She'd threatened, screamed, pleaded with the quickly aging man, all to no avail.

There was no stopping him. No stopping the gambling.

There was nothing left now.

Nothing but her.

And she could not, *could* not, turn a blind eye to those men—to the threat they posed. To the threat they had succinctly delivered. No matter how much she frowned upon what her father did, and no matter how many times she'd promised never again to speak to him about it and he continued gambling anyway, he was her father. Her only family.

Once he'd been a businessman. Respected, admired even. Now it saddened her to think what she'd become.

Virginia didn't know how much he owed. She'd rather not know. All she knew was the deal she'd struck with those three surly men that morning. She had a month to come up with one hundred thousand dollars, during which time they would leave him alone.

In her wildest dreams, Virginia had never imagined coming up with that amount of money, on such little time. But while *she* couldn't, Marcos Allende could.

The little hairs on her arms pricked to attention at the thought of him. Her boss was a quiet, devastatingly handsome man. Some said he was gifted; his touch was that of a Midas. While Virginia had only been his assistant for a year—his third of three assistants, because it seemed one alone couldn't handle the daunting task of having him as boss—in that length of time, she had seen enough of him to agree.

The man was out of context.

He was bold, ruthless and proud. Single-handedly, he'd spotted, bought and righted troubled companies, and he'd created an empire. He inspired respect and admiration among peers and fear among his enemies. Judging by the overwhelming number of phone calls he received from the female population of Chicago, Virginia could tell they adored him. And in Virginia herself, the man inspired things she dared not consider.

Every morning when she stepped into his office, he would study her with that dark, compelling gaze and disturb every inch and atom of her body with the hot intimacy in his eyes. She would always try to act professionally, to look away when his stare became inappropriately long. But his eyes had a way of undressing her, of speaking in silence, of summoning visions in her mind about him and her and skin and sweat. Yet tonight she was on her way to him for one purpose only, and she reminded herself that her visit to his lair at such a late hour might not be welcome.

With his assistants he was always the firm, quiet boss, but Marcos Allende was reputed to have a hell of a temper, one she might witness tonight for the very first time.

Her stomach clenched when the car pulled into the ample driveway of one of the Windy City's most luxurious apartment buildings, situated on the heavily trafficked Michigan Avenue. A uniformed valet opened the door.

She mumbled a quick "thank you" and stepped out of the car, walking into the sumptuous apartment building with an eerie calm that belied every one of the roiling emotions inside her.

She made no eye contact with the people milling around the area, but instead focused all of her attention on the polished bronze doors at the far end of the lobby.

"Mr. Allende is expecting you."

An elevator attendant waited for her. He slipped a card into the top slot inside the confined elevator space and lit the top *P* before stepping out with a bow. "Good evening, madam."

The doors closed and Virginia stared at her blurry reflection.

Oh, God, please let him help me. I'll do anything. Anything…

Long seconds later, the doors rolled open to reveal the penthouse—a vast room with black granite floors, dimly lit and lavishly furnished. The walls could've been covered in crisp green bills and screamed the owner's net worth just as loudly. To a mortal, his place seemed as inaccessible in price as the owner was claimed to be in character.

Virginia stepped inside. A pair of elegant, willowy bronzes flanked the entry and a massive oil painting with vibrant black brushstrokes hung at the end wall. Before she could absorb the rest of the opulent area, as though drawn by some unknown force of nature, her gaze landed on him. He stood next to the bar at the far end of the living room. He was as elegant and unmoving as the designer furniture surrounding him. Dark, tall, detached. He faced the window, his broad back filling the shoulders of his jacket. Her heart thumped as she took a step forward, the click of her heels on granite magnified in the silence.

"I trust you had a fine ride."

Her flesh pebbled at the hum of his voice. So husky. So mellow. As though he were no threat to anyone. The crackling energy around him dispelled the notion fast.

"I did. Thank you for sending a car, and for seeing me on such short notice," she said quietly.

Starting to shake inside, she advanced toward the living room, stepping lightly across a plush Persian rug. He didn't turn. Virginia wasn't certain she even wanted him to. Every time their gazes met, a bolt of electricity would shoot through her. Sometimes he didn't even need to speak. His eyes did it for him. And in her mind, he said the wickedest things to her.

Now here she was, in his apartment, ready to face that bold, virile man she'd fantasized about. Ready to beg him.

Never mind Virginia had her modestly successful life, which she'd tried to live by the book. Never mind she'd paid her bills on time and tried first and foremost to stay out of trouble. Never mind anything but what had to be done. Saving her father. Doing anything she had to, to make him safe again.

She could've sworn Marcos read her thoughts just now, for he whispered, "Are you in trouble, Virginia?" While still gazing out the window as though mesmerized by the tiny flicker of city lights.

She swallowed, eyeing his back. "It appears I am."

"And you came to ask for my help?"

A ball of unease settled in the pit of her stomach, and the words seemed to be wrenched from her throat. "I do need your help, Marcos."

He turned, and she was rendered motionless by the sheer black power of his stare. "How much?"

Her heart pounded faster. His face was so exquisitely masculine, and there was something so naughty about him—his attitude, his dark good looks, his accent—that a dormant part of her found thrilling and frightening at once. Every inch of his Latin blood showed in his bronzed skin, the very masculinity oozing from his pores.

His inquisitive gaze traveled with interest down the length of her body until she could bear no more. She lifted her chin with pride, though the way she wrung her hands before her wasn't all that convincing. "I—I don't expect anything for free. I wanted to see you about an advance. A loan. Perhaps I could do more work for you. Special projects."

His eyelids dropped as he sighted her lips. "You're very pretty tonight, Virginia."

The low seduction in his words made her heart clench in a fistful of thrill. She fought the thrill, telling herself he was a sexy, virile man—and that he must look at all women this way. Which was why they called him. All. The. Time! When those eyes were on her, he made her feel like the sexiest woman alive—like the only woman alive.

"I'm trying to raise…" She paused, summoning all her courage. "I'm trying to raise one hundred thousand dollars. Can you help me?" she asked him then, lowering her face. As she spoke, she felt so…so cheap…so humiliated to be asking for money…

"Is that all you need?" he asked softly. As though it were nothing. A paltry sum. And to him, with all his billions, of course it would be.

He surveyed her in silence. "May I ask why you need it?"

Her gaze flicked up to his, and she shook her head. She couldn't bear it.

His lips twitched and the corners of his eyes crinkled, almost—*almost*—managing to make him less threatening. "You won't tell me?" he prodded.

"If you don't mind," she mumbled. She tugged the hem of her dress to her knees when his gaze ventured to her legs and lingered. "So there's nothing I could do for you? In exchange for this…incredible salary?" God. She couldn't even say the amount it seemed so out of reach.

He laughed, and Virginia didn't think she'd ever heard him laugh before. The sound resembled the roll of distant thunder.

He set his glass on the nearby bar and signaled to the twin leather couches. "Sit."

She sat. Her back was stiff and straight as she tracked his lithe moves around the room. How could a big man move with such grace? How could—

"Wine?"

"No."

He poured two glasses nonetheless. His hands moved skillfully—too skillfully not to notice—and brought one to her.

"Drink."

She grasped the fluted glass and stared at a faraway bronze sculpture, trying not to breathe for fear of what his scent might do to her. He smelled so amazingly good. Earthy and musky and male. She drew in a shaky breath until he dropped onto the couch across from hers.

When he stretched his arms out behind him, he made the couch appear small, his wide frame overwhelming the bone-colored leather designer piece. Under his jacket, the dress shirt he wore was unbuttoned at the top, gifting her with a view of smooth, bronzed skin and a polished gold cross.

She wanted to touch him. She wondered what that bronze skin would feel like under her fingers, if his cross was cold or warm…

Suddenly sensing his scrutiny, she raised her chin and smiled.

Lifting one black brow, Marcos opened his hand and signaled to her. "You're not drinking."

Virginia started, then obediently sipped. "It's…good. Very…um, rich."

"Have I ever bitten you?"

She almost choked on the wine, blinked, and then, then she saw the smile. A prime smile. Rare, like everything valuable, higher on one end than the other.

"I can see this is difficult for you," he said, with a glimmer of warmth in his eyes.

"No. I mean, yes. It is." He had no clue!

He set his glass aside, crossed his arms over his chest, and snuggled back as if to watch a movie. "You don't trust me?"

Her heart skipped a nervous beat.

Trust him? She respected him. Admired him. Was in awe of him and, because of his power, even a little afraid of him. And maybe, she realized, she trusted him, too. From what she'd seen, Marcos—quiet, solid, heart-of-gold Marcos—had proved to be nothing but a champion for his people. A lion protecting his cubs. When Lindsay, assistant two, had been weeping for months after her twins were born, Marcos had hired an army of nannies and sent her off to a second honeymoon in Hawaii with her husband.

Lindsay was still talking about Maui.

And when Mrs. Fuller's husband passed away, the over-wrought woman had cried more tears reminiscing about all that Marcos had done to support and aid her family than she had cried at the funeral.

No matter how humiliating this was, how awful her situation and having him know it, she knew, like nothing in her life, he was as steady as a mountain.

Holding his gaze, she replied in all honesty. "I trust you more than I trust anyone."

His face lit in surprise, and he scraped his chin between two blunt fingers. "And yet you don't tell me what troubles you?"

The thought that he—the man she most honored, esteemed—would know her life was in such shambles squished her heart like a bug. "I would tell you what I need the money for if I thought it mattered, and I would tell you if that is the only way you'll give it to me."

With an expression that would befit a lone hunting wolf,

Marcos rose and strode over, then pried the glass from her fingers. "Come with me."

Unnerved that she couldn't even begin to guess the thoughts in that unique, labyrinthine mind of his, Virginia followed him down the wide, domed hallway of his penthouse, becoming acutely aware of his formidable frame next to her.

And she couldn't help but wonder if maybe she wasn't a little bit the fool for trusting him after all.

Predatorily, Marcos studied her profile, her nose, the untamed, unruly bounce of her curls. She bit her lip in nervousness. Where was he taking her?

Visions of a bedroom flicked across her mind, and her cheeks flamed hot.

He opened the last door for her, and Virginia entered the darkened room, shamed at her own quickening pulse.

"Your home office?" she asked.

"Yes."

He flicked on the light switch, and the room burst to life. Bookshelves lined three of the four walls. A Turkish rug spread across the sitting area. Five glossy wood file cabinets formed a long, neat row behind his desk. No adornments. No picture frames. No distractions. As fine in taste as the rest of his apartment, with a state-of-the-art computer perched atop a massive desk, his office screamed two words: *no nonsense.*

"I like it." She strode inside, the knowledge that this was his private, personal space making her blood bubble. Her fingers itched with the overwhelming urge to organize the stacks of papers on his desk.

"I know about your father, Miss Hollis."

Dread sunk like a bowling ball in her stomach. "You do?"

She spun around, and when he stepped into the room, Marcos achieved the impossible: he made it shrink in size.

"You do not exist in the world I do without being cautious about everyone who comes into your inner circle. I have a dossier on everyone who works in close proximity with me, and I know every detail of their lives. Yes, I know about his problem."

"Oh."

What else did he know?

He passed her as he crossed the room, and she stifled a tremor as if he'd been a cool hurricane wind. "Why didn't you come to me before?" he asked, matter of fact.

"I'm here now," she whispered.

Halting behind his desk, he shoved the leather chair aside and leaned over the surface. His shirt stretched taut over his bunched shoulders and his eyebrows pulled low. "How bad is it?"

"It… The gambling comes and goes." Flushing at his scrutiny, she turned to busy herself with the books on the shelves, and then said, as if he'd expertly unlatched a closed door which had been near bursting with secrets, "He's out of control. He keeps betting more than what he has and more than I could possibly earn."

"Is that the only reason you're here?"

His voice grew so textured, a jolt of feminine heat rippled through her. She spun around—shocked by the question. Shocked by the answering flutter in her womb.

Her breath stopped.

His gaze. It was open. Raw. Revealed a galvanizing wildness, a primitive hunger lurking—lurking *there*—in the depths of his eyes, like a prowling beast.

Pent-up desire rushed through her bloodstream as he continued to stare. Stare at her in a way no man, ever, should look at a woman and expect her to survive. "Is that the only reason you're here tonight? Virginia?"

As if in a trance, she moved forward on shaky legs, closer to his desk. "Y-yes."

"You want nothing else? Just the money?"

How to talk? How to think? Breathe? Her heart felt ready to pop from the pressure of answering. "N-nothing."

In the back of her mind, she vaguely realized how simple and unassuming her needs sounded as she voiced them. When they were not. They were tangled. They had grown fierce with his proximity. Out of reason, out of context, out of *control*.

"Will you help me," she murmured as she reached the desk, and somehow the plea sounded as intimate as if she'd asked for a kiss.

"I will." Deep and rough, the determination in his answer flooded her with relief.

He was going to help her.

In her soaring mind, Marcos was mounted on a white charger holding up a flag that read "Virginia."

And she...well, hers might be a banner. A neon sign. A brand on every inch of her body and possibly her heart. Marcos Allende. God, she was a fool.

"I don't expect something for nothing," she said. Her voice throbbed even as a tide of relief flooded her.

It was as if some unnatural force drew her to him, pulled her to get closer and closer. Did the force come from him? From her? If it weren't for the desk—always the desk between them—where would she be?

No. The obstacle wasn't a desk. It was everything. Everything. Nothing she could ever arrange or fix or clean.

Marcos raked one hand through his hair, then seized a runaway pen and thrust it into an empty leather holder. "I'll give you the money. But I have a few requests of my own."

"Anything," she said.

His gaze was positively lethal. His hands—they made fists. "There's something I want. Something that *belongs* to me. Something I must have or I'll lose my mind with wanting it."

A shiver ran hot and cold down her spine.

He wasn't speaking of her—of course he wasn't—but nonetheless, she felt something grip inside her as though he were. What would it feel like for Marcos to want her so fiercely? "I...understand."

"Do you?"

He smiled bleakly at her, then continued around his desk.

He swept up a gemstone globe from the edge and spun it around, a lapis lazuli ocean going round and round. "Here." His finger stopped the motion, marking a country encrusted in granite for her eyes. "What I want is here." He tapped.

Tap tap tap.

She stepped closer, longingly lifting a fingertip to stroke the length of the country he signaled. Travel had seemed so far down the line of her priorities she hardly gave any thought to it now.

"Mexico," she whispered.

His finger slid. It touched hers. He watched. And she watched. And neither of them moved. His finger was blunt and tan, hers slim and milky. Both over Mexico. It wasn't even a touch, not even half a touch. And she felt the contact in every fiber of her lonely, quivering being.

He turned his head, their faces so close that his pupils looked enormously black to her. A swirling vortex. He whispered, as though confessing his every hidden desire and sin, "I'm after Allende."

She connected the name immediately. "Your father's business?"

"The business he lost."

He set down the globe, and again, his finger. This time the back of it stroked down her cheek. Marcos touching her, Marcos looking so strangely at her, oh, God. He smelled so good she felt lightheaded.

"And you believe I can help?" she asked, one step away

from him, then two. Away from his magnificent, compelling force, away from what he made her want.

He scraped a restless hand down his face. "The owner has managed it poorly and contacted me for help." A tiny muscle ticked at the back of his jaw. "I'm usually a sucker for the ailing, I admit, but things are different in this case." Disgusted, he shook his head. "I do not intend to help her, you understand?"

"Yes." She didn't understand, exactly, but rumors around the office were that *no one* mentioned Allende to Marcos unless they wanted their head bitten off.

He paced. "I'm taking it hostilely if I have to."

"I see."

"I could use an escort."

Escort.

"I need someone I can count on. Most of all—" he crossed his arms and his enigmatic black gaze bored into hers "—I need someone willing to pretend to be my lover."

Lover.

Her hands went damp and she discreetly wiped them at her sides. "Lover." When his long steps brought him over to her, she instinctively backed away until her calves hit a small ottoman.

Unperturbed, Marcos headed over to the bookshelf, his strides sure and unhurried. "Would you be interested in doing this for me?"

Her head whizzed with unwelcome, naughty thoughts. Thoughts of Mexico and Marcos. Martinis and Marcos. Mariachis and Marcos. "Yes, definitely." But what exactly did he mean by *pretend?* "So what would you expect of me, for how long?" An unprecedented thrill was trickling along her veins.

He rummaged through the books, moving tome after tome. "A week as my escort in Monterrey, and perhaps some work after hours until I'm able to close. I'll be sure to handle your…little problem."

"That's all?"

He shot her a look of incredulity. "That's not enough?"

She just smiled. And waited.

And watched.

The muscles under his shirt flexed as he reached the top shelf and pulled out a huge leather volume.

"Maybe your company at the Fintech dinner?" he continued, winged eyebrows flying up. "Would you mind? Going with me?"

She fiddled with her pearls, unable to stop fidgeting. "You… I can always arrange a date for you."

His lips curved upward as he waved the heavy book in her line of vision as easily as if it were a mere piece of paper. "I don't want a date, Miss Hollis. Here. You can take this—a bit about Monterrey, if you'd like." He set it on the ottoman. He had a lovely, lazy kind of smile, and she felt it curl her toes.

"I feel like I'm robbing you blind," she said, lifting the shiny book.

He paused in the middle of the room and stared at her with his deep gypsy eyes. "If I allowed it, it wouldn't be robbery, would it."

She saw his cool, brief smile and flattened the book tight against her breasts when they pricked. Traitors. But he'd smiled three times tonight. Three. Or more? Three or more just had to be a record.

"You're an asset to my company," he continued in an unnaturally husky voice, stalking back around the desk. "A week of your time is valuable to me. You're hard-working, smart. Loyal. You've gained my trust, Virginia, and my admiration—both difficult feats."

A feathery sensation coursed along her skin. She was certain he used that same self-assured tone in his meetings, but she wondered if it had the same thrilling effect on the members of his board.

When she couldn't seem to find anything useful to do other than ogle stupidly, she automatically did what she always did to cure herself. She set the book aside and began arranging the papers at the edge of his desk—from a messy pile to a neat pile. "T-thank you for the compliments. I enjoy working at Fintech very much. And for you…of course. Which is why I don't want to jeopardize my position."

She continued arranging, aware that he was doing nothing—nothing—but towering a few feet away and watching her. Like he did in the office sometimes. He would stop what he was doing and watch with those black, exciting eyes.

"What will we say at the office?" she rambled.

Gossip could be ruthless at Fintech. To think Lindsay or Mrs. Fuller might believe she'd done something un-professional to land a business trip with Marcos gripped her with unease.

When Marcos didn't reply, she looked up and caught the wicked sparkle in his eyes. She had the strangest sensation that he'd been staring at her bottom. "We will say that I ordered you to accompany me, of course. You are my assistant, after all."

His brows drew together and he peered at her hard, as though daring her to argue with him.

But a pang struck her right where it hurt; she knew she could never be more than an assistant to him. He was Marcos Allende. He could be Zeus himself, he was so unattainable.

Virginia was dreaming if she wanted more than a seat outside his office. Dreaming if she thought the desire in his eyes was for her. Dreaming to think that, even if it were, he'd do something about it and she'd dare let him.

No. She could not, would not allow herself to continue

harboring those foolish nightly fantasies about him. The daily ones had to go, too. It was hopeless, and it was hurtful, and it was stupid. He was offering her an assignment.

When the pile couldn't be a more perfect tower, she straightened it with as much dignity as she could muster. "I'd be happy to be your escort."

He nodded slowly. "Good. Great. Excellent." His voice was strangely terse, so utterly rich it seemed to sink into her body until it pulsed inside of her. "I knew we'd come to an agreement, then."

Dealing with a tumult of emotions without betraying herself proved difficult. Excitement warred with worry, gratitude with desire.

One week with him in Mexico. Playing his escort, his *lover*—a role Virginia had slipped into plenty of times in her mind. But this would be real, a real pretense, where she—inexperienced and naive in the ways of men—would pretend to be lover to a hunk, god and legend. Where she could even seize the moment, do something reckless she would no doubt come to regret and plant a kiss on the lips of the man who was unknowingly responsible for Virginia not wanting others. Did she dare? Did she fly? Did she have magic powers?

Was there even the possibility of being a good pretend lover to him after he'd dated actresses, duchesses, centerfolds?

Growing more and more unsettled at her new assignment, she picked up the book, *Monterrey: Tras el Tiempo,* and headed for the door, stealing one last glimpse of him. "Thank you, Marcos. For...everything. Good night."

"Virginia." When she was halfway down the hall, he caught up and seized her wrist, urging her around. His clasp sent a shiver skidding up her arm. "It's a five-hour flight. I mean to leave tomorrow afternoon. Can you be ready by then?"

Ready, she thought wildly.

She could be a virgin Mayan princess prepared her whole life for this ultimate sacrifice, be an Anne Boleyn laughingly led to her beheading, and she would *still* not be ready for Marcos Allende.

But she smiled. Her nod came out jerky.

He seized her chin and raised it slightly. She sucked in a breath at the contact, and the tips of her breasts brushed against his chest. "Will you be ready, Virginia?" he persisted.

Her legs quivered. All kinds of things moved inside her body. His breath was hot and fragrant on her face, and his lush, mobile mouth was so close, a moan rose to her throat, trapped there. Like the wanting of a year, trapped there.

How would he *feel* against her? His mouth? His hands?

He was so hard all over, so unlike any other man she'd known. He made her feel safe and protected and special, but he also made her burn, frightened her with the way she needed *something* from him more than she could possibly bear or understand.

She suppressed a shiver. "I'll be ready," she assured, a nervous excitement flourishing in her breast as she took a healthy step back. "Thank you. I know...I know you could ask someone else to do this for you. And I doubt you'd have to pay for her company."

His eyes smoldered, and his face went taut with some unnameable emotion. "Yes, but I want you."

I want you.

A ribbon of hope unfurled inside her. It feathered from the top of her head down to the soles of her feet. She didn't trust it. Marcos didn't mean the words the way they had sounded to her ears. Ears starved for anything he ever said to her.

She told herself, firmly, until it was embedded in her brain, that Marcos wanted someone trustworthy, someone biddable, and his lionlike instinct surely prodded him to help her.

And, oh, how she had wanted to be different. To him. Not

charity. Not like his stepbrother, a reckless playboy Marcos had to rescue time after time—not like all the strangers and friends who called him every day, seeking his counsel, his power, his help.

Everyone wanted something of Marcos Allende, for underneath the hard exterior lay a man with a strong, solid heart of gold. His faith in people was inspiring, his ruthlessness rivaled only by his mercy. Marcos...took care of you. And those early mornings when Virginia had stepped into his office to find his broad shoulders bent over the desk, his shirt rolled up to his elbows, his silky black hair falling over his forehead, his voice husky and his eyes tired from lack of sleep, her heart had ached with wanting to take care of that big, proud warrior. *Who gives you back what you give, Marcos Allende?*

Is there anyone out there who takes care of you for a change?

Now she determined that whatever he wanted, she would give. "You won't regret it, Marcos," she softly promised. "Helping me, I mean."

His lips twitched. That amused smile did things to her stomach, but it didn't seem to reach his eyes. Those remained hooded, unreadable. He ran the back of one finger down her cheek, the touch sparking fire. "It is I who hopes you never regret this visit."

Two

"Your new lover?"

Silent, Marcos stood at the living room window and broodingly watched the car pull away with Virginia inside it. From the penthouse, the Lincoln looked like a sleek black beetle, slipping into the intermittent traffic before the apartment building.

The pressure in his chest mounted with the distance.

His blood still pumped hot inside his veins and his head swam with a thousand thoughts, all of them X-rated.

"Or a mistress maybe?"

Twisting around, he faced his newest guest, the inquisitive Jack Williams—ex-corporate spy and now self-made millionaire. He was helping himself to a bag of nuts he'd obtained from the bar.

"My assistant," Marcos said tonelessly, swirling his newly poured Scotch in his hand. The cubes clinked in the glass.

Jack had arrived promptly at eleven as promised—the tall, blond Texan was never late, and, like a golden retriever listening to a particularly silent whistle, he had cocked his head when he spotted Virginia almost in Marcos's arms. As she whispered goodbye, Marcos's own instincts had flared to life and whispered that she wanted to stay.

But when "Williams the Bastard"—as the press had dubbed him—said he'd deliver, he delivered. And unfortunately what Marcos expected couldn't wait.

Still, he couldn't allow his friend to get the wrong impression of her, so he lifted his glass in a mocking toast. "She makes good coffee."

Jack popped an almond into his mouth and munched. "Aha. In bed?"

Marcos crossed the living room and headed back into the office, Jack trailing behind him.

Cranky, frustrated and exhausted, he set the glass atop a stack of papers on his desk and sank into the high-backed leather seat. "I'm not that man, Jack. Never mix business with pleasure, remember?"

But Virginia's sweet, fragrant scent lingered in the air. A torment to his straining body. A mockery to his words.

He respected his employees, took pride in being regarded as a man with moral fiber. And yet when it came to Virginia Hollis, it seemed he was reduced to the instincts of a caveman.

His friend's smooth, easy chuckle coming from the threshold somehow cranked up his frustration. "I remember. But the question is: do *you?* Should I have fetched a spoon, buddy? You looked ready to eat her."

Marcos would have scoffed. He certainly didn't welcome the canny twinkle in Jack's eye. But then he remembered the desperate urge he'd had to kiss Virginia…the exquisite scent of her skin, so close to his…the surprisingly fine feel of her in his arms, stirring and enticing beyond belief…

His chest cramped with emotion as he dragged a hand down his hot face. "Perhaps the old adage is true, and some rules are meant to be broken—especially if you're the moron living by them."

"Don't go there, Marcos." Jack pushed away from the door, dead serious. "I've been there. Not fun, man. Not fun for you, definitely not fun for her. Office affairs always end badly—no matter how well you plan them when you begin."

Marcos pondered the massive, crowded bookcase on the wall across from him. A near bursting sensation was lodged in the pit of his gut. He didn't want to hurt her. Hell, he hadn't wanted to *want* her.

Diablos, but he'd been sexually frustrated since the day he'd hired her. She was demure, desperate and determined, and Marcos had feared she'd be a distraction. But he hadn't counted on the fact that his primitive response to her would reach such a fever pitch.

"I've never gotten involved with an employee in my life— but she's different, Jack. And yes, I am aware of how that sounds."

Reclining in his seat with a grimace, he opened his cuff buttons and rolled up his sleeves.

He was actually considering, perhaps he was even past considering and had already made up his mind, giving them both what they'd wanted for months.

He was a man, flesh and blood like all the others. There was only so much he could stand. And Virginia…no matter how energetically she tried to conceal her reactions to him, she responded. Viscerally, primitively—a woman underneath the tidy assistant after all. A sweet, lovely woman who knew instinctively when a man wanted her. No, not wanted— Marcos *burned* for her.

And now he'd asked—practically demanded—she spend a week with him. Pretending to be his lover. At a time when all his energies, all his attention, needed to be on the one prize he'd sought to gain for so long.

Allende.

He hadn't been certain whether to ask her as escort. She was too much a temptation to play lovers with, and in order to successfully achieve his goals, focus was key.

But tonight the lovely Virginia—alone and financially abandoned by her family, something Marcos could identify with—had turned to him for help.

Tonight, as he'd gazed into her bright, fierce eyes, he couldn't deny himself any longer.

He wanted her.

He'd offered her a position for a week, true, but that was merely a guise for what he really wanted to do.

Her powerful effect would linger with him long after he left his office at night. He thought of her continually, every hour. He relived their encounters in his mind sometimes, enjoyed hearing her laugh at Lindsay's antics when his office doors were parted. He could not push her image away at night and loathed to see her in trouble when she seemed to seek so little of it for herself.

He'd made a mental list long ago with plenty of valid reasons to leave her alone.

She was an innocent, he was not. She was vulnerable, he could hurt her. She was his employee, he was her boss. There were dozens of reasons to stay the hell away from Virginia.

The ways she'd looked at him tonight pulverized them all.

"Here. I have just the thing to cheer you up." Jack stepped outside and returned rummaging through his leather briefcase. He yanked out a manila folder and held it out. "There you go, big man. Your wish is my command."

Marcos plucked the file from his hand and immediately honed in on the name printed across the tab. Marissa Galvez.

He smiled darkly. "Ah, my rainmaker. Everything here, I assume?"

"Everything on Marissa and her sleazy little deals. She's quite a busy little bee. You'll find it to be riveting reading. Took me a while, as you can see—but I did give you my word to have it ready by tonight."

Marcos skimmed through the pages, not surprised that the file was as thick as the woman was scheming.

Marissa Galvez. A shaft of anger sliced through him. The lady had hopes of a reconciliation before discussing numbers?

Of course she did. She read *Forbes*. Was smart enough to realize the son was worth more than the father she'd left him for, not thousands or millions, but billions. She knew the company, which should have rightfully been *his*, was prime for takeover and it wouldn't take much but a few savvy connections to learn it had been Marcos who'd been buying the outstanding stock.

Unfortunately, insulting Marissa's renewed interest in him wouldn't do to accomplish his goals. But a beautiful, smiling lover would slowly and surely take care of her dreams of reconciliation—and let them get down to the real business at hand.

Allende. *My company.*

"Mind telling me how you're going to convince the delectable woman to sell? Without succumbing to her request for some personal attention before discussing numbers?" Jack queried.

Marcos lunged to his feet, waving the evidence in the Texan's face. "With this. It's my game now, my rules." He met his friend's sharp, blue-eyed stare and his lips flattened to a grim, strained line. "Allende is in a vulnerable position. Sooner or later, she'll have to sell."

"Not to you, she doesn't."

Marcos shrugged disinterestedly. "She knows she's game for a hostile takeover. And she knows I'm the shark after her.

She wouldn't have called if she didn't want to get on my good side."

And I've got my pretty, green-eyed "lover."

"Will she?"

And her pretty little mouth. "What?"

"Get on your good side?"

"When you start wearing a tutu, Jack. Of course not."

Distaste filled him as he recalled her phone call. Dangling Allende up to him like bait, proposing they discuss it in her bed. She'd played with him as a naive, noble, seventeen-year-old boy, but it would be an ice age in hell before she played with the man.

"She called because she wants you back," Jack pointed out.

"Fortunately, I have an escort," he said and headed to the window, a part of him somehow expecting to see the Lincoln. "Being I will be conveniently taken, we'll have to forego the personal and get down to the numbers."

"I see now. So the lovely lady is key."

Those eyes. Big, bright, clear green, and so expressive he thought she'd pummeled his gut when she'd looked at him so adoringly. She made him feel…noble. Decent. Desperate to save her ten times over in exchange for another worshipful gaze.

When she'd called to request a moment of his time only hours ago, he'd allowed himself a brief flight of fantasy. He fantasized she'd been ready to succumb to him, ready to admit what already threatened to become inevitable. Even as he allowed himself the luxury of the fantasy, he knew she was too cautious and respectable for that.

It was up to him now. What was he going to do?

He shot Jack a sidelong look. "Marissa will get what's coming to her." And Virginia…

Jack swept up his briefcase with flair. "The devil on a Falcon jet, yes." He saluted from the threshold and flashed his signature I'm-Jack-the-Ripper grin. "I'll let you pack, my friend."

"My gratitude to you, Williams. And send the bill to Mrs. Fuller this week, she'll take care of it."

When Jack said an easy "will do" and disappeared, Marcos swallowed the last of his Scotch, his eyebrows furrowing together as he thought of the demure strand of pearls around Virginia's neck tonight. His woman wouldn't wear such little pearls. She'd wear diamonds. Tahitians. Emeralds.

With a swell of possessiveness, he brought to mind the lean, toned form of her body, watched countless times across his office desk, countless times when it had been by sheer determination that he'd forced his scrutiny back to his work.

A size six, he predicted, and promptly pulled his contact list from the top drawer and flipped through the pages.

If she was playing his lover, then one thing was certain: Virginia Hollis would look the part.

In the quiet interior of the Fixed Base Operator which specialized in servicing company jets, Marcos stood with his hands in his pockets. He brimmed with anticipation and gazed out the window from the spacious sitting area while the Falcon 7X jet—a sleek, white dove and one of his faster babies—got fueled.

He'd like to blame his simmering impatience on the deal he was about to negotiate. But the truth was, his assistant was late, and he was impatient to see *her.*

Now a door of opportunity was wide open for them. An opportunity to interact outside the busy, hectic pace of his office. An opportunity to step out of their roles and, if they chose to, temporarily into a new one.

She'll pretend to be my lover.

That she had accepted to aid him in this manner made

him feel heady. For how long would they be able to pretend and only pretend? Three days, three hours, three minutes?

In the back of the room, the glass doors rolled open. The sounds of traffic sailed into the building and Marcos swung around. To watch Virginia stroll inside.

A balloon of protectiveness blossomed in his chest.

The only thing untidy about his assistant today was her hair. Wild, windblown and uncontrollable. The ebony curls framed a lovely oval face and eyes that were green and clear and thick-lashed. Hauling a small black suitcase behind her, she paused to store a bag of peanuts in the outside zippered compartment. The mint-green V-neck sweater she wore dipped sexily to show the barest hint of cleavage. His mouth went dry.

She straightened that agile body of hers and swiped a wave of ebony curls behind her shoulder. The scent of citrus—lemons, oranges, everything that made him salivate—wafted through the air as she continued hauling her suitcase forward. Christ, she was a sexpot.

"Virginia," he said.

Her head swiveled to his. "Marcos."

He smiled. The sight of her face, warm in the sunlight, made his lungs constrict. She wore no makeup except for a gloss, and with her curls completely free, she was the most enchanting thing he'd ever seen.

Licking her lips as he came forward, she pulled the suitcase up and planted it at her feet—a barrier between their bodies. "You got a head start on me," she said. She spoke in a throaty, shaky voice that revealed her nervousness.

He eyed her lips. Burnished a silky pink today, inciting him to taste.

"I apologize, I had some last-minute work out of the office."

Dragging in a breath, he jerked his chin in the direction of the long table down the hall, offering coffee, cookies, napkins—all that Virginia liked to toil with. "Fix yourself coffee if you want. We'll board in a few minutes."

"You? Coffee?"

Somberly he shook his head, unable to prevent noticing the subtle sway of her skirt-clad hips as she left her compact black suitcase with him and walked away.

He was fascinated. By the sweet-smelling, sexy package of Virginia Hollis. Five feet four inches of reality. Of *pretend* lover.

Cursing under his breath, he snatched her suitcase handle and rolled the bag up to his spot by the window. The pilots were storing his luggage, consisting mostly of shopping bags from Neiman Marcus.

He crossed his arms as he waited for their signal. The file the infallible Jack Williams had given him last night provided him with more than enough ammo to persuade Marissa to sell, yet even the knowledge of emerging victorious didn't make this particular task any easier. You could crush a bug in your fist and it still didn't mean you would enjoy it. But Allende—a transport company on its last breath, flailing for help—had his name on it.

It was his. To resuscitate or to murder.

Virginia drew up beside him and he went rigid, inhumanly aware of her body close to his. She was a subtle, scented, stirring presence.

Without so much as moving his head, he let his eyes venture to the front of her sweater. The fabric clung to the small, shapely, seductive swells of her breasts. A wealth of tenderness flooded him. Virginia had come dressed as his assistant in the sweater, her typical knee-length gray skirt, the simple closed-toe shoes with no personality. "I'm afraid this won't do," he murmured.

A smile danced on her lips as she tipped her face up in bewilderment. She seemed animated today, no more the worried siren begging for his assistance last night. "What won't do?"

Virginia. With her perfect oval face, creamy, elegant throat and bow-shaped morsel of a mouth that invited him to nibble. It really seemed easier to stop breathing than to continue saying *no* to those marshmallow-soft lips. "The sweater," he said quietly, signaling the length of her body with his hand. "The skirt. The sensible shoes. It won't do, Miss Hollis."

She set her coffee cup and napkin on a side table, then tucked her hair behind her ear. "I did pack a few dresses."

"Did you." His eyebrows furrowed together as he surveyed her pearls. "Designer dresses?"

"Why, no."

He raised his hand to the pearl necklace. "How attached are you," he whispered, trailing his finger across the glossy bumps, "to wearing these?"

She watched him for a moment, a telling wariness in her voice. "They were Mother's."

"Pretty. Very pretty." The pent-up desire that blazed inside him textured his voice. "You see, my lover…might wear something else." He was playing with fire. He didn't care. "My woman—" he plucked a pearl between two fingers "—would wear Tahitians. Diamonds. Emeralds."

Her eyes danced. "Are you afraid I won't look presentable?"

He dropped his hands and shot her a dead-serious look. "I'm afraid you will look too much like my assistant and not my lover."

But she kept on smiling, kept on enchanting him. "I see."

He frowned now. "Understand me, Virginia. If I'd wanted to be seen with my assistant, I'd have brought Mrs. Fuller."

This made her gasp, and the gasp did not make his scowl vanish. He nodded towards the Falcon. "Your new wardrobe is in the plane. There's a room in the back. Change."

Three

Of all the highhandedness, of all the *arrogance,* of all the bosses in the world—she had to be in debt to *Marcos.* Undoubtedly the most complicated.

While the jet motors hummed in the background, Virginia slipped into the slinky patterned dress inside the windowless little room at the back of the plane. Damn him. She had agreed to his request, but how was she supposed to reply to his autocratic commands? Worse, the clothes were divine. She couldn't in her right mind stay annoyed at a man with such exquisite taste. Her knight in shining armor.

Enthralled by how slight and satiny the dress felt against her body, she ran three fingers down the length of her hips, wishing there was a mirror to let her visually appreciate the dress's exquisite, plunging back. *And how is this necessary to his plan?* she wondered.

Gathering her courage with a steady intake of breath, she forced herself to step outside.

Throughout the tasteful wood and leather interior, the air

crackled with the suppressed energy of his presence. His head was bent. His powerful, well-built body overwhelmed a cream-colored, plush leather seat, and his hair—abused by his hands during the flight—gleamed in the sunlight as he read through a massive leather tome. He was clad all in black, and the short-sleeved polo shirt he wore revealed tanned, strong forearms corded with veins. Watching him, big and proud and silent, completely engrossed and unaware of her gaze, she felt like sighing.

With a quick mental shake, she walked down the wide plane aisle, noting the screen embedded in the wood-paneled wall behind Marcos's seat. The electronic map showed the plane just three red dashes away from the little dot of Monterrey. At least one more hour.

As she eased in between their seats, intent on taking her place across from him, one huge hand shot out and manacled her wrist. She was spun around, and she gasped. Then there was nothing to pry those glimmering eyes away from her, no shield from the scorching possessiveness flickering in their depths.

"No," he rasped, his voice hoarsened by how little he'd spoken during the flight.

A melting sensation spread down her thighs, his accent too delicious to not enjoy. *No, don't sit yet,* she thought he meant, but she couldn't be sure. No one could ever be too sure of anything with Marcos. Maybe it was *no* to the dress!

Aware of her chest heaving too close to his face, she tried to pry her wrist free but failed miserably. "I changed. Wasn't that what you wanted?"

He cocked his head farther back and stared, his grip loosening slightly. "You're angry at me."

"I…" She jerked her chin toward the book on his lap, wanting, needing him to remove his hand. "Please. Read."

For a woman who'd strived to become invisible for years, the last thing she felt now was unseen. The filmy Issa London dress hugged her curves subtly, the wrap-around style tied with a bow at her left hip. The fabric felt so feminine she became utterly conscious of her body—and how he peered at it in interest.

"You approve of the clothes I bought you, *amor?*" he said huskily.

Amor? A jolt went through her at the endearment. Panicking, she tugged with more force and whispered, halfheartedly, "You can let go of me now."

His gaze pierced her, his unyielding hand burning her wrist. By the way his touch spread like a wildfire, her boss may as well have been touching her elsewhere. Where her breasts ached, where the back of her knees tingled, where her nerves sparkled and where she felt hot and painfully aware of being empty.

He released her. So abruptly she almost stumbled.

Still reeling, Virginia sank into her seat like a deflated balloon. Her pulse thundered. Her hands shook as she strapped on her seat belt.

His intense regard from across the aisle became a living, breathing thing. "Does a man's interest offend you?" he asked silkily.

Blushing furiously, she propped her purse on her lap. "Did you know Monterrey has over five million people now?" She shoved the maps she'd printed at the office and lists of Spanish words back in her purse.

He slapped the book shut and let it drop with a resounding thump at his feet. "Would *my* interest offend you, Virginia?"

She squinted at him, expecting a laugh, a chuckle, a smile at least.

He was perfectly sober. Excruciatingly handsome and sober.

Oh, no. No, no, no, he wouldn't do this. She was prepared

to do a job, but she was not prepared to allow herself to become a man's…plaything.

No matter how much she fantasized about him in private.

With a nervous smile, Virginia shook a chastising finger at him, but it trembled. "Mr. Allende, the closer we've gotten to Mexico, the stranger you've become."

Silence.

For an awful second, her blatant claim—part teasing and part not—hung suspended in the air. Virginia belatedly bit her lip. What had possessed her to say that to her boss? She curled her accusing finger back into her hand, lowering it in shame.

Sitting in a deceptively relaxed pose, he crossed his arms over his broad chest and regarded her with an unreadable expression. Then he spoke in that hushed, persuasive way of his, "Do you plan to call me *Mr. Allende* when you're out there pretending to be my lover?"

Self-conscious and silently berating herself, Virginia tucked the skirt of her dress under her thighs, her hands burrowing under her knees. "I didn't mean to insult you."

"I'm not insulted."

She racked her brain for what to say. "I don't know what came over me."

He leaned forward with such control that even a glare might have been more welcome by her. "You call me Marcos most of the time. You call me Marcos when you want my favors. Why now, today, do you call me Mr. Allende?"

She looked away, feeling as if her heart were being wrung. He spoke so quietly, almost pleadingly, that he could be saying something else to her—something that did not smack her with misery.

Because I've never been alone with you for so long, she thought.

She hauled in a ragged breath and remained silent.

The plane tilted slightly, eventually coming in for a landing as smoothly as it had flown. Its speed began to ease. If only her hammering heart would follow.

They taxied down a lane decorated with large open plane hangars, and she fixed her attention on the screen behind him, resolved to smooth out the awkwardness. "Do you believe Allende will be a safe investment for Fintech?" she asked. She knew it was all that remained of his past. His mother had passed away long before his father had.

"It's poorly managed." He extracted his BlackBerry from his trouser pocket and powered it on. "Transport vehicles have been seized by the cartels. Travel is less safe these days in this country. For it to become successful, strict security measures will need to be put in place, new routes, new personnel, and this will mean money. So, no. It isn't a safe investment."

She smiled in admiration as he swiftly skimmed through his text messages. He oozed strength. Strength of mind, of body, of purpose. "You'll make it gold again," she said meaningfully, still not believing that, God, she'd called him *strange* to his face!

He lifted his head. "I'm tearing it apart, Virginia."

The plane lurched to a stop. The engines shut down. The aisle lit up with a string of floor lights.

Virginia was paralyzed in her seat, stunned. "You plan to destroy your father's business," she said in utter horror, a sudden understanding of his morose mood barreling into her.

His hard, aquiline face unreadable, he thrust his phone into his pocket and silently contemplated her. "It's not *his* anymore." His face was impassive, but his eyes probed into her. "It was meant to be mine when he passed away. I built it with him."

This morning, between phone calls, coffee, copies and errands, she'd gotten acquainted with Monterrey from afar. Learned it was a valley surrounded by mountains. Industrial, cosmopolitan, home of the wealthy and, at the very outskirts of the city, home of the poor. Indisputably the most prominent part of northern Mexico. Conveniently situated for Allende Transport, of course, as a means to import, export and travel—but also conveniently situated for those who imported and exported illegal substances. Like the cartels.

Allende wasn't a bouquet of roses, she supposed, but she'd never expected Marcos willingly to attempt to destroy it.

"You look as if I'd confessed to something worse," he noted, not too pleased himself.

"No. It's only that—" She checked herself before continuing this time. "That's not like you. To give up on something. You've never given up on Santos no matter what he does."

His intense expression lightened considerably. "My brother is a person—Allende is not."

Mightily aware of how out of character this decision was, Virginia ached to remind him he'd dedicated his life to helping companies in crisis, had taken under his wing businesses and even people no one else had faith in but Marcos, but instead she rose to her feet. Unfolding like a long, sleek feline just awakened to the hunt, Marcos followed her up. And up.

"Virginia, this isn't Chicago." He loomed over her by at least a head. His face was impassive, but his eyes probed into her. "If you want to sightsee, you'll be accompanied by me. Too dangerous to be alone here."

Dangerous.

The word caused gooseflesh on her skin.

Remembering her research on the city, she peered out a window as two uniformed *aduanales* and twice as many armed *militares* marched up to the plane. She'd heard military men customarily accompanied the Mexican customs agents but she was still floored by the intimidating sight. The copilot unlatched the door up front and descended to meet them.

She couldn't see much of the city at this late hour, but what she'd read online had mesmerized her. She would have even thought the setting romantic if his careful warning weren't dawning on her. "Dangerous," she said. "What must it be like for the people who live here?"

"Difficult." He rammed his book into a leather briefcase and zipped it shut. "Kidnapping rate has risen alarmingly during the last couple of years. Mothers are lifted outside the supermarkets, kids out of their schools, members of both government and police are bribed to play blind man to what goes on."

A rope of fear stretched taut around her stomach. "That's so sad."

She took one last look out the plane window. Nothing moved but the Mexican flag flapping by the customs building.

"It looks so calm," she protested.

"Under the surface nothing is calm." As he stood there, over six feet of virile overpowering man, he looked just a tad tired, and human, and so much sexier than behind his massive desk. He looked touchable. *Touchable.*

Under the surface nothing is calm. Not even me.

"Mrs. Fuller said you grew up here," she remarked as she eyed the fruit assortment on a table near the front of the plane.

"From when I was eight to eighteen," he answered. He stared, mildly puzzled, as she grabbed two green apples and slipped them into her purse.

"In case we get hungry," she explained sheepishly.

His eyes glittered with humor. "If you get hungry, you tell me and I'll make certain you're fed."

"What made you leave the city?" Leave a place that was beautiful and deadly. A place that gave out the message: Don't trust. You're not safe. And the one that had built a man like Marcos Allende, with an impenetrable core.

He braced one arm on the top wood compartment, waiting for the pilots to give them leave to descend. "Nothing here for me. Nothing in España either."

She loved the way he pronounced that. España. The way his arm stretched upward, long and sinewy, rippling under his black shirt before he let it drop. Somber, he gazed into her eyes, and the concern she saw in his gave her flutters. "Are you tired?"

"I'm fine." *You're here,* she thought.

The look that came to his eyes. The way he appraised her.

Virginia could've sworn there could be no flaw in her entire body. Nothing in this world more perfect to those dark, melted-chocolate eyes than she was.

His eyes fell to her lips and lingered there for an electric moment.

"Virginia." He closed the space between them. One step. All the difference between breathing or not. All the difference between being in control of your senses and being thrust into a twister.

He leaned over as he pried her purse from her cramped hands. His fingers brushed the backs of hers and a sizzle shot up her arm.

"Why are you nervous?" The low, husky whisper in her ear made her stomach tumble. She felt seared by his nearness, branded, as though he were purposely making her aware that his limits extended to breaching hers. She felt utterly... claimed. "You've fidgeted all day."

So he had been aware of her?

Like...a predator. Watching from afar. Planning, plotting, savoring the prey.

Why was this exciting?

His breath misted across the tender skin behind her ear. "Because of me?"

Her muscles gelled. *Because I want you.*

She took a shaky step back, singed to the marrow of her bones but smiling as though she was not. "I always get a charge after being rescued."

"Ahh." He drew out the sound, infusing it with a wealth of meaning. "So do I. After...rescuing." He swung his arm back so her purse dangled from one hooked finger behind his shoulder.

When the pilot announced they were clear, he signaled with an outstretched arm toward the plane steps. "Ladies first."

She warily stepped around his broad, muscled figure. "I admit I'm not used to your silences still."

His gaze never strayed from hers as she went around. "So talk next time," he said. "To me."

Right. Next time. Like he inspired one to make intimate revelations. And like he'd have another company to take over with the help of a "lover."

As both pilots conversed with the customs officials, Virginia stopped a few feet from the gaping doorway. Warmth from outside stole into the air-conditioned cabin, warming her cool skin. But she found she couldn't descend just yet.

She'd do anything to get her father out of his mess, yet suddenly felt woefully unprepared to play anyone's lover. Especially Marcos's lover. No matter how much she ached for the part and planned to get it right.

She pivoted on her heels to find him standing shockingly close. She craned her neck to meet his gaze. "Marcos, I'm going to need you to...tell me. What to do."

He wore an odd expression on his face, part confusion and part amusement. The smile he slowly delivered made her flesh pebble. "You may step out of the plane, Miss Hollis."

Laughing, she gave an emphatic shake of her head. "I mean, regarding my role. I will need to know what you suggest that I do. I'm determined, of course, but I'm hoping to get some pointers. From you."

His lids dropped halfway across his eyes. He lifted a loose fist and brushed his knuckles gently down her cheek. The touch reached into the depths of her soul. "Pretend you want me."

A tremor rushed down her limbs. Oh, God, he was so sexy. She was torn between latching on to his tempting, unyielding lips and running for her life. "I will, of course I will," she breathed.

A cloak of stillness came over her—so that all that moved, all she was aware of, was his hand. As he trailed his thumb down to graze her shoulder and in a ghost of a touch swept a strand of hair back, he swallowed audibly. "Look at me like you always do."

"How?"

"You know how." There was so much need in his eyes, a thirst she didn't know how to appease, which called to a growing, throbbing, aching void inside of her. "Like you care for me, like you need me."

"I do." She shook her cluttered head, straightening her thoughts. "I mean, I am. I *will*."

She shut her eyes tight, fearing he would see the truth in them. Fearing Marcos would realize she'd been secretly enamored of him all along. Since the very first morning she'd stepped into his office, she had wanted to die—the man was so out of this world. So male. So dark.

And now…what humiliation for him to discover that, if he crooked his finger at her, Virginia would go to him.

He chuckled softly—the sound throaty, arrogant, male. "Good."

His large hand gripped her waist and urged her around to face the open plane door a few feet away. She went rigid at the shocking contact. Longing flourished. Longing for more, for that hand, but on her skin and not her clothes, sliding up or down, God, doing anything.

Dare she dream? Dare she let herself long just a little,

without feeling the remorse she always did? Like she could indulge in a healthy fantasy now and then?

She wiggled free, sure of one thing: dissolving into a puddle of want was not what she should be doing just now.

"But…what do you want me to do, exactly?" she insisted, carefully backing up one step as she faced him. His eyebrows met in a scowl. He didn't seem to like her retreating. "This is important to you, right?" she continued.

"Señor Allende, pueden bajar por favor?"

Spurred to action by the voices on the platform, Virginia descended the steps. Marcos quickly took his place beside her.

They followed two uniformed officials toward a rustic, one-story building rivaled in size by Marcos's jet. A small control tower, which looked abandoned at this hour, stood discreetly to the building's right. A gust of hot, dry wind picked up around them, bouncing on the concrete and lifting the tips of her hair.

Virginia grabbed the whirling mass with one hand and pinned it with one fist at her nape. Marcos held the glass doors open for her. "No need to pretend just now, Miss Hollis," he said. "We can do that later."

His eyes glimmered dangerously with something. Something frightening. A promise. A request.

Her heart flew like the wind inside her, bouncing between her ribs, almost lifting the tips of her feet from the ground. Warily she passed through the bridge of his arm, one word's haunting echo resounding in her mind. And for the dread that began to take hold, it might have been a death sentence.

Later.

Fifteen minutes later, after a brisk *"Bienvenidos a Mexico"* from the *aduanales*, they were settled in the back of a silver Mercedes Benz, their luggage safely tucked in the trunk.

"A Garza Garcia, si?" the uniformed driver asked as he eased behind the wheel.

"Por favor," Marcos said.

His palm tingled. The one he'd touched her with. The one that had reached out to cup the lovely curve of her waist and caused Virginia to back away. From his touch.

Frowning, he checked his watch—it was ten past midnight. Wanting had *never* been like this. You wanted a watch, or a house, or money, but wanting this particular woman was no such whim. It was a need, something pent-up for too long, something so valued you were hesitant to have, or break, or tarnish, or hurt.

The car swerved onto the deserted highway and Virginia tipped her face to the window, lightly tugging at the pearls around her neck.

"You had a decent trip, Señor Allende?" their driver asked.

"Yes," he said, stretching out his legs as far as he could without bumping his knee into the front seat.

Miles away, the distant core of the city of Monterrey glowed with lights. The sky was clear and veiled with gray, its shadow broken by a steady stream of streetlights rolling by.

"It's lovely here." Virginia transferred her purse to the nook at her feet then tapped a finger to the window. "Look at the mountains."

Her skin appeared luminous upon every brisk caress of the streetlights, and in the shadows her eyes glittered uncommonly bright. They sparkled with excitement.

He felt a tug at his chest. "I'll show you around tomorrow in daylight," he said curtly.

Her eyes slid over to his, grateful, alive eyes. "Thank you."

A heroic feeling feathered up his chest, and he pushed it aside.

During a lengthy quiet spell, the driver flicked on the radio and soft music filled the interior of the car. Virginia remained way over on the other end of the seat.

Not near enough…

He studied her figure, becoming fixated on the rounded breasts swelling under her clingy dress, the curve of her thigh and hip and small waist. Swirly black bits of hair tickled her shoulders. Her long, shapely legs had a satin shine to them, inviting him to wrap them around his body and spill days and weeks and months of wanting inside her.

He whispered, in a low murmur that excluded the driver, "Are you afraid of me?"

She stiffened. Pale, jade-green eyes rose to his for a second before her lashes dropped. "No. Why would you ask?"

Her shyness brought out the hunter in him, and it took effort on his part to keep under control. Go slowly with her… His heart began to pound. He patted his side. "You could come a little closer."

Ducking her head to hide a blush, she smoothed her hands along the front of her dress. Then she flicked a tiny knot of fabric from it. "Just haven't traveled in ages."

"You cringe at anyone's touch, or merely mine?"

She blinked. "Cringe? I'd never cringe if you…touched me."

The words *touched me* hovered between them like a dark, unleashed secret, an invitation to sin, and when Marcos at last responded to that, the thick lust in his voice was unmistakable. "You moved away when I urged you out of the plane. And when I helped you into the car."

"I was surprised." Her throat worked as she swallowed. Her eyes held his in the darkness. "I told you to tell me what to do."

She was whispering, so he whispered back.

"And I asked you to come closer just now."

A tense moment passed.

In silence, Marcos once again patted his side, this time more meaningfully.

After a moment's debate, Virginia seemed to quickly make up her mind. Thrusting out her chin at a haughty angle, she began to edge toward him. "If you're thinking I'm not good at this, I'll have you know I can pretend just fine."

Her scent stormed into his lungs. His nostrils twitched. His heart kicked. His temperature spiked.

Cautiously, as though petting a lion, she turned his hand over and set her cool, small palm on his. She gingerly laced her fingers through his. Lust kicked him in the groin at the unexpected touch. His head fell onto the back of the seat, a groan welling up in the back of his throat. Crucified by arousal, he dragged in a terse, uneven breath, squeezing his eyes shut.

She inched a little closer, tightening her grip. Her lips came to within a breath of his ear. "Does that satisfy you, Your Highness?"

He didn't let it show, the emotion that swept through him, but it made his limbs tremble. He said, thickly, "Come closer."

He wanted to jump her. He wanted all of her, right here, right now.

He inhaled deeply, his chest near bursting with the aroma of her. Clean, womanly, sweet. "Closer," he said, hearing the growl in his own words.

When she didn't, he glanced down at their joined hands. Hers was tiny and fair, nearly engulfed by his larger one. He ran the pad of his thumb along the back of hers, up the ridge of her knuckle, down the tiny smooth slope. She felt so good. And he felt eighteen again. "Soft," came his trancelike murmur.

Transfixed, she watched the movement of his thumb, her breasts stretching the material covering them as she inhaled. He dipped his head and discreetly rubbed his nose across the shiny, springy curls of her hair. Christ. Edible. All of her. He could smell her shampoo, wanted to plunge all ten fingers into her hair, turn her face up and kiss her lips. Softly, so he could savor her breath, go searching deep into her mouth.

Ducking his head so the driver wouldn't hear him, he whispered, "You might try to appear to enjoy my touch."

Their bodies created a heat, a dark intimate cocoon in the confined car interior, enhanced by the warmth of their whispers. "Marcos…"

His hand turned, capturing hers as she attempted to retrieve it. "Virginia."

Their gazes held. Like they did across his office, over the tops of people's heads, in the elevators. Those clear, infinite eyes always sought out his. To find him looking right back. Their fingers brushed at the pass of a coffee mug, a file, the phone. At contact their bodies seemed to flare up like matches—tense, coil, heat up the room. Even with a wall separating them, his awareness of her had escalated to alarming levels. And she'd been more fidgety with him than she had in months.

"We're pretending, remember?" he said, a husky reminder.

Pretend. The only way Marcos could think of that wouldn't involve her feelings, or his. The only way they might be able to—hell, what was this? It had been going on so long it felt like surrender—without anyone hurting in the end. Without their lives changing, breaking or veering off in separate ways because of it.

"Yes, I know."

"Then relax for me." Lightly securing her fingers between his, he delved his thumb into the center of her palm with a deep, intense stroke, aware of her audible intake of breath as he caressed. "Very good," he cooed. "I'm convinced you want me."

"Yes." Her voice was but a whisper, hinting at how the

sinuous, stroking circles of his thumb affected her. "I mean… I'm trying to…appear that I do."

But she seemed as uncertain and startled as a mouse who didn't know where to run to, and Marcos was very much taking to the cat's role. He wanted to play, to corner, to taste.

He glanced up. "Don't tax yourself too much, hmm."

Her warm, fragile fingers trembled in his. The excitement of a new country had left her eyes, replaced by a wild, stormy yearning. "I'm trying not to…get bored."

His thumb went deep at the center then eased back. "Hmm. Yes. I can see you're fighting a yawn." His eyes ventured up along the top of her head, taking in its gloss. "You have pretty hair. Can I touch it?"

He did. It felt soft and silky under his fingers, tempting him to dig in deeper, down to her scalp.

She made a sound in her throat, like a moan. A hunger of the worst, most painful kind clawed inside him. She had a way of staring at him with those big eyes like he was something out of this world. It was a miracle he'd resisted her this long.

"A man," he gruffly began, massaging the back of her head as he greedily surveyed her features, "would be lucky to make you his."

Her eyes sealed shut so tightly she seemed to be in pain. She squirmed a little on the seat and, unbelievably, came nearer. "You don't have to convince me. I'm already pretending."

Her breasts brushed his rib cage, and the heat of her supple body singed his flesh through their clothes. He intensified the strokes of his fingers. "A man would be lucky to make you his, Virginia," he repeated.

Her lashes fluttered upward, revealing her eyes. Pale green, ethereal. Distrustful. "What are you doing?"

His gut tightened. *What does it look like I'm doing?* He

wanted to yank her onto his lap, feel his way up her little skirt, and kiss her mouth until her lips turned bright red. Her face blurred with his vision. With his need. He had to force himself to leave her hair alone.

She exhaled a string of broken air, then relaxed somewhat, shifting sideways on the leather seat. Facing him. Her smile faded. "Who are we fooling, Marcos, with this charade?"

"Marissa Galvez, Allende Transport's owner."

And maybe you. Definitely me.

He retrieved her hand from where it had gone to wring the hem of her dress and secured her wrist in his grip as he raised it. He turned it over and set a soft, lingering kiss at the center of her palm. A tiny, breathless gasp came from her.

"We must practice," he murmured, gazing into those deep, bottomless eyes.

"Oh." She shivered. Not moving away, and not moving closer, she allowed him to drag his lips along her open palm. She watched him through her lashes, her lips shuddering on each uneven breath.

"And why must we fool her?" Her question was a silky wisp.

"Because she wants me," he huskily answered. She tasted divine. Her skin was smooth and satiny under his lips, and he predicted every inch of her body would feel just like it. Perfect. "It wouldn't do to insult her." Against his mouth and lips, he felt the vibrant tremor that danced up her arm. Emboldened by her response, thirsting for more, he opened his mouth and gently grazed his teeth at the heel of her palm. "I happen to want someone else."

"I'm sure—" she began, swallowing audibly. "I'm sure you can have anyone you want."

"If I want her bad enough and put myself to task, yes." His lips closed and opened against her hand. Before he could restrain himself, he gave a lick at her palm. Pleasure pummeled through him. "And I've grown to want her…bad," he strained out, swallowing back a growl.

"Oh, that was…" Her hand wiggled as she tried prying it free. "I don't think…"

"Shh."

He held her wrist in a gentle grip and raised his head. He watched her expression soften, melt, as he whisked the pad of his thumb across her dampened palm, getting it wet. He lifted the glistening pad of his thumb to her lips, his timbre coated with arousal. "Pretend you like it when I do this."

A sound welled in the back of her throat as he stroked. She nodded wildly, her lips gleaming at each pass of his thumb. "Yes, yes, I'm pretending," she breathed.

He'd never seen a more erotic sight, felt a more erotic sensation, than playing with Virginia Hollis's quivering pink lips in the back of a moving car. "Umm. Me, too. I will pretend…you're her."

"Aha."

"And I very much want her." God, he enjoyed her unease, enjoyed seeing her pupils dilate, her breath shallow out.

"O-okay."

His thumb continued glancing, whisking, rubbing, right where his mouth wanted to be. He bent to whisper, to conspire together, just him and her. "Let's pretend…we're lovers, Virginia." His voice broke with the force of his desire, came out rough with wanting. "Pretend every night we touch each other…and kiss…and our bodies rock together. And when we find release—"

"Stop!" She pushed herself back with surprising force, sucking great gulps of air. "God, stop. Enough. Enough pretending tonight."

He tugged her closer. They were breathing hard and loud.

"You should kiss me," he said gruffly.

"Kiss you." She absently fingered his cross where it

peeked through the top opening of his shirt. He went utterly still—the gesture too sweet, too unexpected, too painful.

Her fingers reached his throat, then traced the links of the thick chain.

Too aware of this now, he dropped her hair and squeezed her elbow meaningfully. "Virginia. Your mouth. On mine."

They'd had foreplay for a year—with every glance, every flick of her hair, every smile.

She drew back and laughed, a choked, strained sound. "Now?" She couldn't seem to believe her eyes and ears, seemed stumped for words to deny him.

The car halted at a stoplight. A few cars drove up beside them. Marcos went still, glancing at her quietly until their car continued.

He had never wanted to feel a body as much as he wanted to feel hers.

And her mouth—he'd give anything to taste that mouth, was being for the first time in his life reckless, selfish, for that very mouth. A mouth that promised all the innocence he'd never had, trust, beauty, affection he'd never had.

Without any further thought, he pulled her close. "One kiss. Right now."

"But you're my boss," she breathed, clutching his shirt collar with a death grip. But her bright, luminous green eyes gazed up at him. And those eyes said yes.

Her lips were plush, parted, eager for his. He brought his thumb back to scrape them. "Just pretend I'm not him."

"But you *are* him—"

"I don't want to be him, I want to be…just Marcos." Their relationship had been wrapped in rules, limited by their roles. What if Virginia had been just a woman? And he just a man? She would have been his, might still be his. "Only Marcos."

The passing city lights caused slanted shadows to shift across her face—she looked splendid, wary, wanting.

"A kiss is harmless, Virginia." His vision blurred with desire as he stretched his arm out on the seat behind her and dipped his head. Their breaths mingled, their mouths opened. "People kiss their pets. They kiss their enemies on the cheeks. They kiss a letter. They even blow kisses into the air. You can kiss me."

"This is a little unexpected."

"God, I'd hate to be predictable." His arm slid from the back of the seat and went around her shoulders, loosely holding her to him. His fingers played with the soft, bouncy curls at her nape. His accent got unbearably thick—like his blood, a terse string of lust flooding his veins. It took concentration to give her a smile meant to disarm. "Stop thinking about it and kiss me."

Her curls bounced at the shake of her head. "We don't have to kiss to pretend to be...together. I can pretend convincingly without kissing."

No kissing? Christ, no. He had a fascination with her mouth, the delicate bow at her upper lip, the ripe flesh of the bottom one. He'd been kissing that mouth for days, weeks, months, in his mind.

"You're wrong, *amor*." He bussed her temple with his lips, aware of his muscles flexing heatedly under his clothes, his skin feverish with pent-up desire as she continued clinging to his shirt. "We must kiss. And we must kiss convincingly."

"I— You didn't mention this before."

He caressed her cheekbone with the back of one finger and noted the frantic pulse fluttering at the base of her throat. Christ, once again she was fixated with his mouth, and he wanted to give it to her. Now. Right now. Slam it over hers, push into her, taste all of her. "Kiss me, Virginia. Kiss me senseless." He barely held himself in check with his ruthless self-discipline.

She hesitated. Then, in a burdened breath, "Only a kiss."

His heart rammed into his ribs at the realization that she had agreed. To kiss him. *Ay, Dios.*

He urged himself to ease back on the seat and stifled the impulse to take matters into his own hands. He was a second away from losing his mind. A second away from tearing off her clothes, the necklace at her throat, his shirt, everything that separated them. Still, he wanted to be sure, sure she wanted this. Him. Them.

He groaned and said, "Kiss me until we can't breathe."

"I... The driver could see us." She sounded as excited as he, and the breathless anticipation in her voice plunged him even deeper into wild, mad desire.

"Look at me, not him."

"You're all I'm looking at, Marcos."

He didn't know who breathed harder, who was seducing whom here. She laid her hands over his abdomen. He hissed. The muscles under her palms clenched. His erection strained painfully.

Her hands slid up his chest, a barely there touch. *Fever.* She cradled his jaw with two cool, dry palms...and waited. Hesitant, inexperienced. In a ragged plea, she croaked, "Close your eyes."

He did. Not because she asked, but because her fingers lovingly stroked his temple, down his jaw. Her hands drifted lower and curled around his shoulders, rubbing along the muscles so sensually he gritted his teeth. This was murder.

She had to stop. She had to go on.

"Do it. Do it now." The helpless urgency in his voice startled him as much as the other emotions coursing through him. Arousal ripped through him like a living beast.

Then he felt the warm mist of her breath on his face, sensed the nearness of her parting lips, heard through the roaring in his ears her tremulous whisper. "I'm a bit out of practice—"

He didn't let her finish. He reached out and slipped a hand beneath the fall of hair at her nape and hauled her to him. "Virginia," he rasped, and slammed her mouth with his.

Four

Virginia had meant for a quick kiss. Only a taste. A taste to satisfy her curiosity. Her need. A taste because she could not, could never, deny this man. But when he pulled her down and his mouth, so strong and fierce and hungry, touched hers, there was no stopping what came over her.

They'd been panting, laughing; he'd been teasing her, had pulled her onto his lap. Pretending had been so easy, but now...now this mouth, this man, the hands gripping the back of her head, were too real. Rough. Raw. Devastating.

She moaned helplessly as he slanted his head, murmuring something indiscernible to her, and his warm, hot tongue came at hers, and his hard need grew larger and stronger under her bottom, and the realization that he really *wanted her* barraged through her.

He began to take little nips, and those lush, sure lips moving against hers set off the flutters in her stomach, the fireworks in her head. *"Sabes a miel."*

He spoke in an aroused rasp against her lips. She clung to

his neck and tried not to moan as his warm breath slid across her skin, heating her like a fever.

"Te quiero hacer el amor," he murmured, running his hands down the sides of her body, his fingers brushing the curves of her breasts, his chest heaving with exerted restraint. *"Toda la noche, te quiero hacer el amor."*

She had no idea what he said, but the words pulsed through her in a wave of erotic pleasure. Her breasts swelled heavy, her nipples in such pain she pressed them deeper into his chest and she opened her mouth wide, moving instinctively against him, and she knew this was wrong, so wrong, would not happen again, which surely must be why she incited it. "What are you saying to me..." she murmured into him.

His breath was hot and rapid against her. "I'm saying I want to make love to you. All evening, all night." He groaned and twisted his tongue around hers as their lips locked, the attachment intense, driven, absolute.

She sucked in a breath as his palms engulfed her straining nipples, felt his desire in every coiled muscle, in the rough way his palms kneaded, the thrusts of his tongue as his mouth turned ravenous on hers.

He groaned, appearing decidedly out of control for the first time since she'd known him. He stroked the undersides of her breasts with his thumbs and whisked his lips along the curve of her jaw, and she cocked her ear to his nibbling lips, shuddered when he murmured to her. "Your gasps tear me to pieces."

"Marcos..."

She was hot and burning inside.

He made a grinding motion with his hips, and her thighs splayed open as he desperately rubbed his erection against her.

His tongue plunged into her ear, wet, hot, sloppy. "Stop me, Virginia." One determined hand unerringly slipped through the V of her dress and enveloped her breast. "Virginia. Stop me, Virginia."

He squeezed her flesh possessively, and when his palm rubbed into her nipple, her eyes flew open in shock. The feel was so delicious, so wrong, so *right,* she hid her heated face against his neck and almost choked on the sounds welling at the back of her throat. Sensations overpowered her body, her mind struggling to comprehend that this was really happening with Marcos Allende.

"That's your hotel up ahead, sir."

Swearing under his breath, Marcos gathered her closer. His ragged breaths blasted her temple. He squeezed her. "We'll finish this upstairs."

Virginia pushed back her rumpled hair. Upstairs? God, what were they even doing?

Chuckling at the look on her face, Marcos bussed her forehead with his lips as his gentle hand stroked down her nape, trembling slightly. "I should've known we'd be combustible," he murmured.

The Mercedes pulled into a wide, palm tree–lined hotel driveway and Virginia fumbled for her purse while Marcos stepped out and strolled to her side, reaching into the car and helping her to her feet.

His glimmering, dark gaze didn't stray from her face, not for a second. *We kissed,* his dark eyes said. *I touched you. I know you want me.*

And for an insane second, all she wanted was to forget why she was here and who she was and be swept away by this one man, this one night, in this one city.

As though discerning her thoughts, Marcos cupped half of her face in his warm palm, and his eyes held something so wild and bright it almost blinded her. "Upstairs," he said again.

The promise plunged into her like a knife as he moved away to discuss something with the chauffeur, and Virginia stood there like someone in a hypnotized state, watching his big, tanned hands at his sides. Hands she'd felt on her.

She gritted her teeth, fighting the lingering arousal tickling through her. He was playing with her. He was *pretending*. He was a man who'd do anything to win—and he wanted Allende.

Marcos seemed oblivious to her frustration when he returned, slowly reaching behind her, his fingers splaying over the small of her back as he led her up the steps.

She followed him and no, she wasn't imagining him naked, touching her, kissing her in the exact way he'd just done—no, no, no. She studied the beautiful hotel and the potted palms leading to the glass doors with the intensity of a scientist with his microscope.

The lobby and its domed ceiling made her lightheaded. It was so…so… God, the way he'd touched her. With those hands. As if that breast were his to touch and his hand belonged there. How could he pretend so well? He'd been so hard he could've broken cement with his…his…

"Do you like it, Virginia?" he asked, smiling, and signaled around.

She gazed at the elegant but rustic decor. "The hotel? It's beautiful."

His eyes twinkled, but underneath it all, he wore the starved look of a man who'd hungered for a very long time and intended to feast soon. He looked like a man who could do things to her she didn't even imagine in fantasies, like a man who would not want to be denied.

And he would be. He had to be.

"It's very…charming," she continued, anything to steer her mind away from his lips, his mouth, his gaze.

They wound deeper into the marbled hotel lobby. A colorful flower arrangement boasting the most enormous sunflowers she'd ever seen sat on a massive round table near the reception area.

Virginia could still not account, could not even fathom, that she'd just kissed him. Her!—woefully inexperienced, with her last boyfriend dating back to college—kissing Marcos Allende. But he'd been cuddling her, whispering words so naughty she could hardly stand the wanton warmth they elicited. No matter how much resistance she'd tried to put up, he was the sexiest thing on the continent, playing some sort of grown-up game she had yet to put a name to, and Virginia had been close to a meltdown.

It had all been pretend, anyway. Right?

Right.

Trying to compose herself, she admired his broad back as he strolled away, the shoulders straining under his black shirt as he reached the reception desk and leaned over with confidence, acting for the world as if he were the majority stockholder of the hotel. The two women shuffling behind the granite top treated him as if they agreed.

Virginia quietly drew up to his side, her lips feeling raw and sensitive. She licked them once, twice.

A lock of ebony hair fell over Marcos's forehead as he signed the slip and slid it over the counter. "I requested a two-bedroom suite—it would appease me to know you're safe. Will this be a problem?" Facing her, he plunged his Montblanc pen into his shirt pocket, watching her through calm, assessing eyes.

She saw protectiveness there, concern, and though her nerves protested by twisting, she said, "Not at all." Damn. What hell to keep pretending for a week.

"Good."

In the elevator, as they rode up to the ninth floor—the top floor of the low, sprawling building—his body big and commanding in the constricted space, the silence whispered, *we kissed.*

In her mind, her heart, the choir of her reason, everything said, *kiss kiss kiss.*

Not good, any of it. Not the blender her emotions were in, not her tilting world, not the fact that she was already thinking, anticipating, wondering, what it would feel like to kiss again.

Freely. Wildly. Without restraint.

She would have to stall. Abstain. Ignore him. God. If she did something to compromise her job, she would never forgive herself. And nothing compromised a job like sex did. And if she compromised her heart? She stiffened, firmly putting a lid on the thought.

Mom had loved Dad with all her heart—through his flaws, through his odd humors, through his drunken nights, through all the good and bad of which there was more of the latter, her mother had loved with such steadfast, blinded devotion Virginia had secretly felt...pity.

Because her mother had wept more tears for a man than a human should be allowed to weep. Appalling, that one man could have such power over a woman, could take her heart and her future and trample them without thought or conscience.

Even on her deathbed, sweet, beautiful, dedicated Mother had clutched Virginia's hand, and it seemed she'd been hanging on to her life only to continue trying to save her husband. "Take care of Dad, Virginia, he needs someone to look out for him. Promise me, baby? Promise me you will?"

Virginia had promised, determinedly telling herself that if she ever, ever gave away her heart, it would be to someone who would be reliable, and who loved her more than his cards, his games and himself.

No matter her physical, shockingly visceral responses to Marcos, he was still everything she should be wary of. Worldly, sophisticated, ruthless, a man enamored of a challenge, of risks and of his job. The last thing she pictured

Marcos Allende being was a family man, no matter how generous he'd proven to be as a boss.

Down the hall, the bellhop emerged from the service elevator, but Marcos was already trying his key, allowing her inside. He flicked on the light switch and the suite glowed in welcome. Golden-tapestried walls, plush taupe-colored carpet, a large sitting area opening up to a room on each side. *"Gracias,"* he said, tipping the bellhop at the door and personally hauling both suitcases inside.

Virginia surveyed the mouthwatering array of food atop the coffee table: trays of chocolate-dipped strawberries, sliced fruit, imported cheeses.

A newspaper sat next to the silver trays and the word *muerte* popped out in the headline. A color picture of a tower of mutilated people stared back at her.

Marcos deadbolted the door. The sound almost made her wince. And she realized how alone they were. Just him. And her.

And their plan.

Suddenly and with all her might, Virginia wished to know what he was thinking. Did he think they'd kiss again? What if he wanted more than a kiss? What if he didn't?

Feeling her skin pebble, she shied away from his gaze, navigated around a set of chairs and pulled the sheer drapes aside. The city flickered with lights. Outside her window the hotel pool was eerily still, the mountains were still, the moon still. She noted the slow, rough curves and the sharper turns at the peaks, lifted her hand to trace them on the glass. "Do you come here frequently?" she asked quietly—her insides were not still.

"No." She heard the sunken fall of his footsteps on the carpet as he approached—she felt, rather than saw, him draw up behind her. "There wasn't reason to."

He could be uttering something else for the way he spoke so intimately. Inside, a rope of wanting stretched taut around her stomach and she thought she would faint. The proximity of his broad, unyielding hardness sent a flood of warmth across her body, and the muscles of her tummy clenched with yearning. His body wasn't touching hers; there was just the threat of the touch, the presence that created a wanting of it.

In the darkness of her bedroom, very late at night, she'd wondered if Marcos was as ruthless when he loved as when he did business. And if his kiss…was as dark and devastating as his eyes had promised it would be.

It was. Oh, God, it was.

The air seemed to scream at her to turn to him and *kiss*.

The close contours of his chest against her back, the scent of him, were an assault to her senses. He laid his hand on her shoulder, and the touch was fire on his fingertips. "This is a safe neighborhood—I won't lose sight of you, Virginia."

But outside the danger didn't lurk. It was in her. It was him. She locked her muscles in place, afraid of leaning, moving, afraid of the magnetic force of him, how it felt impossible not to turn, touch. "What was it like for you when you were young," she said, softly.

His hand stroked. Fire streaked across her skin as he drew lazy figures along the back of her arm. "It wasn't as dangerous back then. I grew up in the streets—I kept running away with my father's workers, looking for adventure."

Did he move? She thought he'd grown bigger, harder, nearer. She sensed his arousal, the thundering in his chest almost touching her back. Or was it her heart she heard?

He lowered his lips and briefly, only a whisper, set his mouth on her neck. A sharp shudder rushed through her. "Now even bodyguards aren't safe to hire," he whispered on her skin. "Wealthy people have armored cars and weapons instead."

She closed her eyes, the sensations pouring through her.

"No-man's-land?" Just a croak. A peep from a little bird who couldn't fly, would willingly be lured in by the feline.

He made a pained sound and stilled his movements on her. "Were you pretending just now when you kissed me?"

Oh. My. God. They were actually discussing it.

Her nod was jerky.

Marcos hesitated, then huskily murmured, "Do you want to…?"

She sank her teeth into her lower lip to keep from saying something stupid, like yes. "To what?"

His whisper tumbled down her ear. "You know what."

"I don't know what you mean." But she did. Oh, dear, she did.

"Kiss…" Thick and terse, his voice brimmed with passion. "Touch…"

Shaking like a leaf in a storm, she wiggled free and walked around him, her insides wrenching. "I told you I could pretend just fine."

Heading for the couch and plopping down, she surveyed the food once more, but her eyes didn't see anything.

Was she supposed to stay strong and resist what her body and heart wanted when she had a chance to have it? Was she supposed to say no and no and no?

Marcos plunged his hand into his hair. "That was *pretense?*"

"Of course." He sounded so shocked and looked so annoyed she might have even laughed. Instead, her voice grew businesslike. "So you left. And your father stayed here? In this city?"

For a moment, he released a cynical laugh, and when he gradually recovered, he roughly scraped the back of his hand across his mouth as if he couldn't stand remembering their kiss. Reluctantly, he nodded. "You're good, Miss Hollis, I'll give you that."

"What made you leave here?" she asked, blinking.

One lone eyebrow rose and this time when he laughed, she knew it was at her attempt at conversation.

"Well." Propping a shoulder against the wall and crossing his arms over his chest in a seemingly relaxed pose, Marcos exuded a raw, primal power that seemed to take command of the entire room. "Allende Transport was taken. By my father's…woman. It was either her or me—and he chose her. But I promised myself when I came back…the transport company would be mine."

His voice. Sometimes she'd hear it, not the words, just the bass, the accent. Marcos was larger than life, large in every single way, and Virginia could pretend all she wanted but the fact was, she'd be stupid to forget her position. And she had to make sure the car incident would never again be repeated.

"Marcos, what happened here and in the car was—"

"Only the beginning."

She started. The beginning of what? The end? She ground her molars, fighting for calm. "We were pretending."

"Aha."

"Yes," she said, vehemently. "We were."

"Right, Miss Hollis. Whatever you say."

"You asked me to pretend, that's what I'm here for. Isn't it?"

His silence was so prolonged she felt deafened. Was she here for another reason? A reason other than what he'd requested of her? An intimate, wicked, naughty reason?

She could tell by the set of his jaw that if he had a hidden agenda, he wouldn't be admitting to it now.

Walking off her conflicting emotions, she fixed her attention on the food. The scents of lemon, warm bread, cheeses and fruit teased her nostrils, but her stomach was too constricted for her to summon any appetite. Usually she'd be wolfing down the strawberries, but now she wiped her hands on her sides and put on her best secretarial face. "At what time should I wake up tomorrow?"

"We have a late lunch, no need to rise with the sun," he said.

She signaled to both ends of the room, needing to get away from him, wishing she could get away from herself. "And my room?"

"Pick the one you like."

She felt his gaze on her, sensed it like a fiery lick across her skin.

She went over and peered into a room: a large, double-post bed, white and blue bedclothes. Very beautiful. She went to the other, feeling his eyes follow. The lamplight cast his face in beautiful mellow light. He looked like an angel that had just escaped from hell, like an angel she wanted to sin with.

"I guess either will do," she admitted.

She smiled briefly at him from the doorway, and although he returned the smile, both smiles seemed empty.

And in that instant Virginia was struck with two things at once: she had never wanted anything so much in her life as she wanted the man standing before her, and if his lips covered hers again, if his hands touched her, if his eyes continued to look at her, she would never own her heart again.

She said, "Good night." And didn't wait to hear his reply.

The room she chose was the one with coral-pink bedding and an upholstered headboard. She didn't question that, for appearances, he would wish him and his "lover" to appear to share a room. But she quietly turned the lock behind her.

As she changed, she thought of what she had read about Marcos and Monterrey. She arranged the clothes in the large closet, each garment on a hanger, and eyed and touched the ones he'd bought her.

She slipped into her cotton nightgown, ignoring the prettier garments made of silk and satin and lace, and climbed into bed. Awareness of his proximity in the adjoining room caused gooseflesh along her arms. A fan hung suspended from the ceiling, twirling. The echo of his words feathered through her, melting her bones. *I'll pretend…you're her.*

She squeezed her eyes shut, her chest constricting. *It's not you, Virginia,* she firmly told herself.

She touched a finger against her sensitive lips and felt a lingering pleasure. And in her heart of hearts, she knew she was. She was her, the woman Marcos wanted. She'd dreamed of him in private, but dreams had been so harmless until they came within reach.

Marcos Allende.

Wanting him was the least safe, most staggering, worrying feeling she'd ever felt.

And one thing she knew for certain was that to her, Marcos Allende was even more dangerous than his beautiful, deadly city of Monterrey.

Sleep eluded him.

The clock read past 1:00 a.m. and Marcos had smashed his pillow into a beat-up ball. He'd kicked off the covers. He'd cursed and then he'd cursed himself some more for thinking one kiss would be enough to rid himself of his obsession of her.

Then there was Allende.

He had to plan, plot, leave no room for error. He had to stoke his hatred of Marissa, to be prepared to crush her once and for all.

But he could not think of anything. Memories of those kisses in the car assailed him. The fierce manner in which his mouth took hers and her greedy responses, the moans she let out when he'd touched her. How his tongue had taken hers, how she'd groaned those tormenting sounds.

He lay awake and glared at the ceiling, his mind counting the steps to her room. Twenty? Maybe fewer. Was she asleep? What did she wear to sleep? Was she remembering, too? Jesus, what a nightmare.

He shouldn't have asked her there.

He'd thought nothing of Allende, nothing of tomorrow, but had kept going over in his mind the ways she'd kissed him and the ways he still wanted to kiss her.

He sat up and critically surveyed the door of his room. He wanted her to give in. Wanted something of hers, a stolen moment, something she hadn't planned to give him, but couldn't help but relinquish. She was cautious by nature. She'd fear ruining everything, all she'd worked so hard for, all she'd tried to achieve. A steady job, security, respect. Could he guarantee this would remain solid when they were through? Could they even continue working together—flaring up like torches like this?

Their kiss had shot him up into outer space; obviously he still couldn't think right. In his drawstring pants, he climbed out of bed and slipped into his shirt.

He meant to review his numbers once again, ascertain that the amount he planned to offer for Allende was low, but fair enough to secure it.

Instead he ignored his files and found himself standing outside his assistant's bedroom door, his hand on the doorknob, his heart beating a crazy jungle-cat rhythm.

He turned the knob, smiling at his certainty of her, her being always so...orderly, having locked it against him.

His heart stopped when he realized Virginia Hollis's door was unlocked. Now all that kept him from Virginia Hollis were his damned scruples.

Five

"Sleep well?"

"Of course. Wonderfully well. And you?"

"Perfectly."

That was the extent of their conversation the next morning over breakfast. Until Marcos began folding his copy of *El Norte*. "A favor from you, Miss Hollis?"

Virginia glanced up from her breakfast to stare into his handsome, clean-shaven face. *A kiss,* she thought with a tightness in her stomach. A touch. God, a second kiss to get rid of that haunting memory of the first.

With her thoughts presenting her the image of him—Marcos Allende—kissing her, she flushed so hard her skin felt on fire. She toyed with her French toast. "Nothing too drastic, I assume?" she said, some of the giddiness she felt creeping into her voice.

"Drastic?" he repeated, setting the morning paper aside.

She shrugged. "Oh, you know...murder. Blackmail. I don't think I could get away with those."

Eyes glinting with amusement, he shook his head, and his smile was gone. His elbows came to rest on the table as he leaned forward. "What kind of boss do you take me for?"

One I want, she thought. *One who kissed me.*

Those broad, rippling muscles under his shirt could belong to a warrior.

God just didn't make men like these anymore.

She'd lied. She hadn't slept one wink.

If she'd been camping out in the dark, naked, within ten feet of a hungry lion, maybe she'd have been able to sleep. But no. She had been within a few feet of her dream man, and her lips had still tingled from his kiss, and her body seemed to scream for all the years she hadn't paid attention to letting someone love it.

After lying on the bed for what felt like hours, for some strange reason she had bolted to her feet and rummaged through the stuff he'd bought…and slipped into something sexy. A sleek white silk gown that hugged her like skin. Heart vaulting in excitement, she'd unlocked the door. Returned to bed. And waited. Eyeing the door.

The knob had begun turning. Her eyes widened, and her pulse went out of orbit. She waited minutes, minutes, for the door to open, and yet the knob returned to place again. Nothing happened. He changed his mind? Her heart sped, and then she flung off the covers and stepped out of bed.

The living room was empty—silver in the moonlight. And then, torn between some unnamable need and the need for self-preservation, she'd quietly gone back to bed.

Now, looking like a well-rested, sexy billionaire, he asked what kind of boss she took him for.

"One who's never bitten me," she blurted, then wished to kick herself for the way that came out sounding. Like an invitation. Like…more. Damn him.

He chuckled instantly, and Virginia pushed to her feet

when she totally lost her appetite. He followed her up, uncurling slowly like he always did.

"I like the dress," he said, studying the fabric as it molded around her curves. It was a very nice dress. Green, to match her eyes, and one from a designer to please His Majesty.

"Thank you, I like it, too."

His gaze raked her so intimately she felt stripped to her skin. There was a silence. Her heart pounded once. Twice. Three times. Virginia couldn't take a fourth.

"Name your favor," she offered.

Eyes locked with hers with unsettling intensity, he wound around the table, and his scent enveloped her—not of cologne and definitely not sweet—but so intoxicating she wanted to inhale until her lungs burst inside her chest.

Gently, he seized her chin between his thumb and forefinger, tipping his face back to hers. An unnamable darkness eclipsed his eyes, and an unprecedented huskiness crept into his voice. "Just say, 'Yes, Marcos.'"

Her breath caught. His voice was so ridiculously sexy in the morning. Virginia pulled free of his touch and laughed. "You," she accused, tingles dancing across her skin. "I don't even know what I'm agreeing to."

His arms went around her, slow as a boa constrictor, securing her like giant manacles. "Can't you guess?"

Something exploded inside her body, and it wasn't fear.

Lust. Desire. Everything she didn't want to feel.

His breath was hot and fragrant on her face, eliciting a little moan she couldn't contain. Oh, God. He felt so hard all over, so unlike any other man she'd known.

His voice was gentle as he tipped her chin up. "Yes to my bed for a week, Virginia. Say yes."

Was he insane? "Wow," she said, almost choking on her shock. "I've never had such a blatant come-on."

The determination on his face was anything but apologetic. "I don't want to play games with you." He studied her forehead, her nose, her jaw. "I intend to please you. I've thought of nothing else. Tell me," he urged, caressing her face as he would a porcelain sculpture. "Are you interested?"

Interested? She was on fire, she was frightened, confused and scared, and she hated thinking, realizing that she was no match for him.

She should've known that if Marcos ever made a move for her, he'd come on like he always did—strong, like a stampeding bull charging to get his way. Her breasts rose and fell against his chest as she labored to breathe. Her legs were so weak they couldn't support her, and she remained standing only by her deathly grip on his arms. "One week?"

"Seven days. Seven nights. Of pleasure beyond your imagining."

"A-and what if I can't give you this pleasure you want?"

"I will take any pleasure you can give me, Virginia. And you will take mine."

There was no mistaking. His deep, sexy voice was the most erotic thing she'd ever heard. "A-and if I say I'm not interested?"

He chuckled softly—the sound throaty, arrogant, male—melting her defenses. "If that is what you wish." His gaze pierced her, as though searching for secrets, fears. "You haven't wondered about us?" He lowered his head and skimmed her lips lightly, enough to tease and make her shiver when he retracted. "You unlocked your door last night, and I was so close to opening it, you have no idea."

"Oh, God," she breathed.

His lips grazed hers from end to end. "You wanted me there, you wanted me in your room, your bed."

"I—I can't do this."

His hands lowered to the small of her back and pressed her to his warm, solid length. "You can. Your body speaks to me. It feels soft against mine, it molds to me. Say it in words."

There was no escaping his powerful stare, no escape from what raged inside her. "I can't, Marcos."

Growling, he jerked free and for a blinding second she thought he was going to charge out of the room, he seemed so frustrated. Instead he carried himself—six feet three inches of testosterone and lust and anger—to the window and leaned on the frame. "The first moment I set eyes on you, you planted yourself in my mind. I'm going insane because once, Virginia, once I was sure you were crazy about me. So crazy. You can't help the way you look at me, *amor*. Perhaps others don't notice, but I do. Why do you fight me?"

Her eyes flicked up to his and she was certain her anxiety reached out to him like something tangible. His muscles went taut. "Do I get an answer?" he demanded.

She smiled, shaking her head in disbelief. "You're proposing we mix business and pleasure."

He wanted her desperately, she realized. Like she'd never been wanted before. And she might enjoy allowing herself to be wanted like this.

So, with a pang of anticipation in her left breast, she said, "I'll think about it over lunch."

The floral arrangement in the lobby had been replaced with one chock-full of red gerberas and bright orange tiger lilies bursting amidst green. They navigated around it, Marcos's hand on her back.

"If you want everyone to know you're nervous, by all means, keep fidgeting."

"Fidgeting? Who's fidgeting?"

He grabbed her trembling hand and linked his fingers through hers, his smile more like a grin. "Now no one. Smile, hmm? Pretend you like me."

Her pulse skyrocketed at the feel of his palm against hers, but she did not reject the touch and held on. *This should be easy. Easy,* she told herself. One look at her and everyone would think she was in love with him.

Impulsively she breathed him in, feeling oddly safe and protected. They'd had a wonderful morning, talking of everything and nothing as he accompanied her to the shopping mall across the street. The morning had flown by in casual conversation, which had been a good thing particularly when the night had seemed endless to her.

Now they entered the restaurant. Past the arched foyer entrance stood the most beautiful woman Virginia had ever seen. Tall and toned, blonde and beautiful. Her lips were red, her nails were red. She was clad in a short leather jacket teamed with a white miniskirt and a pair of heels Virginia was certain only an acrobat could walk on. Her face lit up like a sunbeam when she saw Marcos, and then it eclipsed when she saw Virginia.

She swept to her feet and came to them, her walk as graceful as the swaying of a willow tree. All other female eyes in the restaurant landed on Marcos.

"You're bigger." Her eyes became shielded, wary when they moved to her. "And you're...not alone."

In one clean sweep, Marissa took in the entire length of Virginia's knee-length emerald-green designer dress.

Marcos drew her up closer to him and brought those inscrutable eyes of his down on Virginia, his gaze sharpening possessively. "Virginia Hollis, Marissa Galvez."

He gave Virginia such a male, proprietary look she felt stirrings in all manner of places in her body. Nervous, she offered the woman a nod and a smile. Marissa's hand was slim and ringed everywhere. They shook hands and took their seats.

The awkwardness had a strange beat—slower somehow, and heavy like lead.

Over the sunlit table, Virginia tentatively slid her hand into Marcos's, sensed him smile to himself, then felt him give her a squeeze of gratitude which Marissa might have taken as affection. A silence settled. Every minute was a little more agonizing. Marcos's thumb began to stroke the back of hers, causing pinpricks of awareness to trail up her arm. Sensations of wanting tumbled, one after the other. What would it be like if this were real? Sitting here, with such a man, and knowing the name of the shampoo he showered with and the cologne he wore?

Marissa's blue eyes shone with a tumult of emotions. "Why didn't you come to him? He begged you to."

Virginia's spine stiffened. Whoa. That had been quite a hostile opening line. But then what did she know?

Marcos answered coolly, reclining easily in his upholstered chair. "I did come."

"A day too late."

The corners of his lips kicked up, but the smile was hard somehow, and it didn't reach his eyes. The air was so tense and dense it was scarcely breathable. "Perhaps if he'd really sent for me, I'd have come sooner—but we both know it wasn't him who summoned me."

Surprise flickered across the blonde's face. "Why would he not call his son on his deathbed?"

"Because he's an Allende."

She made a noncommittal sound, rings flashing as she reclined her chin on her right hand. Her eyes dropped to Virginia and Marcos's locked hands over the table, and finally the woman shrugged. "He died with his pride—but I could see him watching the door every day. He wanted to see you. Every time I came in he…" She faltered, pain flashing across her face as she lowered her arm. "He looked away."

Marcos was idly playing with Virginia's fingers. Did he realize? It seemed to distract him. Comfort him, maybe. "He didn't want to see you, Marissa?"

Her eyes became glimmering blue slits. "He wasn't

himself those last days." She smiled tightly. *"No se que le paso, estaba muy raro."*

Even as Marcos replied in that calm, controlled voice, Virginia sensed his will there, incontestable, allowing for nothing. "You ruin your life for a woman—I suppose you're bound to have regrets. And to be acting strange," he added, as though referencing the words she's said in Spanish.

A waiter dressed in black and white took their orders. Virginia ordered what Marcos was having, wishing she could try everything on the menu at least once but embarrassed to show herself as a glutton. When the waiter moved on, Marissa's eyes wandered over her. She tapped one long red fingernail to the corners of her red lips.

"You don't look like Marcos's type at all," she commented matter-of-factly.

Virginia half turned to him for a hint of how to answer, and he lifted her hand to graze her knuckles with his lips, saying in a playful murmur that only she seemed to hear, "Aren't you glad to hear that, *amor?*"

She shivered in primal, feminine response to the smooth touch of his lips, and impulsively stroked her fingers down his face. "You didn't see your father before he died?" she asked quietly.

His eyes darkened with emotion. "No," he said, and this time when he kissed the back of her hand, he did so lingeringly, holding her gaze. Her temperature jacked up; how did he do this to her?

The moment when he spread her hand open so her palm cupped his jaw, it felt like it was just them. Nobody else in the restaurant, the hotel, the world.

"You'd never abandon your father," he murmured as he held her gaze trapped, pressing her palm against his face. "I admire that."

Her chest moved as if pulled by an invisible string toward him. Had she ever received a more flattering compliment?

His pain streaked through her as though she'd adopted it as hers, and she ached to make him feel better, to take the darkness away from his eyes, to kiss him…kiss him all over.

She stroked his rough jaw with her fingers instead, unable to stop herself. "Perhaps he knew you loved him, and he understood you kept to your pride, like he did," she suggested.

"Marcos? Love? He wouldn't know love if it trampled him," Marissa scoffed and frowned at Marcos, then sobered up when he swiveled around to send her a chilling look. "It's my fault anyway. That you left. I've paid dearly for my mistake, I guarantee it," she added.

He didn't reply. His gaze had dropped to where his thumb stroked the back of Virginia's hand again, distracting her from the conversation that ensued. He seemed to prefer that touch above anything else. He kept stroking, caressing, moving her hand places. He put it, with his, over his thigh, or tucked it under his arm. Longing speared through her every single time he moved it according to his will. He genuinely seemed to…want it. Was he pretending? When his eyes came to hers, there was such warmth and heat there.… Was he pretending that, too?

Marissa mentioned Allende, and Marcos, prepared for the discussion, immediately answered. His voice stroked down Virginia's spine every time he spoke. Her reaction was the same: a shudder, a quiver, a pang. And she didn't want it to be. She didn't want to have a reaction, she shouldn't.

While the waiter set down their meals, she thought of her father, of how many times he'd disappointed and angered her, and she thought of how hurt she'd have to be in order not to see him again. Sometimes she'd wanted to leave, to pretend he didn't exist to her, and those times, she would feel like the worst sort of daughter for entertaining those thoughts.

Marcos wasn't a heartless man. He stuck by his brother

no matter what he did. *My brother is a person, Allende is not,* he'd told her. But his father had been a person, too. What had he done to Marcos to warrant such anger?

She had her answer fifteen minutes later, after she'd eaten the most spicy chile relleno on the continent and swallowed five full glasses of water to prove it. She excused herself to the *baño* and was about to return to the table when she heard Marissa's plea from the nearby table filter into the narrow corridor. "Marcos...if you'd only give me a chance..."

"I'm here to discuss Allende. Not your romps in my father's bed."

"Marcos, I was young, and he was so...so powerful, so interested in me in a way you never were. You were never asking me to marry you, never!"

He didn't answer that. Virginia hadn't realized she stood frozen until a waiter came to ask if she was all right. She nodded, but couldn't make her legs start for the table yet. Her chest hurt so acutely she thought someone had just pulled out her lungs. Marissa Galvez and Marcos. So it was because of a woman, because of her, that Marcos had never spoken again to his father?

"You never once told me if you cared for me, while he... he cared. He wanted me more than anything." Marissa trailed off as if she'd noticed Marcos wasn't interested in her conversation. "So who is this woman? She's a little simple for you—no?"

He laughed, genuinely laughed. "Virginia? Simple?"

Virginia heard her answering whisper, too low to discern, and then she heard his, also too low, and something horrible went through her, blinding her eyes, sinking its claws into her. She remembered how difficult it was as a little girl to cope with the whispers.

The father is always gambling...they say he's crazy...

Now they talked about her. Not about her father. About her. She didn't hear what he said, or what she said, only felt the pain and humiliation slicing through her. Her father had put her in this position once more. No. She'd put herself in it. Pretending to be lovers with a man she truly, desperately wanted...and then looking the fool in front of someone she was sure had really been his lover.

Jealousy swelled and rose in her. She had no right to feel it, had never been promised anything, and yet she did feel it. Their kiss yesterday had been glorified in her mind and she'd begun to wishfully think Marcos had wanted to be with her this week. Silly. She'd even told herself she might like sharing his bed for a week.

She felt winded and strangely stiff when she reached the table. She sat quietly. She focused on dessert, tried to taste and enjoy, and yet her anger mounted, as if she really were his lover, as if she had anything to claim of him.

When he reached for her hand, it took all her effort, it took her every memory of having gone to beg him for help that evening, not to pull it away.

If she weren't sitting she'd be kicking herself for being so easy. She sucked in air then held it as he guided that hand to his mouth and grazed her knuckles with his lips.

Her racing heart begged for more, but Marcos's kiss was less obvious than last night, more like a whisper on her skin. Every grazing kiss he gave each knuckle felt like a stroke in her core.

A slap in the face.

They say her father's crazy...

By all means, Virginia would pull her hand away in a few seconds. She just wanted...more. More hot breath and warm lips on the back of her hand. More fire between her legs. A place so hot and moist it could only be cooled by—

Something moved.

His phone.

His lips paused on her for a breathless second before he

set her hand back on her lap and whispered, "It's the office. I have to get this."

Virginia made a strangled sound which was supposed to be an agreement and clearly sounded more like a dying woman. She watched his dark silhouette move between the tables and disappear down the hall so quickly. She already missed him. She scanned her surroundings. Everybody was eating, carrying on conversations. The world hadn't stopped like she'd thought because of those tiny kisses on her knuckles.

She sank back in her seat, agitated when Marissa watched her. She brought her hand to her mouth, the one he'd kissed, and closed her eyes as she grazed her lips in the exact same places his lips had touched.

Eyes popping open to meet the other woman's canny gaze, she straightened, readjusted the hem of her knee-length dress, and mentally cursed this pretense from here to Alaska and then to Mars. Was he seducing her? Or was this all for Marissa's sake?

"So," Marissa said. "You love him."

Virginia was about to jump in denial, frantic to save herself from this accusation, which of course implied that she was stupid, needed therapy and more, and then she realized he was counting on her to pretend that she did.

Love him.

"I…" Her lips couldn't form the words *I love him*. Her tongue seemed to freeze. Seemed to want to say only one thing, and that was *I hate him*.

She hated him and this stupid plan and how he touched her and how well he pretended to want her.

So instead she nodded, and let Marissa think what she would.

His powerful scent reached her long before he sat down beside her again. Virginia stared straight ahead like a horse with blinders. And just to prevent any more stoking of the staggering anger building inside her, she tucked her hands under her thighs. There. See if the man could touch her knuckles now.

She remained quiet the rest of the meal.

She heard Marissa invite them to a party the next day while she considered Marcos's offer.

She told herself she didn't care to know what kind of offer he'd made.

Six

Something had changed.

Virginia had changed. She was different, and yet, it was all the same with him. The twisting sensation in his gut, the demented beat of his heart, the itch in his hands, the coiling want in his body.

Alert, clever, perceptive and spirited...now his assistant seemed to be struggling to comprehend what she'd witnessed as they reached their rooms.

They'd had such an enjoyable time this morning, he'd been certain he knew where they were heading tonight.

He wasn't sure anymore.

He wasn't sure of anything—very unlike an Allende.

He took her to the middle of the living room and just stood there, his jacket in one hand, looking at her. His every muscle felt stiff and pained, his hard-on merciless, and when he moved the slightest bit, arousal lanced through him. He set his jacket aside and felt as if the air was being squeezed out of his lungs. She was disappointed he'd been such a bad son to his father? He'd lost her admiration? Her respect?

His insides twisted at the thought. He stepped forward, toward her, his thoughts congested, tangled like vines. The heat of her angry breaths made his insides strain in his want to drink it, feel it, appease it. It sent him teetering into an aroused state he couldn't fathom, much less understand. Eyeing her in silence, he tugged at his tie, stripping it from his neck, breathing harshly.

"I'd say that went well."

She tilted her head, her eyes fierce, something there marking him as loathsome. "She didn't believe us for a moment, that we…" She turned away as if disgusted. "She didn't buy it."

He narrowed his eyes—watching the tantalizing rise and fall of her chest. How would they feel to the touch? Soft. Yes, God, soft and small. Perky? Yes, that, too. His mouth watered. "Whether she believes it or not is of no consequence now."

Her eyes flashed a glittery warning. "You wanted to make her jealous."

"Jealous," he repeated, puzzled by the accusation. "Is that what you believe?"

She shoved her hair back from her forehead. "Yes, it is. And I'm sorry I disappointed, Marcos."

His blood raged hot and wild. He'd never seen her like this. Almost out of control, begging for…something he wanted to give her. Suddenly he'd give anything to hear her utter his name in that same haughty, do-me tone. He'd do anything to just…bury this ache inside her.

"I look at her and feel nothing—not even anger anymore. I didn't want her jealousy, but I didn't want her insinuating herself into my bed either."

"Because you want her there. Otherwise you wouldn't need me standing between you!"

He grabbed her arms and jerked hard, spurred by every ounce of pent-up desire in him, harbored for too long. "Listen to you!" She slammed against him with a gasp. Her eyes flamed in indignation and his body roared to life, singed by her lushness, her mouth so close. "There's only one woman I want in my bed—one. And I've wanted her for a long, long time."

"Then go get her!"

He backed her toward the bedroom. "Oh, I will—and I'll have her right where I want her." He dragged her closer and pulled her dress beneath her breasts and her scent, sweet and warm, washed through his senses. He seized a nipple with two fingers and pushed her breast up to his mouth and sucked.

He paused briefly to say, "The thought of you has me tied into knots. I want to taste you. For you to give me your lips, feel my body in yours. I want you coming with my name on your lips, coming over and over, with me."

She caught his head and moaned. He could see the needs, the emotions, rising in her and darkening her eyes to storms. His hands caught her wrists and pinned them over her head and tightened. "Share my bed."

"Marcos…"

A throbbing sensation pulsed through him, aching in his erection, his chest, his head. His voice grew hard, fierce as his cheek pressed against hers and he murmured in her ear. "I won't beg, not even for you, I won't ask again, Virginia. I have a craving for you…it's running wild and out of control. You share this craving. You crave me, you crave me so much you tremble with the force of it. Don't deny us. Don't deny me."

His breathing was ragged, hers wild. The gleam of defiance died out in her eyes as she gazed at his lips. He groaned and pulled her head to his as he swept down. His kiss was bred by passion, rampant with lust. The raging desire threatened to consume his mind, his sanity. He was undone by her kiss, her taste. His mind raced, his thirst for her sweeping through him. Her response was wholehearted, fiery, and it almost sent him to his knees. Her mouth sipped, her hands took what he wanted to give her. He called upon restraint but there was only passion here. Over and over he thought of being gentle, over and over her answer was to intensify, demand more.

He grabbed her and thrust her onto the bed, bouncing, and he was ripping at his shirt.

She climbed to her knees, her hands on her dress, fumbling to unbutton.

He whipped his shirt off, meeting her glimmering green gaze, stripping naked. "Do you want me?"

"Yes."

He unbuckled his belt and sent it slapping to the floor. "Lie back."

His heart thundered as he waited for her to, aware of the erection straining before her, listening to her sharp inhale. She backed away, her dress riding up to show her blue panties. And she was... There were no words. That lacy blue stuff looked delicious on her.... He wanted to use his lips to pry it off, his teeth... No, he couldn't wait; he needed to feel her skin.

He fell on her and trapped her under him, yanking her arms up, his pelvis arching into her. "You'll take what I can give you, all of it, *amor*."

"Yes."

She struggled against him, but he tamed her with his mouth, pinning her with his weight, stretching out naked on top of her. He grabbed her hair and held her still, and it felt like silk between his fingers. "I'm going to love doing this with you."

She sighed and rubbed against him like a cat. "I'll pretend to like it."

Her voice was husky, full of longing, inviting him to do

things to her. He cupped the full globes of her lace-covered breasts, dragging his teeth across that delectable spot of skin, licking the curve between her neck and shoulder. "Oh, you will. I'll make sure you do." Her nipple puckered, and he pinched to draw it out even more. "This little nipple pretends very well."

She lay back, all skin and hair and woman, drawing him to her warmth. Her arms were around him, her hands on his back, kneading the bunched-up muscles. He shuddered. He could lose himself in those eyes, in that body, in her, and he demanded, "Say 'Marcos.' Whisper my name to me."

"Marcos."

She wasn't sure from what part of her had come this determination, this courage or this desperate want, she only knew she needed him. He annihilated her mind, her senses. She hadn't realized what she'd do, how she'd fight to be with this one man until she'd seen Marissa.

She hadn't yet finished saying his name, a word that echoed the passion roaring through her, and he was there already, growling "Virginia" and taking her mouth in a fierce kiss. A flock of butterflies exploded in her stomach when their lips met. Her head swam as the flames spread, his tongue thrusting precisely, strongly, fiercely inside, emotion hissing through her, weakening her, overwhelming her.

Growling, he deepened the kiss as he tugged the bow loose at her hip, and she felt the fabric of her dress unfurl until it opened and hung at her sides. "It's important your body becomes familiar with my touch. All of it. You want Marissa to believe us, don't you? If you want others to believe it you have to believe it yourself. Your body has to know to respond when I touch it."

A strangled sound echoed in the silence and in the back of her mind Virginia realized it came from her. He cupped one lace-encased breast. Oh, it was so wonderful. So bad. So everything. She'd stop him in a minute…in one more minute…no, she'd not stop him, not tonight, maybe not ever.

Utterly possessing her lips, he slid his free palm down the flatness of her stomach and below. "It's important I know your curves…the texture of your skin…"

She could feel every sinew of his muscles against her. His fingers…sliding downward. Deep, forgotten places inside her clenched in waiting for his touch. Opening her mouth, she flicked her tongue out to his. "Marcos."

"Here you are. Soaked."

His voice grew husky. Desire trembled there. His hand between her legs began to slide under her panties. She arched involuntarily when he feathered a finger across the soft, damp spot at the juncture of her thighs. Every pink, throbbing part of her pinged at his touch. She moaned in her throat and sank back deeper into the bed as he caressed more deliberately.

She'd never known a touch could feel like fire, spread through her until every inch throbbed and burned. Involuntarily she moved her hips, filling his palm with the dewy softness between her legs.

"Marcos…" It was a plea, and it carried in it the fright she experienced in what he made her feel.

"Shh." His lips grazed her temple. "Open up to me." His free hand tugged at her bra and bared her left breast to him. Her disbelieving gaze captured the instant the rosy peak of her nipple disappeared between his lips. A thrilling jolt rushed through her as the moist heat of his mouth enveloped her. Her head fell back on a moan.

Instinctively she reached up to cup the back of his head, cradling him with the same gentle care he used to suckle her breast. He groaned profoundly in his throat and continued to fondle her with his mouth, lips nipping, tongue swirling, mouth suckling.

His hand moved lightly, expertly, his fingers unerringly

fondling her through her panties. Hot little shivers rushed through her.

One long finger began to stroke her dampness. Open her with little prods of the tip.

She squirmed in shock, a little in agony, seeking ease for the burn growing inside her. "I hurt." Blindly, her parted mouth sought more of the warmth of his lips. He penetrated her. With his tongue. His finger. She arched and cried out, shocked by the sensation. An explosion of colors erupted behind her eyelids. His mouth melded to hers harder. Skin, heat, ecstasy.

Her skin felt damp while every cell in her body felt hot and tingly. With a low growl, he delved a hand into her hair and pulled her head back, moving his mouth up her neck. It was damp and velvety on her flesh, licking as though her skin were his only sustenance. In her ear he rasped, "I'm filling you."

"Yes." Against his throat.

"You crave me to fill you." His finger was thrusting, possessing—his body incredibly hard against hers. "You need me to take away the hurt."

Pleasure ripped through her, and her back arched helplessly as she moaned. "You make me reckless, Marcos, you make me..."

"Burn." He opened his mouth. Giving her the mist of his breath. "I can't believe how ready you are. How slick. Are you pretending? Are you, *amor?*"

"No."

He gave her his tongue. She could hear the soaked sounds his touch caused and felt embarrassed and aroused all at once. "Shh. Take my finger," he huskily murmured, the graze of that finger so bare and fleeting across her entry she mewled with a protest to take it in again. "Soon I'll give you two. Do you want two?"

"No," she lied. Her body ruled now, screamed, shivered against his.

"Hmm." He inserted the first, then the second deeply. "I'll pretend that was a yes."

Her thoughts scattered. "Marcos, please…"

"My God, you're responsive." His hands continued to work their magic as he looked down on her. "You were jealous for me."

The burn intensified. The clench in her womb unbearable. "Yes," she breathed, closing her eyes.

His groan sounded like a growl. "I like that."

"Marcos."

He was watching her, the effects of what he did to her. Every time she gasped, or let go a little moan, his face tightened with emotion—and alternately, something clenched tightly in her. She'd never known the extent of her passion, was surprised at how shamelessly she took pleasure from him.

Gently, he pried her fingers away from his neck and brought her hand between their bodies. "Touch me."

"Where? Where do I…"

"Here." He shifted over her. The sheets slid well below his hips and their every inch, shoulder to hips, became perfectly aligned. The very hardest part of him pushed against her hand. "Feel me," he strained out. "Feel how I want you. This isn't for her, Virginia, this is for you."

He ground his hips against hers unapologetically. When she let go, his rigid length grazed her moistness through her panties. They groaned at the contact. He pressed closer, ground himself harder, wide and long against her. She wanted to die.

By the erratic heaves of his chest, Virginia suspected even though he was larger and more powerful, he was as defenseless to their chemistry as she was. Under her fingers, his skin was warm and slightly damp. Shyly, she continued to explore him, sifting her fingers through the dark hair at his nape, amazed at the soft texture.

His hands covered her breasts. The calluses on his palms were palpable through the lace, and her breast swelled ripely under his kneading.

Turning her cheek into the pillow, she let her eyes drift shut as she fought the intimacy of it all, the swelling tenderness that washed over her as he touched her. It was difficult to imagine that he was not her lover and she wasn't entirely, completely, indisputably his.

Burying his face between her breasts, he gnawed at the tiny bow at the center of her bra. She felt the unmistakable graze of his teeth on her skin. He used them to scrape the top swell of her breast and a very startling whimper escaped her.

His mouth shifted to the peak, pointy and obvious under the fabric, and he licked her. The hot dampness of his tongue seeped into her skin. She shuddered. A thrilling heat fanned out from her center.

He reached around her and unhooked her bra. When he peeled it off her, she instinctively covered herself with her palms.

"I want to see." He pried her hands away and placed them on his shoulders. His dark, heavy-lidded eyes regarded each of her breasts with interest. His breath fanned across one exposed nipple. "So pretty."

She drew in a ragged breath as he brushed the little bud with the pad of his thumb. It puckered under his finger. If possible, his eyes darkened even more. "Do you want my mouth here?"

"I d-don't know."

He swiped his tongue across the tip. "Yes, you do." He closed his eyes and nuzzled her with his nose. "Do you want my mouth here?"

"Yes."

He licked gently. "Like that."

"Yes."

He grazed with his teeth. "Or like that."

She squeezed his shoulders, staring to shiver. "B-both."

He nibbled using his lips then drew her fully into his mouth. "Hmm. Like a raspberry."

Her eyes shut tight. The sensation of being devoured entirely by his mouth had her melting.

Could he say something wrong, please? Could he not lick her…like that? Could his hands be smaller, less thorough, less hot, less knowing?

Turning to suckle her other breast, he delved one hand between her legs and slipped into her panties. "I want my mouth here, too," he murmured, searching her pliant folds with strong, deft fingers.

She gasped and thrashed her head, seized by a mix of shame and pleasure as he unerringly found, opened, invaded that most intimate part of her. "N-no…no mouth there."

"But I can touch?"

Quivering and warm, she sensed him watching her as he gently eased one finger into that moist, swollen place that craved him.

She gulped back an enormous clog of emotion. "Yes."

"*Chiquita.*" It was a reverent whisper, full of wonder as he stretched her. "*Chiquita mia.*"

She arched, shamelessly offering herself. As he continued his foray inside her, a marvelous pressure gathered at her core.

His nostrils flared. "One minute," he rasped as he searched under her dress for the silken string of her panties. She was weightless on the bed when he tugged them off her legs. "And I put us both out of our misery."

His chest gleamed bare when he leaned over her, his shoulders bunched with tension as he grasped her calves.

He stared into her eyes, his expression tight as he guided her legs around his hips. "Hold on to me. Don't let me go."

The way he asked to be held made her think she'd never let him go, she'd make him love her, she'd hold on to him.

He pulled her to his hips and she felt him, hot and thick and rigid, pressing into where she was pliant and damp. A wildness raged inside her when he ducked his head to suckle a breast—suckle hard the instant he pushed in. She bucked up to receive him, urging him in with her hands and legs.

They moaned in unison when he entered, their breaths mingling as he angled his head to hers, their lips so close that all he had to do was bend his head an inch to capture her mouth and the whimper that followed when he was fully inside her.

"Yes," he growled.

"Yes," she breathed.

A fullness took her, bringing the discomfort of being stretched more than she could bear, and then he was moving inside her and the unease transformed to pleasure. Waves and waves of pleasure.

And in that instant she loved what he did to her, how he brought her every cell and atom to life, how he offered her ease. Ease for this wanting.

She'd longed for that ease more than anything.

As he moved in her, touched and kissed her, she gave encouraging sounds that seemed to tear out from within her—and he continued. Taking. Giving. Expertly loving her.

Braced up above her, his arms rippled with tension, his throat strained, his face was raw with the semblance of pleasure. All were memorized in her mind.

Vaguely, in her blanked, blissful state, she knew sex would never again be like this. Would a man ever live up to this one?

A sound that was purely male vibrated against her ear as he placed his mouth there to whisper, "Come for me."

Moving deftly, he pushed her higher and higher, murmuring carnal, unintelligible words in Spanish that melted her bones like the silk and steel thrusts of his body. *Mia. Suave. Hermosa. Mia. Mia. Mia.*

All Virginia could say was "Marcos." In a plea, a murmur, a moan. *Marcos.* Over and over again. *Marcos* as he increased his pace, driving faster, more desperately into her. Vaguely she felt the warmth of him spill inside her, the convulsions that racked his powerful body as ecstasy tore through them both, the pleasure consuming, making him yell, making her scream, scream "Marcos."

"Marcos" as he kissed her breasts, her lips, her neck. "Marcos" as the pressure spread. "Marcos" as she shattered.

Seven

Darkness: it was hard to leave it. But a strong, familiar scent wafted into her nostrils. Tempting. Tantalizing. Beckoning her awake. Coffee. Yes. Strong and rich and ready. Virginia stirred on the bed. She stretched her arms first, then her legs, sighing when it hurt pleasantly to do both.

"...in an hour...yes...we'll be there..."

Virginia bolted upright on the bed when she recognized that particularly deep baritone voice. Her head swam. *Lips tugging at her nipples, fingers pinching, touching, pleasuring...whispers...* A throb started between her legs. She squeezed her eyes shut and swung her feet until her toes touched the carpeted floor. *Calm down.* She would not, could not, panic.

Sunlight glowed in the living room, making her squint as she entered. He stood by the window in his shirt and slacks. His raven-black hair looked damp from a recent bath. He held one arm stretched above his head, his tan hand braced on the windowsill. His was a solid presence in the room.

Sturdy as an ox, that was the way he looked. That was the way he was.

"Good morning," she muttered.

He turned, smiled.

She set her coffee on a small round table beside the desk and lowered herself to a chair, Marcos coming forward and kissing her forehead.

"Did you order the entire kitchen contents up here?" she whispered.

He stroked her cheek. "I wanted to be sure I ordered what you liked."

A blush was spreading up her neck because she remembered cuddling against him after she'd gone on and on saying *please*. God, no.

His eyes were full of knowledge, of satisfaction of having loved his lover well and hard for a night. Her skin pebbled with goose bumps as she realized he was remembering everything they'd done through the night: the kissing, the laughing, the kissing, the eating cheese and grapes on the carpet, the kissing.

They had made love until Virginia thought she'd pass out from bliss.

And hours before waking up, when she had cuddled in and draped one leg across his hips, he had made slow, lazy love to her again, and whispered words to her in Spanish she could only dream of finding the meaning of.

He lifted her chin, studying her. "Did I hurt you last night?"

With a small smile, she tugged on the collar of her pajama top and showed him his bite. His forehead furrowed.

"That has to be painful."

"Only in the most pleasurable way."

Settling down, she took a healthy sip of coffee, then set the cup back down. "What?" she pressed.

He was looking at her strangely.

"What?"

"You begged me to take you last night."

"And?"

"And I liked it."

Her stomach muscles contracted. Suddenly her lips felt puffy and sensitive as she remembered just how thoroughly he'd kissed her. "Marcos, this will be very complicated in Chicago."

"It doesn't have to be."

A thousand butterflies fluttered in her chest. "You expect we can keep this up?"

"We touched. We made love four times in one night. Do you expect we can stop by Monday?"

They'd touched. His tanned, long hands had been somewhere in her body, and hers had been somewhere in his. She couldn't bear to remember. "What do you...suggest?"

"Nobody has to know about us. And my suggestion is to continue."

Her body trembled. Little places zinged and pinged as though reminding her just, exactly, where his hands had been. "Continue."

He leaned against the window and his hand slowly fisted high up on the windowsill. "I swear I've never seen anything lovelier than you, naked. Your breasts."

She closed her eyes, sucking in a breath, willing herself not to remember what he'd done there. How he'd squeezed or cradled or...

"Marcos..."

"You cried out my name when I was inside you."

Oh, God. Yes, she had, yes, she had. Had she no honor? No pride when it came to him? No digni—

"I couldn't sleep for wanting to take you again." He smiled sadly. "You kept cuddling against me and I kept growing hard. I had to...shower."

Wrapping her arms around her shaking frame, she asked, "Do you want to?"

"To what?"

"Make love to me again."

And he said...

"Yes."

Her stomach exploded. He wanted her. Still. More than yesterday? Marcos still wanted her. But they couldn't continue in Chicago. They couldn't.

His arm fell at his side as he spun around and pinned her with a smile. "Eat up, though. We're going sightseeing."

She set down her coffee mug before she spilled it all over herself. "Really?"

"Of course. Really. We're flying over the city on a chopper first. Then we'll lunch downtown."

"A chopper."

"Are you concerned?"

"Actually, no. Excited."

She dug into the eggs, the waffles and the tea.

Marcos was piling his plate as though he hadn't been fed since his toddler years. "Would you like a tour of Allende," he asked casually.

Allende. She grinned. "I thought you'd never ask."

It occurred to her she had never imagined she could ever have one of these mornings with Marcos. Such a lavish, elegant hotel suite and such a clear, sunny day outside, a beautiful morning. Like husband and wife. Talking. Smiling. Laughing as they enjoyed breakfast. But they were boss and assistant, embarking on what had to be wrong. The air around them was charged with sexual tension. Really, it could very well be lightning in there.

"Did she...agree to your bid?" Virginia asked, breaking the silence. This watching him eat was a little too stimulating to her mind.

He popped a grape into his mouth. "She will."

"She didn't seem interested in even discussing business."

"It's a game." His eyes skewered her to her seat. "She wants me to demand Allende and I won't."

"So you'll play this for the entire week."

"Not likely." He spread cream cheese atop his bagel. "I'll leave with an offer and let her think it over."

Were he any other man, Virginia was sure a woman like Marissa could handle him. But he was Marcos. Nobody could think straight with him near and he was as manageable as a wild stallion to a child. "If she rejects your offer?"

He diverted his attention from his tower of gluttony and selected a newspaper among the three folded ones, calmly saying, "She's not getting a better one, trust me."

He yanked open *El Norte*. "What angered you? Yesterday?"

The cup paused halfway to her lips then clattered back down on the plate. "I heard you…discussing me. I've always found that annoying."

Slowly he folded the paper and set it aside. The intense stare he leveled on her made her squirm. Those gypsy eyes, they did magic in her. Black magic.

"You're blushing."

"I'm not."

But her face felt hot and so did other parts of her.

His jaw tightened and a muscle in his cheek flexed. "Is it the attention? You do not like this?"

She drew in a deep breath because unfortunately there was no brown bag she could cover her face with. She had to pretend he was hallucinating. "It's the whispering behind my back."

"You cannot control what people whisper." He popped a piece of his bagel into his mouth and then picked up the paper again.

"You are wrong." How could he think that? "You can

control your actions. You can give them no cause to...to whisper."

"You'd let gossip hurt you, Virginia?"

His voice was full of such tenderness she actually felt it like a stroke. "You've never been hurt by words before?"

Once again, the paper was lowered. This time his eyes burned holes through her. "I said words to my father. I'll bet my fortune that yes, they hurt."

Something distressed her. His gaze. His tone. "You wish you took them back?"

He considered with a frown. "No. I wish he'd have taken them for what they were. The words of a wounded boy determined to break him."

She had never known Marcos to be cruel. But he could be dangerous. He was predator, and he had been wounded. "You could never make amends with him?"

His smile was pantherlike, almost carrying a hiss. "Because of her."

"Marcos," she said again after a moment, even more alarmed at the harsh set of his jaw and ominous slant of his eyebrows. "Marcos, why do you want to destroy the company? You could make amends with it. Save it, mend it."

"It would take too much effort." He waved her off with a hand, went back to the paper. "Eat up, *amor,* I'm eager to show you the city."

"You're eager to get back and have your way with me," she quipped.

He threw his head back and gave out a bark of laughter, his expression so beautiful her heart soared in her chest. "So we understand each other, then."

He couldn't tear his eyes away from her.

She was the same woman he'd wanted for so long, and yet she had become someone else. A sexy woman who was comfortable in his presence, smiling, laughing, open to speaking her mind.

Eyes sparkling as the helicopter touched the ground, Virginia pulled his headphones down to his neck. "That's Allende?" she yelled through the rotor noise.

He glanced out the window, squeezing her fingers with his. Impossible, but her excitement was rubbing off on him. "That's it, yes."

Once they climbed out of the helicopter, Marcos surveyed the vast industrial building that sat on two hundred acres of land. It was smaller than he remembered it—but then he'd been so much younger.

The sun blazed atop their heads. Virginia's raven mane gleamed. And in that moment Marcos didn't see how aged the building appeared, or notice the grease on all the trucks and carriers that were parked in endless rows across the parking lot. He saw his father and himself, discussing the delivery schedule. A strange heaviness settled in his chest, weighing him down.

"Are we going in?"

Pulled from his thoughts, he looked at his assistant. How she managed to stand there—sexy and innocent—while he felt so unsettled was beyond him.

Bracing himself for whatever greeted him inside, he led her toward the double glass doors beneath a metal sign that read *Transportes Allende*.

Within minutes the two guards unlocked the door and ushered them in. Marcos and Virginia were free to roam the old wide halls. An attractive blush tinted her cheeks as she eagerly drank in her surroundings.

There was nothing to say about the structure, except that it was bare bones, obsolete and old. *Horrible.*

New installations were a must. A more recent fleet of carriers to strengthen their position as a link to the U.S. market. New—

"This is terribly spacious," she said, leaning a hand on a red brick wall that served as a room division.

Marcos reined himself back. What in *the hell* had he been thinking?

He didn't want to restore the company to its former glory; he wanted it gone.

He frowned darkly while Virginia swayed her hips and went peeking from room to room. All were vacated for the morning under Marcos's instructions. An encounter with Marissa was the last thing he'd wanted today—and thankfully she was smart enough to have obliged.

Virginia tucked her hair behind her ear, her forehead creasing as she peered up at the rafters on the ceiling.

Rather than notice the paint was peeling off the walls and making a list of fixing that—Miss Hollis was probably already cataloguing that for him, in any case—Marcos focused on her reactions.

Something warm and fuzzy stirred in him. Virginia would be a pitiful poker player. Her expressions were too untrained for intrigue—and her father's past had given her a loathing for the game.

"My first office," he said then, without tone.

She spun around in the doorway as he spoke, wide-eyed. "This one? With the view of the front gate?"

He followed her into the small space and tried to see it through her eyes, old and dirty and cluttered, but then it just appeared like what it was: a promising place in need of some attention.

Marcos could've kicked himself for mentally volunteering to give it some TLC. No. Hell, no.

He wouldn't.

All he wanted was to eliminate it, like wiping out his past in one fell swoop. Swoosh. Gone. Presto!

But judging by the interest that swam in Virginia's eyes,

she approved of the place, too. "It fits you somehow," she said. "Rough around the edges."

They shared a smile.

The fuzzy feeling inside him grew to incredible proportions.

"How many transport units does it have?" she asked. "Approximately?"

He watched her sail to the window. His eyes tracked her progress for a moment and then he followed her.

She was peering through the blinds, scanning the vast loading area, when he came up behind her.

He buried his face in the side of her neck and enveloped her in his arms, biting back a groan. "There are two thousand and forty cargo carriers—plus hundreds of smaller units for simpler deliveries."

She smelled of a soft, powdery fragrance, her hair scented with his travel shampoo. The combination flew up to his head like an aphrodisiac.

He'd never imagined the days they spent together would be like this. Lust and desire constantly had him on edge, true, but there was also the delightful peace and pleasure of her company.

Gently, he guided her around to face him. "As soon as we land in Chicago, I will have the funds transferred to your personal account. I want those men out of your and your father's lives so you can be at peace. Agreed?"

A shadow descended, veiling her eyes. Inch by inch, her smile disappeared.

He cupped her face between his palms. "Something wrong with that?"

Clearly something was. She averted her gaze and gnawed on her lower lip. "Thank you, no, it's all fine. That's our arrangement, right?"

Pretend, she didn't say. But his mind supplied it.

When Marcos did not deny this, Virginia lowered her

face and drew away, suddenly looking very young and very vulnerable. She hugged herself tight. "I'd forgotten I'm being paid for this, that my father's bad habits brought me here."

Marcos knew that a woman like her didn't easily fall into a man's bed. Was she regretting that she had? Or only the circumstances that had brought her there?

A host of male instincts assailed him, urging him to embrace her, take her, appease her, seize the instinctive role of a man and protect her.

With a surge of dominant power, he grasped her shoulders and gave a gentle clench. "You're worried he won't stop gambling—that this will only be a temporary relief from your problem."

She nodded. "I am."

Virginia had been calling her father every day. His insides wrenched in protest at the knowledge of her suffering because of a reckless old man on a suicide mission. "How long since your father had a real job?" They strolled back into the hall, side by side.

"Since Mother died. Several years ago."

They came into the last office—his father's old office. Virginia probably didn't know it had been his because of its ample size, or maybe she suspected, Marcos didn't know. All he knew was that he couldn't bear to look around but at the same time couldn't leave it.

He crossed the wood floor, now covered with a shaggy white rug, and touched the window as he gazed outside. "He's been like this ever since? Your father?"

"It's gotten out of control recently."

Circling around the desk, he stroked the blunt edge with his fingers—he used to sit there and listen to his father talk on the phone. Thoughtfully, he asked, "Has he tried to even get a job?"

"He did. He's tried, but of course he's found nothing. At

least that's what he says, but I suspect his pride won't let him accept the kinds of jobs that have been offered to him."

He frowned. "Sometimes you have to take what you can get."

"I agree." She toed the plush ends of the rug with the tip of her high heels. "I just feel he was hoping for someone to give him a chance at what he used to do. He was a good manager except he spoiled his chance."

Second chances, Marcos thought. People spoke of them all the time, but in reality nobody offered them.

His father hadn't offered it to him.

Nor had he offered one to his father.

Gradually, he allowed his surroundings to filter into his mind. A snapshot of Marissa beside the dormant computer. Frilly female things atop the desk. And he realized with a sinking heart that Marissa had taken possession of his father's office.

There was no picture of the old man who'd raised him. The soccer posters—vintage ones that his old man had collected— were no longer on the walls. She'd taken everything, that heartless witch. *Everything!*

"This is your father's office?" Virginia watched him, and the pity in her eyes made him desperate to eliminate it.

"Not anymore." He smiled tightly, snatching up her hand. "Come on, let's go. The office staff is coming in later."

He escorted her outside. Thinking of how it was too late for his father and him—but maybe not for hers. Marcos's old man had not been a gambler, but his quest for a woman had trampled his own son.

It seemed unfair a child should sacrifice their happiness for a parent. Marcos had not been willing.

He'd *never* accept as a stepmother a woman who'd months before been his lover, *never* accept as a stepmother a woman who was so obviously playing his father for a fool. After numerous heated arguments where Carlos Allende refused to admit his son's view as true, Marcos had packed his bags and left. But Virginia?

When her father fell into that dark gambling pit once more, what was this generous, loyal creature going to do? And what would he be willing to do to help her?

She loved Mexico.

There was something deliciously decadent about the time they spent during the following days poking around little shops, eating in restaurants, walking the city.

This afternoon, as Virginia's heels hit the marbled floors of the awe-inspiring MARCO museum, she drew in a deep, reverent breath. This was a luxury she'd never allowed herself before. She'd rarely allowed herself outings to relax or to stimulate the mind; she'd always been so consumed by worry.

Now she wove through the paintings on exhibit, feeling Marcos's presence next to her, and felt like she'd stepped into an alternate reality.

Every painting that caught her eye, every sculpture she viewed with the eyes of a woman who had suddenly acquired sight. And hearing. And touch. The colors were vibrant, and the themes were all passionate. Even death seemed passionate.

At night, Marcos took her out to eat in a small café just blocks away from the city plaza. After salad, tacos and fries, they walked arm-in-arm through the throng of people.

She'd never felt so safe.

She was in a dangerous city, surrounded by a language she did not understand and among unique, intriguing people, and she felt utterly safe. Her world felt so distant. Her father's debts, the threats, the fact that things could get worse. Nothing mattered when these long, sinewy, rock-hard arms were around her.

She felt, for the first time in her life, protected. *Secure.*

During their ride back to the hotel, she caught Marcos watching her with those eyes and that knowing smile, and a sneaky little voice whispered to her. It accompanied them to their rooms, nestling somewhere deep inside her.

This is as real as real gets, Virginia Hollis. Can you make him see it?

No, she doubted that she could. He viewed the world with the eyes of a man. While she, with those of a woman.

As she struggled to tame her welling emotions, Marcos grasped her chin between his thumb and forefinger and tipped her head back. "Who does he gamble with? Do you know?"

It took a moment for her to grasp his train of thought. She shook her head. "I don't know."

Marcos hadn't dropped the subject of her father for days. It was as though he were intent on avoiding the topic of his own parent and was focusing instead on fixing the troubles of hers.

Shrugging off his shirt, his eyes held hers in the lamplight, his voice a mellow rumble. "You said his gambling put you in this position. In that bed right behind you. My bed. Did you mean it?"

She considered the question at length, and though she'd needed to save her father no matter what, she also softly admitted, as she pulled off her short-sleeved sweater, "I think I brought myself here."

She tossed her sweater aside, then her bra. Even in the flickering shadows, she caught the tightening flex of his jaw and throat. That her nakedness affected him made her smile and move close to him. Her palms hit the smooth velvet of his chest and her fingers rubbed upward. "What do you say about that, Mr. Allende?" she whispered.

With slow deliberation, he turned his head toward hers. As his fingers ventured in a languorous caress up her back, his mouth grazed her cheek and his sweet, hot breath coasted across her skin. "I say you're the sexiest little thing I've ever seen. Miss Hollis. And I want you to promise me—whatever happens between us, you're coming to me if your father's ever again in trouble."

"No, Marcos."

"Yes. You are. I'd make you give me your word you'll not pay debts that aren't yours, but I know that'd be unfair to ask of you. You feel responsible for him, I respect that. Now please understand I feel responsible for you."

Her toes curled at the proprietary gleam in his eyes. "But you're not."

"You're my employee."

"You have thousands of employees."

His knuckles caressed her nipples, and her body flared to life at the touch. "But only one who's been my lover."

The words lingered in the air for a heated moment. She was ready to give up. Just wanted to kiss. Could almost hear the seconds ticking as their time together ran out.

"No contest?" he queried then, sensing his victory.

She yielded, shaking her head, wrapping her arms around him. "None."

By the time their lips touched, she was holding her breath, parting her lips for his smiling mouth to take. He seized them softly and began to entice and torment her with nips and nibbles and gentle little suckles she felt down to the soles of her feet.

When he lowered her to the bed, his mouth became more demanding, spreading fire through her veins. And as his tongue forayed hard and hot inside her, one hand traveled up her ribcage to knead one waiting, throbbing breast with long, skillful fingers. *"Chiquita."*

He scraped his whiskers across her chin, and she sighed.

She was his lover for a week.

She was nothing more and she would never be more.

Braced up on one arm, he used his free hand to unbuckle her slacks. He pulled the zipper low and pulled them off her. His thumb touched the elastic of her panties and made slow, sinuous circles before he eased it down.

Lover for a week. That's all.

Discarding her panties, he urged her down on the bed and rained haphazard, unexpected kisses across her torso. On her shoulder, her tummy, then feasted on the tip of one breast. Virginia dropped her hand and absently caressed the back of his satiny black head as it moved, imagining what it would be like to suckle a baby. Their baby.

She'd always wanted a family.

Virginia, lover for a week!

As he kissed a path down her belly, it struck her with a sweet wrenching pain that she had never sensed her dream of a family so far out of reach. At first the desire had been tucked aside to help her father resurface from his grief. Now it had come to the forefront of her mind and it mocked her.

Because she had become lover to this man.

This enthralling black-haired Spaniard.

And every man in her future would always be compared in her mind to Marcos Allende. Every bed she slept in would not be this one. And she dreaded, doubted there would be a man in this world to kiss her the way he did. Touch her like this, just like *this*.

Realizing his mouth was approaching somewhere dangerous, she squirmed under him. "If you knew what I was thinking," she spoke up at the ceiling, "you'd leave the room."

He lifted his head and met her gaze, his voice frighteningly solemn. "Don't give me your heart, Virginia."

Oh, God. She squeezed her eyes shut. *Don't fall in love with him, don't fall in love with him,* don't fall in love with him. She scoffed, yanked her arm free as she sat up. "What? You think you're all that and then some? That I cannot resist you? I'll have you know…my heart…was not part of our bargain. You're the boss and I'm the…employee and this is…an arrangement."

One callused palm ran up and down the side of her leg. "And yet it's easy to forget who we are here, isn't it? Easy to get confused."

She frowned over the concern in his voice and grabbed his head, defiantly pulling his lips to hers.

Lovers. That was all.

This is as real as real gets, Virginia Hollis. Can you make him see it?

They came to understand each other. Too well, maybe. They talked, but not of the future. They talked, but not of themselves.

They pretended, as they'd agreed to do.

"Did you enjoy yourself this week?"

Riding to the airport in the back of the Mercedes, Virginia sat curled up against Marcos's side and laid her cheek on his shoulder. It was strange—how instinctively she sought this place, and how instinctively Marcos wrapped his arm around her shoulder to offer it to her.

She didn't care if she shouldn't do this, only knew within hours she wouldn't dare. So she did it now.

"It's been wonderful," she admitted and trailed off when he brushed his mouth across her temple and placed a soft, almost imperceptible kiss there. "Unexpected and…surreal and wonderful."

He held her so tight, so intimately, and whispered against her hair, "We should've done this before."

Going pensive at the note of lingering lust in his voice, Virginia played with the buttons on his shirt while Marcos checked his phone and made a call to the office. As he spoke into the receiver, she stole a glance at him.

His voice rumbled in her ear, and his arm around her

was absently moving up and down her bare arm. She'd been unable to keep from staring at him all week, and had been secretly delighted that most times he'd been checking up on her, too.

When he hung up, he gazed out the window at the passing car lights and said, "You'll wire yourself the money from my account and take care of your problem straight away. Promptly, tomorrow morning."

A command. As an authoritative man and, also, her boss.

"Understand?"

She hadn't noticed she'd flattened her hand on his chest until his own big one came to cover hers. She watched their fingers entwine. Lovers' fingers.

God, she'd done the most reckless thing. Look at her— draped all over her boss. Imagine if this ever got out? If people knew? Worse of all, her tummy was in a twist because she loathed for it to stop. And it had to—tonight. "Yes, I'll take care of it right away," she murmured, and on impulse took a good long whiff of his familiar scent.

"I've been thinking." Marcos turned her hand around for his inspection and his thumb began to slowly circle the center of her palm. "I'd like to offer your father a job."

"A job?"

"I figure if he realized he could be useful, he'd break the cycle of vice he seems to be stuck in."

She thought about it, still resting her cheek against his chest, feeling utterly contented and yet dreading tomorrow when that feeling could be replaced with unease. "Why?" she asked then.

He quirked an eyebrow, then narrowed his eyes. "Why what?"

She fingered the heavy cross at his throat. "Why... him?"

"Why not?"

She shrugged, but her heart began to flutter at the prospect. "Maybe he's just hopeless." As hopeless as she was. How would she bear Monday at the office? She was terribly in lust with the man. He was an extraordinary lover, made her feel so sexy and wild she wanted to take all kinds of risks with him, and now he offered her father this incredible lifeline?

"Maybe he is hopeless," Marcos agreed, chuckling.

But no, he was not hopeless, no one was. A smile appeared on her face. "Or maybe he will want one more chance." And maybe she could handle Monday after all.

She'd survived so far, had feigned not to want Marcos for days and weeks and months. Now she'd act as though nothing had happened. As though when he looked at her, her insides didn't leap with joy, and when he smiled at her, her stomach didn't quiver.

He smiled at her then, causing all kinds of happenings in her body, and stroked her cheek with his warm hand. "I've looked into him. He was a smart, dedicated man, and he could be one again."

Virginia contemplated his words, pleased that Marcos was smart enough to look past her father's mistakes and see the hardworking man underneath. And a plan formed in her mind. Her father had managed a large chain store so successfully that, if everything hadn't gone downhill after her mother's death, he'd be CEO by now.

"You know, Marcos," she said quietly, straightening on a burst of inspiration, "I think he might enjoy coming to Mexico."

Silence fell. The car swerved to the left and into the small airport driveway. Virginia remembered the look of grim solemnity in Marcos's face during their tour of Allende and she plunged on.

"He might even enjoy working at Allende," she said. She tossed the bait lightly, hoping to plant some kernel of doubt in him so he'd reconsider his decision regarding the company's future. But he went so still, she almost regretted it.

He stared at her with a calculating expression, then gazed out at the waiting jet. "Maybe."

Neither said another word, but when he pulled her close, ducked his head and kissed her, she fought not to feel a painful pang.

This was where they'd first kissed.

It only made sense it would be where they had their last.

Eight

She was tidying up his office the next morning when Marcos halted at the doorway. The sight of Virginia fiddling with the coffeemaker froze him, then heated up his blood.

As she poured a cup—black, as he liked it—the plain buttoned-up shirt she wore stretched across her breasts in a way that made watching feel like purgatory.

"Good morning."

She glanced up with a soft gasp. "Marcos—Mr. Allende." And there went her breasts again, swelling, pert and lovely as she took a little breath.

His heart thudded as they stared at each other, the words lingering in the air. *Mr. Allende.*

A word meant to erase everything that had happened in Monterrey, Mexico.

Having never expected she would make it this easy, he stepped inside and pulled the doors shut behind him. "Good morning, Miss Hollis."

He really could do this.

They'd pretended to be lovers before.

Now they would pretend they never had been.

Black coffee mug cradled against her chest, Virginia stared at him with the glazed wariness of a woman who feared that a man knew her secrets. "Can I get you anything, Mr. Allende?"

You.

He bit off the word, pulled off his jacket and tossed it onto the L-shaped sofa before he started for his desk. His head buzzed with thoughts of her. Her, smiling up at him from her place on his lap. She had an obsession with tidiness, and it showed. His office was pristine. She was a tidy little box, his Miss Hollis. Who would've known she'd be such a wanton in bed? So uninhibited? So sexy? So addictive?

"I hear you arrived home safely," he said, his groin stirring at the memory of their lovemaking. *Dammit, don't go there, man.*

"Yes, thank you." She flashed him one of those smiles that made his thoughts scramble. "And I caught up on my sleep a little."

"Excellent. Excellent."

His body clenched at her admission, for *he* hadn't had a wink of sleep since their return. He kept remembering her, innocent, cuddled up against him.

Diablos, he had never imagined he'd once again look at Monterrey with longing. Now he did.

He longed to be there with his assistant for another week where he knew exactly what to do with her.

Lips thinning in disgust at his own erotic thoughts, he took the coffee cup from her hands when she passed it to him and dismissed her with a wave. No use in delaying their parting. "That will be all. Thank you, Miss Hollis."

And with a painful wrench of mental muscle, he tore his eyes away and pushed her from his mind.

He had a business to take over.

* * *

Chicago felt different. The wind was the same, the noise, the traffic, and yet, it felt so different. She'd had to face Marcos at the office again today. Yesterday, their nonchalance toward each other had been so borderline pathetic she'd felt nauseated by the time she got home.

This morning, unable to stomach coffee, she made her way down the hall. The door to the extra bedroom where her father had been sleeping for the past couple of months was shut, and Virginia pressed her palm against it for a long moment, wondering if she should wake him. Let him know she was leaving for work. That everything had been taken care of and his debt absolved.

She decided she would call later instead and carried her small black duffel bag outside where the taxi waited, remembering Marcos's offer to give her father a job.

It had been easy then, to accept anything he'd wanted to give her. They'd been…involved. Now, Marcos Allende could calmly forget about it, as he'd forgotten the rest.

Worst of all was it hurt.

Even when she'd expected it.

As she stepped onto the amazingly busy Fintech nineteenth floor, Virginia hoped every employee would be in their usual flurries of movement and therefore too busy to notice she was fifteen minutes late.

But notice her they did.

The very moment her heels hit the carpet, a quiet spread throughout.

For the second day in a row, people glanced up from the copy machines. Behind their desks, heads lifted. The fact that everyone, everyone in the vast open space, knew and had probably discussed the fact that she had spent a week with Marcos in Monterrey became brutally evident. Deep inside, where all her fears were kept in a tight little bundle, she heard something.

They say she's his lover...

Had someone spoken that? Was she putting words and thoughts into their mouths because of her own regrets?

Dragging in a calming breath, she crossed the sea of cubicles, then went down the art-packed hallway. At the far end, to the right of the massive carved doors that led to Marcos's office, three identical rosewood desks stood. She slid in behind hers. The savvy Mrs. Fuller, who'd been with Marcos "longer than his mother has," was quick to make her way around her own tidy work place and greet Virginia. "He's very strange today," the older woman said, wide-eyed. "He smiled at me and he said 'thank you.'"

The words didn't diminish the kernel of fear settled in the pit of Virginia's stomach. If she so much as stepped out of her boundaries this week and onward…if she was fool enough to even remind him of Mexico…she dared not think of who would be sitting behind her desk next week.

"Then the deal must be going in his favor." Virginia attempted a teasing smile as she turned to get settled.

Lindsay, a young redhead near Virginia's age who'd also become her friend, drew up next to Mrs. Fuller. Their expressions were those of genuine excitement. "How was Mexico?" the older woman asked as Virginia sank into her chair and gazed at the top of her desk. A picture of her mother. A fake orchid. Her yellow markers sticking out of a silver can.

"Was it hot? I hear it's sweltering this time of year," Mrs. Fuller insisted. Virginia hadn't seen the woman yesterday since they'd reached Fintech later than normal.

"Yes," Virginia said, having no other answer to give a woman who was known through the entire building as levelheaded and kind.

As Mrs. Fuller's concerned gray eyes bored into the top of Virginia's head, she wished she could have been spared this encounter with even more fervor than she'd wished to avoid her last one with the dentist.

"He's been gazing out the window all morning, and with so much to do, that is so unlike him," Lindsay confessed under her cinnamon-scented breath. "And he asked me where you were."

Virginia was spared having to reply when the phones began their usual music. Struck as though by lightning, both Lindsay and Mrs. Fuller were spurred to action. They jumped behind their desks and began tackling the calls.

Ignoring the telephone ringing equally obnoxiously on her desk, Virginia tucked the duffel into the nook under the computer. She would not, could not, think of his mood meaning anything. Their deal would be over soon, after the Fintech dinner, and they would forget Mexico. He had promised it would not affect her job.

Inspecting her drawers and taking out her personal notepad and the colored clips she'd bought in a burst of secretarial enthusiasm, Virginia felt her throat close at the sudden memory of her mother. That hopeful light always in her eyes. Her warm, caring smile. She had always had a saying to cheer Virginia up. Would she have one for Virginia today? One about there always being something better out there? Better than Marcos?

"Miss Hollis, I hear you were out with the boss?"

She started in surprise. Fredrick Mendez, one of the youngest accountants, had propped his hip onto the corner of her desk and was eyeing her with a combination of amusement and mock despair.

"For a week," she stressed as she straightened in her chair.

"That's too much, Miss Hollis. Too much time without you. So, did you bring me a key chain?"

"Did you ask for one?"

"All right, at least show us some pictures," Fredrick

insisted. But when Virginia's usual friendly smile just would not come, he fell to his knees and clutched a hand to his chest. "Oh, Virginia, thy eyes shalt truth reveal—"

"Am I running a circus here, Mendez?"

The deep, clear voice, but most of all, the distinguished accent, struck Virginia like a cannon blast.

Her eyes flew to locate the source. Inches away, exiting the conference room and on his way to her, Marcos Allende was a sight to behold. Power and sophistication oozed from his every pore. His stride was slow and confident, his expression perfectly composed. And his every step kicked up her heartbeat. Six of his top lawyers followed.

Upon realizing who'd spoken, Fredrick's pale complexion turned in the space of a second to a tomato-red. He jumped to his feet and smoothed a hand along his polka-dot tie. "No, sir. I was just welcoming Virginia back on our behalf."

"Our?" He said the word as though Fredrick had no right to include himself in something he hadn't been invited to.

Turning to where Virginia sat with perfect poise behind the desk, Marcos thrust his hands into his pockets and silently contemplated her. "Don't you have work to do other than hound Miss Hollis," he said softly, and there was no doubt whom he addressed.

Fredrick took off with a mumbled "Yes, sir."

Without removing his eyes from her, he also said, "Brief me on the new stipulations when they're in."

In unison, the lawyers expressed their agreement and dispersed.

Without the buffer of their presence, there was nothing to pry those jealous black eyes from hers, no shield from the scorching possessiveness flickering in their depths.

Suddenly breathless, Virginia wondered if the blouse she wore today might be too white, or a little sheer? If her skirt was too short, her hair too unruly, the silver hoop earrings inappropriate for Fintech?

Meanwhile Marcos was the epitome of the worldly businessman.

He filled his black Armani like it had been tailor-made for those broad, square shoulders, which tapered down to his lean waist and narrow hips.

God! She could not believe the dark, breathtaking creature before her was her lover from Mexico.

Suddenly, as their gazes held, their eyes screaming with something dark and sinful, Virginia was certain the entire room thought she had slept with him. *They say she's his lover...*

Please, God, let no one ever know.

"Marcos," she said, moderating her tone. "I'm sorry I'm late, but I—"

Hands planted on the desk, Marcos stretched his arms out and in a single fluid move leaned forward. As his face neared her, Virginia saw Mrs. Fuller's eyes turn to saucers, and Lindsay almost fell back in her chair.

When the tip of his nose almost touched hers, she could focus on nothing else but six feet three inches of Marcos Allende. He ducked his head.

"Do you remember our deal?"

The murmur couldn't have been heard by anyone else. But she felt as if the clock, the world, stopped.

The feel of his breath on her face sent a torrent of warmth through her singing veins. "Yes, of course, I remember."

He leaned back a bit, regarding her as though he expected the same illumination he seemed to have experienced to have struck her, too. "After-work hours were included, weren't they?"

She couldn't explain the thrill she experienced, this inspiring and overwhelming happiness. He was asking for more, more from her, and not until this moment when she had his full attention had she realized how thirsty she'd been for it. "They were. Why do you ask? Is it that you need some assistance?"

His smile, slow in reaching completion, was meltingly sexy. "I do."

They say she's his lover...

She was plunging into a bottomless pit where surely there was nothing but heartache, and still, her blood was thrilling in her veins. "I'm always happy to be of assistance."

He gazed directly at her—the intent in his eyes unmistakable. "Be certain you present yourself at my apartment this evening. There's much to do."

She flushed beet-red, and scribbled in a yellow Post-it, *Is this what I think it is?*

He read it and tucked the note into his jacket, not before stroking her thumb with his, and sent her a look of such emotion and longing she almost wept. "Six p.m. sharp, Miss Hollis. I'm afraid it's an all-nighter."

He'd already started for his office when she blurted, "I can handle all-nighters."

"Good. This one's particularly hard."

When the doors closed shut behind him, whispers erupted, and Mrs. Fuller jumped to her feet and raced toward her in a flurry of mortification.

"Virginia. Please don't tell me this is what I think it is."

Heart pumping irregularly, Virginia grabbed her notepad. "I'd better go. The sales projections start in a few minutes and Marcos will want my notes." Oh, God, they had seen and heard all that, hadn't they?

Virginia, like putty in his hands. Marcos, suggesting she go to his place to...to...behave wickedly.

But the woman caught her by the shoulders and clenched tight with her fists, her face stricken. "Oh, sweetie, please say it isn't so!"

"Mrs. Fuller," Virginia said in a placating voice, patting

one of her hands for good measure. "I don't know what you mean, but there is nothing going on here, *nothing!*"

"Yes, there is. I've seen the way you look at him. You're a sweet young girl, an innocent little lamb, and Marcos is…a wolf! He's emotionally detached and you can't possibly—"

Virginia turned her head to hide her blush only to catch half the office staring at them. But Lindsay was smiling in glee behind her desk and sticking her thumbs up as though Virginia had just won the lottery.

Lowering her voice to a whisper, Virginia confessed, "I can handle wolves. I can handle a pack of them, I promise you. And this is nothing like what you think."

"Vee. Sweet, sweet Vee." Mrs. Fuller's hands trembled when she framed her cheeks between them. "I adore Marcos like a son. He has been a kind boss to me, and when my poor Herbert died…" She sighed, then shook her perfectly coiffed head and got back on track. "But he is not the kind of man a woman like you needs. There hasn't been a single woman in his history he's kept around for more than a month. You'll end up with a broken heart and even lose your job."

That her last comment struck a nerve was a given.

"I'm not losing my job for anything." Virginia forced a smile to her face and much needed courage into her heart. She wanted him. She wanted him so bad she had to have him, would seduce and remind him. "He's my boss, and he wants me to assist him, and so I will. Please don't worry, Mrs. Fuller, or your heartburn will act up. I'll be fine. And be sure everyone, *everyone* knows there's nothing going on here."

But even as she stepped into the projection room, she couldn't help wondering how well they'd be able to hide it for as long as it lasted.

And what would happen to her when it was really, truly finished.

Nine

After the longest work day of his entire life, and one during which he'd gotten exasperatingly little work done, Marcos arrived home to find her waiting in his living room.

Of course. His assistants had his key code—why shouldn't she be here?

With the sun setting behind her, her feet tucked under her body on the couch, and a book spread open on her lap, Virginia Hollis was a welcoming sight.

When he stepped out of the elevator that opened into the penthouse, she came to her feet, her hands going to her hair—to her rich, curly black hair, which was deliciously tousled as though she'd been running her fingers through it all day.

He fisted his hands at his sides, his mouth going dry. Good God. She wore drawstring pants and a button-up shirt with little ice cream cones. The colorful, almost childish pattern was also stamped all across the pajama pants. And on her, that weathered, warm-looking thing was the sexiest garment he'd ever had the pleasure of gazing upon.

He hadn't intended to sleep with her. Or had he? He'd wanted to see her, damn it. And now he could hardly believe what she was so obviously offering to him.

When he finally spoke, his voice came out rougher than he'd anticipated. "Have a good day?"

She set her book on the side table. Nodded. Then, "You?"

God, this was so domestic he should be climbing back into the elevator right about now. And getting away from there as fast as he could.

Why didn't he?

Because his hands itched to touch her. His guts felt tight and he was hot and hard with wanting her. He'd wanted to drag her into his office today, feel his way up her little skirt, kiss that mouth until her lips were bright red. He couldn't stay away, had now determined he was a fool to.

She wanted him, too.

Removing his jacket, he draped it across the back of a chair, nodding, as well.

"I brought my notes," she said quickly. "Just in case."

He gazed into eyes that were green and bottomless, and slowly advanced. "Good. Notes are important," he offered in return, and because he had missed the enticing, arousing sight of her all day, he gruffly added, "What else did you bring me, Miss Hollis?"

The soft smile that appeared on her lips trembled. Her hands smoothed her pajamas all along her hips and his eyes greedily swept up and down the length of her. "I like that… thing you're wearing." More than that, he was warming up to the idea of tearing it off her and licking her like vanilla ice cream.

"Thank you." She signaled at his throat. "I—I like your tie."

He wrenched it off, tossed it aside, then closed the space

between them. "Come here," he said quietly, wrapping an arm around her waist and drawing her flat against his body. "Why are you so shy all of a sudden?"

She set her hands lightly on his shoulders, barely touching him. "I—I don't know. I shouldn't have slipped into my pajamas."

Lust whirled inside him. She had a way of staring at him with those big eyes, like he was something out of this world. And she felt soft and womanly against him, her scent teasing his lungs as he buried his face in her hair. "I've wanted this, Virginia. God, how I've wanted this."

As she tipped her head back to him, he covered her lips with his.

Employing every ounce of experience and coaxing power at his disposal, he began to feast on that little mouth, drink of her honey.

Hesitantly she dipped her tongue into his mouth and a pang of longing struck in his core at how sweet she tasted, how entirely she succumbed and fitted her body to his.

In his need, he didn't hear himself, the way his voice turned hoarse with longing as he spoke to her, cupping the back of her head gently. *Delicioso...besame...dame tu boca...*

She tasted of warmth and hunger, and responded like a woman who'd thought of him all day—wanted him all day.

Just as he had thought of ways of devouring her, too.

The kiss went, in the space of three seconds, from a hard quest to a need that left no room for finesse. While he took thirsty sips of her mouth, his hands went places, one to cup a plump buttock, the other to work on her shirt.

Her eager hands tugged his shirt out of the waistband of his pants and slipped inside, making him groan when her cool, dry palms caressed his chest up and down.

He imagined lifting her, wrapping her legs around him and taking her, and she jumped as though she were thinking the same thing, kissing him like no woman had ever kissed him before. She curled one shapely leg around him, and his hands went to his zipper.

"Damn." He halted, then set her slowly on her feet. Restless, as he drew back, he rubbed the straining muscles at the back of his neck.

They were breathing hard and loud.

Her hand flew up to cover her moist, glistening lips. "I… I'm sorry. I didn't mean to bite you."

That little bite had made him want to bite her back, in every place imaginable. Damn. He rubbed his face with both hands, his blood thrumming in his body. He'd undone three buttons of her pajama top, and the flesh of one breast threatened to pop out.

Marcos regarded the creamy flesh while an overwhelming urge to dip his fingers inside the cotton and weigh that globe in his hand made him curl his fingers into his palm.

"Marcos?"

He jerked his eyes away, stared at the top of her head. "I had a long day." *And I thought of nothing but this moment.*

He'd been out of his mind with jealousy at the sight of her flushed cheeks, that clown Mendez begging at her feet. How many men had stared at her, wanted her, like Marcos did?

Oblivious to the rampant storms of his thoughts, Virginia followed him down the hall and into the bedroom. He was a mass of craving and thirst and he'd never felt so perilously close to losing control before.

Crossing the length of the room, he braced a hand on the window and gazed out at the city. If she ever dared make a fool of him…if she ever dared so much as look at another man while she was with him…

"Marissa was after me for years."

A quiet settled, disturbed by the rustle of her clothes as she moved around. "I'm sorry."

Yes. Well.

So was he.

Such humiliation, the way she'd played him. "I didn't know my father wanted her," he said, unable to conceal the disgust in his voice, "until they were already...involved."

When he turned, she was standing by the bathroom door. She'd grabbed a brush and was pensively running it through her hair. The lights shone on the satin mass.

Entranced, Marcos watched the curls spring back into place after a pass, and he wanted to plunge his fingers through that hair and wrap it in his hands.

"Don't do that."

She stopped. It took him a moment to realize the hoarse, ragged plea had come from him. She lowered her arm.

"Do what?"

The cotton molded to her chest, rose and dipped in the most attractive places. Aware of how hard he was, how hot under his clothes, he feared his own instincts when she set the brush on the nightstand and directed her full attention on him.

"I'm not Marissa," she said, coming toward him.

He liked how candid she was. How she smiled with her eyes. How she walked. Talked. No, she was not Marissa.

Getting a grip of his thoughts, he shook his head. "I didn't say that." But it would be worse with her. If she ever hurt him. Deceived him. Betrayed him. He'd never trusted so fully, had never felt so many things at once.

"Marcos," she said softly. Her eyes were examining his stiff shoulders, the stony mask on his face, as she halted before him. He was shocked at the raw emotion shining in her eyes. Not only desire. But tenderness. Concern. Caring.

Caring that tugged at some little strings inside him.

Caring that begged him to care, too.

Damn.

She was his lover. He had a right to touch her, take her,

come with the pleasure of being inside her. It was all this was. Lust.

Lust lust lust.

"Never—" He could hardly speak as he lifted a hand to her silky, raven hair. She gasped at the touch, went very still.

"—ever—" he said gruffly, and tangled his fingers, fisted that lovely hair in his hand, using his knuckles to push her head up to where his lips waited "—lie to me."

He took her gasp, rubbed her lips farther apart, and traced their seam with his tongue. They were flavored with toothpaste and mint, and they were wet and hot. "Never lie to me with this mouth."

He licked into her, and she moaned. "I love this tongue, never lie to me with this tongue."

She inhaled a ragged breath and his tongue followed its path inside her, searching deep. In one instant her hands curled wantonly around his wrists, went higher up his arms, opening around the width of his biceps. Her fingers bit into his shirt and skin.

It was instinct, need, something fierce he couldn't understand, that pressed him to slam her back against the wall, take her, make her his mistress. It was so consuming to him, this passion, he was afraid if he followed it, he would break her apart. Or maybe he would break apart, feeling this—for her. With her.

Was this what his father had felt for Marissa? Was this why he'd given everything for her, everything to her? Let her slowly finish him off...so long as she kept on kissing him, looking at him, touching him like this?

When a cell phone rang, he tore his mouth away and she fumbled in a purse she'd left by the nightstand to answer. "Yes?"

His hand flicked the buttons of his shirt as she walked away and softly spoke into the receiver.

His heart rammed into his ribs, his blood a thick, terse boil in his veins. He was losing his head—and he didn't like it. He considered retiring to his study to work, put distance between them. No. No. He wanted her. He walked forward, shrugging off his shirt.

"Yes…yes, I didn't want to wake you…and yes, I'll see you…um…I'm working late and I don't know how long I'll be—" Silence. A soft, very soft, "Good night."

She came back, smiled.

"You're spending the night," he said, rendering it a statement when in fact he wanted confirmation. She was seducing him—in her pajamas, brushing her hair, staring with those green, green eyes.

Gritting his teeth against the flaring lust, he readied himself briskly, his erection springing free.

He grabbed her hand and put it on himself. If that didn't tell her, show her, how far gone he was, then he didn't know anything anymore. Still, he recalled Monterrey, all those nights with her, the days, and gruffly spoke. "You're staying the night here—with me."

She nodded and met his gaze, her eyes bright and fiery. She stroked his chest with soft, fluttering hands, dragging her lips across his jaw, his chin. "I want you in me, Marcos."

A primal hunger had overtaken his mind, his senses, until he felt as instinctive as an animal. An animal tantalized by the nearness of his mate. "You came to seduce me, didn't you? You like being at my beck and call. You came to please me, service me."

Smiling, she stepped back, and her hands went to her shirt, and Marcos watched as she began to unbutton it farther. Her fingers pulled another button free, then the next, and his eyes flicked up to hers. "I'm crazy about you," he rasped.

Virginia didn't seem to hear the truth in his words, the worry they carried. He felt out of control, and he didn't like it.

"C-can I try something with you?" she asked hesitantly, easing her top off her shoulders.

He nodded, mute with desire and anticipation.

"Would you stay still, please?" she asked.

"What are you going to do to me, Miss Hollis?" he asked in a guttural voice. He fisted his hands at his sides, watching her hands like a man about to die under them. He stood utterly still, admiring her flesh as she revealed it. His voice was barely audible, his eyes on the gentle curves of her breasts as she stepped out of her pants and at last stood as naked as he.

"Just don't move, okay?"

So he waited, his chest expanding on each breath. She trembled when she stepped closer. "Can I touch you?"

He swallowed thickly. "Please."

He sucked in a breath when she set her hand on his chest and began kissing his neck, his ear, his jaw. His breathing became a wild thing. He was motionless as her hands began to roam down his chest. She hesitated at his waist.

His jaw clamped, his nostril flared, when she wrapped her hand around him.

"Is this okay?"

Ecstasy surged through him in a tidal wave. His breath made a strange whistle. "Yes."

"Do you want—"

His head fell, forehead against hers. "Just keep touching me."

She eased her fingers between his parted thighs, to gently cup him in her palm. She began to rub.

He hurt under her stroking hand. His mind spun with images of her and him, losing themselves in his bed like he'd wanted to. His hands idle at his sides, he softly, so softly, said, "You're not pregnant, are you, *amor?*"

She tensed for a moment, and he frowned. He reached down and pried her hand away.

"Are you? We didn't use protection the first time, and I'd like to know if there were consequences."

Ignoring him, she took his shoulders in her little hands and urged him down on the mattress. "The only consequence is this, Marcos. Me. Wanting more."

He sat there, on his bed, like a man in hypnosis, and watched her straddle him.

They kissed.

Marcos was dying with pleasure, his body rocking as he feasted from her lips, lips that were soft and warm against his, lips that were wide open for his tongue to search in deep, so deep. Her sex cradled his hardness, her legs twined around him as tight as her arms while he ran his hands up her sides, into her hair, groaning at the way she whimpered his name. Marcos. All he could say was, "Virginia." Oh, Virginia.

He pulled roughly at her hair.

"Why?" His voice was a cragged sound.

"I…I don't know what you're talking about."

"Why do you look at me like this? What are you playing at?"

Watching him through heavy, sooty lashes, she kissed his nipples, his abs. She was smiling—teasing him with her teeth. Her tongue. Driving him out of his mind. Out. Of. His. Mind. "Must it be a game for you to enjoy it, Mr. Allende?" she purred. "Must we play at another pretense for you to let me in?"

He snatched her hair to halt her wandering mouth, suddenly trembling with thirst for not only her body, but for something else. Something he'd always, always, seen and sensed and tried to grasp in her eyes. "Are you trying to drive me insane?" he demanded.

She pulled free and lovingly cupped his jaw, kissing him softly on the lips. "I'm trying to make you remember."

He framed her face, engulfing it between both hands, and before he took her lips in the hard, hot way his screaming soul demanded, growled, "I'm trying to *forget*."

Ten

"With luck, the negotiations will advance, then my lawyers will fly down to…" Marcos trailed off as Virginia strolled into his office the next morning, bringing those long legs with her, her raven curls bouncing with each tiny step her tapered, knee-length skirt allowed.

She stopped to check discreetly on the coffeemaker—directly in Marcos's line of vision. A bolt of lust arrowed to his groin. *Marcos, oh, please, more, more.*

Her gasps of last night echoed in his head.

This morning they'd gone at each other like—hell, like two wild animals—before they'd separately headed for the office. He'd asked her to buy something special to wear to the Fintech dinner, to splurge. She hadn't seemed to be impressed. He wanted to please her, to give her something, and yet the only thing Virginia Hollis seemed to want was him.

Damn, he was totally taken—in a way not even Marissa had taken him before. Virginia's moans, her body, writhing against his, with his. It maddened him. Heated him. Excited him. Appalled him.

Aware of the abrupt silence in the vast carpeted space, a quiet that magnified her noises as she innocently fiddled with spoons and cups, Marcos jerked his eyes back to the open proposal and tapped his Montblanc pen against the sales projection chart. He cleared his throat. "Where was I?"

"Allende. Marissa Galvez. Negotiations," Jack said, sprawling on a chair across from his desk.

"Of course." He dropped his pen and lounged back in his high-backed leather chair, stacking his hands behind his head. He met the Texan's electric-blue stare. "As soon as negotiations take on a serious note I'll call in the cavalry and we—"

Virginia leaned down to refill Jack's coffee, and her proximity to the man made Marcos's jaw clamp in anger. He felt ridiculously jealous. Yes, *diablos,* he was totally had.

"We'll close," he finished tightly, and slapped the proposal shut. She had no idea, no idea.

Or was she doing this on purpose?

The sunlight that streamed through the floor-to-ceiling windows of the Art Deco building shone over her loose hair. But she was frowning, he realized then, somehow worried, and the noose tightened around his neck.

"Miss Hollis," he said. Last night's seduction? That ridiculously simple but mouthwateringly sexy outfit? Was all this some sort of plan of hers?

She spun, shocked as if from out of her thoughts. "Yes?"

He reclined in his seat and crossed his arms. She was pale this morning. Guilt assailed him. He hadn't let her sleep much, had he? "I was telling Mr. Williams about Monterrey."

She spared a fleeting glance at Jack's lean, jeans-clad figure, and he shot her one of his disarming grins. "How nice," she said absently, and lifted the glass coffeepot to Marcos. "More coffee?"

He shook his head, searching for warm emotions in her expression, all of which usually showed on her face as she experienced them. There were none this morning either.

Her desperation last night, her need, her wanting…he'd felt them all. He'd throbbed with every one of them. Today she looked distant. Why?

I'm not Marissa…

His body clenched. No. No. She was not. Virginia was even more dangerous.

"Marissa Galvez is flying in this weekend," he then offered. Why did he offer this information? Because deep down, her words continued to pull at his heartstrings. *Mend Allende. Make it gold again.*

Did he dare? Did he even want to?

"Oh. How nice. I'm sure she'll be more agreeable this time."

The reply was so noncommittal and so lacking in generosity of feeling that he frowned. When the carved oak doors shut behind her, Jack murmured, "I see."

"Hmm?" Marcos took a long, warm gulp of coffee.

"I see," Jack repeated, propping a shiny lizard boot atop his knee.

He drank again, savoring the scent, the warmth of her coffee. Was she sick? "Mine, Jack."

"Yes, I see."

Marcos grunted. Jack wouldn't even begin to comprehend the pain of his sexual frustration. The looks she gave him— tenderness, desire, admiration, respect. When would he tire of her? He'd expected to tire within the week, and yet it had been over a month now. He could not get enough of her. Was she tiring of him? Good God, was that a possibility?

His friend's dry chuckle wafted in the air. "I assume your

plan worked with Marissa. She no doubt thought you were taken with Virginia."

Marcos pushed to his feet and headed to the wide bay window, his coffee cradled against his chest. "My bid has been rejected, Jack."

Silence.

His chest felt cramped with anger, frustration. "She controls the board and somehow made sure they declined."

"Ahh. Then I assume we're getting hostile? Why are we even discussing Allende if not?"

"We are getting hostile." He spun on his heel. "If we could."

Jack made a scratching noise. "Meaning?"

Damn Marissa and her sneaky ways. Marcos had discussed for the tenth time the purchase of her shares, and she still held off selling to him. In the back of her warped mind, she no doubt believed she could bend Marcos like she'd bent his father—who else would save her company but the son? What else would ensure her continued ownership but marriage?

No. She wouldn't get away with it, not anymore, and yet even in the midst of this surety, the fact that a woman would have power over his future made his blood boil.

"Meaning I must pressure her to sell, Williams. She's flying to Chicago this weekend—I invited her to the Fintech dinner. As long as she owns the majority of the shares, a hostile takeover is close to impossible. She must sell, and she must sell to *me*."

"Pardon my slowness, but you invited her to Chicago?"

"I want Allende, Jack."

"You want to kill it," Jack added.

Marcos absently scanned the busy sidewalks below. "And if I don't?"

Jack's usually fast retorts seemed to fail him this time.

Marcos's mind raced with every new discovery he'd made about Hank Hollis today. The man had lost his way—not unusual after the heartache of losing a beloved wife, Marcos supposed. But he'd been visiting AA meetings, seemed to be struggling to get his life back on track. He'd been a risk-taker on the job, and ruthless when it came to disciplining those beneath him. Years ago, he'd pushed his chain of stores, every single one of them, to be better, more efficient, and the admirable numbers he'd produced for them didn't lie.

"What if I told you," Marcos began, "that I'd save Allende. What if I told you I've found a man to do the dirty work— one who's driven and who's thirsty to prove something to someone?" *Maybe he'd enjoy coming to Mexico.*

"Marcos, I'm on your board as a professional, not as a friend. The same reason you're on mine."

"Of course."

And Virginia would be free of the pain her father had been causing. She would be free to be with him. Marcos.

"Well, as both, I have to tell you," his friend continued in a thickening drawl. "It's that damned prodigal apple. Any opportunity man *or* woman has to get a bite out of it, ten out of ten times, they *will*."

"Amen."

"I'm serious."

He swung around. "All right. So we get to play gods and kick them out of the kingdom. New management, new rules, no thieving, no blackmailing, no mafia."

"I agree. But who's heading new management?"

His eyebrows furrowed when he realized there was no clear space on his desk to set down his cup of coffee. The last fifteen years of his life—hard, busy years—were in this desk. A heavy oak Herman Miller, the first expensive designer piece he'd bought after his first takeover. It was old—he was superstitious—and it was a keeper and it was *packed*. The surface contained no photo frames, no figurines, nothing but a humming computer and piles and piles of papers that would later go into a roomful of file cabinets. He planted the mug over a stack of papers. "You are," he flatly repeated.

Jack's gaze was razor sharp. "Me."

His lips flattened to a grim, hard line as he nodded. "You. And a man I consider may be hungry to prove himself."

Jack hooked his thumb into his jeans pocket. "Go on."

Marcos folded into his chair, grabbed a blue pen and twirled it in his hand as he contemplated. "I negotiate for Marissa's shares and agree to allow her to stay in the company temporarily, while you and Hank Hollis will get the ropes and start a new team."

"Hank Hollis." His eyes narrowed to slits. "You're not serious."

He smiled the very same smile the Big Bad Wolf might have given Little Red Riding Hood. "Oh, but I am."

Hank Hollis would redeem himself in Virginia's eyes, right along with Allende. Marcos would make sure of it.

If Virginia had had any worries regarding her poor emotional state for the past twenty-four hours—other than having stupidly, blindly, foolishly fallen in love with Marcos Allende—she now had more proof for concern.

Pale-faced, she walked into the long tiled bathroom to stare for the twentieth time at the sleek white predictor test—the third one she'd used today—sitting next to the other two on the bathroom sink.

Pink.

Pink.

Pink.

All three were *pink*.

Of course. Because when it rained, it *poured*. Because when one thing went terribly wrong, *everything* went wrong. Because when your world collapsed on top of your head, really, *nothing* you could do would stop the crash.

Letting go her breath while the sting of tears gathered

in her eyes, she leaned back on the white tiles lining the bathroom walls and slowly, weakly, dragged her body down its length until she was sprawled on the floor.

She was very, undeniably pregnant.

With Marcos's baby.

There could be no more solid proof of her naïveté. She'd walked into his penthouse one evening with little in the way of emotional shields, without protection and without standing a chance. She might as well have torn out her heart and offered it in her hand. What had she expected would come out of it? Of all those pretend kisses, the laughter, the moments she could not forget?

Did she think he would say, "Step into my life, Virginia, I want you in it forever?"

Did she think he would say, "Marry me, *amor,* where have you been all my life?"

Oh, God. Covering her face with her hands, she considered what he would do when he found out about this.

A vision of him suggesting something bleak made the bile hitch up in her throat. She choked it back and shook her head, wrapping her arms around her stomach, speaking to herself at first, then below at the tiny little being growing inside her.

"I have to tell him." And when a wealth of maternal love surged through her, she ran a hand across her stomach and determinedly whispered, "I have to tell him."

Maybe she was more of a gambler than she'd thought. He might be furious, and he could turn her away, but still she found herself righting her hair and her clothes in front of the mirror, preparing for battle. Gathering up all the tests in the plastic bag from the drugstore and stuffing it in her purse, she once again headed back to Marcos's office.

She knocked three times. "Mr. Allende?"

His friend Jack seemed to have left already, and now, as she entered, Marcos pulled up a file from a stack on his desk, studied it, set it back down, rubbed his chin then finally stared at her.

"Close the door," he said, all somber.

She couldn't read that expression. She tried for flippant and saucy. "I'm under orders to spend a lot of money on anything I fancy."

"Are you now." He frowned. "Who is this man who orders you around? Seems to me you should run far and fast away from him, Miss Hollis."

The unexpected smile he shot her made her grin. "Did I mistakenly put whiskey in your coffee?" she asked, nearly laughing.

His eyes sparkled. "You might want to sit on my lap while you investigate."

She approached his desk, thinking about the baby, his baby, growing inside her body. "I was wondering if you were busy tonight. I'd like for us to talk."

"Virginia." He leaned forward and gently lowered her to his lap. "You have me. I'm at your disposal every night."

"Marcos…" The words *I want more* faltered in her throat.

He must have misinterpreted her concern, for Marcos dropped his hands to his sides and sighed. "Nobody knows about us, Virginia, please don't fret. I'm trying to keep things running smoothly. My office won't be abuzz with gossip, I won't allow it."

Gossip. Could everyone be gossiping? Whispering? Her stomach clenched in dread. "But you keep stealing touches and people are noticing." That much was true. And soon… how would she hide a pregnant belly?

Marcos boldly raked her figure with his gaze, reclined in his seat and said, "Then I should give these people something more to do."

She blinked, then realized he was teasing her, and she

forced her lips into a smile. But it wasn't funny. Soon they'd notice she was pregnant. Soon she'd be waddling around.

He scraped two fingers across his chin as he studied her. "You look worried."

She couldn't do this here—she felt as emotionally stable as a compass gone berserk. "Maybe the Fintech dinner isn't such a good idea," she suggested.

"It was part of our arrangement, Miss Hollis."

She swallowed and snatched up his files, deciding to postpone this for…tonight. Tomorrow. Never. "The projection room is ready."

"You have your notes?"

"Of course. And yours."

He stormed down the long hallway with her, and as people smiled at her in a "Yay, you" kind of way, her unease grew tenfold.

During the meeting, Virginia tried to concentrate on the images flicking on the projection screen. Sales charts with numbers. But Marcos sat unbearably close.

"Is it the dinner?"

She stiffened. "What?"

"Why you're worried. Is it?"

"I… No."

"The outfit? You're afraid you won't find one you like?"

She shook her head. "No."

He leaned forward. He tapped her pad. "Reading your notes here. 'Colorful charts.' Very observant, Miss Hollis. Now why are you worried? Tell me."

She attempted to take more notes but her mind was elsewhere.

"Now, you see the hedge fund study we just passed?" he said when she, apparently, was not going to talk. "We lost a little, but the fund was heavily invested in metals, as well, and the gold price has been rising, so we closed with a positive number nonetheless."

"Yes, I understand. You lose some and win some. Like... gambling."

He chuckled. "Indeed. It's all a game of risk, Miss Hollis. You weigh the benefits against the risk. And decide how to move forward. You may lose, but at least you played the game. Or you may win...and the prize is exquisite."

She did the exercise in her mind. Risk—her job, her self-respect, her body to a pregnancy, her heart...no, it was too much to bear to even think it. Benefit—save her father, who didn't deserve saving, and share a wonderful week with the most wonderful, wonderful man.

She would have liked to think that if she remained cool and aloof, she would not be risking anything. If she behaved like her usual self, there was no reason the office would speculate. If she ignored his scent, his lips and his eyes, and the fact that she'd fallen in love with him, then she could settle for the benefits. Eventually.

Except already, there was a child.

Their child.

And she wouldn't be able to hide his growing presence much longer.

Eleven

"That's supposed to be a dress?"

She sensed Marcos at the doorway, actually heard a whoosh of air as though the sight of her had stunned him, and she continued tugging the fabric down her hips, her legs, carefully avoiding his gaze as she stepped into it.

"Hello? Fintech dinner? You said buy something to dazzle them. Splurge. Buy the dress of your dreams." *Before I blow up like a balloon and have your bastard baby.*

"The key word was *something*," Marcos growled, "That is nothing."

In the middle of his spacious, carpeted closet, standing before a mirror in a satiny green dress that was making her smile and Marcos frown, Virginia flicked her hair and scoffed at his words.

His glare deepened. "I'm not taking you looking like this."

"Excuse me?"

"I'm serious."

"This is all I have, I spent a fortune on it. You told me—"

"I don't care what I said. I am saying right now, I'm not taking you…into a party with half the city…in that…that scrap."

"Don't be absurd, it's perfect."

A muscle ticked in the back of his jaw. He grabbed her arm and pulled her close. "Do you have any idea what a man thinks of…at the sight of you in that dress?"

"I thought it was elegant, but seductive, if I'd thought it was—"

He grabbed her by the waist and pressed her to him, and the shock of feeling every lean, hard inch of him against her made her gasp. "He thinks of peeling it off with his teeth. He imagines your breasts without the satin over them, and he imagines you, wrapped all around him, with your hair all across his bed."

Her bones melted inside of her.

Marcos, in a tuxedo, was easily the sexiest thing she'd ever seen. She wanted to beg him to peel the dress off her fevered body with his teeth and to wrap her limbs around him with his weight crushing her on the bed.

She tipped her face back, remembering an entire month of making love to Marcos.

In the morning. At midnight. Evenings when he got home. Coupled with those memories, she had others of him with the morning paper spread across the table, coffee cup in hand. Him shaving. Him taking a shower. With her.

She could not remember a thought that didn't make her tummy constrict.

Feeling her thighs go mushy, she stroked her fingers up his cleanly shaven jaw. "You're so handsome," she whispered.

His eyes roved her face, cataloging her flushed cheeks, the telling glaze in her heavy-lidded eyes. "I want you." His hands tightened, and she became excruciatingly aware of his erection biting into her pelvis. His eyes were so hot they were like flames. "I want you every minute of every godforsaken day and it's making me grumpy."

When she gasped, he let her go. A muscle flexed in the back of his jaw as he clenched hard. He shook his head. "Damn."

It took an effort to stand on her own two feet while quietly nursing the sting of his rejection, but she thrust her chin up with a little dignity. "This is all I have to wear."

God, she had turned into a wanton. She only wanted to touch and touch and touch him. To be kissed until her breath left her.

Flushing, she pulled open the carved-wood closet doors and began to rummage through the shoe rack.

Marcos paced the area and raked a hand through his hair. "The pearls have to go."

She straightened, a hand coming to stroke a smooth pebble at her throat. Her father had stripped out every material memory of her childhood, of her mother, the life they'd once had. He'd pawned her mother's engagement ring. The pearl earrings to match the necklace she always wore. He'd sold off the nice clothes, even the locket they'd given Virginia as a little girl.

"Are they too old-fashioned?"

"They're not you."

He pulled out a box from a drawer, and she blinked. The box was sky-blue in color, with a silken white bow on top. As his long, tanned fingers tugged the edges of the bow and the shimmering ribbon unfurled in his hand, the unmistakable words *Tiffany & Co.* appeared.

Within seconds, he'd opened a velvet box and held up the largest, most dazzling diamond necklace Virginia had ever seen. Its sparkle was blinding. Its sheer magnificence just made her breath, her brain, her everything scatter.

The piece was worthy of old Hollywood, when the women

would wear their finest evening dresses and most impressive jewels for the night. A large, oval-shaped green pendant hung from rows and rows of large, brilliant diamonds that fell like curtains and lace in the most exquisite workmanship Virginia had ever set eyes on.

"I… It's lovely."

"It's yours."

She shook her head. "I can't."

But he stepped behind her and began to fasten it around her neck. His lips grazed the back of her ear as his fingers worked on the clasp. When he was done, he turned her around to face him. "You're mine to spoil. It's yours. Tomorrow. Next week, next month, next year. It's yours."

This was him, announcing, in a way, that he was sleeping with her. No one who saw her would have any doubt. Why would he do this tonight? Why would she allow it?

She experienced a horrible urge to touch him, an even more intense one to ask him to hold her, but that would only bring the tears gathering in the back of her eyes to the forefront. She didn't understand these tears, or the desperate sensation of having lost before she'd even fought for him.

Her eyes dropped to his chest as she felt a blush creep up her cheeks. His cross lay over his chest, glinting bright gold against the bronzed skin. His breath stirred the hair at the top of her head. The warmth of his body enveloped her.

His hands framed her jaw, lifting her face to his. "I bought you earrings and a bracelet, too."

As he seized her wrist with his long, tanned fingers, she watched the thick cuff bracelet close around her. Oh, God, no wonder mistresses were always so sexy and smiling, when all their men treated them just like this!

"I can't," she still said. Because it felt so wrong. So intimate. So personal. It made her mind race with thoughts she did not—should not—think of. She was lying to him, or at least, withholding something important.

And it felt so odd, the weight of the diamonds and the forest-green emerald on her. It felt like a chain around her neck—Marcos's chain on her. And her baby. And her future.

You're mine to spoil…

"I insist, Virginia," he sternly said, and drew her at arm's length to take in the visual.

Self-conscious, Virginia dropped her gaze and tugged at a loose curl on her shoulder. The dress hugged her body like a lover's embrace, the jewels refracted thousands of little lights and for the first time in her life Virginia felt like a fraud. A woman desperate to be anyone, anyone, that the man she loved could love.

"I don't know what to say."

His chuckle was full of arrogance, but it made her melt all the same. "Then get over here."

When he drew her close and kissed her with a passion that buckled her knees and had her clinging to his shoulders, she didn't say anything at all. But her mind screamed, "We're having a baby!"

"Marcos, I'd like to talk to you, tonight."

He fixed his powerful eyes on her, his face unreadable. He seemed to have forgotten about the dress, and she wondered if he'd been jealous. Marcos wasn't surrounded by the aura of relaxation of a man who'd spent an entire night feasting on his lover, but with the tension of one who wanted more. The air felt dense between them. "I have other plans for tonight," he admitted.

She could not even smile at that. "Still, I'd like for us to talk."

He cradled her face, forced her to meet his gaze. "What is it?"

The concern in his eyes, the gentleness in his voice, only made her crave his love with more intensity. She did not want to crave it with such intensity, did not want to feel the emptiness growing inside her, realizing she lacked his love at the same time as their baby grew bigger.

Their agreement was over once she accompanied him to the Fintech dinner. And maybe they would be over, too.

She drew in a tremulous breath. "After the party."

"All right," he said, smiling. "In fact, there's something I'd like to speak to you about, too."

Inside the lavishly decorated lobby of the glass-and-steel skyscraper smack in the center in Michigan Avenue, Marcos guided Virginia through the throng of people, nodding to a few. "That's Gage Keller, he's a developer. His company, Syntax, owns half of Las Vegas now. The young woman with him is his wife."

"Second, I presume?"

He grinned. "More like sixth."

He brought her around to where a group of men and women stood by a spectacular ten-foot-tall wine fountain. "The woman drowning in jewels over there is Irene Hillsborough; she owns the most extensive collection of Impressionist art in the States. Old money, very polite."

"Very snotty?" Virginia added when the woman lifted her head to stare at her then promptly glanced away.

An appreciative gleam lit up his eyes as he smiled down at her and patted her hand. "How perceptive."

"Allende." A bearded middle-aged man Marcos had presented her to just moments ago—Samuel…something— came back to slap his back. "Haven't seen much of Santos lately. What is that troublemaker up to?"

"I wouldn't know," Marcos said with a rather bored intonation, then uncharacteristically offered, "You can ask him later if he shows." He steered Virginia away, and an immediate image of Santos—surely gorgeous and bad, so bad—made her ask, "Santos is coming?"

"If only to be a pain in the ass, yes." He said it so decidedly, so automatically, her eyes widened in surprise.

He then urged her around, and a woman with silvering hair and an ecstatic look on her face was fast winding her way toward them.

"That would be Phyllis Dyer," he continued, "the director of donations and—"

"Marcos," the woman said, lightly laying her hand on his shoulder as she kissed one cheek, then the other. Her voice quivered with excitement. "Marcos, I can't thank you enough for your generosity. I heard from the Watkinson Center for Children today and they were all wondering why the early Christmas. It was so kind of you, as usual."

Marcos gave her a curt nod. He then brought Virginia forward. "May I present Virginia."

The woman's soft gray eyes went huge. "Oh, well, how lovely to meet you. I believe this is the first time I have had the pleasure of meeting one of Marcos's girls." To her, she leaned forward to whisper, "This one's a keeper, darling, if you know what I mean."

"Oh, I'm not his… I'm actually his—"

After a bit more small talk, Phyllis left with an encouraging pat on Virginia's shoulder, and Virginia ventured a glance at him. "Why didn't you tell her I was your assistant?"

Tucking her hand into the crook of his arm, he guided her toward the sweeping arched doors that led out into the terrace. He didn't answer her.

Stepping past an elegant trellis, he led her across the terrace, illuminated with flickering gas lanterns that lined the perimeter.

When he loosened his hold on her, Virginia stepped forward and leaned on a cement banister and gazed out at the fountain. A breeze stirred the miniature trees in the nearby planters, the chilly air making her flesh pebble with goose bumps.

Unconsciously, she rubbed her arms up and down, listening to the soft piano music audible through the speakers. Somehow, the notes couldn't completely mute the faint rustle of water.

She drew in a steadying breath. "Aren't you up for a speech soon?"

Through the corner of her eye, she followed his movements as he set his wineglass on the flat surface of a stone bench. "Yes."

She gasped at the feel of his hand, warm and strong, curling around hers, tugging her forward. In a haze, she found herself slowly but surely gravitating toward him, captivated by the play of moonlight on his features and the gentle, insistent pull of his hand.

"I want us to dance, and I had a feeling you'd say no if I asked you in there."

"Dance," she parroted, mesmerized.

He smiled. Manly appreciation sparkled in his eyes as he curled his arm around her waist and pulled her even closer. *"Te ves hermosa, ven aqui."*

Anything Marcos told her in Spanish Virginia did not understand, but she felt the words so deeply, as though he were telling her a secret her instincts knew how to decode.

Both arms enveloped her and their bodies met in a visceral move, seeking a fit of their own volition. Surrounded by the piano music, feeling the cool breeze on her skin beside the fountain, Virginia suddenly wondered if she would ever experience this again. Everything. What he made her feel. The flutters inside her when she became the sole focus of those pitch-black eyes.

"Marcos," she began to protest.

"Shh. One dance."

Her involuntary squirms only made him tighten his grip on her, press her closer, urge her to move against his tall, hard body in a very slow, sensual dance. He trailed one hand up her back and delved into her hair, his fingers caressing her scalp in a light, hypnotic massage.

His hands shifted on her back, splaying wide, keeping her flat against his solid length. Virginia remembered when they had been sweaty and hot and needing each other last night. She trembled at the memory and he tightened his hold on her. She knew, sensed, felt, that he also remembered.

His eyelids drooped suggestively as he ran his knuckles down her cheek. His lips hovered over her mouth and lightly skimmed side to side. "I can't wait to take you home with me."

A feeling unlike any other bloomed inside her. She trembled down to her knees as she fought to quell it, afraid of what would happen if she set it free.

"Take me home…like a stray?" she ventured. Was this the full-moon fever? Her hormones? She'd never thought love could feel like this. So total. So powerful.

Marcos let go a rich, delicious chuckle. "More like the loveliest treasure."

She guided her fingers up his taut, hard-boned face, not daring to hope that he might…

"What is it you wanted to tell me tonight? You said you wanted to speak with me, too?"

His smile didn't fade, but a soft tenderness lit up his eyes. "Can't you guess, *chiquita?*"

"Can you give me a hint?"

He nodded, calmly explained, "It's about us."

The tender but possessive way he held her, the warm, admiring way he gazed down at her, prodded her on. "Is there…an us?"

A tingle drummed up and down her body where they touched.

His eyes went liquid, hot with tenderness as he tipped her face back. "You tell me."

I'm pregnant with your baby. She could not say it, needed to know what he had to say first.

He stroked her cheek with one knuckle. "I know what a woman like you wants," he said softly. "I can't give it to you, Virginia, but I'd like…" He trailed off when they heard a sudden noise.

Virginia's stomach tumbled with the need to hear the rest. What had he meant to say? For a single disconcerting moment, she worried he'd sensed the sudden, alarming, fragile emotions she was struggling with and this made her even more determined to hide them.

Next she heard the echoing footsteps of someone approaching. Virginia trembled when Marcos released her, her heart gripping when she spotted Marissa. Her hair streamed behind her, and her smile was provocative. And suddenly Virginia felt very small and very pregnant.

To Marcos, with wry humor, Marissa handed her arm as though he'd asked her to dance, and slyly purred, "I hope I'm interrupting something."

Bad form. Bad, bad form.

Marcos couldn't make his proposition to Virginia here. *Diablos*—where was his head? On Allende? No, it was not even there, and Marcos was shocked at the discovery.

Somewhere during the past month…somewhere between a headache, when Virginia had smoothed his hair off his brow and "knew the perfect thing to take care of that headache" for him…somewhere between one morning and another, when they sipped coffee in silence…somewhere between the sheets, when he was lost inside of her in a way he'd never thought humanly possible…somewhere between one of her million kinds of smiles…somewhere between an exchange of files…something had happened.

Marcos had let down his guard. He'd allowed himself to trust a woman, fully and completely, in a way he'd sworn he'd never trust another human. He'd allowed her to filter his mind, his thoughts, to the point where his goals had shifted... shifted and shifted until he no longer knew if they were his or hers.

"I need your help."

Marissa's soft, pleading words registered out on the terrace, and yet his eyes followed Virginia's lovely figure as she glided back into the crowded room. He'd noticed the frustration in her jade-green eyes when she stepped away, saw her struggling to hold her temper in check. She was a curious one, his Virginia. No doubt she craved to know what he'd planned to say. He smiled to himself as she wound her way away from him, into the room, her bearing as regal as a queen's.

She was wearing the most amazing, breathtaking, heart-tripping dress he'd ever seen, and he was dying to take it off her.

"Should we talk inside?" he asked curtly, shifting his attention back to Marissa, who in turn was eyeing him speculatively.

"Of course."

He led her into the decorated space. An orchestra played. Couples danced in harmony to the tune. Amongst the round tables, people mingled.

Heading toward the conference hall at the south end of the lobby, they crossed the room. He greeted several acquaintances, nodded his head at a few more and kept a close eye on Virginia. Her hair fell down to cover part of her face. Her profile was exquisitely feminine, like a doll's.

Taking in her visage, he felt a slow, throbbing ache spread inside of him, and contrary to most of the aches she gave him, this one had nothing to do with physically wanting her.

When he secured Allende, he could mend it, and he could mend her father along with it. He could give her safety and peace and pride.

The intensity with which he wanted to give this to her shocked him to his core.

Whereas before Virginia Hollis had been something to be observed but not touched in his office, a Mona Lisa behind glass, she was more real to him now than his own heartbeat. She was flesh and bones and blood. She was woman.

His fierce attraction to her, kept tightly on a leash, had spiraled out of control the moment he'd put his lips right over hers, or perhaps the moment she'd called him and Marcos had known, in his gut, he was going to have her.

Fierce and unstoppable, the emotions raged within him now, under his muscles, and the urge to cross the room and sweep her into his arms became acute.

With an effort, he tore his eyes away from Virginia, tried to steady the loud beat of his heart.

A man, notoriously tall, athletic and dark, with a smile that had been known to break a woman's heart or two, caught his attention.

Santos Allende was the only person in the world who would not wear a tie to a black-tie event. As he ambled over, he lifted a sardonic brow at the same time he lifted his wineglass in a mock toast. "Brother."

Marcos nodded in greeting, drained his drink, and introduced Marissa and Santos even though they needed no introductions. They loathed each other.

"How's the hotel business?" Marcos asked him without even a hint of interest.

"Thriving, of course."

Though Santos was irresponsible and wild, Marcos held no antagonism towards his brother, and usually regarded his exploits and antics with amusement. Except tonight he wasn't in the mood for Santos. Or anyone else.

Too smart for his own good sometimes, Santos chuckled at his side.

"So. Is that one yours?" Santos lifted his glass in Virginia's direction, and Marcos gazed at her again. His chest felt heavy and his stomach tight.

"Mine," he confirmed.

"I see." Santos smiled and rammed a hand into his pants pocket. "Mistress or fiancée?"

"Mistress," he snapped.

But his mind screamed in protest at those words.

Would she agree to his proposition to become his mistress? Live with him, be with him? She'd turned his world upside down, inside out, in over a month. He wanted her every second of the day—not only sexually. Her laugh brought on his laughter, her smiles made him smile, too. He was…he didn't know what. Enraptured. Charmed. Taken.

By her.

"That would make her your first mistress, eh, brother?" his brother asked. "No more fiancées after Marissa here."

Marissa whipped her attention back to Marcos. "You mean she's just a fling? Your girlfriend?"

He set the glass down on the nearby table with a harsh thump. "Unless you want me to leave you in prison the next time you're there, don't push it, little brother."

And to Marissa, with a scowl that warned her of all kinds of danger, "I say we've played games long enough, you and I, and I'm not in the mood for them any longer. You have something I want. The shares that belonged to my father—I want a number and I want it now."

She's his submissive, been like this for years…

Old lover demanding she be fired…competition… Allende…

Allende and Galvez…

It was easy at first, to pretend she hadn't caught bits and pieces of the swirling conversation. But after she'd heard it over and over, ignoring the comments popping up wherever she went became impossible.

It hurt to smile, and to pretend she wasn't hearing all this. But then, he'd taught her to pretend just fine, hadn't he? And she was doing quite well. Had been commending herself all evening for remembering people's names and keeping up with their conversations. And smiling her same smile.

But when the whispers were too much, she pried herself away from a group of women and strolled around the tables with her mind on escaping, finding Mrs. Fuller, Lindsay, a friendly face, but even they seemed engaged in the latest gossip.

She stopped in her tracks and frowned when a young man approached. He was over six feet tall, lean but muscled. He moved with slow, lazy charm, his smile oozing charisma. Rumpled ebony hair was slicked back behind his ears, his hard-boned face and striking features prominent. Laser-blue eyes sparkled with amusement as he halted before her and performed a mock bow.

"Allende. Santos Allende."

He spoke it the way Agent 007 would say, "Bond, James Bond," and it made her smile. So he was the elusive Santos.

"Virginia Hollis."

Drawing up next to her, he signaled with a cock of his head, a glass of red wine idle in his hand. "The bastard looking at you is my brother."

"Yes, I'm his assistant. You and I have spoken on the phone."

Santos had the looks of a centerfold, the kind that modeled underwear or very expensive suits like Hugo Boss, while Marcos had the very appearance of sin.

As if reading her mind, his lips quirked, and he added, "He didn't mention that."

"He mentioned me?"

Her eyes jerked back to Marcos; it seemed they couldn't help themselves. She always caught herself staring at him.

He was weaving toward the hallway with Marissa. When Marcos ducked his head toward her, Virginia's stomach clenched with envy and a sudden, unexpected fury.

He glanced back over his shoulder and when their gazes collided, a strange wildness surged through her. His face was inscrutable and his tuxedo was perfectly in place; only an odd gleam in his eyes spoke of his inner tumult. And in her mind, Virginia was positively screaming at him. *Everybody knows! Everybody knows I'm your stupid…silly…*

No. It was her fault, not his.

She'd wanted him, and she'd gambled for the first time in her existence. She knew his scent, the feel of his hair, the sounds he made when he was in ecstasy with her.

She knew his mouth, his whispers, knew he slept little but that he would remain in bed beside her, watching her.

She knew he liked to put his head between her breasts, knew he made a sound of encouragement when she stroked his hair.

But she did not know how to make this man love her.

This man with all these secrets, all of the locks and bolts around his heart.

He wanted Allende. To destroy it. He wanted her. To play with.

She was just his toy. Something to fool around with. Once, she might have jumped with glee. But now she wanted so much more from him, thought there could be no greater treasure in this world than to be loved by him.

"So did the affair come before he hired you or after?"

Santos phrased his question so casually and with such a playful gleam in his eyes that Virginia could only blink.

He grinned and shrugged his shoulders. "I'm sorry, I'm just terribly curious. I have to know."

Cheeks burning with embarrassment, Virginia ducked her head and tried to get away. "Excuse me."

With one quick, fluid move, Santos stepped into her path

and caught her elbow. "Marissa wants him, you do realize this?"

She stepped back, freeing her arm from his, hating that it was so obvious, so transparent on her face. "I can't see why you think I'd care."

But his curling lips invited her to mischief. "She offers something my brother wants very badly. What do you offer?"

She frowned. "I wasn't aware this was a competition—"

"It's not." He tipped her chin up, those electric-blue eyes dancing with mirth. "Because I think you've already got him."

When she hesitated, he bent to whisper in her ear, sweetening the offer with words she found she could not resist.

"My brother is very loyal, and if you managed to steal his heart…no ten businesses would top it."

But Virginia knew that one business, one woman did— when she heard the news announced later in the evening that Fintech would be taking over Allende.

Twelve

They rode to the penthouse in dead, flat silence. Marcos seemed engrossed in his thoughts, and Virginia was deeply engrossed in hers.

It took her ten minutes, while he made phone calls to Jack and his lawyers, to pack the meager belongings she'd once, mistakenly or not, left in his apartment.

She was calmer. Immobile on a tiny corner of the bed, actually, and staring at the doorway, nervously expecting him to come in any minute. But calmer.

Though she didn't know whether the nausea inside of her was due to the pregnancy or to the fact that she would not be sleeping with Marcos for the first night in over a month.

She just couldn't do this any longer. Every little word she'd heard tonight had felt like whiplashes on her back; she could not believe her colleagues would speak this way about her. And then Marcos…offering her a necklace, but not his love. Him telling his brother she was his…his…

No.

She refused to believe he would refer to her as something tacky. But the truth, no matter how painful, was the truth. Virginia was his assistant—one of *three*—and she was sleeping with her boss. It didn't matter if she'd spent the most beautiful moments of her life with him. It didn't matter that every kiss, every touch, she had given with all her might and soul. It didn't matter that she'd loved him before and loved him now.

She was sleeping with her boss, and she'd never be respected if she continued. She'd never respect *herself.*

If only she were able to tuck her determination aside for a moment and enjoy one last night with him. The last night of a month she would not ever forget. The last night with the man she had fallen in love with, the father of her unborn child.

Drawing in a fortifying breath, she left the bedroom and went searching for him.

She'd heard him in his office, barking orders to Jack over the phone, laughing with him, even—he was not concealing his delight over his deal.

The door of the study was slightly ajar, and she slipped inside in silence.

He sat behind his desk at the far end. He looked eerie behind his computer, concentrated, the light doing haunting things to his face. Her stomach clenched with yearning. "Marcos, may I talk to you?"

He stiffened, and his head came up. Her breath caught at the devastating beauty of his liquid black eyes, and her heart leapt with a joy that quickly became dread when he remained silent. There was lust in those orbs, desire, and she seized on to that with all her might before he jerked his gaze back to the computer. "I'm very busy, Virginia."

She tugged at the hem of her dress, uneasy of how to proceed. She tried to sound casual. "Marcos, I thought we could discuss…something. I may not spend the night and I really feel it's important—"

"Jesus, do we have to do this now?" His hands paused on the keyboard, then he dropped his face and rubbed his eyes with the heel of his palms. "I'm sorry. Right. Okay. What is it, Virginia?"

Her eyes widened at his condescending tone. The thought that he'd always put Allende and his business before her made her stomach twist so tight she thought she would vomit. She'd forgotten she was his plaything. If she produced money maybe he'd give her five minutes now?

"We were going to discuss…us." Her voice trembled with urgency. "At the dinner, you mentioned wanting to say something."

He leaned back, his expression betraying no flicker of emotion, no hint of what was going through his mind. "Can't us wait a day? Hmm?"

"No, Marcos, it can't."

He sat up straighter, linked his hands together, and kept silent for what felt like forever. His calm alarmed her. He was too still, too composed, while his eyes looked…indulgent. "What is it you want to say to me?" he at last asked.

Suddenly she felt like young Oliver Twist, begging, "Please, sir, I want some more." And she hated him for making her feel like that.

Her voice broke and she swallowed in an attempt to recover it. "Look, I realize what kind of arrangement we have," she began. "A-and maybe it was good for a time. But things change, don't they?"

He nodded, his entire face, his smile, indulgent.

She dragged in a breath, trying not to lose her temper. "Marissa, Marcos."

"What about Marissa?" His eyes were so black, so intense, she felt as though they would burn holes through her.

Are the rumors true? she wondered. *Did she force you*

into a marriage bargain only so you could once again own Allende? "You loved Marissa. Do you love her still?"

A frustrated sound exited his throat as he flung his hands over his head. "I'm not discussing Marissa now, of all times, for God's sake!" he exploded.

But Virginia plunged on. "I think it very tacky to jump around from bed to bed, don't you?"

His eyebrows drew low across his eyes, and he nodded. "Extremely."

To her horror, her throat began closing as she pulled her fears out of her little box and showed them to him. "She hurt you, and maybe you wanted to use me to hurt her back—" Why else would he want Virginia? She was not that smart, not that special, not that beautiful, either!

She tried to muffle a sob with her hand and couldn't, and then the tears began to stream down her cheeks in rivers. With a muffled curse, he rose and came around the desk, walking toward her. His face and body became a blur as he reached her, and though she tried to avoid his embrace, her back hit the wall as she tried escaping.

He bent over her, wiped her tears with his thumb. "Don't cry. Why are you crying?"

The genuine concern in his voice, the soul-wrenching tenderness with which he cradled her face, only made the sobs tear out of her with more vigor. "Oh, God," she sobbed, wiping furiously at the tears as they streamed down her face.

When he spoke, he sounded even more tortured than she was. "Don't cry, please don't cry, *amor.*" He kissed her cheek. Her eyelashes. Her forehead. Her nose. When his lips glided across hers, she sucked in a breath of surprise. He opened his lips over hers, probed her lightly with his tongue, and said, in a tone that warned of danger, "Please give me ten minutes and I'm all yours. Please just let me…"

When he impulsively covered her mouth, she opened for

the wet thrust of his tongue, offering everything he didn't ask for and more. His kiss was hot and avid, and it produced in her an amazing violence, a feeling that made her feel fierce and powerful and at the same time so vulnerable to him.

The possibility that he was feeling some kind of pity for her made her regain some semblance of control. She pushed at his wrist with one hand and wiped her tears with the other. "I'm all right."

"You're jealous." He took her lips with his warm ones, nibbling the plump flesh between words. "It's all right. Tell me that you are."

She shook her head, not trusting herself to speak.

"I was when you danced with Santos," he rasped, "jealous out of my mind. Out. Of. My. Mind." His teeth were tugging at her ear, and he was making low noises of pleasure as his hands roamed up her sides, following her form, feeling her.

She dragged her mouth across his hair, softly said, "I can't do this anymore, Marcos."

He froze for a shocked moment.

In one blindingly quick move, he lifted her up and pressed her back against the wall, pinioning her by the shoulders. "Is this your idea of getting my attention?"

Her heart thundered in her ears. "I can't do this any longer. I want more." *A father for our child. A man who'll always stand by me. Someone who cares.*

A nearly imperceptible quiver at the corner of his right eye drew her attention. That was all that seemed to move. That and his chest. Her own heaving breasts. They were panting hard, the wild flutter of a pulse at the base of his throat a match to her own frantic heartbeat. "What more do you want?" His voice was hoarse, more a plea than a command.

She grasped the back of his strong neck and made a sound that was more frustrated than seductive. "More! Just more, damn you, and if you can't figure out it's not your money then I'm not going to spell it out for you."

He stared at her as though what she'd just said was the worst kind of catastrophe. Then he cursed in Spanish and stalked away, plunging his hands into his hair. "You picked the wrong moment to share your wish list with me, *amor*."

"It's not a long list," she said glumly. She felt bereft of his kisses, his eyes, his warmth, and wrapped her arms tightly around herself. "We said we'd talk, and I think it's time we did."

"After midnight? When I'm in the midst of closing the deal of my life?"

"I'm sorry about the timing," she admitted.

She swallowed hard for some reason, waiting for him to tell her something. He didn't. His back was stiff as he halted by the window. His breaths were a frightening sound in the room—shallow, so ragged she thought he could be an animal.

But no, he wasn't an animal.

He was a man.

A man who had ruthlessly, methodically isolated his emotions from the world. She did not know how to reach this man, but every atom and cell inside of her screamed for her to try.

But then he spoke.

"Virginia." There was a warning in that word; it vibrated with underlying threat. It made her hold her breath as he turned. There was frustration in his eyes, and determination, and his face was black with lust. "Give me ten minutes. That's all I ask. Ten minutes so I can finish here and then you'll get your nightly tumble."

His words jerked through her, one in particular filling her with outrage. *Tumble!*

She began to quake. A chilling frost seemed to seep into her bones.

Stalking around her, he fell back into his chair, was sucked back into his computer, and began writing.

"Tumble," she said.

He set down the pen and met her gaze. The man was mute as wallpaper.

She signaled with trembling fingers. "For your information." She wanted to fling her shoe at his face, to shred every single paper on the pile she'd neatly organized atop his desk, but she clenched her eyes shut for a brief moment. "I do not want a tumble!"

Several times, Virginia had imagined how their parting would be.

Not even in her nightmares had she imagined this.

She couldn't bear to be in the same room with him, didn't dare glance up to make note of his expression.

Stricken by his lack of apology, she choked back words that wanted to come out, hurtful things she knew she would regret saying, words about being sorry she'd met him, sorry she loved him, sorry she was pregnant by him, but staring at the top of his silky black hair, she couldn't. Instead she said, "Goodbye, Marcos."

And Marcos…said nothing.

Not *goodbye*. Not *chiquita*. Not *amor*.

But as she waited by the elevator, clutching her suitcase handle as though it was all that kept her from falling apart, a roar unlike any other exploded in his study. It was followed by an ear-splitting crash.

The clock read 1:33 p.m.

He had what he wanted, Marcos told himself for the hundredth time. Didn't he? And yet the satisfaction, the victory, wasn't within reach. Perhaps because what he really wanted was something else. Someone else.

The pressure was off his chest—the lawyers were currently sealing the deal. Allende for a couple of million. Marcos now owned every single share of stock in the company, had recovered every inch and centimeter and brick and truck of what Marissa had taken from him.

It had not taken much at all to bend her to his will; the woman had nothing to bargain with. Marissa had to sell or she'd go bankrupt. She'd held no more attraction for him, as she'd thought, no temptation. After a few harsh words from him and a few tears from her, there had finally been a bit of forgiveness between them.

And with that, everything had changed. By her admittance to defeat, she'd unwittingly granted Marcos the opportunity to color his past another shade that wasn't black.

He felt...lighter, in that respect. But heavy in the chest. So damned heavy and tortured with a sense of foreboding he couldn't quite place.

"You needed me, Mr. Allende?"

His heart kicked into his rib cage when Virginia strolled into his office five minutes after he'd issued the request by phone.

Yes, I need you. I do. And I'm not even ashamed to admit it anymore.

Dressed in slimming black, she held a manila file in her hand, and a few seconds after she closed the doors behind her, Marcos spoke. "You left before the ten minutes were over."

Silently she sat and fiddled with her pearls, her eyes shooting daggers at him when she spared him a glance. "I realized you wanted your space, so I indulged you."

Those last words came barbed, as though he'd once spoken them in sarcasm and she were flinging them back at him. She looked tired, his Miss Hollis, he noted. As though she'd slept less than an hour and tossed around for all the rest. Like he had.

He didn't understand her anger very well. But they'd had plans to speak afterward, had been sleeping together so delightedly he hadn't expected the loss of her last night to affect him like it had. Were ten minutes too much to ask?

"Ten minutes, Miss Hollis. You can't even grant me that?"

"You were being—" As though offended by her own thoughts, she bolted upright in the chair, spine straight. "Something of a jerk."

He choked. "Jerk! This spoken by an opinionated little brat I've spoiled rotten?"

The blow registered in her face first, crumpling her tight expression. Marcos raked his fingers through his hair and shot up to pace his office.

He felt like celebrating with her, like marking this momentous day in his career with something even equally outstanding for him personally. But somehow he sensed he had to make amends with her first.

Virginia had wanted him last night. First, he'd been occupied with Marissa. Who'd deceived and lied to him. And who had become so insignificant in his life, he'd forgiven her. After he got what he wanted from her.

All this, thanks to Virginia.

Suddenly, Marcos felt a grieving need to explain, to placate her, to restore the sparkle in her pretty green eyes. Staring around his office, at the papers scattered across the desk, he quietly admitted, "Virginia, I want to make you a proposition."

Her slow and deep intake of breath was followed by a dignified silence. This was not the way he'd intended to ask her and yet suddenly he had to. Here. Now. Had to know she would belong to him, only him.

They were fighting, the air between them felt electric, charged with anger and lust and something else he couldn't quite place. Something fuzzy and warm that made him feel close to her even when she annoyed him.

He strode over to her chair and bent, put his palm on her

bare knee, and said, with fervor, "Would you be my mistress, Virginia?"

The way she automatically breathed the word *no,* he'd have thought he'd slapped her. Her eyes shone with hurt and her mouth parted as though she wanted to say something else but couldn't. "No," she said again, on another breath, this one made of steel.

"I don't think you understand what I'm saying," he said gently, stroking her knee and moving his hand up to clasp hers where it rested on her lap.

"Don't!" She said it in such a fierce voice that he halted. Even his heart stopped beating. She shook her curls side to side, her face stricken. "Don't touch me."

What was this? What was this?

He caught her face in one hand, his heartbeat a loud, deafening roar in his ears. "Darling, I realize you might have misinterpreted my interests in speaking to Marissa, which I assure you were only business. It's you I want, only you. And I'm very prepared to give you—"

"What? What will you give me?" She stood up, her eyes shooting daggers at him. "Do you even realize that the only thing I've been pretending all this time is that I don't love you?"

His heart vaulted, but his voice sounded dead as he stepped back. The confession felt like a bomb dropped into his stomach. "Love."

She chose to look out the window. And at last handed him the file. "Here's my resignation."

She set it atop his stacks and started for the door, and Marcos tore across the room like a man being chased by the devil. He caught her and squeezed her arms as his paralyzed brain made sense of her words.

"If you're telling me you love me," he said through gritted teeth, "look at me when you say it!"

She wrenched free. "Let go of me."

He caught her elbow and spun her around, and she screamed, *"I said don't touch me!"*

Worried the entire floor may have heard that, he let go of her. His chest heaved with the cyclone of feelings inside of him. He curled his fingers into his hands and his fingers dug into his palms, his knuckles jutting out.

"You want me," he growled.

"No." She backed away, glaring at him.

"You tremble for me, Virginia."

"Stop it."

"You want me so much you sob from the pleasure when I'm inside you."

"Because I'm *pretending* to enjoy your disgusting *tumbles!*" she shot. She was flushed and trembling against the wall, her nipples balled into little pearls that begged for his mouth. But in her voice there was nothing but pain.

"Pretend? When the hell have we pretended?" He crushed her against him, squeezed her tight even as she squirmed. "We're fire, Virginia. You and I. Combustion. Don't you understand English? I'm asking you to stay. With me. And be my mistress," he ground out.

Did she even realize he'd never in his life said this to a woman before? When her lashes rose and her gaze met his, the damaged look in her eyes knocked the air out of him. He didn't expect the slicing agony lashing through him at her next words.

"I'm not interested in being your mistress."

When she disengaged from him and pulled the doors open, he cursed under his breath, raked a hand through his hair. All noise across the floor silenced, and he immediately grabbed his jacket, shoved his arms into it as he followed her to the elevator.

He pushed inside before the doors closed, and she turned her face toward the mirror when he demanded, "Do I get two weeks to convince you to stay? I want you here. And I want you in my bed."

"You want. You need." Her voice quivered with anger, and its tentacles curled around him so hard he could've sworn it would kill him. "Is that what you wanted to speak to me about? Becoming your...*mistress?*"

His heart had never galloped this way. His plans had never veered off so unexpectedly, so decidedly. Their gazes met. Hers furious. His...his burned like flames. He grabbed her shoulders. The need inside him was so consuming he saw red. "Say yes. Christ, say yes now."

But the way she looked at him wasn't the same way she always did. "Do you think that's what I want?" she asked, so softly he barely heard through the background elevator music. "Did I ever give you the impression I would...settle for...such an offer?"

Stunned that she would look at him like he was a monster, he took a step away from her, and another. His body burned with the want to show her he meant not to punish but to love her with every graze of his lips and every lick of his tongue.

And he said, out of desperation, impulse, the exact second the elevator halted at the lobby floor, "I love you."

And the words, magic words, ones he'd never, ever said before, didn't have the effect he'd predicted.

Her laugh was cynical. "See, you're so good at pretending, I don't believe you."

And she spun around and walked away, out of the elevator, away from him, away from it all.

Stunned, he braced a hand on the mirror, shut his eyes as he fought to make sense of the rampaging turmoil inside him.

What in the hell?

Thirteen

Alone in his Fintech offices, motionless in his chair, Marcos stared out the window.

The nineteenth floor was empty. It was 3 a.m. But there was no power on this earth, no way in hell, that he'd go back alone to his apartment. His penthouse had never felt so cold now that Virginia Hollis was gone. The sheets smelled of her. He'd found a lipstick under the bathroom sink and he'd never, ever felt such misery. The sweeping loneliness that had accompanied that unexpected find was staggering.

He'd stormed out of his home and now here he was, inside his sanctuary. The place where he evaluated his losses and plotted his comebacks. Where he'd conquered the unconquerable and ruthlessly pursued new targets. Where, for the last month, he'd spent countless hours staring off into space with the single thought of a raven-haired temptress with pale, jade-green eyes.

And now he stared out the window, blinded to the city below, and he told himself he did not care.

He told himself that a month from now, he would forget Virginia Hollis.

He told himself this was an obsession and nothing more. He told himself the gut-wrenching, staggering throb inside him was nothing. And for the hundredth time, until the words rang true and his insides didn't wince in protest every time he thought them, he told himself he did not love her.

But it was a bluff. A farce. A lie.

Virginia had her money. Their arrangement had culminated at the Fintech party and had left him with an overwhelming sense of loss he couldn't quite shake. She'd left him wanting. Wanting more.

Marcos, I love you.

She hadn't said it in exactly those words—but in his mind, she did. And he'd never heard sweeter words. More devastating words. Because suddenly, and with all his might, he wanted to be a man who could love her like she deserved.

The pain in her eyes—he'd been the one to put it there. Touch of gold? He scoffed at the thought, thinking he destroyed anything he touched that had life. He'd put that misery in Virginia's eyes and he loathed himself for it.

His proposal, what he'd offered her, not even half of what he'd truly wanted from her, sickened him.

All along, he'd wanted her. He was a man accustomed to following his gut, and he did it without a conscience. He knew when he saw land and wanted it. He knew what he looked for when he bought stocks. He knew, had known from the start, he wanted Virginia in his bed, under his starved, burning body. But now, clear as the glass before him, he knew what else he wanted from her.

He wanted it all.

He wanted a million dances and double that amount of her smiles.

He wanted her in his bed, to see her when he woke up, to find her snuggled against him.

He wanted to pay her credit card bills and he wanted her with a baby in her arms. His baby. His woman. His *wife*.

Mia. Mia. Mia.

He'd been alone his entire lifetime, pursuing meaningless affairs, convincing himself that was enough. It had all changed. Slowly, almost imperceptibly, but surely, ever since the day he'd hired Virginia Hollis.

Now he had broken her heart before she'd truly admitted to having lost it to him. He should've treasured it. Tucked it into his own and never let it go.

Sighing, he pushed his chair around and stared across his office. A dozen plasma TV screens hung on the wall to the right. They usually enlivened the place with noise and light, but were currently off. They lent a gloom to the area that Marcos found quite the match to his mood.

In fact, a morgue was quite the match to his mood.

He stalked outside, and made his way to a sleek wooden desk. Her items were still on it. He scanned the surface—polished to a gleam, all orderly, all her, and he groaned and let his weight drop into her chair.

Her rejection felt excruciatingly painful. Not even the day Marissa Galvez had stared up at him from his father's bed had he felt such helplessness.

What in the devil did she want from him?

As he stroked a hand along the wood, he knew. Deep in the closed, festering pit of his emotions, he knew what she wanted. Damn her, she'd been playing him for it! Seducing him, delighting and enchanting him, making him love and need and cherish her.

And now he couldn't even remember why he had thought she didn't deserve everything she wanted. Because she was a woman, like Marissa? Why had he thought his bed would be enough for everything she would lack? Had he grown so heartless that he would rob her of a family?

He began opening and closing the desk drawers, looking for some sign of her. Something—anything—she might have left behind.

For the first time in his life, someone else's needs seemed more important than his, and he loathed the overwhelming sense of loss sweeping through him like an avalanche.

If he had an ounce of decency in him, if he was not the unfeeling monster she thought him to be at this moment, Marcos would let her go.

And just when he was certain it was the right thing to do, just when he was determined to forget about her and all the days they'd pretended and all the ways they'd been both wrong and right for each other, he spotted the boxes crowded into the back of her bottom drawer.

And the three test strips. All of them had the same result.

"Nurse, is my father out in the hall?"

Virginia had been transferred to a small private room in the west hospital wing, where she'd slept for the night hooked up to an IV drip, and this morning the one person she longed to see hadn't yet made an appearance. She wanted to go home already—she felt tired, cranky, lonely—and still the nurse kept delaying her departure.

The balmy-voiced nurse fidgeted around the bare room, organizing the trays. "I believe he's outside. I'm sure he'll come in shortly."

Virginia sighed, the sensation of having been run over by an elephant especially painful in her abdomen and breast area. She cupped her stomach. Amazing, that the baby already had its heartbeat. Amazing that just as she left its father, the baby had tried to leave her body, too.

"Virginia?"

She went completely immobile when she heard that.

There, wearing a severe black turtleneck and slacks, stood Marcos Allende in the doorway. Her heart dropped to her toes. She felt the urge to snatch the sleek red carnation her father had set on the side table and hide her pale, teary face behind it, but she was too mesmerized to pull her eyes away. Large, hard, beautiful—Marcos's presence seemed to empower the entire room, and she suspected—no, knew—everyone in this hospital must be feeling his presence.

He stood with his feet braced apart, his arms at his sides, his fingers curled into his palms. And something hummed. Inside her. In her blood, coursing through her veins.

"An acquaintance, miss?"

The nurse's tone gave a hint of her preoccupation. Did she feel the charge in the air? Was the world twirling faster? The floor falling?

Virginia nodded, still shocked and overwhelmed by this visit, but as she stared at the sleek-faced, long-nosed young woman, she hated her mind's eye for gifting her with another, more riveting image of Marcos's dark, cacao gaze. His silken mass of sable hair. Long, tanned fingers. Accent. Oh, God, the accent, that thick baritone, softly saying *Miss Hollis...*

"I'll leave you two for a moment, then."

Oddly close to being devastated, Virginia watched the nurse's careful departure, and then she could find no excuse to stare at the plain white walls, no spot to stare at but Marcos.

If she had just been torpedoed, the impact would have been less than what she felt when he leveled his hot coal eyes on her. He stood as still as a statue.

Why didn't he move? Was he just going to stand there? Why didn't he hold her? Why was he here? He was angry she quit? Angry she hadn't collected her items? Did he miss her just a little bit?

She sucked in a breath when he spoke.

"I'm afraid this won't do."

The deep, quiet, accented voice washed over her like a waterfall. Cleansing. Clear. Beautiful.

Oh, God. Would she ever not love this man?

She pushed up on her hands, glad her vitals were no longer on display or else Marcos would know exactly how hard her heart was beating. "Marcos, what are you doing here—"

He looked directly at her as he advanced, overpowering the room. "I had to see you."

She sucked in breath after breath, watching him move with that catlike grace, his expression somber. Her body quaked from head to toe. The unfairness of it all; he was so gorgeous, so elegant, so tempting. So unreachable. And she! She was so...so beat-up, tired, drained. Hospitalized. Oh, God.

Her lips trembled. As if she weighed next to nothing, he bent and gently scooped her up against him, and Virginia liquefied.

I almost lost our baby, she thought as she wound her arms around him and buried her face in his neck.

He inhaled deeply, as though scenting her. Then, into her ear, his voice ringing so low and true it tolled inside of her, "Are you all right?"

Only Marcos could render such impact with such softly spoken words. Her entire being, down to her bones, trembled at his concern. And then came more. It was just a breath, whispered in her ear, and he whispered it with fervor.

"I love you."

Her muscles clenched in protest, and her head swiveled to her father's when she spotted him at the open doorway. The weathered man's face was inscrutable and his suit was perfectly in place; only the ravaged look in his eyes spoke of what he'd done.

He'd told Marcos about the baby?

"You lied to me, you left me, and yet I love you," Marcos

continued, his voice so thick and gruff, as though he were choking.

After the fear, the cramps and the possibility of losing her baby, Virginia had no energy. She just wanted him to speak. The sturdiness of his hard chest against hers gave her the most dizzying sensation on this earth. She'd thought she'd never feel his arms again and to feel them around her, holding her so tight, was bliss.

She didn't realize she was almost nuzzling his neck, breathing in his musky, familiar scent, until her lungs felt ready to explode.

"Do you think we could pretend," he whispered into the top of her bent head, "the past two days never happened, and we can start again?"

More pretending? God, no! No more pretending.

But she refused to wake up from this little fantasy, this one last moment, refused to lift her face, so instead she rubbed her nose against the side of his corded neck. A strange sensation flitted through her, like the soaring she felt when she played on the swings as a child.

His voice was terse but tender as he wiped her brow with one hand and smoothed her hair back. "And our baby?"

Shock didn't come close to what she experienced. Her nerves twisted like wires. "P-pardon?"

"You lost our child?"

For the first time since Marcos had come through that door, Virginia noticed the red rimming his eyes, the strain in his expression. Even his voice seemed to throb in a way she'd never heard before.

She moved not an inch, breathed no breath, as her mind raced to make sense of his question. Then she glanced out the small window, not at what lay beyond, just at a spot where Marcos's face would not distract her. "What makes you say that?" she asked quietly, her fingers tugging on themselves as she scanned the room for the possible culprit behind this misunderstanding. Her father.

"Look at me." Marcos's massive shoulders blocked her view as he leaned over the bed rails. His breath stirred the top of her head as he scraped his jaw against her hair with absolutely no restraint, and then he spoke so passionately her middle tingled. "Look at me. We'll have another baby. I've always wanted one—and I want one with you." He seized her shoulders in a stronghold, his face pained and tortured as he drew away and forced her to meet his gaze. "Marry me. Today. Tomorrow. Marry me."

"I— What do you mean *another* baby?" After many moments, she pinned Hank Hollis with her stare. "Father?"

Wide-eyed, her father hovered by the opposite wall, shifting his feet like an uncertain little boy. He opened his mouth, then snapped it shut, then opened it again, as if he were holding on to great words. "I told him you'd lost the baby."

She gasped. What a horrible thing to say! "W-why? Father! Why would you do that?"

The man rubbed the back of his neck, pacing the little room. "So he'd leave. You said you didn't want any visitors."

While the honest words registered in her foggy mind—the first protective thing her father had done for her in ages—Virginia stared at the aging man. Her heart unwound like an old, twisted shred of paper.

For years, she had been so angry at this man. Maybe if she hadn't changed, become pregnant, fallen in love, she'd still be. But now—she didn't want resentment or anger. She wanted a family, and she'd take even one that had been broken.

Virginia leveled her eyes on the beautiful, thick-lashed cocoa ones she'd been seeing in her dreams and straightened up on the bed, clinging to that fine, strong hand. "Marcos,

I'm not sure what he told you, but I'd like to assure you I'm all right. And so is the baby."

When she pictured telling Marcos about a child, she hadn't expected an audience, nor having to do it in a hospital room.

Still. She would never, in her life, forget this moment.

Marcos's expression changed, metamorphosed, into one of disbelief, then joy. Joy so utter and pure it lit his eyes up like shooting stars.

"So we're expecting, then?"

The term *we* coming from his beautiful mouth made her giddy with excitement.

He smiled, and it was brilliant, that smile, that moment. Did this please him? Yes! She'd bet her life on it.

She nodded, her heart fluttering madly, a winged thing about to fly out of orbit. "I'd like to go home now," she admitted, and although her father stepped forward to offer assistance, the words weren't meant for him.

She gazed up at Marcos—quiet and mesmerizing—as she eased out of the hospital bed with as much dignity as she could muster.

His attention was no longer hard to bear. She wanted it; she wanted him.

Virginia Hollis knew this man. Inside and out, she knew him. How true he was to his word. How dedicated. How loyal. And how proud. She didn't need any more proof than his presence here, his touch, the look in his eyes and the promise there.

Rising to her full height, she linked her fingers through his and squeezed, feeling flutters in her stomach when he smiled encouragingly down at her. "Yes, Marcos Allende. I'll marry you."

Epilogue

The day arrived three months before the baby did.

Walking up to the altar, with the music shuddering through the church walls, Virginia had eyes only for the dark, mesmerizing man at the far end of the aisle. Tall and smiling, Marcos stood with his hands clasped before him, his broad shoulders and solid arms and steely, stubborn jaw offering love and comfort and protection.

Virginia was certain that nobody who watched him would be blind to the way he stared at her. Least of all she.

They shared a smile. Then her father was letting go of her arm.

Soon Marcos was lifting the flimsy veil to gaze upon her face and into her eyes, eyes which she used to fervently tell him, *I love you!*

Their palms met, their fingers linked, and the moment they did he gave her a squeeze. She felt it down to her tummy.

I, Virginia, take thee, Marcos, to be my lawfully wedded husband…

When he spoke his vows, the simplest vows, to love and cherish, her eyes began to sting. By the time the priest declared them man and wife, she was ready—more than ready—to be swept into his arms and kissed.

And kiss her he did. The priest cleared his throat. The attendants cheered and clapped. And still he kissed her.

Virginia let herself take her first relaxed breath once they were in the back of the limo. Gravitating toward each other, they embraced, and tiny tremors of desire spread along her torso and limbs. She'd had this fool idea of waiting to be together again until they married—and she was dying for him to touch her.

As they kissed, Virginia found her husband already dispensing with her veil. "There we go," he said contentedly. "Enjoy the dress because I assure you, it is coming off soon."

Actually relieved to be without the veil and anxiously looking forward to Marcos dispensing with the dress, she leaned back on the seat and cuddled against him. "I never knew these things were so heavy," she said. The skirt ballooned at her feet but thankfully there was no volume on top to keep her away from the man she most definitely intended to jump at the first opportunity.

"Come here, wife." He drew her close as the limo pulled into the street and the city landscape slowly rolled past them. Staring absently outside, Virginia sighed. His arms felt so good around her, being against him so right. Being his wife.

Both protectively and possessively, Marcos pressed her face to his chest and with his free hand, reached out to rub her swelling stomach. She'd noticed the more it grew, the more he did that. "How is my little girl today?" he asked against her hair.

Her eyebrows drew into a scowl. "We're having a boy,"

Virginia countered. "A handsome, dashing boy like his daddy. No girl would kick like this little guy does, trust me."

"Your daughter would, you saucy wench," he said with a rolling chuckle. "And my instincts tell me we are having a plucky, curly-haired, rosy-cheeked daughter. She'll run my empire with me."

Virginia smiled against his chest and slid a hand up his shirt to find the familiar cross lying at his throat and play with it. "Father keeps asking how many grandchildren we plan to have, he's obsessed with wanting it to be at least three."

Marcos laughed, and that laugh alone warmed her up another notch.

"Ahh, darling," he said. "He can rest assured we'll be working on that night and day." The praise in his words and the suggestive pat on her rear filled her with anticipation of tonight and future nights with her complex, breathtakingly beautiful, thoroughly giving and enchanting husband.

"He's so changed now, Marcos," she admitted, feeling so relaxed, *so* happy.

"His work in Allende has been impressive, Virginia. Even Jack is amazed."

"And you?"

He snorted. "I got to say to the moron 'I told you so.'"

She laughed. Then she snuggled closer and said, "Thank you. For believing that people can change. And for forgiving that little fib he told you at the hospital."

He nuzzled the top of her head. "He was trying to protect you—he didn't know me yet, and I respect that. Your father deserved a second chance, Virginia. We all do."

She sighed. "I'm just glad he's put all his efforts into making the best of it. And I'm proud of you, dear sir, for being wise enough to put the past behind you and keep Allende."

And for being most decidedly, most convincingly, most deliciously in love with her.

* * *

The band played throughout the evening, and the guests at the reception laughed and danced and drank. Hardly anyone would notice the groom had kidnapped the bride, and if they did, Marcos sure as hell didn't care.

He still could not understand why Virginia had gotten it into her head to play hard-to-get leading up to the wedding, and even less could he comprehend why he had obediently complied.

But now in the cloaked shadows of the closet, he had Virginia right where he'd always wanted her. In his arms. His mouth feasted on her exposed throat while his hands busily searched her dress for access—any access—to the smooth, creamy skin beneath.

"Careful!" Virginia screeched when he yanked on the delicate zipper at the back and an invisible button popped free.

He laughed darkly and maneuvered through the opening. "You're not wearing it again, *reina*. I could tear it apart and dispense with all this silliness." The guests had been crowding them for hours when all Marcos wanted was to be with his bride. Now his hands stole in through the opening at the small of her back, where he instantly seized her cushy rear and drew her up against him. "Come here. You've been teasing me all night."

"How kind of you to notice."

"Hmm. I noticed." He kissed the top of her breasts, all evening looking lush and squeezable thanks to Christian Dior, and then used his hands to gather the volume of her skirts and yank most of them back.

She automatically wrapped her stockinged legs around him when he pressed her against the wall. "You're incorrigible," she said chidingly, but he could hear the smile in her voice and the little tremble that said how very much his wife wanted to be ravaged by him.

He brought his hands up front and lowered them. "I'm open to being domesticated."

"Luckily I'm open to attempting that daunting task. In fact—no, not the panties!" A tear sounded, Virginia gasped, and his fingers found what they were looking for.

"Bingo," he purred.

"Oh, Marcos." Slipping her hands under his jacket and around his shoulders, she placed fervent little kisses along his jaw. "Please."

With a rumbling chuckle, he found her center and grazed it with his fingers. "Please what, *chiquita?*"

Against his lips, she mumbled, "You know what, you evil man."

"Please this?"

"Yes, yes, that." She left a moist path up his jaw and temple, and in his ear whispered, "I was aching to be with you all day."

"Shame on me." He turned his head and seized her earlobe with his teeth, tugging. "For keeping you waiting."

"I adore what you do to me."

He groaned at the husky quality of her voice. "No more than I, darling." Unable to wait, he freed himself from his trousers and, grasping her hips, began making love to her.

A whimper tore out of her, and she clutched his back with her hands.

"Chiquita." He wound his arms around her and was in turn embraced and enveloped by her silken warmth, completely owned and taken by the woman who had single-handedly stolen his heart.

No matter how quiet they tried to be, they were groaning, moving together. Marcos closed his eyes, savoring her, his wife and partner and mate and woman. When she exploded in his arms with a gasp, crying out his name into his mouth, he let go. Gripping her hips tighter, he muttered a choked, emotional *te amo* then let out a satisfying, "Hmm."

"Hmm," she echoed.

Inconspicuous minutes later, the bride and groom exited the closet. The ballroom brimmed with music and laughter, most of the guests who remained being the people closest to them.

With an appreciative eye, Marcos noticed the bride looked deliciously rumpled. Her cheeks glowed bright, and the fancy hairdo she claimed had taken endless hours to achieve had become magnificently undone.

As if reading his thoughts, she shot him a little black scowl. "I'm sure that everyone who sees me now will know—" she rose up to whisper into his ear "—that you just tumbled me in the closet. Really. Is that how your wife should expect to be treated, *Señor* Allende?"

Smiling into her eyes, he lifted her knuckles to his lips. "My wife can expect to be treated with respect and admiration and devotion."

With a dazzling smile, she let him drag her to the dance floor when a compellingly slow song began. "I believe this dance is mine," he said, and meaningfully added, "So is the one afterward."

She stepped into the circle of his arms, finding her spot under his chin to tuck her head in and sliding her arms around him. "You are a greedy fellow, aren't you?"

His lips quirked, and his eyes strayed toward the arched doorway, where his little brother stood, barely visible through the throng surrounding him. "With Santos around, I don't plan to let you out of my sight."

Virginia laughed. "He's already told me everything. Even about the time you broke his nose and chin. I swear that man loves to make you out as the ogre." She glanced past her shoulder and wrinkled her little nose. "Besides, he seems pretty busy with the two he brought tonight…and the dozen others he's trying to fend off."

Grateful that for the moment the guests were oblivious

to them as they danced amidst so many familiar faces, Marcos ran a hand down her back and glanced at the firm swell between their bodies. "How do you feel?" he asked, somber.

She smiled as she canted her head back to meet his gaze. "I feel...perfect." She kissed his lips and gazed up at him with those same green eyes that had haunted him. Their sparkle surpassed the blinding one of the ring on her finger, and her smile took his breath away—like it did every day. "You?" she asked.

His lips curled into a smile, and he bent his head, fully intending to take that mouth of hers. "A hundred thousand dollars shorter," he baited. He touched her lips, and his smile widened. "And I've never felt so lucky."

* * * * *

A sneaky peek at next month...

Desire™

PASSIONATE AND DRAMATIC LOVE STORIES

My wish list for next month's titles...

> 2 stories in each book - only **£5.30!**

In stores from 16th September 2011:

❑ Ultimatum: Marriage – Ann Major

& For the Sake of the Secret Child – Yvonne Lindsay

❑ Expecting the Rancher's Heir – Kathie DeNosky

& Taming Her Billionaire Boss – Maxine Sullivan

❑ The Billionaire's Bridal Bid – Emily McKay

& Million-Dollar Amnesia Scandal – Rachel Bailey

❑ At His Majesty's Convenience – Jennifer Lewis

& Her Little Secret, His Hidden Heir – Heidi Betts

Available at WHSmith, Tesco, Asda, Eason, Amazon and Apple

Just can't wait?

0911/51

  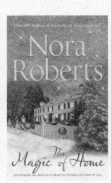

New Voices is back!

MILLS & BOON
romanceisnotdead.com

New Voices

returns on
13th September 2011!

For sneak previews and exclusives:

 Like us on facebook.com/romancehq

 Follow us on twitter.com/MillsandBoonUK

Last year your votes helped Leah Ashton win
New Voices 2010 with her fabulous story
Secrets & Speed Dating!

Who will you be voting for this year?

*Visit us
Online*

Find out more at
www.romanceisnotdead.com

We're looking for talented new authors and if you've got a romance bubbling away in your head we want to hear from you! But before you put pen to paper, here are some top tips...

Understand what our readers want: Do your research! Read as many of the current titles as you can and get to know the different series with our guidelines on www.millsandboon.co.uk.

Love your characters: Readers follow their emotional journey to falling in love. Focus on this, not elaborate, weird and wonderful plots.

Make the reader want to walk in your heroine's shoes: She should be believable, someone your reader can identify with. Explore her life, her triumphs, hopes, dreams. She doesn't need to be perfect—just perfect for your hero...she can have flaws just like the rest of us!

The reader should fall in love with your hero! Mr Darcy from *Pride and Prejudice*, Russell Crowe in *Gladiator* or Daniel Craig as James Bond are all gorgeous in different ways. Have your favourite hero in mind when you're writing and get inspired!

Emotional conflict: Just as real-life relationships have ups and downs, so do the heroes and heroines in novels. Conflict between the two main characters generates emotional and sensual tension.

Have your say or enter New Voices at:
www.romanceisnotdead.com

Visit us Online

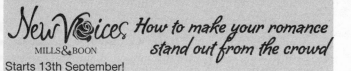

Avoiding the dreaded cliché

Open your story book with a bang—hook your reader in on the first page and show them instantly that this story is unique.

A successful writer can use a conventional theme and twist it to deliver something with real wow factor!

Once you've established the direction of your story, bring in fresh takes and new twists to these traditional storylines.

Here are four things to remember:

- Stretch your imagination
- Stay true to the genre
- It's all about the characters—start with them, not the plot!
- M&B is about creating fantasy out of reality. Surprise us with your characters, stories and ideas!

So whether it's a marriage of convenience story, a secret baby theme, a traumatic past or a blackmail story, make sure you add your own unique sparkle which will make your readers come back for more!

Good luck with your writing!

We look forward to meeting your fabulous heroines and drop-dead gorgeous heroes!

For more writing tips, check out:
www.romanceisnotdead.com

Visit us Online

NEWVOICESTIPS/B

Have Your Say

You've just finished your book.
So what did you think?

We'd love to hear your thoughts on our
'Have your say' online panel
www.millsandboon.co.uk/haveyoursay

- Easy to use
- Short questionnaire
- Chance to win Mills & Boon® goodies